SIX TRAINS OF NO RETURN

SHORT STORIES AND NOVELLAS

Immigrant Worlds & Texts

Other Titles in this Series

Hyam Plutzik and the Mosaic of Time, edited by Victoria Aarons, Holli Levitsky, and Hilene F. Lanzbaum

Two Hundred Brand New Shiny Cadillacs, by Pavel Lembersky

Memoirs of a Jewish District Attorney from Soviet Ukraine, by Mikhail Goldis, edited and translated by Marat Grinberg

Nabokov on the Heights: New Studies from Boston College, edited by Maxim D. Shrayer

For more information on this series, please visit:
https://www.academicstudiespress.com/immigrant-worlds-texts/

SIX TRAINS OF NO RETURN

SHORT STORIES AND NOVELLAS

MAXIM
MATUSEVICH

ACADEMIC STUDIES PRESS
BOSTON
2026

Library of Congress Cataloging-in-Publication Data

Names: Matusevich, Maxim author

Title: Six trains of no return / Maxim Matusevich.

Description: Boston : Academic Studies Press, 2026. | Series: Immigrant worlds and texts

Identifiers: LCCN 2025037750 (print) | LCCN 2025037751 (ebook) | ISBN 9798897830787 (hardback) | ISBN 9798897830794 (adobe pdf) | ISBN 9798897830800 (epub)

Subjects: LCGFT: Short stories | Novellas

Classification: LCC PS3613.A8734 S59 2025 (print) | LCC PS3613. A8734 (ebook) | DDC 813/.6--dc23/eng/20250905

LC record available at https://lccn.loc.gov/2025037750
LC ebook record available at https://lccn.loc.gov/2025037751

ISBN 9798897830787 (hardback)
ISBN 9798897830794 (adobe pdf)
ISBN 9798897830800 (epub)

Book design by PHi Business Solutions
Cover design by Ivan Grave

Published by Cherry Orchard Books, an imprint of Academic Studies Press
1007 Chestnut St.
Newton, MA 02464, USA
press@academicstudiespress.com
www.academicstudiespress.com

To my parents, Lena and Grisha.

Contents

The Apartment*

And that's how a life begins . . . Dad was born in the early 1920s in Moscow. His parents and their three boys lived in a wooden house on the outskirts of the city, which at the time still felt quaint and provincial. They shared the house with several other families, at least some of them part of the massive Jewish resettlement wave that left the Pale and reached many Russian cities soon after the civil war. They were poor (who wasn't?)—the mother worked at the central post office and the father, some thirty-five years her senior, rarely left the house, where he set up a one-man knitting workshop. The kids spent much of their time playing out in the street in front of the house, and that's where little Grisha (my father) met with an accident that would change (and likely save) his life. One day, while playing tag with a neighborhood kid, he tripped over and fell into an uncovered manhole—then as now a common sight in the streets of Russian cities. He never played tag again. In fact, over the next few years he would develop a crippling bone disease that would confine him to various hospitals and sanatoria into his late adolescence.

He would spend years surrounded by other disabled kids, never quite alone. At the famed Bobrov clinic in Alupka (Crimea), where he stayed between 1929 and 1931, he bonded with another sick child—her name was Mura and she was dying of bone tuberculosis. For almost two years Mura and Grisha played a daily game of greeting the rising sun from their adjacent little beds on an open veranda. The girl's father—famed children's author, Kornei Ivanovich Chukovsky—was a busy man, but he visited quite frequently from Leningrad; and when Mura's condition took a turn for the worse, he talked the doctors into allowing him to sleep on a cot next to his dying daughter. The three of them (my dad, Mura, and Mura's father) became very close. My dad's parents were too exhausted and too busy eking out a living and building their lives around the needs of a disabled son to give him much besides their unequivocal love and commitment, so Chukovsky became a surrogate parent of sorts, the person who, in the midst of a personal tragedy, turned my

* First published as "The Apartment," *Bare Life Review* 2 (Spring 2019), 74–85.

father on to culture. For hours, Kornei Ivanovich recited poetry and told the children stories about his life in London and other travels. He introduced my father to the wonders of chess, an enduring passion he would carry with him through life. And then Mura died . . . After the funeral, Chukovsky stopped by the ward and dropped a stack of Mura's books on my dad's bed. One of them was signed: "Grishenka, get well and never forget about the sun!"

After Dad was discharged from the clinic the family, following Chukovsky's advice, moved to Leningrad and eventually settled into two rooms in a communal apartment just a stone's throw from the Winter Palace. As far as communal apartments go, theirs was quite decent, as they claimed two small rooms and eventually grew to be very friendly with their neighbors. There was no privacy, of course, but father was not concerned. Besides, until his high school graduation in 1939, he didn't spend much time at home, confined to a by now established routine of surgeries followed by stints at various rehabilitation facilities, mostly in Leningrad.

Four important events happened in 1939: Dad's father, an elderly unobtrusive man, died of a heart attack, Dad was proclaimed "cured" by the doctors at the Turner Institute, he graduated high school with a coveted "gold medal" (straight *A*s), and, on the strength of his academic record, was accepted into a prestigious optical engineering college. The next two years were the happiest in his life. The four of them (his mother and three brothers) continued to occupy the two rooms on Khalturina Street. Grisha and Naum (his eldest brother) were now college students, while the youngest, Volodya, a shy and unassuming boy, stayed close to his mother. My father relearned how to walk using specially designed footwear and a sturdy cane and apparently took full advantage of his newly gained mobility—I found a couple of cute little love letters in the family archive, dating from 1940–41, one from a *myshka* (little mouse) and another from *glupyshka* (little silly one).

All the silliness ended on Sunday, June 22, 1941, the day before his last final—a balmy June morning that also became the first day of the war. Within a few weeks the family broke up, not to reassemble again until the fall of 1945. Naum volunteered for the self-defense force and survived the first horrific winter in the besieged city, digging trenches and intermittently attending night architecture classes. In March 1942, having buried his college girlfriend in a common grave and weighing about one hundred pounds, he left for the front, and the family wouldn't hear from him until 1943.

His two brothers, the one disabled and the other a teenager, accompanied their mother to the industrial city of Stalingrad where they moved in with their close relatives, sharing a two-room municipal flat with a family of three. The man of the house turned out to be the boys' half-brother David, from their late father's first marriage. David was the city's most celebrated journalist (hence the municipal flat) and a man of rare integrity. He would survive the war. But not his wife . . . In 1946 he would come to Leningrad for a quick visit and invite my dad for a walk in the Mikhailovsky Garden. It was there, by the yellow-and-white chess pavilion that they had a "talk." "Stalin," David said, "is a monster, a blood-sucking viper. We didn't beat the Fritzes because of him but rather despite him. I hope there is a hell and I hope he burns in it—eternally." Dad always said that this was the most important conversation of his life. For days he walked in a daze. He never saw David again.

In the meantime, the family's hopes to find safety in Stalingrad proved to be illusory. The Germans were closing in, and after a winter marked by the record freeze, a near fatal bout of meningitis and a nasty case of scurvy, Dad, his mom, and his little brother were on the move again—boarding one of the last boats out of the nearly encircled city. As the boat drew away from the main pier, he saw a neat formation of low-flying planes coming in from the north; they passed at great speed over the boat, strafing the length of the Volga, then slowly banked around and returned to the city. When the boat neared a bend of the river, the pier, now some two to three kilometers away, went up in smoke and dim flashes. Theirs was the second to last boat out of Stalingrad. The last boat never left.

It took them almost a month to reach the small village in the Urals which would become my dad's home for the next two years. They traveled by boat, freight train, and occasional truck, and, as they got closer to the continental divide, more and more often by horse-drawn *telegas*. They encountered the best and the worst of humanity, but Dad always insisted that the best invariably prevailed . . . by a wide margin. In the Urals, he became the breadwinner for the family of three, working as a math and geography teacher at the local school, whose student body was evenly divided between the village kids and the evacuees. There were some tensions between the emaciated, often Jewish urbanites and the local boys, but they dissipated over time. Dad's teaching stint yielded several commendations and, as he later insisted, greatly improved his ability to walk—the school was some three kilometers from the house, a distance he covered several times a day. My dad, his mom, and his brother rented the back room of a log cabin, belonging to a woman whose husband had been killed in the early months of the war. Dad remembered her as unwaveringly kind.

Within a year after their arrival in the Urals, Dad began to send out letters to his former college professors, inquiring whether the resumption of his studies was possible. The war had begun to roll west, but Leningrad remained under siege. His college had temporarily relocated to Moscow and he finally received an invitation (and a transit pass) to reenter the program as a junior. In early 1944, he embarked on a return journey to European Russia, leaving behind his mother and younger brother. Among his possessions was a beat-up chess set. The trip lasted for several weeks, much of the time spent at various provincial train stations, choked with war transports and medical trains. In Moscow, his acceptance papers were processed with an uncharacteristic speed, and within a few days, he resumed his studies and moved into a dorm. There were ten roommates in his room, most of them recently maimed soldiers discharged from the front. For the first time in his life, my father's disability attracted no stares, no awkward questions. As he put it, there were nineteen arms and eighteen legs between the eleven of them. The oldest was twenty-four.

On Wednesday, May 9, 1945, the day of Germany's surrender, Grisha woke up in his dorm bed to see his mother and younger brother perched on a stack of suitcases and grinning exuberantly. For a drowsy second, it occurred to him that he was back at the Bobrov clinic in Crimea, holding his friend's little hand, watching the sun rising over the choppy vastness of the Black Sea . . .

In September 1945, the family returned to Leningrad. A few weeks later, Dad's eldest brother Naum, now a decorated and freshly discharged artillery sergeant, joined them. His war ended in Potsdam. The family's building had been hit in the bombardment, but miraculously, the old apartment survived unscathed. Well, not entirely unscathed—the prewar friendly neighbors were gone, their place taken by a new clan that in years to come would play a rather sinister role in the family saga. "I never met people more vile, more unreasonable, more thuggish, more antisemitic than Frosya"—the matriarch—"and her offspring," remembered Dad (who was very much used to being liked) years later. "They absolutely loathed us, and there was nothing we could do to escape this hatred. It's a strange experience to live for twenty years next to human beings who hate you so much. Well, some marriages are like that, I suppose . . ."

By the 1960s, Dad had to face Frosya's wrath all alone. His mother died soon after the war, both his brothers married and moved out. Dad tried to limit his presence in the apartment to a minimum. Most of his waking time was spent either working or playing chess. During Stalin's last few years he had had to bear the full brunt of the anti-Jewish campaign, and that was when David's stark warning became Dad's own deep-seated conviction. A brilliant engineer, he was fired from his job and his scheduled PhD defense was scrapped. For almost two years, he remained unemployed, surviving on his meagre disability pension and the occasional illegal proceeds from pickup chess games. After Stalin's death in 1953, his prospects improved most dramatically: grudgingly he joined the Party, defended his thesis (Party membership was a prerequisite), and found a promising new job at a research institute. Being single and fairly well paid he spent his summers down in Crimea—playing chess on the beach, reading, and, judging by several yellowed pictures found in the closet, having his photograph taken in the company of an assortment of vacationing beauties from places like Krivoj Rog and Belgorod. And then, rather late in life, he met my mother.

Once this new woman entered the picture, Frosya changed her tactics from low-grade harassment to all-out assault. Things were getting out of control and decidedly more physical. On one particularly harrowing occasion the crazed neighbor hurled a boiling kettle at Dad's young wife. She was now pregnant and Dad feared for her safety and the safety of their unborn child. If they wanted to have a family they would have to find a new place to live—another communal apartment, of course. "I don't care if it's larger and noisier, so long as it's safer," he said.

The new apartment (the one I grew up in) was indeed larger and noisier. My parents had to downsize—swapping two rooms next to the potentially murderous Frosya for one room in what used to be the service quarters of one Baron Ginzburg, one of the wealthiest and therefore emancipated Jews in prerevolutionary St. Petersburg. I'm not sure what the place was like on the baron's watch, but in 1968, the apartment housed five families, all beneficiaries of the grand Soviet experiment that brought millions of human beings of a variety of ethnic backgrounds, dramatically different levels of education, and often incompatible hygiene habits, to live under one roof. The kids were screaming, the toilet was perpetually occupied, and our bath day was Thursday. However, when compared with the homicidal Frosya and her kin, the new abode qualified as an improvement. The neighbors, in any event, were generally nice and mostly friendly. Dad was well respected for his bookishness and prowess in chess, Mom's joviality was contagious. I think we were quite popular. And there was one additional benefit of great importance: besides the room, we also got to use a tiny alcove, formerly a broom closet under the baron. The space was just big enough to fit in a small desk, a chair, and a couple of bookshelves filled with Dad's chess library. There was no ventilation so the door (a flimsy cardboard affair) had to be kept open at all times to let in air (but also the sounds and the smells of the communal toilet some five feet away across the hallway). To say that Dad was emotionally attached to the broom closet would be a gross understatement. A few hours spent in his "study" made life worth living—a chess set, a chess clock, an open and heavily bookmarked copy of Mikhail Botvinnik's *Analytical and Critical Works, 1937–1970*...

In the late 1970s, Dad's already limited ability to engage his leg muscles began to weaken and by the end of the decade he graduated to crutches, a development that did not upset him at all—he kept boasting that now he could walk faster than me (he could). Some twenty years later, while on a trip to Israel, he would join an excursion touring Masada. The guide offered to call in some young assistants to carry him up the hill to the fortress, but Dad brushed him off: "Don't you mind me, I'm far more steady using these"—he raised his crutches in a celebratory salute to the group—"than your regular two-legged tourist." When they reached the top the guide paused, waiting for the rest of the group to catch up with him, then pointed at the heavily perspiring but broadly smiling Dad: "*Haverim,* I am supposed to talk to you about perseverance and sacrifice, about the survival of the Jewish people, I'm expected to say something inspirational, but this gentleman has made my task so much easier. All we have to do is acknowledge his presence in our midst. In a way, he embodies the message of Masada."

But in 1979, we were still years away from his Israel junket or from that pleasantly temperate day in June when, now pushing eighty, he spent some eight hours climbing the hills of San Francisco, taking in the view of the Golden Gate bridge and marveling at the extravagantly dressed denizens of the Castro district. In 1979, other concerns preoccupied us. That year, the building housing my grandma's communal apartment was slated for renovation and the residents were offered a choice of either a private flat on the outskirts of the city or a room in a newly renovated communal apartment in the same neighborhood. After much agonizing the family opted to keep Grandma in the center. Now I understand that the way my parents (and I) felt about the so-called "new districts" was not much different from how native or transplanted Manhattanites view parts of Queens or New Jersey. We belonged in the city center, even if the price for the privilege was a continued lack of privacy.

The summer of the Moscow Olympics (like most other furtive dissidents, Dad fervently supported the US-led boycott), Grandma moved to a new communal apartment where she claimed two rooms. There was only one other neighbor—an old, frail Ukrainian woman, who mostly kept to herself and, as the time passed, increasingly to bed. One morning as I was getting ready for school (at that point I was spending a lot of time at Grandma's place) the old woman knocked on the door. "Sweetie," she said, "I'm getting so old and my memory is just no good. Who was the architect of the chess pavilion in the Mikhailovsky Garden?" This was probably the first time we ever talked, and I was appropriately stunned. "Rossi," I mumbled. "God bless you, sweetie. I have just spent the whole night thinking about that pavilion. I even asked my nephew yesterday, but he only understands about plumbing. You are very smart and will have a long and interesting life. Now run to school." She delicately closed the door. I heard the sound of the door latch. Then quiet. By the time I got back home from school, the ambulance had already taken the old woman's body to the morgue. Her nephew was sitting in the kitchen—talking quietly to my parents, who seemed extremely nervous.

And thus launched the great real estate battle that would stretch over the next two years and eventually yield the ultimate luxury of private accommodations. The war of wills between my parents and the municipal bureaucracy started with an offer that my father believed the city would never refuse: we give up a much larger room in our communal abode in exchange for the ownership of the old woman's room in Grandma's apartment. The nephew had no objections, his malleability, I vaguely suspected, somehow connected to my mom's frequent trips to a basement pawnshop across the street from Vladimirskaya metro station. My father, a disabled "labor veteran" and "scientific worker," was apparently entitled to some sort of preferential treatment in such matters. Since he had never previously experienced anything that could even remotely qualify as preferential treatment, he convinced himself that "now was the time" and that "these lowlifes" (the term he employed rather indiscriminately when referring both to the cogs and the operators of Soviet state machinery) would cave in. He should've known better. Within a month of the old woman's passing my parents' application was denied and soon after the municipal workers visited Grandma's apartment and sealed the room of the deceased.

What ensued was a flurry of activity, a quest of historic proportions to claim the room as our own. Hope would flicker for a few days, only to give way to despair only to be rekindled again by some offhand remark by a passing party apparatchik, whose office my parents besieged with a determination worthy of Wehrmacht troops on the outskirts of Leningrad. I learned the names of our district deputies and party bosses, there was something dizzying in realizing that they were real people. Or sort of.

A few months into the campaign things were not looking up for the "scientific worker." The city notified us that the municipal authorities were about to issue a "tenancy order" for a family of two to occupy the ill-starred room. Dad stopped playing chess and fell into a morose state from which he would occasionally emerge to issue uncharacteristically theatrical pronouncements. He threatened to purchase an axe to prevent the "family of two" from moving in. He promised to write to Ronald Reagan (whom he, as many other armchair Soviet dissenters, regarded with an unbounded admiration) and thus "embarrass the hell out of the lowlifes." Thankfully, his audience was mostly limited to me and my mom as none of these declarations of intent would've augured well for the family if overheard in public.

Just as my parents' dreams of living in a private apartment were about to drift off into the milky vapor of the white nights, some intriguing news arrived from Moscow. The story of our epic struggle had reached the family patriarch—my mom's uncle, who happened to be a famous Soviet playwright and, in the past (and to my father's abiding contempt), a winner of the Stalin Prize. A. was a kind and loving man, but he inhabited the world of Moscow privilege—far removed from our own. For decades, his presence in our life had been more mythical than real. Visiting him and his wife in their enormous four-room private apartment in the Writer's House by the Aeroport metro station was one of my childhood's secret joys. And did he have stories to tell . . . In March 1942, he took a few days off from his assignment as a war correspondent embedded with the Baltic Fleet to sneak into encircled Leningrad. Taking full advantage of his numerous connections and pulling his colonel rank he tracked down his brother (my grandfather), who was dying of starvation in a military hospital on the Obvodnyi Canal. True to form, he brought with him a parcel of food—some bread, a few cans of sardines, chocolates. Years later he assured me that my grandpa had a nice last meal . . .

As a matter of course, we never bothered our famous relative with trivial requests; and generally he never volunteered his assistance—a combination of discretion and reserve that made for a pleasantly amicable relationship. Besides, who would dare to complain about someone who had risked his life to deliver the last meal to a dying brother? So the news that A. was apparently concerned about the outcome of my parents' real estate odyssey came as a complete surprise. He called in the morning and that very evening Dad and Mom boarded an overnight train to Moscow to hold a palaver with the distinguished old man. I never learned the exact content of that conversation, but evidently it was something of a strategy session, and my parents returned from Moscow agitated beyond belief and armed with a new plan of action. The plan centered on one particular individual—the beloved Soviet actor Kirill Lavrov, my great uncle's close friend and, by useful coincidence, our city deputy. A. prepared a letter to Lavrov, which, he insisted, had to be delivered to him in person. One of the nation's biggest celebrities, Lavrov was not easy to approach and his busy touring schedule turned the task of securing an audience with him into a veritable logistical nightmare. The summer months of 1982 would be spent in unrelenting pursuit.

I didn't see much of my parents that summer. They used up their vacation time trailing the famous actor around the Soviet Union—Moscow, Tallinn, Tula . . . Trains and buses, nights spent in bedbug-ridden hovels or in train stations. Like in a bad (good?) Hollywood screenplay, each time their target seemed within reach, something interfered: they were either late, or the actor was busy performing, or the performance had been cancelled, or he had been called off to a movie set down in the Caucuses. Finally, the fateful encounter took place on the windswept steps of the Theater of Drama in Riga, Latvia. I wonder what Lavrov made of this couple: a slight, madly grinning man on crutches, with a mane of wavy hair and wearing a beige turtleneck; a woman with piercing navy-blue eyes and standing in dramatic posture (she always dreamed of becoming an actress). As far as my parents were concerned, the whole scene was decidedly anticlimactic. It had to be. The actor graciously accepted the letter in its well-worn envelope and patiently listened to the story. He couldn't make any definite promises or commitments, but he assured them he would "put in a word."

This "word" travelled through the inner world of municipal bureaucracy for a good portion of 1982. By the time "The Letter" arrived, my parents had long since made peace with the futility of their mission. Dad had resumed playing chess and was spending much of his time dissecting the latest Korchnoi-Karpov match (he detested the officially approved Anatolii Karpov and rooted desperately for his childhood friend Victor Korchnoi). The letter arrived in an official-looking envelope and was quite short. Dad put on his glasses (he only started wearing them after he had turned sixty) and slowly opened the envelope. His hands were trembling, his voice having lost a register slipped to falsetto. The city had relented; we had the permission to give up our room in the communal apartment and move in with Grandma. Dad was crying. There would be no desperate dashes to hardware stores, no plaintive letters to the US president. "I will even forgive him playing Lenin," Dad sniffled. He was speaking of Kirill Lavrov.

The day we completed our move, I was late coming home from school. In fact, I stopped by the old communal apartment to say tearful goodbyes to our neighbors. We had spent fifteen years living side by side, in intimate proximity, all of us close yet dreaming of privacy. We knew each other's smells and tastes, we shared food and medicine. We feuded and reconciled, we gossiped about each other, we ignored each other's presence. From this communal living, I gained my first understanding of the frailty and durability of human connections, I learned about the historical drama of people thrown together by the will of the state, sharing space and life experiences with random strangers. I learned about sex. What a rite of passage . . .

When I opened the door with my newly cut key, the apartment smelled of fresh paint and was deathly quiet. I could hear the vague murmur of television coming from Grandma's room. Mom was still at work. In the living room (yes, we now had a living room), Dad slouched awkwardly in a recently acquired armchair—his deformed legs couldn't bend so learning how to get into and out of this new piece of furniture would take some practice. His chess set was at the ready in front of him. As always, when engrossed in his beloved game, he remained completely oblivious to his surroundings.

"Papa," I said. He looked up startled, tidied his hair (as he always did, obsessively), then smiled: "Ah, you're home."—"Yes, I'm home. So . . . how do you like it?"—"Like *what*?" He looked at me uncomprehendingly. Well, I thought, this quiet—no running kids, no screaming neighbors, no kitchen noises, no Tamara Vasilievna, who always flushed the toilet with a particular vengeance, and . . . no dying invalid children in a bed next to you, no wailing wounded soldiers loaded on a hospital train at the Saratov railroad juncture, where you spent a week hoping to catch a freight to Moscow, no vicious Frosya . . . The quiet, you know. "Oh, *that*?" He looked around—surprised? bemused? Still thinking of the Alekhine defense for which he had lately developed a new appreciation? "I don't know," he said with a shrug. "I guess this feels . . ." He looked distracted, searching for words that usually came to him easily. "I guess it feels . . . *normal*?" He let the word hover between us. Yes, it was the right word and he didn't mind repeating it: "It feels normal . . . absolutely normal."

Arthur or Night on Earth*

By far, by far he was the most dazzling, the most charismatic man of the cohort. Just a couple of years older than the rest of us, Arthur comported himself with suave dignity. He was tall, lanky, mischievous-looking, with broad, fashionably stooped shoulders. A slight overbite rendered his mouth a perpetual sensual pout. He spoke slowly, deliberately, in a deep baritone ("What a beautiful velvety voice," my grandma would intone each time he called me at home), which presented a strange and alluring contrast to his youthful looks. Arthur advocated self-reliance and independence from parents. He was the only person I knew who rented his own apartment and visited his parents on the weekends. Even though not Jewish he worshipped his mother with whom, he insisted, he conversed in French, the language in which he claimed fluency.

He dressed with studied and confusing shabbiness—confusing because even his threadbare suit fit him snugly; he always looked stylish. He was a *fartsovschik*—a smooth, black-market operator who haunted the hotels and restaurants frequented by foreigners with whom he engaged in mysterious commercial transactions. By his own admission he got a particular satisfaction out of "playing on contrasts"—usually coming to class wearing a beat-up pair of shapeless Skorokhod shoes but then showing up the next day at the CP History seminar sporting brand-new Swedish sneakers and impossibly cool Lee jeans.

Arthur worshipped late nineteenth-century French poets and German automobile engineering. He despised *Sovok*, but his objections to the Soviet regime were not of a political nature, at least not outwardly. He treated my dissident protestations with slight contempt. "You see," he would say, "you keep whining about freedom and various Sakharovs, but you really are a pawn of the system. You wear crap, you take money from your parents, if you ever get a date what are you gonna do with the girl? Can you pick her up in a car (even in a Zaporozhets)? Take her to a restaurant? Bribe the bouncer and get

---

* First published as "Arthur or Night on Earth," *Kenyon Review* (July/August 2017).

her into a bar at some Intourist hotel? No? I didn't think so. What am I even talking about . . . you've never *been* to a restaurant, you'll never *own* a car." "Listen," he would continue, "the problem with this regime is not that they lock up the occasional dissident, the problem is the complete, total lack of quality. This fucking country is built on crap and manufactures crap. In huge quantities. What? The Hermitage? Who fucking needs the Hermitage when the best they can do is steal a Fiat design and even then fuck it up and produce some piece of Zhiguli junk? Stop listening to the BBC, learn to be a man."

Easier said than done. My one foray onto the Galyora—the second-floor gallery at the shopping center Gostiny Dvor, a place where illicit trading was conducted by an array of shady characters—resulted in a loss of fifty rubles and any further ambition to be a *fartsovschik.* (I also spent a night at the nearby police station, puzzled by the seeming intimacy of the interactions between the area drunks and prostitutes and their uniformed captors.) By the second semester Arthur and I had settled into a strange sort of friendship, with him playing the role of an older and far more experienced comrade who recognized both the potential and the many limitations of his protégé. I continued to listen to the BBC and accept money from my parents. My love life was infused with white nights sensibilities—romantic and therefore unglamorous. Arthur continued to regale us with the stories of his entrepreneurial successes and amorous conquests; his commitment to materiality had evolved into an elaborate personal philosophy of consumption. While clearly cherishing our friendship, he nevertheless cultivated a distinct separateness, a strategic compartmentalizing of his social engagements. I never met his parents or any of his numerous girlfriends. That is, until he moved in with Nika.

That Arthur would end up dating (and eventually marrying) Nika stood to reason. A year our senior, Nika had an air of someone much older (and wiser) and seemed to inhabit a galaxy far removed from our own. She was a child of privilege—her father worked for the merchant marine and spent the better part of the year traversing foreign seas and disembarking in exotic ports. This rare access to foreign lands manifested itself in Nika's tasteful outfits and in her air of detachment from the quotidian. In the drab, stale-smelling hallways of the History Department she looked out of place. And she knew it. She perfected a classy retro look; her fleeting smile was hard to decipher, but I chose to interpret it as mildly disdainful; years later I would recognize the type in late Woody Allen films. Whenever I would work up enough courage to chat with her, Nika's demeanor remained friendly but distant. Of course, I had a crush on her, but somehow it was not sexual—more of a fascination with a delicately beautiful and enigmatic specimen. To us mere mortals, she was completely inaccessible. Not to Arthur, though . . . In the spring of our sophomore year, during a mind-numbingly dull lecture on Russian medieval history, he solemnly confided in me that he and Nika were an item. In fact, they had been dating for months but by mutual agreement had kept their intimacy a secret. I suspect the reasons for such equivocation had less to do with any notion of privacy and more with Arthur's weakness for French Symbolist poets, especially his famously debauched namesake. To tell the truth, the intrepid black marketeer was a closeted romantic. Like the rest of us.

Arthur made a big show of hosting me for dinner at Nika's apartment, which, as I discovered, was located just a few blocks from my own. The nights were already growing short and pale, and at 10:00 p.m. there was no need for light. The apartment was classical old St. Petersburg—full of books and dark, dusty nooks and crannies. Apparently it belonged to Nika's family since before the revolution—a rare but not unheard-of case of private ownership surviving in some stunted form the vagaries of Soviet rule. Arthur played the role of man of the house with gravity (and barely concealed delight), and if he wanted to make an impression on his younger friend he certainly succeeded beyond all expectations. They were the first "real" couple of roughly my age that I knew—a couple who shared their own space, slept next to each other, made love in their own bed, took turns in the shower, and then sat together to breakfast in the morning—so Remarque-like (we were mad about Erich Maria), so indomitably adult. There was no trace of Nika's usual aloofness; she chatted freely and animatedly, and I had some trouble reconciling this sweet and vivacious girl with the enigmatic *Great Gatsby* character I had been admiring from afar over the previous couple of years. They addressed each other with cute pet names—Little Birdy for Nika and Little Piggy for Arthur—which somehow didn't strike me as corny but rather preternaturally cool, and again . . . so adult. The evening was precious and dreamlike, and I responded to it the way I (and most of my friends at the time) responded to most of life's memorable events—by composing a poem. Years later I still remember the first line (but not much else): "Белой ночью и кошки белые, и вокзалы стоят прощальные . . ." ("During the white nights even the cats turn pale, and the railway stations bid their farewells . . .").

We talked about their plans, which included marriage and the acquisition of a used German-made automobile. We talked about my plans, which didn't exist, as I was about to be drafted into the army. Both Arthur and Nika sounded alarmed by this prospect, and Arthur, who had secured a deferment thanks to an opportunely diagnosed congenital heart condition, scolded me for not making an effort to dodge the draft: "It's not for you, it's not for people like *us*. Do you get it? Do you know how they treat guys like us, especially those whose nose is shaped like yours? What if you get shipped down south? Did you see what they did to Vitalik?" Vitalik was our war veteran classmate who had recently returned from a tour in Afghanistan and exhibited some disturbing signs of psychological instability. His temper tantrums were legendary, and we all swore not to let him anywhere near alcohol. When drunk, Vitalik turned into a menace—to himself and anyone who happened to be within his peripheral vision. When sober, he remained morose and withdrawn. Obviously, we didn't understand at the time that he likely suffered from an acute case of PTSD. No, I didn't want to be like Vitalik, and I most certainly didn't want to end up on a dusty, sun-scorched hill somewhere in Kandahar.

Unbeknownst to Arthur, my father and I had been planning just for such an eventuality. The planning process reflected my father's deep-seated phobias and geographical naivete; it also captured a degree of idealism that even at the time I found endearing. Ever since the draft papers arrived earlier in the spring my father and I engaged in a strange weekly ritual of charting out my possible escape routes from Afghanistan. In planning this defection, we primarily relied on the 1951 edition of the *Great Soviet World Atlas* that bore a Stalin quote on its title page. The plan, as I understand it now, was sheer madness, but it did have the benefit of being comfortingly simple (it also ignored such salient features of regional geography as insurmountable mountain ranges, extreme aridity, and drastic temperature fluctuations).

Having spent hours poring over the dated map we produced two possible itineraries: one seemed to be the most straightforward and would have taken me from Kabul to Islamabad via Peshawar. Of course, for it to become feasible I would have to be stationed in or close to the capital. Plan B envisioned a more daring escape from Kandahar to Karachi, via Quetta. Thankfully, we had no access to Google Maps or Earth, which when applied to the area in question provides a quick reality check to any would-be adventurer. But then again, my father was not just an armchair explorer. Well, he may have been an armchair explorer in 1986, but in 1944, as a disabled twenty-two-year-old man (his lower extremities disfigured by an acute case of bone tuberculosis) he hitch-hiked from a tiny village in the Urals, where he had been working as a teacher since his evacuation from Leningrad in 1941, all the way to Moscow—a passage that took him more than three months to complete. Some forty years later he was devising another harrowing journey across another country devastated by war. The hair-raising scheme owed its madness to my father's Manichean vision of a world torn asunder by a momentous struggle between good and evil, in which the side of good was dramatically represented by the Congress of the United States and America's sitting president. Father's fondness for Ronald Reagan knew no bounds, and in that he was no different from most other Soviet Jews of a dissident persuasion. Needless to say, he fully expected that his affection, which he experienced as uniquely personal, was widely shared across races and national borders. In accordance with this conviction, the magic phrase "I love Ronald Reagan" should have secured my safe crossing from Afghanistan into Pakistan and onto the grounds of the US embassy in Islamabad or US consulate in Karachi.

Luckily for everyone involved I never got to test the Reagan magic on either the Pashtun shepherds or the Pakistani military police. A few weeks after the unforgettable farewell dinner with the cute, young couple a specially requisitioned train deposited me, along with some six hundred other disoriented recruits, on the spit-covered, cigarette-butt-strewn platform of a drab provincial Russian town that was to become my home over the next couple of years. After the first few months, when it did feel on occasion that my parents' (and Arthur's) worst fears were not all that far-fetched, the service settled into a predictable pattern of great boredom and uneventfulness punctuated by sporadic (and usually quickly extinguished) flare-ups of violence, some of it interethnic.

Writing and receiving letters was our sustenance; my carefully preserved army archive still holds close to a thousand epistolary items. Arthur wrote to me twice. The first letter arrived a couple of months after my call-up. Arthur sounded concerned but supportive; he suggested I convert my new experiences into poetry. He mentioned his idol, the poet-turned-entrepreneur Rimbaud, whose poetic, sexual, and business exploits in Arabia and Harar Arthur found both fascinating and instructive. As far as I could judge, there were some fairly obvious differences between Kovrov and Aden, but I got his point. Arthur and Nika had gotten married and Little Piggy had finally purchased a car—alas, not the much-desired Mercedes-Benz 500SE but a Soviet-made Lada Model 7 ("Made in Sovok but will do for now"). The wedding was a modest and apparently secretive affair, attended only by the families. A black-and-white wedding picture fell out of the envelope: Arthur and Nika stood holding hands on what appeared to be a boating dock somewhere in the countryside (Nika's dacha?). Arthur appeared to be on the verge of bursting out laughing, Nika squinted against the sun, which gave her a knowing, sarcastic look. Both were dressed casually. Arthur was holding something tiny in his free hand; I looked closer and studied the photo. There could be no doubt—Arthur was holding the car keys.

I received another letter from Arthur almost two years later, less than a month before my final discharge. It arrived in a strange-looking, bluish envelope; the two stamps on the upper-right corner showed the profile of a middle-aged man with a mustache. The word *SVERIGE* appeared underneath the image. It was clear that I was not the only one intrigued by the foreign origin of the letter—the envelope had been tampered with, the flaps torn open and then politely reattached with a small piece of Scotch tape. The letter was most certainly not short on news; in fact, I needed a few minutes to absorb the magnitude of the changes in Arthur's life, and even then it all seemed pretty surreal. Arthur and Nika had gotten divorced about a year earlier—the reasons were murky, presented with deliberate vagueness (something about diverging life trajectories). Arthur was married again, though, to a Finish woman "a little bit older" than he, and he . . . had left the country. The newlyweds had settled in Helsinki ("One of the best neighborhoods, fantastic sea views"), but Arthur's new job with a Swedish consulting firm often took him to Stockholm and beyond. In fact, he had just returned from a couple of months in Tangiers (God, where is the 1951 *World Atlas* when you need one?) and Paris. Arthur's business partner, impressed with his fluency in Russian, Finnish, French, and English, wanted him to open another office in Oslo, but Arthur was not sure—his wife had booked a summer villa south of Florence, and he felt he should probably spend more time with her, even though he got sick and tired of Italy on his previous business trips. There was a PS: my friend now owned a Mercedes.

I reread the letter a dozen times and still found it incomprehensible. I had spent the past two years removed from real life and, as a result, lost much of a sense of reality. We were stuck on an island, complete with barracks and marching grounds and BMP repair shops, but beyond the perimeter fence the world had shifted, it was full of mysteries and promise. I wondered if I would ever see Arthur again.

***

I saw Arthur again on a snowy night in Helsinki in the early 1990s. We were returning to the States after our first post-emigration visit to St. Petersburg and had planned the trip so that we could spend a couple of days in this Nordic city, whose alluring forbiddingness had captivated us throughout our childhood and early youth. In fact, I don't think I ever got over its mystique—maybe that's why watching the Helsinki-based vignette in Jarmusch's *Night on Earth* still constitutes the ultimate cinematic experience for me.

In January, Helsinki was steeped in quiet and cozy melancholy. We booked an inexpensive hotel near the municipal park; the frosted-over windows of our room faced a generously lit skating rink where well-behaved kids and their parents solemnly glided in circles. The music from the rink mixed with the gentle screeching of late trams that circumnavigated the park before swishing off into the night of the city: night on earth. We had agreed to meet Arthur at an Italian place around the corner. The restaurant was almost empty; besides the three of us (my wife, myself, and our little son) there was just one other couple seated on the opposite side of the room. They were young, roughly our age, sitting very straight and hardly exchanging a word over a dinner of spaghetti and meatballs. Their dignified poise made us feel self-conscious—we were making too much noise. Arthur walked in just as we were finishing dessert. He wore a heavy parka but was hatless. We embraced—it's been, what, seven years? He gave me a quick once-over. "Where are your famous curls?" he said. "You're beginning to lose hair."—"I know," I smiled. "I know."—"I told you, it's the army, it's the fucking army." We laughed and embraced again.

Arthur's car was parked outside next to a snowbank. It was immediately clear that he was proud of his car and wanted us to be impressed. Having spent the previous two years delivering pizzas in Oklahoma, I still knew precious little about cars, especially the ones blanketed in Finnish snow. "It's a Mercedes, right?" I ventured a guess.—"You must be kidding me, right? It's a Peugeot, a special luxe edition. Don't you know the difference? Well, I suppose some people never change . . . I know a guy in Turku, who had it imported for me from Sochaux. It's custom-made. Custom-made just for Arthur." He wanted to make light of it but sounded tense, nervous. We agreed to a quick tour of nighttime Helsinki, followed by a nightcap at his apartment. We drove aimlessly around for at least forty minutes—the city seemed frozen to its core, the occasional blinking neon sign only accentuated the arctic darkness of the place, its strange immobility. Arthur tried to make conversation but kept getting distracted, veering off topic, interjecting non sequiturs. I asked him about his work. He shrugged: "Things are sort of in transition right now. You see, once you've achieved a certain level you can't just take any job. I'm not like one of these fucking lumberjacks (I figured that's how he referred to all Finns). I'm not gonna rot away in some damn Suomi office. So, right now I'm working on a few leads, serious money, you know." We fell silent for a few minutes. "Are you in touch with Nika?" he asked.—"No, haven't seen her since that dinner at her place. How is she?"—"Dunno, we're not really on speaking terms. Or should I say, she won't speak with me . . . But she is OK, remarried, got herself a kid. The husband, I hear, is loaded. Good for her."

As we were getting closer to our final destination (Arthur's apartment), he was growing visibly gloomy, his anxiety filled the car and was kind of hard to bear. We soon parked in front of a two-story apartment building. My wife gasped—it looked remarkably similar to our own low-income apartment complex back in Oklahoma. I had no idea this sort of residential architecture—a long balcony running the length of the building, with rows of individual apartments opening up onto it—was a transcontinental affair. Arthur led the way upstairs, explaining as we mounted the steps that no, this was not a permanent abode—things, as he already mentioned, were in transition; he had a crew working on a new house out in Tammisalo ("You ever heard of Tammisalo? Lots of diplomats live in that neighborhood, so it's expensive but worth every fucking mark, and it costs lots of marks to build there"). The construction will go on for a few more months, a lot of materials need to be imported, particularly from Italy, which takes time; in the meantime they are using this place as a point of transition, a temporary pad before their final leap into the luxury of the new house in Tammisalo. Most of their furniture was in storage; in the apartment they keep only a few of the most expensive items. "Basically it's all about insurance, you know," he declared with tragic finality, stopping in front of one of the numerous apartment doors that pockmarked the façade of the building and rummaging for the keys in his parka pocket.

I remembered that Arthur's Finnish wife was a "little bit older" than him, but I didn't know she was approximately my mother's age. Christina had been expecting us: a bottle of wine, four glasses, and some snacks were set on a small coffee table. The apartment was neat and sparsely furnished. They had a dog—a nervous Italian greyhound, whose state of agitation upon our entrance into the apartment matched Arthur's. After the initial introductions Arthur immediately switched to Russian, which made me uncomfortable—his wife clearly did not speak a word of it. But Arthur wanted to talk about his dog—a very rare breed, which had to be imported from Italy (I couldn't help but marvel at how much my friend's life had come to depend on Italian imports). He didn't think my son should be playing with the dog, who had a particularly delicate nervous system and, according to Arthur, had to be flown to Milan for regular checkups. He also thought the kid should be careful not to spill his juice on the coffee table, which had been made to order at a Norwegian woodshop specializing in exotic mahogany: "You know, one of those high-end custom-made products—hard to make, easy to ruin." We drank some wine, which Arthur explained came from a medieval cellar in Burgundy—he had it shipped to Helsinki in a batch that cost him a small fortune, but it was worth it because now he had something of quality to share with an old friend. The conversation meandered and exhausted me greatly; we kept trying to draw in Arthur's wife, while he kept slipping into Russian. His obliviousness to her silent presence infuriated me. The phone rang. Arthur got up quickly and headed for one of the two bedrooms. "Pardon me. I'm expecting a phone call; it's my business partner in Stockholm. I guess the deal is on, things are beginning to roll. Be right back." He closed the door tightly behind him. In a few seconds we could hear the quiet murmur of a conversation, punctuated by prolonged silences. Arthur was speaking in Russian.

"It's his mother," said Christina. Her English was surprisingly fluent.—"His mother?"—"Yes, she calls him every evening." I couldn't quite figure out whether she was annoyed with this frequency of parental contacts or simply felt compelled to state the obvious. With Arthur out of the room Christina came alive. She had lived in the States back in the '70s and still harbored fond memories of a small college town in Pennsylvania where she spent two semesters as an exchange student. She was happy to welcome Arthur's friends into her home; she knew how much he missed Russia and thought that reconnecting with old friends would do him a lot of good: "You've probably noticed, he is a bit nervous." We chatted some more. Arthur was still on the phone, and I thought we should start thinking of getting back to the hotel. "It is getting late, the kid needs to go to bed soon, and you're probably tired too." Christina smiled politely: "Yes, I suppose it is late. I'm a schoolteacher and used to getting up early, but it's a challenge for Arthur—his morning shift starts at eight."—"His shift?"—"Yes, his shift. He works at the post office. Didn't he tell you?"

We called a taxi that arrived just as Arthur ended his phone call. He apologized profusely for leaving us alone with Christina, and we agreed to see each other again the next evening, our last in Helsinki.

The next day we spent the few daylight hours available to us walking and riding trams around the city, whose snowy monotony was becoming familiar. In the port, our boy ran dutifully through the empty, skeleton-like stalls of the open-air market and threw snowballs at a colony of phlegmatic ducks huddled together on a floating ice sheet that covered much of the harbor. Then we climbed up the slippery hill to the cathedral, where the square was all white, with occasional patches of blackish ice, and completely bare of humans. Down below, the Gulf stretched out past the island fortress and into the Baltic whiteness. A Tallinn ferry had just left its berth and, oblivious to the ice and snow, was heading out into the sea. The streetlights came alive at three and by four the city was dark. We headed back to the hotel—to pack for an early flight and wait for Arthur.

It was close to 10:00 p.m. and we had largely given up on waiting for Arthur when he finally called from the front desk—he was in the lobby. Arthur was drunk. Not intoxicated, not inebriated. Drunk. And he wanted to talk. He asked me if I still wrote poetry and was relieved to learn that I didn't ("Such a waste of time, and, anyway, none of us will write better than Rimbaud or . . . even, you know, that punk Blok"). He wanted to know about America but had no patience listening to my story. Generally, he had come to hold Americans in an extremely low esteem ("All fakes, all ignorant bumpkins, just as bad as these fucking Suomi lumberjacks"). I disagreed, but he didn't want to argue. His unhappiness, heavy as a shroud, enveloped us, made our little group too big and unwieldy for a tiny hotel bar.

"So . . . tomorrow," Arthur tapped the empty glass with his index finger. As usual but even more so, he enunciated his words with deliberate precision. "Tomorrow, this time tomorrow you'll be . . . where?"—"Dallas," I said.—"A-a-ha, Dallas . . . Dal-las . . . If there's hell on earth it's probably called Dal-las. No . . . wait, wait . . . it's probably called Hel-sin-ki! Did you hear the *ki*? It's really important—it's the *ki* that makes it hell." He was making no sense, but I didn't want him to leave in this state. At least not by himself. "Should I call Christina?" I asked.—"Christina?" He looked confused. "I know no one by that name. And what a horrid, horrid name it is: Chris-ti-na. So churchy . . . reminds me of Rimbaud's last days in that charity hospital in Marseille . . . Did I ever tell you? The priests finally got him just before he died."—"Anyone else I can call to come and get you?" His smile was vacant, self-absorbed.—"Yeah, call Nika, tell her to put on a pair of skis and come up and get her Little Piggy, who is stuck in the fucking hellll . . . sinkkkki."—"Anyone else?" There was a girl—Olga, a prostitute, someone he had known during his glory days back in Leningrad, another lost soul transplanted to this indifferent frozen city. On a third try I was able to extract her phone number from the increasingly incoherent Arthur. She asked no questions and twenty minutes after the phone call entered the lobby; the taxi was waiting outside, its engine purring peacefully, its headlights capturing from the night a haphazard and nervous dance of the millions of perfectly shaped snowflakes, each one of them precious, each one holding a promise of a snow queen-like metamorphosis. Olga was tiny and seemed painfully shy, but she helped me hoist Arthur to his feet with remarkable strength and alacrity. "Don't worry," she said, "I'll take him home, I know where he lives." Arthur and I embraced, and I was startled to see that the unflappable Arthur was crying. He struggled to say something, but his usual eloquence had abandoned him; words were not coming easily. "Those lumberjacks, those fucking, fucking lumberjacks," he kept whispering, as Olga and I led him to the car.

***

There were a few times over the next twenty years when I thought of Arthur. Not the Helsinki Arthur, but the one I had come to admire in Leningrad—the suave charmer with velvety baritone; the rakish black-market profiteer who generously dispensed life lessons and pointed me towards adulthood; the wise, older friend whose easy cynicism I found so exasperating, yet so attractive. On my visits to Russia, I often asked about him, but no one could say anything definitive. The stories ranged from the ludicrous to utterly unbelievable: Arthur had left Helsinki and moved to Stockholm (oh, wait, was it Oslo?); Arthur had a run-in with the Chechens and fled to South America, where he now sells used cars; poor Arthur had drunk himself to death; Arthur was killed in a bar brawl in Majorca; Arthur was back in St. Petersburg, teaching high school French and Finnish (high school Finnish?). There was no trace of him. He was my very first Google search, and it yielded nothing. Some years later I discovered that there was a sales associate with the same last name at a trendy furniture store in Stockholm. I called the store. The person on the phone was friendly but could not help me—indeed, there had been a Russian man working at their showroom a few years earlier, but he had long since left and they had no idea of his whereabouts. Eventually I gave up searching and, truth be told, I'd probably never searched that hard.

***

Nika had changed. But it was no doubt Nika—the 1920s haircut, the stylish umbrella that she used as a decorative cane (what a statement of elegance!), the same look of sarcastic detachment. I couldn't believe it took us over twenty years to finally bump into each other even though I visited St. Petersburg with great regularity and she, as I quickly learned, continued to live in the same apartment by the Maltsevsky farmers market. She hugged me warmly, then stepped back and shook her head in mock disbelief: "Oh dear, your hair, what happened to the hair?" I had gotten used to my Russian women friends assuming this air of parental authority—like older relatives, they ignored the reality of time passing, they refused to treat you as an adult. Their familiarity was jarring but surprisingly comforting, as if they were inviting you to forget, for a few minutes, the gap of years.

Nika was in no rush; she was on the way home from her biweekly psychoanalysis class ("I'm a Jungian," she explained). It seemed like every other Russian friend I knew was doing something "New Agey," usually with an all-consuming dedication. We walked around the neighborhood in search of a suitable place to talk in quiet. It was an easy task, and its very easiness served as a jolting reminder of the distance separating us from our youth. The tram lines were gone and the area was teeming with cars (most of them foreign-made *inomarki*), parked with no particular concern for municipal regulations. The courtyards of the buildings that I remembered since my childhood were now gated, their façades plastered with flyers advertising escort services, saunas, and massage parlors. There were tanning salons, pretentious boutiques, hipster bars, and a plethora of sushi and ice cream places. We found a quiet café, whose "African" décor was testimony to its owners' flights of aesthetic fancy (and their complete unfamiliarity with the basics of political correctness). Nika made a quick phone call to give her son the address of the café—he would stop by later to pick her up. And in the meantime, we could talk—more than twenty years' worth of catching up. We could talk about our lives that in retrospect appeared to be the stories we wrote, the stories that we continued to be writing. "We were too literary," Nika offered, "too affected by the weirdness of this city, by its ghostlike presence in our lives." I agreed, readily. We talked more—about our travels and distances covered, and jobs, and marriages, and divorces (in that regard, Nika's record of accomplishment far surpassed mine). And, of course, we talked about Arthur.

No, she didn't know where he was, what eventually became of him. In fact, she couldn't say whether he was dead or alive. She heard (many years ago) that he got divorced and left Finland and was drinking heavily for a while ("went on a real bender, you know, gained tons of weight. Can you imagine a fat Arthur? That skinny little piggy suddenly growing fat? Frankly, I can't believe that part—most likely just stupid rumors"), then the trail went cold . . . But before he disappeared, she did see him once. Sometime in the late 1990s, he suddenly showed up unannounced at her dacha on the Gulf of Finland: "It was towards the end of the summer, August probably, because the nights were already dark, early in the morning—2:00 a.m., maybe. He crashed his SUV through the front gate. My husband was livid, pulled him out of the car; I was afraid he would kill him. Arthur was wasted, it's a miracle he was able to drive at all. He looked pitiful—unshaven, disoriented, mumbling incomprehensibly. Of course, we couldn't kick him out; we are not animals. I made him a bed out on the verandah, let him sleep it off. I don't think he even recognized me . . . When I got up in the morning, he was already gone. He had left five hundred dollars on the dining table—I guess in compensation for the gate . . ." Nika fished a cigarette out of her handbag, lit it expertly. It was surprising to see her smoking. The barista pulled a lever on the espresso machine, and for a few seconds the café filled with mighty hissing sounds—some coffee gods puzzling over the human condition, whistling in disbelief. "And that," Nika drew an airy circle with the cigarette, "*that* was the last sighting of the little piggy. He took off, left, vanished, drove off into the sunset (no, wait, it was the sunrise!) in his beloved Mercedes SUV . . . with a bent fender."

Nika's son turned out to be an attractive young man—rather slight but athletic, with a warm and uninhibited charm. One couldn't miss the easy rapport between the mother and the son; there was not a hint of tension between the two—a child and a parent completely comfortable in each other's presence. As the young man approached our table, Nika quickly put out the cigarette and looked up at him with an affected, coquettish bashfulness: "Sorry, dear, it won't happen again, I promise"—"Mom, who told you I take your promises seriously?" He turned to me: "How can one trust women, especially the ones smoking cigarettes in . . ." He scanned the café, shook his head ruefully, and finished with a theatrical sigh, "a rather strange establishment?" This scene was probably performed, at least in part, for my benefit, but their intimacy was real. I couldn't detect a single false note in their playful back-and-forth.

With the little play-acting routine out of the way, it was time for introductions. Nika's face assumed an expression of faux gravity (oh, she was acting up again): "Meet the ultimate arbiter of my morals, my prosecutor and my judge, my son . . . Arthur." For a second, I thought I had misheard her: "What? Arthur? Your son Arthur?" Nika looked at me with unmistakable amusement. Quarter of a century and I still couldn't read her smile. "Your son Arthur?"—"But of course, such a nice name: Ar-thur, Ar-tur-chik. Don't you like it?"—"I do, it's just that . . . you know . . ." I realized how silly it was to be stunned by a name—it was just a name, like any other; there were dozens, possibly hundreds of Arthurs in this city alone. And yet, and yet . . . "Oh, no," it was as if Nika suddenly became aware of my silent question and found it preposterous. "No, no, oh God, *no*!" There was mirth in her voice. There was something about my bewilderment that she found profoundly entertaining. "Stop looking mystified; we harbor no secrets, right, Arturchik? Besides, as you may remember, I'm on my fourth husband."—"Oh, Mom, stop embarrassing me." Arthur rolled his eyes, but his tone expressed only affection for this classy and slightly eccentric woman, his mother.

Talking to Arthur was pleasant. He seemed like a straightforward but thoughtful guy—a bit self-centered (and who is not at his age?) but engaged with the world and full of curiosity. An MBA student at a university in London, he was back in St. Petersburg for the summer break. How did he like London? Oh, he loved it. But it was New York he admired. He had tons of questions about the city. Many of his friends were moving there, and he would love to try it, too, even though what he *really* loved was Silicon Valley. Because, you see, he had a dream, no, forget the dream, a plan—he had a plan to work for the best company in the world: Apple. "You know about Apple, right?" I pointed at my iPhone resting on the table next to the espresso cup. Arthur gave it a quick, expert glance. "4s?"—"What?"—"Your iPhone model's 4s?"—"I guess . . . I don't really know." At first, Arthur thought I was joking, but having realized that I was not, he fixed me with a stern look: "You. Don't. Know. The. Model. Of. Your. iPhone?" Each word fell with the heaviness of an indictment. Clearly, Arthur had little patience for Luddites. "You understand, though," he continued, "what a beautiful product it is?" The question was rhetorical and disagreeing was not an option. Besides, I did like my iPhone. However, Arthur was not done with me, not yet. He wanted to explain: "You see, for me it's all about quality, how quality things are designed, how they get made, how they are," he looked at me reproachfully, "*respected*." He picked up the iPhone, fumbled with it for a few seconds. "It is a thing of quality. Look how elegant it is, how slick; there is nothing superfluous in its design, not one unnecessary feature. When I look at this product, I feel better about us humans . . . also about myself. My life comes into focus and I know what I want."—"And what is it that you want, Arthur?" He smiled mischievously. "Not much. I just want to work for Apple."

Nika was not part of the conversation, but her presence was felt; in some subtle, ill-defined way, she owned the scene, gave it its meaning. She had lit another cigarette. Arthur moved to object, but quickly reconsidered and threw up his hands in mock exasperation: "You see what I have to deal with?" "You see what *I* have to deal with," laughed Nika. "I told you, he is a one-man morality police, keeps tabs on me 24/7. Even from London. Would you believe it, this mama's boy calls me every damn evening! I'm sure his girlfriends think he must be Jewish."—"Am I?" Arthur asked without losing a beat. "*Am* I Jewish?" These two loved needling each other.—"I don't know what you are; you are the damn Grand Inquisitor, but I still love you. Come on, boys, it's getting late."

It *was* getting late, but how would one know? In the summer, the milky Finnish nights turn our understanding of time on its head, make a shameless mockery of it. Memories come floating in through the hastily pinned-up mosquito screen and refuse to leave in the morning, not even when they are supposed to—at the rooster's crow. Distances shrink and one can easily imagine a place untouched by time's passage: a place where the frigid, dark waters caress the icy hulks of container ships in the harbor, where a lonely driver pulls over on a highway just north of Dallas to peer into the pitch black but full of electricity night of the great American Southwest, discerning the familiar shapes of the Milky Way, the same timeless constellation that comforts a sleepy, young sentry guarding unnecessarily a dilapidated BMP park full of rusty machinery. One can also imagine a rundown French hospital where a roguish poet dying of gangrene finds consolation in the simple words of a humble, provincial priest, and, of course, if you try hard enough, if you strain to remember, you will see a deathly quiet old apartment, where two young lovers sit next to each other (so very closely) at a stained kitchen table, mapping out a future that will not be theirs.

The Road to Battambang*

Mme Rancourt is Cambodian, but she has lived most of her life in France, where she moved in 1980, about a year after Vietnamese troops chased the remnants of the black-shirted Khmer Rouge army out of Phnom Penh. She is Cambodian, but she is mostly French, and she is French in a peculiarly French way—in a light, understated, occasionally brooding yet inevitably elegant way. Her weightless tailored linen pantsuits are testimony to her style and easy understanding of the demands of a tropical climate. She looks fit and much younger than her fifty-seven years.

When in Battambang she always stays at Le Pavillon, an old colonial hotel run by a French management company. There is a timeless feel about the hotel's interior, or rather it feels like it's always 1934—the coolness of the checkered black-and-white floor tiles, the whirring of listless ceiling fans, the friendly hotel dog resting by the mahogany reception desk, the clunky black rotary telephone. The doors to the rooms, made of solid wood and curved at the top oval-like, are painted white. Mme Rancourt's room is on the second floor, facing the pool where a couple of elderly guests (French? Scandinavian?) are lounging in the shadow of an old mango tree. It's always the same room, reserved months in advance. Olivia, the hotel manager, originally from Marseilles, will make sure that the room is available to her friend—they have known each other for years and once even vacationed together in Portugal. These days, Olivia doesn't have much time for travel. Le Pavillon has been featured in several guidebooks, and Anthony Bourdain once stayed here during one of his whirlwind tours of Southeast Asia. TripAdvisor ranks it as the #1 hotel in Battambang. More work (which Olivia performs cheerfully and without complaint) is the price of success.

Mme Rancourt lives in Vertou, a fashionable suburb of Nantes, a lovely city in Brittany that *Time* magazine recently determined to be "the most livable in Europe." A reasonably successful real estate attorney, she runs her own agency, which is really just a two-person operation, consisting of Mme

---

* First published as "The Road to Battambang," *New England Review* 38, no. 4 (2017), 46–61.

Rancourt herself and her scatterbrained but loyal assistant of many years, Mme Guillon. Mme Rancourt is married to Pierre Rancourt, an architect, and theirs has been a happy marriage, a marriage of equals, a marriage of mutual respect, of tenderness and understanding, and love of jazz and Italian vacations. They have two grown-up children: Dominique, who is expecting, has recently moved to London with her Swiss-born husband, Daniel, a financial analyst whose joviality and untroubled laughter defy every common stereotype of a Swiss financier. Dominique is a serious and gentle soul, a foil to her outgoing husband. And then there is Bastien, Mme Rancourt's adored son and a kindred spirit, with whom she enjoys a raucous friendship that makes her feel younger than her age. Bastien studies computer science at the prestigious École Normale Supérieure in Paris. He is obsessed with artificial intelligence and Eastern European women; sometimes his mother wonders about the connection between these two preoccupations. And Pierre, her dear Pierre—it's been almost thirty years and not one regret, not a single disappointment. They were introduced at an office party back in 1988 and he immediately won her over with his easy charm and intelligence, his ability to be empathetic and accepting without indulging in liberal grandstanding. They slept together on their second date, which was not like her at all, but being with him, kissing his kind and open face, having him inside of her—passionate but keen on giving pleasure, not hurting—felt like the most natural thing in the world, like finally falling asleep in your own bed after a long absence from home. It was so easy to be with Pierre. It still is.

The Rancourts usually vacation in Umbria, where they own a modest three-room stone house in a sleepy lakeside village, some forty kilometers southwest of Perugia. They both harbor a strong preference for lakes and wooded retreats over crowded beaches and seaside resorts; they both cherish solitude but do not mind having it occasionally interrupted by visiting guests. The children still claim to love the Umbria house, but mostly stopped coming once they left for college. Last year, Bastien showed up unannounced, with a tall Ukrainian girl in tow; they stayed for a few days—roamed the countryside on a rented scooter, swam in the lake, noisily made love at night—then grew visibly bored and eventually departed for the sun-drenched joys of the Amalfi coast. "My, oh, my, that's what it takes to really appreciate the quiet," laughed Pierre after the pair left.

Throughout the year, Umbria beckons, and Mme Rancourt sometimes sees the lake and the stone house and the unkempt garden in juxtaposition to that other trip—a weeklong annual trek she's been taking since 1996, a year when for the first time in more than two decades Battambang became safe to visit. It's a very different journey, and it usually begins at five on a Saturday morning. Against Pierre's vociferous protestations, she absolutely refuses to wake him up so early; instead, she kisses him goodbye before they go to bed because "really, don't be silly, no need to drive me to the station, totally unnecessary, I'll call in a taxi." It's a ritual, of course. He'll wake up around ten (he likes sleeping late on the weekends), and by that time she will have already arrived in Paris, a smooth two-hour dash on a TGV train. Her bus transfer to Charles de Gaulle Airport takes less than an hour, and she finds herself at the terminal almost three hours before the scheduled departure for Hong Kong. After a twelve-hour flight, there will be a two-hour layover in Hong Kong and then another three hours by air to Phnom Penh.

The moment she gets through customs, the noisy crackling of scooter engines, the shabbiness of the buildings outside the airport perimeter, the pungent smells, the humidity, the familiar colors of Cambodia fill her with apprehension and uncertainty, but she gets over them quickly enough. After a moment's hesitation she climbs into one of the waiting taxis—it's only a twelve-dollar ride to Phnom Penh's French Quarter, where she usually stays at a quaint but meticulously maintained guesthouse that's popular with Australian backpackers. For people like her, things are ridiculously cheap in Cambodia, and she could easily afford more luxurious accommodations, but somehow it would feel wrong; she needs some time to transition to Le Pavillon—colonial luxury can wait, at least until tomorrow, until Battambang. Right now, her desires are straightforward and simple: a shower and a bed with clean sheets. The guesthouse is happy to provide both.

By the time the driver carries her luggage into the guesthouse lobby (which doubles as a bar) the sun has already slipped behind the Sorya Shopping Center and the street outside turns nocturnal: the girl bars and techno clubs stir from their slumber, revving up for the coming night; vendors set up food stands; tuk-tuk drivers jostle for fares at hotel and restaurant entrances; foreigners—some looking self-assured (the experienced backpackers and veteran sex tourists), others slightly overwhelmed and disoriented—emerge from their various climate-controlled hideaways, ready to partake of the tropical night's pleasures. All of which holds little interest for Mme Rancourt, who never liked Phnom Penh, for whom the capital has never been anything more than a layover station, its noise but a superfluous soundtrack to less significant segments of her life story. The din outside hardly bothers her—she is that worn out. The blinds are drawn, the room is immediately steeped in comforting darkness, and she keeps thinking that she'll notice the exact moment of transition from wakefulness to sleep. But she really doesn't.

She takes an early morning Mekong bus to Battambang. The Chinese-made bus, comfortable and air-conditioned to a fault, carries her north along the recently repaved National Road #5. Once, she spent almost three weeks walking down the same road. She was going south then; there was no asphalt and no Honda dealership signs; there were no cars, no buses, but there were a lot of people, thousands of them, in fact, bedraggled and emaciated, carrying their meager possessions in wicker baskets or pushing rickety carts. It was a strangely silent crowd; the dispossessed, she learned then, are inclined to silence.

The driver keeps honking to forewarn the occasional motorcyclist, but this honking seems more of a custom than a necessity, as the traffic is light and grows even lighter the farther they get from Phnom Penh. They make frequent stops—restroom stops, stops to let off people, stops to take people on—and those mysterious stops when the driver appears to engage in commercial transactions with people waiting at the curb: packages and massive cardboard boxes are brought onboard or unloaded, dollar bills change hands. Mme Rancourt observes this microcosm of the Cambodian everyday with the detachment of someone who finds it neither foreign nor exotic. She never leaves the bus. By midday, they reach Battambang.

One of Le Pavillon's tuk-tuk drivers, Mr. Samang, is waiting for her at the municipal bus station, which really is just a dusty open field on the outskirts of town. Mr. Samang walks with a distinct limp and drags his right leg, damaged years ago in a motorbike accident, but she knows better than to insist on carrying her bag to the tuk-tuk. He would have none of it; they both pretend that he is not disabled, which is a privilege she can exercise as an enlightened Westerner. Mr. Samang appreciates the well-intentioned insincerity of his foreign clients; he once told Mme Rancourt how lucky he was to work for a Western-owned hotel—no Khmer-owned establishment would ever hire him. For the Khmers, he insists, there is no shame in prejudice. But prejudice doesn't insult him; he sees it as a matter of practicality, also a cultural trait that she suspects he shares. He is just lucky to have landed the job at Le Pavillon.

He drives the same tuk-tuk as he did last year, and the year before—a Chinese-made motorcycle with a two-wheeled canopied carriage attached to it. Mr. Samang takes exquisite care of his tool of the trade. The seats are of genuine Japanese cherry wood; all handles and sidebars and the rims of both carriage wheels are painted gold; the storage compartment underneath the back bench is hidden behind a mahogany panel, covered by intricately carved Angkor snake patterns; and red-and-white leather tassels hang down the handlebars. The circus-like appearance of the tuk-tuk stands in almost comical contrast to Mr. Samang's rather morose demeanor.

It's a twenty-minute ride across town: past the dilapidated colonial mansions, complete with crumbling stucco balconies; past the former governor's residence, now the site of the provincial government; past the weathered Cambodia People's Party signs, featuring two grim-faced apparatchiks; past the stalls of the Central Market, down the River Road; and onto the bridge crossing the Sangkae river. The hotel is a short distance from the bridge, nestled inconspicuously behind a young grove of mango trees, clearly intended to enhance the sense of privacy, and in the shadow of a massive Buddhist wat. It's always cool and quiet inside Le Pavillon, and the staff do not so much talk as whisper, as they glide noiselessly on the smooth checkered tiles. Upon Mme Rancourt's appearance in the lobby, a girl behind the massive mahogany front desk rises with alacrity and performs a quick *sampeah*. Mr. Samang hobbles a few steps behind, hauling Mme Rancourt's bag, his face expressionless; he heads straight for the second-floor room where she always stays. The passivity of his facial expression is not lost on Mme Rancourt. She smiles lightly, hardly concerned—assured, in fact, that he is glad to see her.

There is a slight commotion in the dining hall, a growing din of voices at a volume unusual for this setting. Soon Olivia enters the lobby—her hair cropped, face full of smiles, emitting affectionate cooing sounds—and embraces her friend, kisses her cheeks, pulls her closer, pushes her away jokingly. She scrutinizes her face, nods approvingly, then pulls her closer again. They have a whole year of catching up to do, but later, later—when the bag has been unpacked and a hot shower has washed off the fatigue of the seven-hour bus trip, when the sun sets behind the wat and the sensor lights flicker to life along the pool perimeter, when the guests emerge from their rooms refreshed after a day of sightseeing and ready to settle down for an evening meal of fish amok (the best in Battambang), beef lok lak, and noodle salad. The women will sit by the bar, sipping Olivia's favorite lychee cocktails, swapping bits of news, bits of the year past—and it was a good year, a year when their daughters got married (Olivia's to a mechanical engineer in Nîmes, back in France) and their jobs continued to be secure and satisfying. At the moment, Olivia doesn't have a man in her life and, to be perfectly frank, she likes it that way. An old beau visited from Marseilles a few months ago, they sort of hit it off and he still sends her cute Facebook messages, but they are both divorced and nearly sixty and not prepared for any dramatic changes in their lives, especially when such a change would necessitate a ten thousand kilometer relocation. As always, Olivia does most of the talking, but she remains attuned to her friend's mood; she knows that Mme Rancourt doesn't mind her garrulousness, even finds it endearing and soothing. Olivia knows that her friend is used to measuring her words carefully and admires the precision and clarity of her slightly accented French. "Must be that law school; they trained you well, my dear," she laughs. She knows all that and she also knows (and she is reasonably certain that she is the only person in the world possessing this particular knowledge) that there is someone else in Battambang who looks forward to her friend's annual visits—Mr. Samang, the hotel's tuk-tuk driver and Mme Rancourt's lover.

***

The Khmer Rouge swept into Battambang on April 24, 1975, a week after they had taken Phnom Penh. Within hours the quaint provincial city was being emptied of its population, as people were being moved into the countryside to work in the rice fields and on irrigation projects. The killing started almost immediately after the arrival of the conquering army, but for a while it remained limited in scope and targeted mostly those who were too slow to comply with the evacuation orders. There was none of the gratuitous violence that would soon come to mark the Khmer Rouge rule—people were simply shot. Mr. Chantrea and his wife, the next-door neighbors of Mme Rancourt's family, were executed right by their front porch as they recklessly tried to prevent two young soldiers from commandeering their Peugeot sedan. Mr. Chantrea was a principal at the French Catholic school, the destination of choice for the children of the Battambang elite—the same school where Mme Rancourt excelled as an A-list student and her parents worked as teachers.

By the end of that eventful Thursday, Mme Rancourt and her parents found themselves on the road, surrounded by throngs of other dispossessed and disoriented urbanites, heading north towards Preak Luong. They camped for the night by the monastery in Samrong Knong, and, exhausted as they were, no one could sleep as the quiet was disrupted by bursts of machine-gun fire coming from the direction of the city, just ten kilometers to the south. In the morning, the soldiers, riding motorcycles, caught up with the group and ordered the refugees to stay put—the wat was being converted into a camp to house the relocated, and it was to be headed by Comrade Mok, a twenty-something illiterate peasant from the east. Most of the camp guards were equally young or even younger, some of them barely teenagers. Within a couple of days Mme Rancourt and her parents found themselves working fifteen-hour shifts in the rice paddies. The parents didn't last long. Early on they had been identified by the vigilant Comrade Mok as members of the enemy breed—the "soft hands and glasses," the intellectuals. He and the guards treated them accordingly. As the temperatures soared in May and their productivity fell off precipitously, Mme Rancourt watched in desperation as her parents grew visibly weaker and kept failing to meet their daily quotas. By then, the punitive ritual had been well established: the culprits had two weeks to shape up; failing that, they were taken to the pagoda for "training." No one ever returned from the pagoda.

Her parents disappeared a few weeks after their arrival at the wat. One morning, late in May, she lined up for her work detail and realized that they were not next to her. She looked around furtively but knew better than to ask unnecessary questions. It was not for nothing that she had been a star student (a fact of her biography that she now kept to herself) at her Catholic school; she was a quick learner. She would have preferred not to know what happened to them, at least not the details, but wishes rarely got granted at Samrong Knong. A couple of days after her parents' disappearance, one of the guards approached her in the fields. He was roughly her age but carried himself with the almost comical self-importance of someone who unexpectedly found himself bestowed with unlimited powers over other human beings. He was just a kid, though, and desperately wanted to share and, she guessed, also to impress her with his intimate familiarity with the mysteries of death. No, he didn't do the killing, but he was there to observe it and clean up afterwards. The interrogation at the pagoda didn't last long, they didn't even need to torture them to extract the confession, certainly not like they did with the others—one of those easy, open-and-shut cases of "soft hands and glasses." That same night, just before dawn, comrade Mok and the guards took the pair outside the wat wall where they clubbed them over the heads with long-handed scuffle hoes, the same ones they used in the fields. When comrade Mok finalized the execution by expertly slitting their throats, the bodies didn't twitch, a clear indication that by that point the condemned had already been dead. That last detail of the murder was clearly intended to convey the boy's own expertise in such matters, which she acknowledged with a slow and deliberate nod and which he apparently took for a sign of appreciation. From that point on he invariably treated her with kind consideration, and years later she would wonder sometimes if it was not her willingness to absorb the gruesome account of her parents' murder that helped her survive Samrong Knong.

But even the kindly guard would not have been able to save her had it not been for a timely transfer to a garment shop farther north, in Serei Saophoan, halfway between Battambang and Siem Rip. By the end of 1975, she had lost almost a third of her weight due to malnutrition and chronic dysentery, and meeting her daily quota in the fields was quickly becoming untenable. By the time the transfer order had arrived she figured that she was well on her way to the pagoda. She never really found out why she was chosen for the transfer—maybe it had something to do with her dutiful praying at the French school's early morning masses, which she used to hate with a vengeance, or with the glut of rice production in the province, or some bureaucratic fiat back at the Angkar headquarters in Phnom Penh. Whatever it was, it saved her life.

In Serei Saophoan she was put to work stitching black Khmer Rouge uniforms. She labored the same fifteen hours a day but under less backbreaking conditions than out in the fields and with less likelihood of execution as a standard form of punishment—slackers were beaten up (and quite savagely) by bamboo sticks but rarely killed. Many of the guards at the Serei Saophoan shop were female and on average less enthusiastic about violence than their male counterparts. And then there was the young shop foreman, also a prisoner, but someone who had earned the trust of the provincial Khmer Rouge leadership. Like Mme Rancourt he hailed from Battambang and he too lost his family during the first chaotic weeks of Khmer Rouge rule; just like her he had learned to conceal his educational background (French-language high school and one year at a technical college in Siem Rip) from the black tunics. Not that she knew any of that at the time. Over the next three years the young foreman would come to play an indispensable role in Mme Rancourt's existence, which in essence was little more than a low-grade daily struggle to survive. She was to address him like all the other girls at the shop: Comrade Samang.

***

The routine has remained unchanged through the years. They take daylong trips into the countryside. She never pays him directly; the cost of these trips (twenty dollars a day) will be added to her hotel bill at check out. She never tips him either. He sits solidly astride his Sanya motorcycle, paying close attention to the road, navigating the potholes (leaning out, leaning in—all slow motion), braking for the cattle crossing the road, then picking up speed again, on occasion overtaking other tuk-tuks, some of them carrying Western tourists, others delivering produce to the market. As usual she marvels at the seemingly effortless proficiency of Cambodia's daily life, quaint and self-contained, with a recent overflow of foreign travelers and adventure-seekers keen on discovering it.

A few years ago, after a brief visit to Samrong Knong, they changed their usual route, eliminating points north from their itinerary. The wat had not changed since 1975, but the monks were back, most of them very young—shaved heads, orange robes, battered plastic flip-flops on their feet—sauntering around the premises with no apparent purpose. Initially she didn't mind these visits; there was nothing easier, she thought, than placing oneself outside a memory—she imagined she was reading a book that she could open or close at will. But then, about ten years ago, she was startled by the sight of a new monument erected at the wat—a glass pyramid filled with skulls that hailed (so the inscription claimed) from the adjacent killing field. The monument, in her view, was entirely unnecessary—crude, predictably well intentioned, superfluous, a typical joint undertaking by a well-meaning NGO and some holier-than-thou immigrants in California or Massachusetts. The sight of it made her both irritated and anxious, and for a minute she sensed her usual steeliness sagging under stress. Infuriated, she hastened back to the waiting tuk-tuk—what nonsense; she didn't trek halfway around the globe to subject herself to this sort of endurance test. Mr. Samang looked at her intently, as always his inscrutable face expressing no visible emotion. He touched her elbow, held it for a few seconds, giving her time to calm down and regain her composure. Slowly, slowly, he let her go, gently patted her on the shoulder, then shrugged and started the motorcycle. They would never come back to Samrong Knong again, and by an unspoken agreement stopped traveling north of the city altogether.

Instead, every morning Mr. Samang picks her up by the hotel front gate and they ride south on Riverside Road. They pass the striking Ta Dumbong, the black Buddha of Battambang, and proceed for a while along a busy stretch of the road, where motorcycle dealerships, Chinese restaurants, and guesthouses compete for prime commercial space. Within a few minutes, they leave the city behind, the traffic thins out, and the dusty business frenzy on the city's edges gives way to the tranquility of rice paddies and corn and pepper fields. They cross the river on one of the rickety suspension bridges. Down below, local boys splash in the murky, muddy waters, but when they get closer, she realizes that what she took for play is actually work—the boys set up crawfish nets along the riverbank, slimy and covered by yellowish clay. One after another the young fishermen submerge themselves in the water and stay under for some time, performing some mysterious but necessary tasks in the impenetrable aquatic darkness. They come to the surface wide-eyed and gasping for air, their wet hair splayed over dark-brown foreheads, until soon enough they are ready for another dive. They go about their work in a deliberate and methodical fashion, a display of discipline that strikes her as incongruous with their young age. Her children were never like that, certainly not Bastien. As always, the thought of her son makes her smile.

***

It was a relationship that went unacknowledged and remained unconsummated. Even then a man of few words and formidable poise, Comrade Samang was well suited for just such a predicament. Romantic relations outside marriage were strictly prohibited and the punishment for violators could be grotesquely severe. All marriages had to be initiated and sanctioned by the state. By the end of that first year, they both had come to believe that their physical survival largely depended on their ability to remain in Serei Saophoan. Any wrong move could trigger a transfer, accompanied by a renewed attention to their family histories and backgrounds. At least for her, a transfer back to the rice fields or irrigation works meant an almost certain death. No, they couldn't risk that, especially because Comrade Samang was already taking enormous risks by slightly padding her production tallies in his daily reports. This became clear to her at a self-criticism session at the end of her third week at the shop, an event organized on account of the visit by a deputy secretary of the Northwest Zone. Brother Nai presented each of the gathered women with a summary of her individual performance, and Mme Rancourt was stunned to find out that she had consistently met the quotas. She knew better than to express her surprise or any other discernible emotion, but on the way out of the room she fumbled with her kerchief and paused for a split second in front of Comrade Samang. His expression was stern and vacant; he looked past her towards the podium where Brother Nai was receiving instructions from the visiting dignitary. "Merci," she breathed rather than whispered. Still not looking at her he nodded, barely, and said, "You need to be moving now." For the next three years these chance, fleeting exchanges would become the staple of their interactions, both the form and the content of their secret romance.

***

It's past noon when they reach the foot of Phnom Sampeau, a limestone bluff dotted with cavernous hollows and old Hindu temples. The morning coolness has long since dissipated and the sun is beating down gleefully and unapologetically on the tuk-tuk canopy. As ever, Mr. Samang is conspicuously oblivious to the heat. Somewhere out there, halfway up the hill, there is another memorial of heavy-handed remembrance and contrition, another glass-paneled structure filled with the bones of the bludgeoned. She knows about its existence but has never laid eyes on the site, even though she rarely fails to pay a visit to Phnom Sampeau when she comes to Battambang. When climbing up the slope she always sticks to the main path, ignoring the signs pointing towards the killing caves, now a major tourist destination. In any event, it's too early and too hot to ascend the mountain and partake of what she considers its main attraction—for that, they will return later. For now, they are pressing on south, riding through the harvested fields framed picturesquely by the distant hills. They stop by a roadside stand to buy a small plastic pouch of freshly squeezed bamboo juice and sip it in silence, passing the container back and forth, waving off the persistent blackflies buzzing in the early afternoon heat. Since this morning they have exchanged but a few words and have yet to catch up on the events of the past year; it's been twenty-four hours since he picked her up at the bus depot, and they still remain ignorant of each other's affairs during the last twelve months. There is a shared temptation to keep it this way, but they also know that sooner or later the silence will be broken and they will talk—they always do, eventually.

The moment arrives when the proprietress has removed the emptied bowls of fish soup and brought in a couple of Angkors. They are sitting on the floor of a lakeside cabana, which is really just a simple platform on stilts with a massive roof of thatched palm fronds kept in place by an elaborate contraption of ropes and four bearing polls. The poorly adjusted floorboards are covered by a couple of battered and visibly stained reed mats, which are shriveled enough to leave large sections of the floor exposed. Through the wide gaps they can see the darkish water and the darting shadows of the fish hunting for scraps. Two hammocks are tied to the polls on the side of the cabana facing the lake.

It was in a cabana like this one (maybe it *was* this one) that she first kissed him, almost twenty years ago. He was taking a nap in the hammock after the meal, his open-collar polo shirt showing a bronzed collarbone, his damaged leg stretched out downwards at an awkward angle, resting listlessly on the floorboards. She kissed his impassive face—a kiss of recognition, she thought, that was long overdue—then his neck, the collarbone that felt unexpectedly cool to her lips; slowly, methodically but not neglecting to continue to kiss him reassuringly, she helped him out of his shirt, all the while mindful of his disability, careful not to ruin the moment by inflicting even the slightest pain on him. He never opened his eyes; his lips twitched into a faint smile, but he expressed no surprise, no delight, no impatience. She had seen this smiling face before, replicated 216 times on the stone idols of the Bayon temple in the great dead city of Angkor Thom.

And now they finally talk. The conversation flickers at first, gets momentarily extinguished, then rekindles again like a tiny flame, at first unsure of itself but ultimately resilient and even triumphant. Within minutes they fall into a familiar pattern of swapping family gossip and sharing parental updates.

They never reminisce and almost never talk politics, especially since, about six or seven years ago, Mme Rancourt discovered that Mr. Samang's political views had undergone a peculiar transformation. She was always aware of his leftist sympathies, but the extreme Khmer nationalism that he began to advocate startled her. Most of her life in the West she has been wary of identity fads, and when her own children in their late teens were going through their own "proud to be half-Cambodian" phase she waited patiently for it to be over. Even though the two of them never brought up their past she assumed that they had a shared understanding of the nightmare that cast such a pall over their youth. And that is why his version of it, the version that he revealed to her during one of those languid and erotically charged hours in the cabana, took her by surprise. In his retelling, Pol Pot's reign of terror was nothing more than a Vietnamese plot to subjugate Cambodia and undermine its spirit. The real Brother #1, he insisted, was not a butcher of millions but a Robin Hood figure—a gallant defender of the oppressed, a bulwark against Vietnamese imperialism and capitalist inequities. The horrors of the Khmer Rouge had been perpetrated by the Vietnamese agents who wormed their way into Pol Pot's inner circle. Mr. Samang's soliloquy, and the baroque and clearly nonsensical conspiracy theory it contained, left her speechless. Not that she had been unaware of his economic struggles and resentments, but his willingness to distort and subvert the reality that he resented, to express his disdain for it by resorting to crude historical revisionism and mythmaking, made her realize the depth of his alienation from her own world. It was a disturbing revelation, and it threatened to break the spell of their strange relationship, something she was not prepared to accept. Since then, they have left politics and history completely out of their conversations, and now when revisiting that tense moment a few years ago she can't help but appreciate his tact and eagerness to purge their interaction of even the slightest whiff of unpleasantness.

And it is an easy enough task, too, because they can safely talk about their children. He has two grown-up daughters, and one of them has been giving him plenty of grief lately. She recently met a guy on Facebook ("Who even meets people on Facebook?") and they are now planning to get married. When it comes to his future son-in-law, Mr. Samang intuits a potential conflict. The boy is "no good," a spoiled brat who comes from a privileged Phnom Penh family and whose father works for the government, which is to say he is a crook. The guy drives an SUV ("How can you even afford an SUV on a government salary?") and throws his weight around. The wedding will be paid for by the boy's parents, which places Mr. Samang in a moral bind: this is in keeping with the old Khmer tradition, but he nevertheless resents the nouveau riche arrogance and hubris of his future in-laws. He has an acute sensitivity to humiliation, and in this case fully expects to be humiliated. She is tempted to offer him money but quickly reconsiders, careful not to contribute to his social anxieties. As ever attuned to the ebb and flow of their conversation, he senses the awkwardness of the moment and dispels it with a quick joke: "You don't have these problems," he laughs, "you don't have two daughters to worry about."—"I surely don't," she nods agreeably.—"Just as you always wanted," he continues, "a boy and a girl . . . Remember, you always wanted a boy and a girl? Remember?" This is the extent of his engaging with the past, and she is confident that he won't go any further; he never does. She nods again—of course, she does remember.

***

Not for a minute did she harbor any illusions about the possibly deadly consequences of Comrade Samang's frivolous bookkeeping. The moment she realized that he was helping her survive she felt equally responsible for him—she would have to shield him by becoming an exemplary seamstress. Within a couple of short months her delicate fingers became calloused but nimble, and eventually a day arrived when there was no need for him to fake her production numbers; from that point on she would be meeting her daily quota of sewn uniforms established by Brother Nai.

The passing of the immediate danger remained unacknowledged by them, and the dread that had defined her existence over the past year receded somewhat, transforming itself into a milder, more bearable version. It also helped that now they could afford the luxury of exchanging a few words. These brief encounters, usually at the end of the working day, were heavily scripted and intentionally formal, but over the next three years they added up to a relationship of surprisingly intense if unconsummated intimacy. No touching, no laughing, not even smiling—just a few terse phrases traded as he was marking down her production output for the day on a dirty notepad. Each such exchange yielded a bit of new information about their past lives and, as they got to know each other better, about their plans for some undefined and, frankly, unlikely future. That's how he learned about her simple dream of motherhood—a boy and a girl—and that's how he learned about the teenage Khmer Rouge soldier observing the gruesome execution of two mild-mannered, middle-aged schoolteachers in the shallow killing ravine outside the wat walls. At most a couple of minutes at a time, but almost daily, over a three-year period, it added up to a couple thousand minutes total, some thirty hours of talk whispered in a truncated monotone. By necessity these were quick briefs rather than normal conversations, quite utilitarian in their intention to inform, to add tangible details and meaningful facts to their growing but still inchoate understanding of each other. There were several close calls when other girls in the shop started to gossip, but they remained vigilant and, when suspecting danger, immediately suspended or dramatically abbreviated their encounters. Later in life, she wondered sometimes how much longer they would have been able to keep up the risky charade.

The need to pretend disappeared on January 20, 1979—a Saturday. For weeks the girls had been hearing the distant rumble of the artillery, but they knew better than to ask unnecessary questions. During the ideological hour,

Brother Nai brushed off the sounds of the nearing battle—first as the detonations at a dam construction on the Tonlé Sap River, but later, when the ongoing thunder of explosions and the rattling of machine-gun fire became impossible to ignore, as evidence of the National Army's triumphant efforts to annihilate the unholy alliance of the Russian and Vietnamese revisionists.

That Saturday, upon leaving the barrack on her way to work, walking in a group of other girls, she saw a bulky tank blocking the intersection by the shop's entrance; a red flag emblazoned with a massive five-pointed golden star was hoisted over its turret. The shop was empty—no trace of either Brother Nai or the female supervisors. The young black-uniformed guards were gone too. Suddenly the shop appeared abandoned, an inconspicuous remnant of a bygone era—a meaningless, faded prop from a failed horror show. It was over. She looked around for Comrade Samang, but he was nowhere to be found; she rushed to the men's barrack, but it was empty too. One of the most profound revelations of that Saturday, and the one that she would internalize for the rest of her life, had to do with the fragility of what we think of as permanent. Within minutes the immediate turned into a memory, with all of the memory's necessary accoutrements: spaces abandoned and echoey, facades crumbling, equipment idle and rusting, people . . . gone. Comrade Samang was gone too.

Later that day she was southbound, on the road to Battambang. She was walking close to the curb, passing by the stalled armored columns of Vietnamese personnel carriers and BMP tanks revving and fuming into the approaching night. Moving along she carefully sidestepped the shell craters and took measure of the still smoking hulks of the military vehicles destroyed in a recent battle. She walked right through Battambang; it didn't even cross her mind to stop by her childhood house—there was no past to be revisited. Along with thousands of other refugees she continued to move south, towards the capital city. She stayed on the road for three weeks, sometimes covering thirty kilometers a day but other days too weak to walk. Like others she had to rely on the charity of local villagers who sometimes came to the road to pass around stalks of roasted bamboo filled with sticky rice. She didn't make any friends and hardly talked to anyone—there was no need. In fact, she would go on for another year without talking—at the Red Cross shelter in Phnom Penh, at the Khao-I-Dang refugee camp in Thailand, and finally at her sister's apartment in the thirteenth arrondissement in Paris. A romantically inclined novelist would have imagined her during that year of outward silence holding long internal conversations with Comrade Samang. But she didn't. There was no rich internal drama hidden from the prying eyes of the gawkers and well-wishers, there was no struggle to come to terms with the hardship and loss of the past years. She remained silent simply because she felt absolutely no need to talk.

***

The sun is descending leisurely towards the wooded crest of Phnom Banan, and the interior of the cabana is now steeped in deep lethargic shadows. Other cabanas have emptied of their daytime visitors; it's time for them too to head back to Phnom Sampeau. The trip is a forty-minute ride north, during which the dusk gathers its density and casts the landscape in unexpected shades of purple. By the time they arrive at the hillside, only a crimson semicircle of the quickly disappearing sun is still visible above the ridge. There are tuk-tuks and motorbikes parked in the open field just off the paved road ascending the mountain. Plenty of other tourists—most of them Western, some, as she recognizes at once, her fellow guests at Le Pavillon—are milling around in anticipation of the coming spectacle.

Just like happened last year, she misses the first bat as it alights from the cave shelter and flutters upwards, exultant at the sight of the dying sun. It is followed by another bat, then one more, and soon the sky is filled with a dark quivering mass. The cave continues to disgorge hundreds upon hundreds of tiny creatures, who race impatiently and seemingly at random across the darkening sky, anxious to shake off the heaviness of a daylong lethargy. Guided by a mighty millennia-old instinct, they are ready for a night of tearing through the fragrant air, primed for a hunt. They leave behind the limestone recesses of their hideaways, the quiet of the cave where, during the day, their torpor is only occasionally disturbed by the muffled sounds of visitors' voices or by an unexpected flash of the sun refracted through the glass wall of a boxy enclosure, full of weathered bones.

Within a few minutes, the bats, now many thousands of them, crowd the horizon, expand as a gigantic breathing canvas, then suddenly come together as a heaving cloud made up of darting black dots. But just as soon, the cloud loses its seeming solidity, it fractures and extends in a long arc, far beyond the ridge and the valley, beyond the corn fields, and beyond the sleepy lake surrounded by cabanas. Five more minutes and the arc grows visibly thinner, losing its definition at the outer edges and finally dissipating into nothingness.

The bats are gone; their grandiose exhibition of unity and common purpose has come to an abrupt end, each animal now on its own, fully committed to its own hunting pursuit and its own itinerary through the night.

Their return journey proceeds in complete darkness, barely penetrated by the feeble headlight of the tuk-tuk. But Mr. Samang knows the road well; in fact, he feels so confident in his skill that he rides with only one hand resting on the handlebar; his other hand reaches back into the carriage, allowing Mme Rancourt to hold onto it. She'll let go of it a couple of minutes before they arrive at Le Pavillon. He doesn't follow her into the hotel; in all these years not once has he spent the night in her room overlooking the swimming pool. The king-size poster bed is all hers, and it has already been prepped for the night by the hotel maid—the Siam mosquito net pulled down and its folds neatly arranged in the flowing cascades of white muslin, a glass of water thoughtfully placed on the nightstand, and a bowl of ripe mangos next to it. There are freshly cut flowers (sweet Olivia, dear Olivia) in a porcelain vase atop the writing cabinet. Truly a night of rest to look forward to. But before that there will be a dinner of the divine fish amok, prepared by the incomparable Mme Samang, the hotel's longtime cook, who, according to a recent *Lonely Planet* write-up, has perfected the mysteries of Khmer cuisine better than any other chef in the whole of the northwestern region. And as per a well-established tradition, there'll be lychee cocktails at the bar with Olivia. But not too late; she'll probably turn in early to get a good night's sleep and be ready the next morning when Mr. Samang will pick her up in his glitzy tuk-tuk. And then . . . and then there will be five more days just like the one that is now drawing to an end.

***

The return home seems to her like an accelerated version of her arrival but on rewind. She splurges a hundred dollars on a taxi, as she feels neither need nor desire to leave Cambodia in gradual stages—the sooner the better. Olivia is there to see her off, all teary-eyed because each such departure reminds her of how much she misses her friend throughout the year. Mme Rancourt makes her promise to visit them in Umbria later in the summer—she'll try, she really will, she just needs to find someone to take over at the hotel for a few weeks. "It's a promise?"—"Yes, dear, it's a promise!" Mr. Samang is not there to say goodbye—he left early in the morning with a couple of elderly Australian tourists who were keen to catch the earliest, pre-heat ride on the bamboo train. It's ok; it's even better this way. The taxi arrives, and a few minutes later it carries her down the newly paved National Road #5. The trip is so much faster by car; she'll be at the airport just in time for her evening flight and most certainly she won't be spending the night in Phnom Penh.

They cross the city limits at dusk. Strangely, the smoothly paved highway loses its asphalt as soon as they reach the capital. The taxi slows down to a crawl and the driver, quite chatty up to this point, falls silent and dedicates himself completely to the task of navigating the moonscape of the unpaved road. The air is filled with thick reddish dust that quickly coats the outside surfaces of the vehicle. They drive by an endless procession of sweatshops and modern manufacturing complexes ("Made in Cambodia," "Made in Cambodia," "Made in Cambodia"), interspersed with clusters of dimly lit massage parlors and local beerhalls that are just beginning to come alive. This is the end of the workday and the factories release onto the street crowds of uniformed employees, most of them young women in matching t-shirts and brightly colored kerchiefs. They move around in compact bands—some are walking, jumping over the potholes, climbing the mounds of sand prepared by construction crews that are nowhere in sight. Others are transported to destinations unknown, tightly packed in the open backs of factory lorries; at some point Mme Rancourt notices that the taxi is completely surrounded by these slowly moving freight trucks—in the ruddy sunset glow the scene strikes her as otherworldly, nearly phantasmagorical. Each truck is carrying a cargo of dozens of young women, all standing upright, not a centimeter of daylight between their bodies—the toilers of the global market on their way home from work, the nimble-fingered seamstresses of the new Cambodia.

At the airport she pays the driver and surprises him with a large tip; she also makes him promise that he won't be driving back at night but instead will spend the extra money to pay for a hostel in Phnom Penh. He readily agrees, eager to please her, but she knows that spending the night in the capital is not really an option for him. She picks up her bag and walks into the terminal. Her flight is on time.

During the layover in Hong Kong, she texts Mr. Samang, just to let him know that there are no delays and the connection has worked out as planned. He has never traveled by air; in fact, he has never traveled outside of Cambodia, but she still makes a point of informing him about her airport logistics. He once asked her to do this, and she sees no reason not to oblige.

He never responds to these messages, but she is certain he has received them. Just before she gets on her Paris-bound flight she deletes the outgoing texts. This is the last communication between them for the next year. Or two. Or ever.

***

Pierre is waiting for her on the platform in Nantes—she spots his broad-shouldered, slightly stooped figure as soon as she gets off the train. What a pleasure it is to see his kind and intelligent face, to kiss his tired, droopy eyes. What a comfort it is to be embraced by him, to feel his closeness, to absorb the immediacy of his presence. There is nothing perfunctory about their embrace, nothing hasty or routine. Jokingly he refuses to let her go. "Don't resist, I'm squeezing Indochina out of you," he chuckles.

In the car, he brings her up to date on the affairs of the past week and she is gladdened to learn that they hardly amount to much. Claudia Guillon, her assistant, called twice from the office—frazzled and panicky as usual. Such a klutz, but she has been with Mme Rancourt for almost fifteen years now and it is easier for her to keep sorting out the mess Claudia leaves behind than to part ways with a dedicated employee. "Her loyalty to you is matched only by her incompetence," jokes Pierre. But loyalty *is* important to her, which is good news for Claudia. Pierre's free hand rests on her knee, she cherishes its familiar touch—it's the knowing hand of a talented architect, a perceptive lover, a true friend. By the time they pull into the driveway their bond has been reaffirmed and certified.

The evening will be short—it's an early rising for both of them tomorrow. Some old friends wanted to drop by for a nightcap, but it's getting late now, so they'll have to postpone until the next weekend. Pierre has cooked a simple dinner of pasta and tossed up a quick salad in a glass bowl that she bought last year at a flea market in Saint-Nazaire. He puts on Coltrane's *Blue Train* (her all-time favorite album), pours her some pinot. After dinner they Skype with Dominique and Daniel. Dominique looks and sounds solemn when she feeds them the latest update from her obstetrician. Mme Rancourt cringes a little—to her taste, Dominique is taking her pregnancy far too seriously. Thankfully, Daniel is there to provide some comic relief—they *are* a very good match after all. Later they try and fail to reach Bastien on his mobile. That rascal, one would think that a Sunday evening could be the perfect time to bring it down a notch, to slow down just bit. Oh well, not Bastien. She leaves him an affectionately teasing message; she knows he'll call her back tomorrow. She loves that boy, she really does.

In bed, she lies awake for a little while. They sleep in separate bedrooms now but just across the hall from each other, keeping their doors slightly ajar in case one of them decides to "drop by." She is exhausted, but she would've welcomed Pierre in her bed tonight. For a second she considers paying him a visit, crawling under the blanket next to him, snuggling up against his familiar body, a body that she knows so well and still finds attractive. The house is deathly quiet; she raises up on her elbow and hears Pierre's soft snoring—barely audible. It's all right, she won't wake the poor guy. There is no rush, they have the rest of their life together.

A late car passes by the house, its headlights momentarily sweeping the room, capturing furniture fragments, hovering over them for a second, then dropping them back into darkness. She knows that sleep is near and its promise fills her with quiet joy. But while it's waiting patiently in the shadows, she still has some thoughts to think. These are distinctly pleasant: she thinks about Bastien and her childlike pride in him, she thinks of her daughter and future grandchild and how they will have to plan to stay in London for at least a couple of weeks after the birth. With Claudia, that little boob of an assistant, there will be the usual commotion in the office tomorrow—the files misplaced, the clients that need to be cajoled and pacified. Claudia will probably cry a little, heartbroken over her own ineptitude. As always, she'll have to console her, maybe take her out for lunch—it's a long-established routine with them. And then she thinks about Pierre and her deep affection for him, a confident and self-assured love that has endured through all these years. She thinks of his kindness and generosity, about his almost supernatural ability to understand her and give her exactly the words she needs most. Such a lovely man, such a lovely, lovely man. She couldn't wish for more. And then . . . and then sleep is finally there, she senses its growing presence during her last waking moments as gradually the room fills with a dense vapor of impenetrable stillness. Someone touches her hair and delicately smooths it over the pillow, kisses lightly the nape of her neck, her breasts, then takes her by the hand and pulls her gently—very, very gently—over the edge.

Boris and David on the Beach

To reach the neurological wing of Wolfson Medical Center in Holon you have to walk through a bland mall, which boasts several shops selling beach supplies, a cheap footwear store (not so cheap actually), a pretend American coffee shop, also a McDonald's. Past the McDonald's an elevator will take you up to floors five and six, which house people recuperating from stroke, also people dying from stroke. The concerned relatives of the afflicted march with righteous determination past the shops and towards the elevator. The inside of the elevator smells of formaldehyde, also of kosher hospital food. The visitors' demeanor is unmistakably distinct from that of regular shoppers—they are not tempted by the sight of the colorful inflatable swimming tubes and gaily patterned flip-flops; a display of faux Oakley sunglasses holds limited appeal for them. Some though drop by the coffee shop for a quick caffeine boost before the inevitable ride upstairs. Others stop by for coffee on their way back, before exiting the air-conditioned shopping arcade onto the sun-drenched parking lot, where a pathetic, undernourished Mediterranean cypress provides no shade. Hospital parking is free, most likely because it shares a parking lot with the mall. Shopping and healing and dying exist in symbiotic proximity at Holon.

Boris didn't mind the arcade; he thought its seemingly incongruous presence useful, practical. He was a proudly and self-assuredly practical man, after all. He even bought a pair of gold-rimmed sunglasses on the very first day, after the ambulance had transferred David, now felled by his second stroke, from the overcrowded Barzilai Hospital in Ashkelon to a more "modern" facility in Holon. On one of their last evening walks, a ten-year-old ritual that has now been discontinued, he had spotted a pair of similar sunglasses at a beach-front kiosk on the marina. The one he picked up at the arcade in Holon was twenty shekels cheaper, a remarkable fact that didn't escape Boris's sharp eye—even in distress Boris could score a bargain.

David, of course, possessed none of Boris's practical skills. Throughout his colorful life David consistently (and often enthusiastically) wreaked havoc of small and large proportions: he misplaced wallets, lost passports, locked himself in, locked himself out, forgot boiling kettles on stoves, and missed trains and flights with an almost supernatural regularity. Once, during a tempestuous, two decade-long stint in the navy, he left his standard-issue service pistol inside the latrine of a Yugoslav destroyer that he visited as part of a "friendship" delegation of fraternal naval officers. He came close to a court-martial. Eventually the navy found a way to let him go.

His divorces were messy—not because he harbored any ill will towards his exes (he certainly did not), but mostly because he kept misplacing legal papers and failing to show up for his scheduled court appearances. "And that's David for you, that's classic David, that's David being David," Boris had taken to uttering with mock exasperation within days of their initial acquaintance, an acquaintance that would quickly blossom into the most tender of friendships—a friendship that also doubled as a full-time job for Boris. Boris, a born caretaker and recently widowed problem-solver, welcomed the challenge. He had never had a real friend before and now found the experience of intimate friendship exhilarating. They formed a peculiar couple these two—two aging, speedo-sporting playboys on the beach, basking in the reddish glow of Mediterranean sunsets. "Considering our age, the sunsets are appropriately meaningful," David quipped, and as often was the case, Boris marveled at his friend's easy command of words—he knew that David had "the gift."

Their friendship inspired some puzzlement and considerable jealousy among the "fair ladies of Ashkelon" (a label copyrighted to David), many of whom had their sights set on this rare, almost unheard of, find—two unattached Russian-speaking men, seemingly healthy and not yet seventy-five. The ladies were mostly widowed, eccentric, overweight, and encumbered by broods of "caring" children and "talented" grandkids. The savvy and world-weary Boris smelled trouble and potential financial ruin and, while remaining invariably gentlemanly, kept the seekers at a polite distance, deflecting good-naturedly but swiftly any attempts on his and David's freedom.

In fact, Boris didn't quite know what to do with this freedom, having spent the last forty years of his life doting on his late wife and building a well-feathered nest—first, in his native Moscow, and later, after a spur-of-the-moment decision to move it to a better climate, on the eastern shores of the Mediterranean. The decision was his, just like most of the decisions in their smoothly run marriage. It was his even though he was not Jewish and thus not eligible for repatriation to Israel. For the first time in his life, he found himself dependent on his wife (who *was* Jewish), even if temporarily, and this unexpected dependency turned into the source of many good-natured jokes between them. Bella famously refused to pay attention to anything quotidian and her lack of familiarity with the basics of everyday existence was the point of personal pride for Boris. "She probably was the only woman in the Soviet Union who had no idea how much a kilo of butter cost, well . . . maybe besides those Politburo wives," he confessed to David soon after they first met at an ulpan Hebrew class. David, who for reasons of chronic absent-mindedness could have claimed the same kind of ignorance, whistled appreciatively.

Boris, on the other hand, was intimately familiar with prices. Back in Moscow he operated within an intricate web of connections whose maintenance kept him perpetually busy: car mechanics, butchers, dentists, hairdressers, furniture store clerks, theater box office managers—all floated through his universe, revolving like planets around the solar center of his household. He knew exactly how to approach the right people, how to trade favors, how to flatter, how to humor, how to backslap. He intuited the appropriateness and size of bribes. He was an expert at cute little gestures. Women loved receiving flowers from him because he had perfected the ritual: he would coyly conceal the bouquet behind his broad back and affect a sly smile—as if suggesting that even though they both understood what was about to happen, there still remained a tiny window for something unexpected. And then, like an amateur magician performing for a friendly audience, he produced the bouquet (often carnations but not exclusively) and thrust it forward towards the lucky recipient, a curt officer's bow completing the gallant act of gift giving. He performed a similar trick with boxes of chocolate, cognac bottles, and theater tickets, and almost invariably to the same effect—that is, a feigned gasp of surprise, followed by a cooing sound of a very melodic and insincere "Aww, you really didn't have to."

Bella trusted his good sense and social skills absolutely; it was natural for her to follow his lead, even though, besides his considerable height and exceptional home-improvement skills, there was definitely nothing particularly intimidating about Boris. General consensus had it that Boris was a sweetheart. Had Bella been more attuned to reality she would have noticed how jealous many of her girlfriends were of her good fortune. "God favors holy fools," they grumbled behind her back. Actually, Boris once overheard one of her colleagues at the clinic (he stopped by to pick Bella up after her night shift—as he did several times a week) sharing this bit of folk wisdom with a night nurse. He felt instantly flattered but also concerned for Bella who after all had to work with these people. Even if only for a second, he wondered if his wife's apparent childlessness had not been brought about by all this ill will directed at her. He pushed away the thought—generally, he had little use for superstitions, but at the same time he wouldn't put such meanness past his fellow citizens. Boris may have been a sweetheart and a kindly provider, but his view of human nature tended towards the skeptical. "I am not naïve," as he preferred to put it.

David though was naïve. Oh, *was* he naïve . . . More naïve than any other person Boris has ever met, and that included his late wife, Bella, who was . . . well, exceptionally naïve. That jealous cardiologist at the Moscow clinic, a stout, grim-faced forty-year-old divorcee, would have no trouble recognizing David for what he was—a holy fool. The day they met at the Hebrew class, David had transferred two thousand shekels into the personal account of a woman he recently met on a bus. The woman was launching a matchmaking business out of her hostel apartment in Ashdod and needed investors. As far as Boris could tell, David became the first and only investor in the ambitious enterprise, whose business plan consisted of a hand-written paragraph pledging to connect "soulmates across international time zones and borders." The only romantic connection the entrepreneurial fixer succeeded in establishing was between hers and David's bank accounts, which was likely the whole purpose of the undertaking. Right after class the alarmed Boris convinced David to give his new business partner a call. A sleepy voice on the other end of the line informed them that the matchmaker had a family emergency in Tbilisi and had departed abruptly. Coming back? Oh, no, she won't be coming back . . . So the friendship between Boris and David began momentously with Boris trying to sort out David's financial mess, and that little adventure established a "screw up/rescue" pattern that the two of them would follow for the duration of their friendship—that is, until that March afternoon in Holon.

Outwardly, they couldn't be any more different—the impulsive and reckless David vs. the deliberate and risk-averse Boris—yet they immediately recognized a deeper affinity. Indeed, some similarities in their respective backgrounds were almost uncanny, the function of a shared national history, to be sure, but striking nevertheless. Both lived through hungry wartime childhoods and lost their fathers in the war, both came from urban intelligentsia but early on opted for military careers, mostly to relieve their exhausted mothers from the necessity to feed too many mouths. Both eventually came to detest their military vocation, even if for different reasons: David dreamed of becoming a full-time man of letters, while Boris desperately missed city life and aspired to creature comforts that were not readily available at a remote missile launch base on the frozen shores of the White Sea.

Neither of them was of a dissident persuasion. In his day and in his capacity as a popular poet in a small Soviet republic in the Baltics, David gravitated towards the countercultural types—those whose nonconformist trials (including real trials) and tribulations sometimes made the headlines in the West. They shared a lot of drinks but hardly the worldview, which, in David's case, remained stubbornly optimistic and colored by his intense love of living. He was too much of an egocentric and bon vivant to care about such esoteric subjects as human rights or the Jewish yearning for Israel. He wished Israel well but was genuinely puzzled by some of his more politically engaged friends' willingness to sacrifice for the cause. His poetry, his mad infatuations, his marriages and divorces, his emotional highs and lows presented a form of existence and left no time or energy for self-sacrifice. For him, politics remained slightly distasteful, not sufficiently poetic, and unimaginatively straightforward. His talent or, as Boris would later refer to it, his "Gift" got in the way of politics; he couldn't be bothered. Had someone told him then that he would spend the last ten years of his life walking an auburn-colored mongrel on a sandy Ashkelon beach some two thousand miles away from the more familiar, rain-soaked Baltic sand dunes, he would have taken it for a plot of a subversive sci-fi play that had absolutely zero prospects of ever getting published or staged. Or maybe he would've penned a poem, one of those quirky little poems that he sometimes jotted down in the morning to capture the outlines and the mood of a particularly vivid dream.

And Boris . . . Boris penned no poems and couldn't claim to have any dissident friends. Whether in the Soviet Union or, later, in Israel, he never questioned the legitimacy of the reality that he inhabited. Whatever it happened to be, he accepted the immediate as a given—a natural phenomenon to figure out and manage on the most favorable terms. When he looked back on the first seventy years of his life the historical milestones of the journey barely registered with him. Of course, he remembered the war, and the drab postwar Moscow, and the stampede at Stalin's funeral, and his twenty years in the military service; he remembered the Cuban Missile Crisis (their base stayed on high alert through the end of the year and all leaves were cancelled), he remembered the last, gasping, Soviet years, and the Moscow putsch, and the shock of the collapse and transition . . . he remembered this history, but somehow it never seemed significant to him. What *was* significant, though, were the memories of his ability to navigate the exciting obstacle course of the Soviet everyday. He would've never phrased it this way, and generally he rarely if ever articulated his feelings (eventually, David would be able to do this for both of them), but deep inside he was grateful to the forbidding country that raised him for turning him into a master navigator. Where a less resilient person would have felt emasculated and spent, the resourceful Boris felt empowered and alive. Was there any other country that would have allowed him to hone to perfection his survival skills and sharpen his understanding of human nature? And free of charge? He didn't think so. Boris was thankful for each expertly deflected curveball but also for the opportunities to put his formidable skills at the disposal of the two innocents who most needed them—first, Bella, and then, after that idiot taxi driver ran the red light to end the forty plus years of his selfless service to Bella, David.

At Bella's funeral Boris's mind wandered. He couldn't get over the fact that the tragedy struck on their very first postimmigration return trip to Moscow. Was it symbolic? Was it a sign? He didn't believe in signs, but the cinematic symbolism of Bella's death made him uncomfortable—he hardly knew what to make of its random horror. Was he to blame? Was it his fondness for the Mediterranean breeze and those bloody orange sunsets that had doomed Bella? Bella's niece, ever the mind reader, touched his sleeve, pulled him aside to peck him on the cheek: "Don't torture yourself; you gave her a very good life and Moscow claimed her. There is nothing we can do about it. But she lived well, thanks to you she lived very well." These were the perfect words, and they instantly breached the shroud of his doubt and lifted his spirits: "Yes, she lived well, didn't she? She lived very, very well. Every whim, every desire . . . Do you know that she had no clue how much to pay for a kilo of butter? She had no need to know."—"I do know she was a happy woman, Borechka," smiled the niece. "*You* made her happy." For emphasis, she squeezed his huge palm with both of her hands—this was a delicate moment, a touch-and-go kind of moment that needed to be converted into permanent assurance. "You need to think of yourself now, Borechka. One step at a time—living your life, you see . . . The pain will be there for a while, but you need to live. How do you feel?" Boris was not used to such questions. No one had ever inquired about his feelings and he didn't have the words to describe them. He paused in puzzlement and searched for an appropriate descriptor: "How do *I* feel? How do I *feel*? What a strange question . . . I dunno . . . No, wait, I do . . . I feel like . . . like I've been laid off, I feel like I'm suddenly unemployed."

It never even crossed his mind that he could remain in Moscow after the funeral. The city seemed inexplicably foreign: in the intervening years it had grown even gaudier and more overwhelming, more imperial in its multihued ethnic diversity, but Boris recognized no evident opportunities for conquest. And on whose behalf would he consider reconquering it? Who or what would give his efforts the force of life? With surprise Boris recalled a long-forgotten history lesson from his postwar adolescence—it had to do with Napoleon's ill-fated takeover of the city. History was one of his least favorite subjects at school, but somehow the triumph-turned-downfall story made a strong impression on him. He could barely retain the most basic historical details of the Patriotic War of 1812, but the French emperor's sad predicament captured his imagination. That day after class Boris walked back home from school through the park at Patriarch's Ponds, the old Moscow neighborhood that retained its quaint provincial feel well into the postwar years; he walked slowly, dragging his feet, absent-mindedly kicking up the fallen autumnal leaves that softened his steps on the gravel path. He kept thinking of the lonely, pudgy corporal, the conqueror of Europe, whose conquest of Moscow turned out to be his ultimate undoing. In the fall of 1812, Moscow burned for weeks and Napoleon, stuck inside the emptied Kremlin, looked on—first in awe, then in bewilderment, and eventually with a growing sense of impotence and dread. By self-immolating, Moscow defied the conqueror; it made him feel tiny and insignificant. Even as a teenager, Boris steered clear of profound psychological insights, but on that drizzly late October afternoon he did take note of Napoleon's hubris. He would never make a similar mistake; he would make sure that his ambitions remained modest and didn't provoke the wrath of fiery gods. And now, in his new, "Bella-less" phase (which he understood to be his last), he saw no point in remaining in a city that punished those who ignored its obvious warning signs. The fires of Moscow burned for him too.

A week after the funeral Boris woke up in their small subsidized apartment with a view of the recently restored seaside promenade. He stepped out onto the balcony where they used to have their morning instant coffee with condensed milk and took in the view of the beach that was already stirring to life at seven in the morning. A neighbor was walking his dog and Boris waved at him; the neighbor waved back and greeted him by touching the tip of his straw sun hat. Boris lingered on the balcony and followed the progress of an athletic-looking jogger in a fluorescent sports bra who was pounding the freshly installed boards of the promenade. Habitually he looked up at the sun and noted its slow but inevitable progress across the cloudless horizon—the heat was gathering; soon enough he would have to retreat inside the apartment and turn on the *mazgan*, the air-conditioning. But he figured he still had a couple of hours for errands. He had spent the four hours on the plane preparing a to-do list and was now eager to hit the ground running: first, the National Insurance branch—to turn in the death certificate; then the bank—to remove Bella's name from the account; after that he should have enough time left to drive across town to the old Turkish market, where a jolly Georgian Givi ran a framing shop. Boris had picked out a black-and-white photograph of Bella that he took on their car trip to Crimea back in 1966. That was a good year—a Year of the Horse. They'd bought their first car, the unassuming but durable Moskvitch 408. In the photograph, Bella was wearing a light summery dress covered with polka dots. She posed in front of picturesque Hellenic ruins, smiling expectantly—as if looking for his approbation of the impishly coquettish pose she had just struck. Now he would have the photograph framed; he identified the perfect spot for it—on the bedroom dresser, right next to the silver menorah that Bella bought at that fancy Judaica store in Jerusalem's Old City. So . . . National Insurance, the bank, the framing shop—that would keep him busy for a few hours, until the heat drove him indoors. Oh, he'll manage, he'll manage just fine.

***

David approached him during their first recess, on the very first day of the language classes at the ulpan. He quickly introduced himself and scooted over next to Boris, sliding along the polished bench. Once seated he folded his arms on the desk in front of him, affecting the look of an exemplary pupil. "And here is life for you," he sighed. "My *teudat zehut* clearly states my age—seventy-two, but somehow it feels that I am seven again . . ." He paused for effect. "Well, maybe not seven, more like thirteen or fourteen, because I clearly have developed a crush on our teacher. Have you noticed the hazel hue of her eyes? Her upper lip quivers ever so slightly when she is just about to greet us: *Shalom, haverim* . . . That guttural sound of her greeting, God, it is *so* sensual. And her name—Orit, she swallows her 'r' when she says it, like that: O-i-i-t . . . The 'r' is implied but not quite pronounced; it's like there are these tiny little bubbles in the back of her throat, like champagne. And her figure . . . I can't take my eyes off her. Look, I've written a poem for her. It's in Hebrew. What do you think? You think she'll like it?"

Boris didn't quite know what to think. He picked up the piece of paper produced by his new acquaintance and gave it a cursory look, then he cleared his throat: "I'm impressed that you can write in Hebrew, this is my third ulpan and I'm still struggling with the alphabet." David laughed: "I don't really speak any Hebrew, this is my first day, but I used the words from the printout she gave us at the beginning of class. Look: *Orit, David, eyes, hazel, sea, beach, love, teacher, Russia, sunset* . . . There is more than enough here to compose a decent love poem, don't you think?" As if hypnotized, Boris nodded. He had always prided himself on his ability to "read people," to immediately identify the type he was dealing with and act accordingly. However, on this occasion this faculty failed him, even though he couldn't help but feel that there was something vaguely familiar about David. They had just met, but David didn't look or act like a stranger. He didn't hold anything back and eagerly shared with Boris his youthful agility and the innocence of his blue eyes.

Confused, Boris felt the need to ask a question, and so he did: "So . . . You know how to write poems?" For a moment, David looked at him uncomprehendingly, as if caught off guard: "Do-I-know-how-to-write-poems?" He repeated the question slowly, placing deliberate emphasis on each word, then he sighed in mock desperation. "What a question to ask a poet . . . Listen, let me explain this to you—it's really simple. I know how to drive a car, I know how to cook oatmeal in the morning, I know how to mend a sock (oh yes, I *do*) . . . But poems . . . No, I don't know how to write poems. I don't *need* to know. Can you guess why?" Boris slowly shook his head. "Because I am a *poet*. And even more, I'll tell you so that you know not to ask this question again. I am a *very good* poet. Actually, one of the best I've ever known, and let me tell you, I've known quite a few. Are we on the same page here?" Boris nodded. David gave him the thumbs up. "Excellent! Let's go for a swim after class, the beach is so lovely late in the afternoon, just before dusk. I'll listen to your life story and you'll listen to mine. At our age any self-respecting person should have at least a draft of his life story ready for the final reading. No worries, I'll edit yours for style if you want me to."—"Thank you," Boris mumbled and then, unexpectedly for himself, blurted out: "You see, I recently lost my wife." David looked at him with genuine concern and tapped him comfortingly on his massive wrist. "I'm sorry to hear it. So yours is a tale of loss . . . as expected. Mine is too but of a different kind. I recently left my third wife. She stopped loving me. You know, I can put up with a lot of nonsense, but I cannot not be loved, I cannot live with a woman who doesn't love me. It's like a death sentence this 'unlove'—it empties you of all content, it makes you hollow inside like an almond shell without the seed. Does that make sense to you?" Boris was not certain that it did but bowed his head in the affirmative, just in case. And he found the metaphor catchy: for days to come, he would continue to repeat it under his breath each time he looked at the framed picture propped up on the dresser: "Like an almond shell without the seed, like an almond shell without the seed, like an almond shell . . ."

That afternoon, after Orit let the class out (but not before David handed his poem to her and was rewarded with a hearty hug from the tough-looking hazel-eyed sabra), they went for a swim followed by a long stroll on the boardwalk. The next morning, David, who, as it turned out, also lived on the marina, came over for coffee, which they had on the balcony overlooking the promenade. David didn't come empty-handed; he brought with him a new poem, which he proceeded to recite by heart to Boris. In the poem, the protagonist—an older man, tired of life's burdens—walked his dog on the beach during a rainstorm. The storm raged and sent angry foamy waves crushing against the concrete breakwater; the dog, soaked to its bones, whimpered and pressed itself against the feet of the owner, who was full of foreboding but simultaneously elated by this expression of unequivocal trust.

Boris, usually not big on poetry, nevertheless decided that he liked the poem; he was also struck by David's ability to recite from memory. "How long did it take you to memorize the lines?" he asked. David raised his eyebrows and patted him amicably on the shoulder. Boris didn't mind the condescension of the gesture. "How long? Hah, you and your questions! Borechka, I don't *have to* memorize the lines of my poems, they come to me to stay, they live right here." He tapped the bald dome of his head. "They never leave—just like your family, your friends, like the women who love us, they never go away." Boris caught himself smiling. Why was he smiling? What was it about David's words and the soothing timbre of his voice that made him smile and feel . . . he searched for the right word and as often in such cases came up short. Happy? Could he say "happy"? Such a simple and generic word, but now he has resolved to use it . . . at his own risk. "I feel . . . happy," stammered Boris. He let out the words and they immediately assumed an aerial life of their own, floating over the balcony, absorbing the aquamarine blue of the early seaside morning.

David turned to him with an encouraging smile; at eight o'clock in the morning the color of his eyes matched perfectly the color of the Mediterranean waters down below. "Happy? Really? What a wonderful thing to say, especially in the morning. You know what, Borechka, let's make it our standard morning greeting! Like this: '*Boker tov, haver*! I'm happy!' and then the other one responds: '*Boker tov*! Me too!' Deal?" Boris nodded enthusiastically: "Deal!" For the first time in months, certainly for the first time since that awful Tuesday when Bella's niece drove him to the medical examiner's office on the outskirts of Moscow, he felt at ease, and he believed that it was OK to acknowledge this feeling: being at ease, after all, meant being happy. He was happy. Boris poured more water into the coffee mug that David unceremoniously pushed towards him across the plastic tabletop. Clearly, David was comfortable being served, but that hardly bothered Boris—serving the select few came naturally to him. And David was not obnoxious about it, not at all! Here was a precocious blue-eyed kid who accepted the care of strangers and their little favors as a matter of course. He never demanded special treatment, but at the same time acted as if assured of its inevitability. Bella used to be like that . . .

After months of internal turmoil that saw him unmoored from his routine, life had finally begun to come into focus for Boris. He exhaled with sweet relief as if having resurfaced after a deep-sea dive. He noticed the sudden sharpness of the objects around him and the festiveness of the morning, which reminded him of those other Sunday mornings in their communal apartment in Moscow, soon after the war, when he would wake up decadently late to overpowering kitchen smells and the indistinct gurgle of sounds and marching music emitted by a mounted radio set. He almost relived the sensation of intense and inexplicable joy that permeated his every fiber, the sense of anticipation and wonder he would come to associate with his adolescence and that, sadly, would completely abandon him later in life. "I'm happy," he whispered again and thought himself silly and reckless for uttering such frivolous words. But David didn't mind, he was lounging contentedly on the balcony sofa covered by the leopard-patterned velvet spread—a nod to Ashkelon's reigning aesthetic. Boris wouldn't be surprised if it turned out that David had preserved that gift of childhood joy; quite possibly it was inextricably connected to that other gift he possessed—The Gift in capital letters (as Boris was already beginning to think of it).

A thought startled him: sometime in the course of this morning (or was it last night during their walk on the promenade?), David had ceased being a stranger and entered Boris's life as its permanent fixture. How did *that* happen? Boris gave his new friend a quick once-over, but it was a new, possessive look—an examination by someone who has just completed a valuable purchase. That's how he bought his used Mazda a few weeks after he and Bella had first arrived in Israel. He slowly walked around the car he located at a ramshackle dealership in the northern industrial zone. A major acquisition required extreme thoroughness on his part. He inspected the tires with meticulous care, then he raised the hood and checked the battery, the radiator, and the water pump—he paid attention to every tiny detail, to each minor scratch and imperfection. And in the case of David, there seemed to be an awful lot of imperfections that Boris, in his new proprietary mode, now proceeded to catalogue: the mismatched socks; the stained, fraying at the hem jeans; the nylon watch strap held together by a staple; the watch itself, its face cracked into an intricate mosaic of minuscule lines . . . Boris sighed with feigned resignation: well, well, well . . . he surely had his work cut out for him. Rejuvenated, he breathed in the smells of the sea and whistled at the friendly neighbor's dog rummaging through the shrubbery that marked the edge of the boardwalk . . . David, in the meantime, had dozed off and Boris was careful to move noiselessly around the balcony while clearing away the remnants of their breakfast. It had been a while since he felt so alive.

In his typically systematic manner Boris set about bringing some order to the artistic chaos that passed for David's everyday existence. The sheer magnitude of the task temporarily overwhelmed him, but he quickly regained his bearings, took another deep breath, and plunged forward. They bought a new (used) vacuum cleaner and borrowed a couple of plastic buckets. The friendly dog-walking neighbor volunteered to help them with what David immediately termed the "great Ashkelon cleanup." Boris couldn't help but register the self-aggrandizing way in which David referred to the most routine details of his daily life. Here was someone who never doubted the significance of his earthly presence, which he easily assumed to be of momentous importance for anyone who entered his orbit. David's egotism was devoid of any meanness or premeditation, and, in a strange way, it was profoundly humanistic and therefore attractive. In demanding care and attention to his person David projected an instant amicability and a genuine warmth, as if offering a membership in an exciting and rewarding joint venture. He took it for granted that the people he met (and whom he invariably presumed to be kind, and generous, and desirous of his companionship) would want to co-manage his life—and not because he, David, wanted to shirk his own responsibilities (yes, yes, while a poet of love, he was also a troubadour of physical labor, which he respected and never shirked), but because he simply couldn't imagine that the thrilling adventure of his life held no interest to others. "When I first met you I felt like Alice falling down the rabbit hole and you fall and fall and fall down this tunnel and wait and wait to hit the bottom but the bottom . . . the bottom is not there for the longest time . . .

until you finally reach it and you come to a stop on a heap of sticks or grass or something and you get up and brush off the twigs and straighten your skirt and look around and try to make sense of what's happening to you and all of a sudden you understand that you have landed on the other side of the world and everyone around you walks upside down." That's how a former lover once tried to explain to David the experience of getting caught up in his vortex. The *Alice in Wonderland* metaphor left him puzzled and he still sounded perplexed decades later when relating the story to his friend, Boris, during one of their evening walks on the promenade. Boris, who had never so much as heard of Lewis Carroll, asked for clarification, after which he mulled over the allegory for a few minutes before conceding it to be apt: "You know, little buddy,"—that's how he'd recently taken to calling David (*druzhok* in Russian)—"she had a point there—things about you . . . I don't know how to put it, and I say this lovingly, but they are a bit . . . you know . . . topsy-turvy."

And how exactly topsy-turvy *were* they at the time when Boris resolved to embrace his mission? In layman's terms, David's apartment was a mess, but the word "mess" hardly captures the free-wheeling disarray that reigned supreme within the bleached walls of his one-bedroom rental with a view of the beach, a brazen jumble of objects that spilled over onto the balcony. Layers of fine, dust-like sand covered every available surface, every randomly placed object or broken appliance. The ceramic floor also had a coating of sand and presented clear evidence of David's daily patterns and would have delighted any motion studies researcher: the well-trodden, intersecting paths in the sand connected the bedroom (a mattress placed at an angle on the floor), the bathroom, the kitchenette, the balcony, and the rickety writing desk that featured a dirty computer monitor and a printer with a cracked case. Despite its intimate proximity to the computer, the printer was not connected to it and there was no evidence that the two ever consummated their intended relationship. Stacks of print paper were propped up against the desk, and the walls, and the sliding glass door to the balcony—each time David opened the balcony door, at least one of the stacks collapsed sending the sheets of paper flying across the room. And each time David issued a heartfelt but resigned "f-u-u-c-k" and proceeded to pick up the scattered pieces of paper and reassemble them into an unsteady pile. "Sick and tired of wasting my time on this labor of Sisyphus," he grumbled while picking up the paper. Boris looked on in bemused disbelief. "But you could easily push the pile away from the door," he observed simply, not a note of sarcasm in his voice. "How about . . . right here?" He pointed at an unoccupied niche between the desk corner and the wall. David looked at him with mild irritation: "Oh, really? As simple as that? Borechka, I don't know how to break this bit of news to you, but trust me, few things in life are that straightforward." He never moved the pile, and Boris, still new to the friendship, decided not to press the issue. But the next day he brought over a small cinder block that he picked up at the construction site down in the marina and propped up the stack by the sliding door. David pretended that he didn't notice, pointedly refusing to acknowledge the efficacy of the innovation; but from that point on significantly fewer "fucks" bounced off the whitewashed walls of the apartment.

It took Boris a few weeks to untangle the complexity of David's finances, and there were some bewildering discoveries along the way. For example, David had signed up for the same service with two different cable companies and both were now bombarding him with threatening letters for non-payment. By Boris's count, no less than six different agencies (electricity, water, the tax office, the parking authority, etc.) had resorted to using the word "lawsuit" in their correspondence; but David, whose Hebrew language skills never progressed much beyond his one (successful) stab at writing a love poem to Orit, remained oblivious to the gathering legal storm. His only credit card was blocked because of "suspicious account activity," while his debit card had gone missing and some lucky crook was now making regular monthly withdrawals from his checking account. His car . . . Well, the car was something else altogether—an imposing, if rust-ravaged, 1984 Oldsmobile, which David parked in the underground garage, in a parking space that would've been dangerously tight even for a Honda Civic. Both the Oldsmobile's once-elegant body and the cement walls of the garage stalls exhibited the all-too-obvious signs of David's near misses.

"I can't believe you bought an old American car! A gas-guzzler! In Israel!" fulminated Boris. "*Druzhok*, do you know how much gas it takes?! Oh, what am I saying . . . 'takes' . . . It doesn't *take* it, it *drinks* it, like you and I drink that instant coffee in the morning . . . only more of it and much faster!" David gave Boris a look of mild condescension and walked over to the writing desk. From under one of the paper piles he jerked out a paperback copy of his recently self-published book of short stories. The pile didn't survive the removal of one of its foundational elements and dissolved in a cascade of falling paper leaves. Without saying a word, but with an air of quiet triumph, he thrust the book into Boris's compliant hands: "Here—check out the dust jacket!" The dust jacket bore a couple of blurbs by two individuals of apparent literary distinction. They endorsed the collection in no uncertain terms: one blurb started with "Rarely" and the other one with "Never before." The names of the endorsers meant absolutely nothing to Boris, but he assumed that such testimonials were valuable. Boris cleared his throat: "I see . . . impressive . . . so . . . does it sell well?" David shook his head disdainfully: "No, Borechka, it doesn't sell well. You know why? Because I give away copies for free. By the way, this one is yours, I'll sign it for you later." He sighed: "Ah, Borechka, you and your questions . . . You know, in my time I sold a lot of books, many thousands of copies—and they traveled far and wide, across all the Soviet time zones . . . How many were there? Nine? Ten? . . . Anyway, I'm winding up my life's journey (don't frown, we're in the same age bracket), but the books . . . the books will continue to live on the shelves of provincial libraries or, in some rare cases, in the private collections of individual citizens. So . . . I'm satisfied; I don't need to sell any more books, and that's not why I'm showing this one to you. Again, check out the dust jacket!" Boris did as he was told, and that's when he noticed the photograph of the author in the lower-left corner. In the picture, David was sitting at the wheel of his Oldsmobile, a light white scarf thrown casually around his neck, a white fedora slanted rakishly sideways on his sun-tanned head, his clear blue eyes squinting knowingly into the camera. "So?" inquired David with a sly, subversive smile, "how do I look? Don't tell me you're not impressed." Boris was at a loss for words—men of his background and generation rarely, if ever, complimented each other on their looks. But he felt that the right response had already been given to him and he had no choice but to regurgitate it. Which he did: "You do look . . . impressive, I guess . . ."—"You guessed right, Borechka! It's a killer look. It's the look of an artist of a certain age. It's a Hemingway look. It's a Belmondo look . . . And now *you* tell me: Can one look like that in a Suzuki (which, by the way, gets excellent gas mileage)?" Boris shook his head in a gesture of mock defeat. The rules as he knew and respected them hardly applied to David. And to his great surprise, Boris realized that he was fine with it. As long as he remained next to David, he'd work hard to muffle the blows and limit the damage.

Conversations with David contained occasional references to his past fame. Boris couldn't claim proximity to the higher echelons of the Soviet artistic elite, but having grown up and lived much of his life in Moscow he certainly recognized the names of at least some prominent cultural figures. And in his previous life, David apparently was part of that circle. He never boasted about his connections, and in that he was different from other Russian-speaking immigrants, most of whom, if one was to believe their tales of past grandeur, had spent their Soviet lives occupying the positions of high and even exceptional responsibility. "I've never met so many former army generals and factory directors as on my evening strolls on the Ashkelon boardwalk," joked Boris. David smiled: "I read somewhere that in the 1930s Paris every other cab driver was either an exiled Russian general or an impoverished Russian prince. Some of them probably were . . ." But David . . . David didn't boast, he simply told stories, and he certainly was a master storyteller—he had a joke or a vignette or a quick reminiscence ready for most of life's occasions, and he wielded those seemingly at will, often to great dramatic effect.

David's memory for poetry (especially his own) was prodigious, and he derived obvious pleasure from the act of recitation. But he also derived pleasure from almost any other activity. Boris had never met anyone with such an unapologetic, such a shameless zest for life. In David's rendering, the simplest of pleasures became exquisite: their morning coffee ritual on the balcony (*Boker tov, haver, boker tov*!), their evening strolls on the boardwalk, their themed dinner parties, attended by an ever-growing bevy of "fair ladies of Ashkelon," most of them smelling of the French perfume Climat, all extravagantly in love with David's poems but hardly interested in his colorful persona (the solidly reliable and well-to-do Boris was viewed as a much better catch), a poetry reading at a retirement community in Ashdod, an impromptu game of soccer with a bunch of Ethiopian kids on the beach, a thrice-a-week workout regimen at an open-air municipal gym on the marina . . .

David's childlike enthusiasm for any new experience was infectious; his womanizing—light and festive and gleefully adolescent. "You know, I've been intimate with seventy-six women," he solemnly confessed to Boris soon after they met. Boris was taken aback: "You've kept count?!" He had also kept count until he married Bella, who was number four. There was a one-time indiscretion with a medical nurse, committed after the farewell banquet at an elite, Ministry of Internal Affairs-affiliated sanatorium in Yalta, where Boris underwent an experimental ulcer treatment during the summer of 1978. The fling left him feeling miserable and guilt-ridden, and ultimately served to reinforce his all-consuming commitment to Bella's well-being. So . . . five altogether and . . . really not a topic that Boris, in all his Soviet-Victorian prudishness, would ever consider discussing with others. Even in the army he did his best to steer clear of all the dirty macho talk that was often interwoven with the most routine conversations in the barracks. He possessed an ingrained sense of propriety and decorum, which, he sometimes thought, was one of the reasons why he never had a lot of male friends. But even in this regard, David presented a peculiar exception. His revelations did not offend Boris, there was nothing even remotely "dirty" about them. In David's retelling, his sexual conquests became acts of humble surrender to powers that he could not control—the powers of beauty, and grace, and benevolence. Each affair was a small miracle, a beneficent deed gifted to him by someone of a superior caste. He was profoundly grateful to each of the seventy-six women, he spoke about them with awe as if mystified by their kind and inexplicable generosity. "Whenever I wake up next to a new woman, I'm overwhelmed by this sense of my own unworthiness. I feel like a puny, pathetic worm lying next to a gorgeous creature, and I feel I need to do something to make myself worthy of my luck. You cannot take this happiness for granted; if you don't think you're deserving you have to make an extra effort to work for it. That's why I write poems—to be worthy," he earnestly explained to Boris.

About a year into their friendship a sudden blast from David's past brought his story into focus for Boris. One morning, when David failed to show up for their customary coffee, an alarmed Boris rushed over to David's place. As usual the door to the apartment was unlocked—another manifestation of David's typical negligence, which both irked and delighted Boris. A couple of months prior, two robbers (caught on CCTV camera but never apprehended) had entered the apartment while David was taking his afternoon nap and relieved him of his portable TV and broken printer. "I hope they can find a way to fix it," noted David while surveying the crime scene. "I hope you will finally start locking the damn door," rejoined an irate Boris. David laughed: "Come on, Borechka, you've studied physics at that military academy of yours, you should know that lightening never strikes twice." He was mistaken. The thieves, apparently inspired by the ease of their previous exploit, returned a few days later and made off with his watch (recently fixed by Boris) and some one thousand shekels in cash that David had carelessly left sitting on the kitchenette counter. David thought that the story of double larceny (which he promptly turned into a self-deprecating jocular poem) more than compensated for the loss of property. Boris was of a different opinion . . .

Presently, he softly pushed the door open and took a step back, half-expecting to discover another burglary in progress. But the apartment appeared to be peaceful and crimeless. The door to the balcony was slid open and Boris observed David reclining, his coffee mug in hand, on a beat-up sofa they had recently rescued from undignified oblivion at the dumpster in Afridar and which Boris was now planning to reupholster. A woman was seated on the tile floor next to the sofa—an attractive younger woman, clearly not one of the "fair ladies," probably in her late forties. As he walked through the hallway Boris caught the quiet murmur of a conversation. The woman noticed Boris and turned to him with an eager, welcoming smile: "Oh, you must be Boris, David's friend!" She stretched out her hand in a gesture of determined friendliness: "I'm Marina, the island muse!" Boris stared at her, uncomprehending. For explanation he turned to David who was enjoying the scene. "The island muse?"—"But of course, Borechka! Meet my old friend, Marina. Marina hails from a picturesque little island off the Estonian coast, where she grew up tending to a lighthouse. Or rather her father did, but she was a great little helper, and through her selfless labors she saved in her day many a doomed mariner from a cruel death on the inhospitable granite rocks. Here, have some coffee, make yourself comfortable. And by the way . . . *boker tov, haver*! It's a nice morning indeed."

Marina had recently arrived in the Holy Land with an Orthodox Christian travel group. She dutifully followed the itinerary, which first took her to Bethlehem, and then up and down the narrow cobblestone streets of Jerusalem's Old City, before depositing her and her fellow pilgrims in the courtyard in front of the Church of the Holy Sepulchre. She covered her head with a scarf and entered the echoey church, where she knelt by the Stone of Anointing and touched its smooth cold surface with her lips. "You'll feel a warmth, a bliss swelling inside your gut," their guide had warned them. "Just let it envelope you, give yourself to the sensation completely, be blessed . . ." But Marina felt nothing of the sort; no matter how hard she tried, she couldn't will herself into a state of bliss. To make things worse, some of the pilgrims had grown hysterical—emitting half-suppressed sobs, tears mixed with mascara streaming down their cheeks—and Marina found their behavior distasteful. Her austere childhood on a remote Baltic island had taught her the emotive power of understatement, and in the face of a public display of religious fervor she longed for a different kind of pilgrimage.

She wished for a meaningful encounter that could truly be her own. Inside the church, a different sort of revelation came to her—she remembered why she had planned this trip in the first place. She remembered the heavenly blue of David's kindly eyes; she heard his soothing baritone reciting verses about a weather-beaten lighthouse keeper and his young daughter on a mission to rescue lost sailors . . . She must've been fourteen or fifteen when the bearded poet arrived on the island to give a reading to the locals—a motley crew of fishermen and longshoremen. They listened in silence, their usual Nordic reserve intact. But when David finished no one moved: he took in the scene, nodded contentedly, and continued to read for another hour, and then one more. After the reading David gave away copies of his newly published book of poems—a slim volume with a falling autumnal leaf on its cover. He signed Marina's copy—"to the little lighthouse keeper"—and promised to write a poem about her and her father and their daily vigil at the lighthouse. And he did—the very next morning, before the midday ferry would carry him back to the mainland. When giving her the folded piece of paper, he told her that there was nothing more important in life than art, and love, and their ramshackle lighthouse on a windswept rock jutting out into the dark and stormy Baltic waters. At the time, she didn't quite know what he meant, but the words were calming and reassuring, and she took them as a life lesson to be preserved for later review. After breakfast they walked him down to the wharf, making their way through a maze of tugboat lines and mounds of drying fishing nets with small cork floats attached to them. She was still holding on to his little book, with the folded piece of paper slipped in between its pages. By the end of the day, she had memorized the poem, all twelve stanzas of it, and that's how now, decades later, she remembered her childhood: an island in the early morning fog, her late father fumbling with a gas starter, the piercing screams of the seagulls hovering fretfully over the rocks, and young Marina, still a child, leaning into the wind on the sandy, sprinkled with pine needles path to the lighthouse.

Marina stayed with David for about a week, during which time Boris's whole life seemed to be hanging in the balance. They had moved their morning coffee ritual onto David's balcony, but as far as Boris was concerned the coffee didn't taste the same and the *boker tov* didn't sound nearly as joyous. True to form, David remained completely oblivious to his friend's inner torment, it was natural for him to assume that those closest to him couldn't help but share in his joy. Boris understood that well, but that understanding did little to alleviate his discomfort and the dull pangs of jealousy. In fact, he felt conflicted—simultaneously aggrieved and guilty for begrudging his friend's happiness. All of this was very confusing for Boris, who was not accustomed to experiencing such emotional turmoil and an acute fear of loss. He resolved to pull himself together and calmly assess the situation. After all, Marina was a pilgrim and therefore a creature of transience. Just like her pilgrimage to Jerusalem, her personal hajj to pay homage to an old poet on the Ashkelon beach was bound to come to an end. And that was something that Boris, in his state of angst, intuited despite the lack of any formal religious education. Pilgrims, he guessed correctly, are less threatening than colonizers. Even though smitten with David, Marina laid no claim to him, being content to simply spend a few days seated cross-legged on the warm balcony tiles, within earshot of the splashing waves and right next to someone who once illuminated her youth.

But like most spells, this spell too was bound to be broken. A few more days and the aging poet would become all too corporeal, all too distinct from the bearded, blue-eyed prince of her childhood island memories. The poet would recede into a hazy background and forth would step in David-the-man, in all his unvarnished decay: the loose, ill-fitting dentures (a mental note to make another appointment with that hack of a prosthodontist from Moldova); the bushy untended eyebrows; his wrinkly sun-scorched skin (especially on and around his neck), the ungainly potbelly that he inelegantly sucks in whenever he gets up off that sofa; the thunderous toilet noises that she pretends not to notice but are really quite impossible to ignore. These may have not been Marina's exact thoughts and premonitions, but Boris would eventually ascribe them to her . . . after the fact.

Strangely, the Marina episode cemented their friendship. Her departure necessitated a mini crisis, with David begging Boris to assure him that he could still cast a spell on a much younger woman. Boris did his awkward best to allay David's distress and in doing so inadvertently drew on his decades-vast experience of dealing with Bella's little vanities: "*Druzhok*, what are you talking about? She had to leave, she has a family, remember? It's not you and your looks are just fine. In fact, you look fantastic for your age. How many seventy-three-year-olds out there would have a beautiful admirer travel thousands of kilometers just to spend some time with them? I don't know any such old-timers. No one would trek halfway around the globe to see me, that's for sure! If I were you, I would be s-o-o-o proud of myself." Actually, Boris was being truthful. David's flaws were abundant and glaring, his self-absorption infuriating, but as far as Boris was concerned his "Gift" redeemed him completely and placed him outside the laws that applied to most other people he knew—most certainly, to himself, and to the friendly neighbor, and to the "fair ladies of Ashkelon" and their "talented and successful" offspring. He made or rather used to make one more (partial) exception—for Bella.

Boris would never confess this to David, but once, a few weeks after their first meeting at the ulpan, he subjected himself to a creativity test—he tried to write a poem. It was an important test, a test that could have altered his idea of himself and thus the nature of his budding relationship with David. Inside his small apartment, Boris stripped down to his trunks (he detested the air-conditioning—both the noise and the runaway electricity bills), poured himself a tumbler of Maker's Mark, and powered on a recently acquired refurbished Dell computer. Earlier that day he had seemingly innocently asked David what it took to write poetry. David being David didn't discern any ulterior motive on Boris's part and happily expounded on the importance of sincerity and inspiration: "You cannot be ignorant of your subject. Yes, inspiration is important—that's how a poem comes to you, but you cannot write about things that you don't understand or know or feel intimately. If you do, then no one will ever believe you. Even worse, your readers, at least the ones who matter, will despise you. Insincerity is a crime. And that's why so many 'officially sanctioned' Soviet poets were just that—criminals."—"But weren't *you* one of those 'officially sanctioned' poets at some point? Remember, you were successful . . ." David shrugged: "And who said I was above reproach? But in my defense, I don't think I ever committed any poetic felonies . . . The occasional misdemeanor—yes, possibly . . . but no felonies on my record."—"Ok, I see, one has to be sincere, true to himself, right?" David nodded agreeably: "Exactly, *haver*! Hey, let's go for a swim!"

Thus, fortified with this bit of literary advice from a master and the bourbon Boris attempted to write a poem. The blank screen stared at him uninvitingly. "Be sincere, be sincere, be sincere"—he muttered the mantra under his breath, between the sips of the bourbon. So he needed to write about something that he understood well . . . In his mind, he composed a short list of possible topics. His expertise extended to the inner workings of the internal combustion engine and the perfect mix of Georgian herbs for a barbeque; he knew how to grease the palm of a waiter, or a car mechanic, or a contractor; and he was the master of a variety of classy old-fashioned gestures that melted the hearts of the "fair ladies of Ashkelon" . . . He knew and understood a lot of things, certainly many more than David did—of that he was certain. Yet somehow none of them struck him as worthy of a poetic effort. He needed a subject that could induce in him "sincere feelings." And, of course, there was exactly such a subject, even the blank computer screen couldn't conceal it from him. That subject was Bella.

"Two years without Bella. I miss her," he typed out in a burst of what he took to be a genuine inspiration. The words rang sincere to him—he did miss Bella. Satisfied he leaned back into his mesh office chair and took a long sip out of the tumbler. Ah, that's how you do it . . . That's how *David* does it.

You search deep inside yourself until the right words come to you and give shape to your longings, and then the inchoate yearnings crystallize into letters and syllables, which morph into words and make the felt real. It was time to compose a second line. He glanced at the portable electric clock on the nightstand. Bella had bought it in Riga years ago and it served them well for years. Everyone made fun of him for hauling it here all the way from Moscow, and when it stopped working (which happened within days of their arrival in Israel) that mockery appeared to be justified. A lesser man would've given up on the clock long ago, but Boris was never one to take no for an answer, especially not from some malfunctioning Latvian timepiece. Fixing the damn clock became his mission, and after weeks of obsessive tinkering the recalcitrant device was brought back from the dead. Now it was showing a quarter past midnight. How time flies when you create, he thought. But the second line . . . the second line never materialized. It teased him from afar, presenting itself as a series of mockingly pulsating red dots on the electric clock; it goaded him into polishing off at least half-a-bottle of the expensive bourbon. "I miss her," he whispered obstinately but with slowly evaporating conviction. "I miss her?" The second line winked at him—elusive and unattainable. What was it? He felt his creative energies ebb inexorably, dissolve into a bourbon-induced fog. Another glance at the pulsating electric clock: it was closing in on three in the morning. In a few short hours the sea will catch and reflect the first rosy glare of the rising sun—it'll be another hot day. David will be coming over for coffee soon after seven and Boris better be fresh and ready for his jolly *boker tov*; he'd better make sure those discounted pastries he picked up after hours at the bakery downtown were still edible, and, most importantly, there'd better be no traces left of his failed stab at poetry.

***

In hindsight, Nadia was inevitable. In a way, Boris always knew that it was only a matter of time until David's charm and his insatiable need for admiration would capture the imagination of someone with a similarly impractical mind. He understood such a prospect to be real, albeit somewhat limited by the near absence of impractical minds among the "fair ladies of Ashkelon." But he recognized the danger the moment he spotted Nadia at a poetry reading at a downtown Russian bookstore called The Lower Depths, tucked in inconspicuously between a furniture retailer and a Romanian shoe repair shop, across the street from the old Ottoman mosque.

The store was run by Rosa, a self-described former socialite from Tashkent, whose ambition to reclaim her glory days as a classical music expert at the Uzbek Ministry of Culture ran into the obvious Ashkelon limitations. But Rosa persevered against great odds and hosted regular poetry and literature events at her money-losing establishment (her husband was a prominent practicing pediatrician, so she could afford to take the loss). For the purpose, she kept a stable of local poets and memoirists whose literary achievement generally aligned with the name of her bookstore. Despite such challenges Rosa had a keen enough eye for artistic quality to immediately recognize David for what he was—a rare, brightly colored tropical fish swimming happily and absent-mindedly in the muddy and stale waters of the Ashkelon literary scene. Even at her post-Balzacian age Rosa remained assured of her feminine powers (and the skills of the French plastic surgeon in Herzliya) and once made a straightforward pass at David. David demurred but responded the next day with a grateful limerick—a thank you note that was so witty and friendly that Rosa couldn't possibly carry a grudge. She turned David into the star attraction at her gatherings and granted him a lifetime 40 percent discount on any purchase at the store, which David promptly transferred to Boris. Boris knew how to use a discount, even a bookstore discount.

Nadia languished in Rosa's employ, overseeing the store's everyday operations and processing the occasional sale. Rumor had it that Rosa exploited and underpaid Nadia, who was unassuming and timid to a fault. Nadia's appearance in Ashkelon was the result of a failed marriage back in Yekaterinburg and an attempt (also ultimately futile) to keep her troubled teenage son off drugs. By Ashkelon consensus, she was a "strange bird"—delicate and painfully self-conscious in her demeanor. She possessed none of the decisiveness and chutzpa that the same consensus held was indispensable to functioning successfully in a society presumably built on such values. At the bookstore reading, Nadia listened to David with rapt attention, and Boris, with a sinking sense of premonition, observed her mouthing along with the verses. He'd been around David long enough to instantly recognize her type—a besotted fan and a genuine poetry lover. His powers of observation proved to be astute when a week later he spotted Nadia exiting David's apartment building soon after sunset, half an hour before their scheduled evening walk. Boris's heart sank. Nadia was not some eccentric tourist, passing through in search of her adolescent memories; quite to the contrary—she was real and present.

Boris had a key to David's apartment (in theory, David had one to his; in reality, though, he had long since lost it) but knew better than to use it; he simply pushed the door and stepped into the hallway. David was out on the balcony, leaning on the rusty rails, peering dreamily over the horizon still slightly reddened by the glow of the disappeared sun. He was smoking a cigarette. "Are you insane?!" Boris was startled by the intensity of his own anger; his frustration was palpable. "Put out that poison right away! What are you? Seventeen?" Unperturbed by the outburst, David gave Boris his most angelic smile: "Borechka, you ever smoked after sex? It's divine. I don't care if it gives me cancer, the pleasure is too intense to trade for a clean bill of health." What was one supposed to make of this sort of innocence?

Boris sighed dejectedly and crossed the balcony to take up a spot next to David. He grabbed the handrail and jiggled it a little to test its sturdiness. The rail failed the test—the brackets had come loose and the carrying rods wobbled freely inside the sockets. Boris squatted heavily in front of the offending rail and studied its structural imperfections with the grave look of a concerned citizen. "I'll have to fix this," he finally grumbled. "It's a small job, really: a couple of small screws—here and here, then a socket bolt—right in there, and afterwards just a dollop of cement and it'll be as good as new. Also, the rust; I'll have to do something about the rust . . . No biggie, just sand it off and then repaint, maybe a couple of coats, I would say: no more than an hour, two at the most from start to finish, that's all." David didn't mind, he never did. He smiled serenely and gave his friend's shoulder a reassuring rub: "You do that, Borechka, you do that."

They stood like that, leaning against the wobbly guardrail and on each other, in the gathering darkness of the Levantine night, the warm sea breeze on their faces, the cutout silhouettes of container ships lining an invisible horizon—deck lights twinkling in the dark indicating their slow-motion progression towards the Ashdod port. What could one possibly do about this man-child, this perpetually adolescent septuagenarian, the blue of whose eyes remained untouched by age and stayed . . . well, so blue? How could one be cross with him or be jealous of his explosive infatuations and predictable infidelities? Boris would have to adjust to Nadia and if for some David reason a new status quo emerged, he would have to adapt to that too. Boris's angst began to subside—he knew he would manage; he was exceptionally skillful at adapting to changed circumstances. He'd just hoped that this time around he wouldn't have to.

As Boris had feared Nadia had joined their life as its permanent fixture. Her staying power rested in her timidity and an implicit readiness to be cast aside. Nadia's intimacy with David didn't make her brazen or presumptuous; when she knocked on David's door her tap was never insistent or self-assured but tentative—as if she were not certain that she was knocking on the right door or would be allowed to enter, as if she were prepared to withdraw at a moment's notice. Nadia reminded Boris of a girl he knew in Moscow more than fifty years ago. She was dating his cousin, a spoiled Muscovite brat, the scion of a well-to-do academic family and a serial womanizer, whose hip brashness both repelled and attracted the young Boris. He once showed up at his cousin's four-room, centrally located apartment unannounced and was surprised to be let in by a pretty but bashful and quiet girl who looked (and, as far as he could tell, felt) out of place in the magisterial surroundings of the professorial flat. She led him into the kitchen and put a kettle on the stove. His cousin, she explained, was taking a bath and would be out in a few minutes. Would he care for some tea? Theirs was a prudish generation, a generation of sordidly virtuous Soviet Victorians and Boris, still at the time a virgin, felt overwhelmed and depleted by this happenstance brush with the adult world. He also couldn't help but register the contradiction between the girl's painful shyness and her status as a moral transgressive—someone who was giving her unwed body (as a teenager Boris didn't dare to think about sex in less literary terms) to an arrogant and privileged cad. That long-forgotten girl—then desirable and morally compromised, now, if still alive, someone's cherished grandmother, relieved by the cleansing powers of old age from the "human stains" of her youth—that lost and hesitant soul has now, half a century later, washed up on the Ashkelon beach.

Some consolation came from the quick realization that Nadia was incapable of taking over someone else's life; she barely had a grip on her own. Nadia's protracted uphill struggle to save her son from an addiction took up most of her time and sapped much of the energy that, as Boris expertly assessed, had never been in abundant supply. She was a delicate creature, born to be a muse and a poet's "safe deposit box" (a line from David's poem dedicated to her). She was not born to fix bathroom leaks or negotiate with car mechanics at the repair shop in the northern industrial zone.

A couple of weeks after he had first spotted Nadia leaving David's apartment at sunset Boris had the chance to observe a scene that largely alleviated his most immediate concerns. He was mounting the stairs on his way to David's place when he caught the unmistakable smell of burning plastic. In his experience, there was only one apartment in the building that reliably produced an unending string of electric malfunctions, gas leaks, and plumbing mishaps. He rushed up the last flight of stairs and burst into the smoke-filled hallway of David's apartment. It took him less than a second to identify the source of fire—a charred kettle on a burning stove, boiled dry, its plastic handle melted into a grotesque smoldering lump. In two or three expert moves Boris terminated the disaster in the making and slid open the balcony door to let out the noxious fumes and let in fresh air and . . . immediately saw David and Nadia.

The pair were cuddling on the sofa, quite oblivious to the fiery drama unfolding just a few meters away from them. Nadia was lying cozily under David's welcoming arm and had her legs stretched out the remaining length of the sofa. With a free hand David was holding a few sheets of paper, his reading glasses (one of the broken hinges held together by a tiny piece of copper wire) perched on the tip of his nose. David raised his eyes above the page from which he was reading and greeted Boris with his usual affability: "Borechka, how good of you to stop by! Look, I've written a new poem, it's in free verse, because you know, love in our . . . hmmm . . . advanced age—it demands new artistic forms. Give it a listen; I think it's lovely and Nadyusha here agrees. As she should because guess to whom it's dedicated?"—"David!" Boris sounded impatient. "You've nearly burned down the damn place! Again! Didn't you or . . . *her* smell the burning plastic? You left the kettle on the stove . . ." Boris knew better than expect an equally concerned response from David, who never saw such close calls as threatening—for him, they constituted the integral elements of his daily routine, as inevitable and thus impossible to prevent or resent as any other natural manifestation of a circadian rhythm. Frustrated, Boris turned to Nadia: "Alright, David is being David but you, Nadia, didn't *you* notice that the house was about to burn down?!"

During their brief exchange Nadia had moved away from David's calming embrace and now huddled in the corner of the sofa—a frightened cornered bird, looking concerned and disoriented: "Oh, I'm so sorry, I didn't smell anything. David's poetry is just so . . . so exquisite, I got completed absorbed in it, it felt like my soul has left my body and floated above the balcony, like this here-and-now was no more—an out-of-body experience . . . I didn't smell anything. I'm so sorry, Borechka . . ." She was calling him by the diminutive now, just like David. These frightened little birds got some nerve; the self-effacing ones are the ones who stay. You take them in and give them shelter from the storm raging outside and then they stay, they cower in the corner—these bright wounded birds—and they never leave, they . . . stay. But there was a silver lining that didn't escape Boris's shrewd eye—Nadia, in her dreaminess, in her David-like impracticality posed no danger of a hostile takeover. The scope of his duties may have to expand now to provide care for two individuals hopelessly underequipped to tend to their needs but Boris—grudgingly, not enthusiastically at all—accepted this added cost of his friendship with David. All things considered it was a small price to pay for the continued privilege of saving David from himself. He would make it work.

And he did. Following the first few weeks of (occasionally awkward) adjustment and accommodation they settled into a pattern that was not very different from the one they enjoyed before the appearance of Nadia. Between her bookstore job and the twists and turns of the unending saga of her troubled son, Nadia had very little free time. Eventually Boris and David resumed their morning coffee ritual and they had never really abandoned the evening stroll on the boardwalk. Nadia usually came by bus on Friday mornings and would stay through the Shabbat. On those occasions, Boris, first reluctantly but soon enough out of a newly acquired habit, began to include her in his morning greeting: "*Boker tov, haver*! *Boker tov, havera*!" He even, to his considerable surprise, once caught himself thinking of their trio as a "we." Nadia remained steadfastly focused on David or rather, as Boris suspected, on David-the-poet, but she possessed enough tact and natural diffidence to spare Boris the trouble of defending his turf. As far as such arrangements go, they managed just fine. Better than fine actually. A day arrived when Boris offered her a Friday morning ride to the marina—an offer that she, after a lot of bashful fluttering and half-hearted refusals, gratefully accepted. The moment the two of them together crossed the threshold of David's apartment their partnership had been cemented—an important development in the internal dynamic of their little group and one completely lost on David who took it for granted that those who loved him couldn't possibly dislike each other.

As his initial apprehensions diminished Boris gradually warmed up to Nadia's intermittent presence on the marina. And there were some tangible benefits too: David appeared to be genuinely happy and brimming with joie de vivre even more than usual. The three of them expanded the repertoire of the themed parties and added to them weekly poetry readings. The readings were well attended and having quickly grown in popularity presented an unexpected competition to events at The Lower Depths. Rosa didn't take kindly to what she perceived to be a double betrayal by David, and as a result Nadia's position at the store grew even more precarious. But David was hardly aware of any of that. He was exultant and eager to share his happiness with Boris, and that included a jubilant account of the intimate details of his suddenly reinvigorated sex life. At sunset, as they strolled down the promenade David marveled loudly how much joy he was able to find in the body of a sixty-year-old woman and sang enthusiastic praise to the inventors of Viagra—"miracle workers, every single one of them, down to the last lab assistant."—"Everything is a miracle to you, you pup. Lower your voice, please!" griped Boris. But he was not cross with his friend, not anymore, just concerned that David's chemically assisted erectile triumphs do not become the talk of the town. And even that concern was hardly for David's sake—he had no doubt that such talk wouldn't offend David in the least, quite on the contrary. No, he was not concerned about David's reputation. He worried (and that worry came as a surprise to him) about Nadia, whom he had recently begun to think of as "our Nadia." He realized he had a need to shield her from gossip: on occasion and contrary to their best stated intentions, the "fair ladies of Ashkelon" could be a mean-spirited bunch, especially when it came to strange, wounded birds like the timid bookstore assistant.

***

David had a unique, almost supernatural gift for losing money. His life's path was strewn with dropped wallets and wads of cash left unattended on kiosk counters, in subway cars, and at ATM terminals. Coins slipped through the holes in his pockets and marked his advance from point A to point B like the traceable grains of wheat in a German fairy tale. Perpetually distracted, he was every pickpocket's wet dream. Despite his decades of experience suffering monetary loss at the hands of ex-wives, publishers, and perfect strangers his belief in the general goodness of human nature remained unshaken. David's gullibility appeared so extreme, so comical, but also so consistent that Boris sometimes wondered if all his misadventures were not some creative ploy to attract the world's sympathy. By relinquishing any personal responsibility for his own solvency David tempted fate and fate responded in kind, that is, erratically but not always viciously. Observant Boris couldn't help but discern a pattern—David's financial fiascos were on occasion followed by unexpected and sometimes bizarre windfalls: a winning lottery ticket that Boris rescued from a trash bag a second before David was about to dump it into the garbage chute; a delayed royalty payment from an Estonian publisher of whose existence David had long since forgotten; an accumulated housing dividend that David neglected to claim over three years and that now amounted to a handsome sum . . . It almost seemed like each foolhardy loss was bound to be sooner or later compensated by some whacky gain.

The unopened letter in a bluish envelope, with a German return address, clearly belonged in the latter category. Boris discovered it in a pile of discarded advertising leaflets that David tossed into an overflowing garbage bin. Boris was not in the habit of throwing away pieces of mail without first familiarizing himself with their content—such diligence cost him a lot of time but spared the occasional headache. The letter contained a short notice addressed to David, whom the letter identified as a "Holocaust survivor," eligible for a compensation from the German government. "I *am*? Are they serious? How did they track me down?" David was genuinely puzzled. He spent the war years as an undernourished Jewish kid, evacuated from besieged Leningrad to the Urals. Years later he published a slim book of poetry, in which he ruminated on his family's wartime travails, on the loss of his father; he wrote about his exhausted mother working multiple jobs to feed her three fatherless children, he wrote about the Jewish kids, and the Russian kids, and the Armenian kids, and the Uzbek kids—all robbed by the war of their childhoods, many (most) of their fathers. A couple of poems from that volume became canonic during the 1960s, and certainly not because they singled out the wartime Jewish suffering (of which he, as many other Soviet Jews, was only vaguely aware), but simply because they resonated with the experiences of so many readers—of all ethnic backgrounds. No, he declared solemnly to Boris—while grandstanding in the middle of the living room, wearing nothing but his trunks—he was neither a victim nor a survivor, he laid no claims on the German government so many decades after the war ended, and he was quite satisfied with the historical fact of Germany losing that damn war; they owed him absolutely nothing.

The more he discoursed on the subject of historical and poetic justice, the more self-righteous and implacable he sounded. He would have none of their money, none at all, they could go ahead and spend it on some real survivors because he wouldn't be one of them. He theatrically tossed the letter back into the garbage—a gesture of proud defiance that failed to impress Boris, who promptly fished it back out and proceeded to methodically lay out his case for accepting the reparation payment. "Come on, *druzhok*," he pleaded with David. "It's money. Someone wants to pay you, why would you refuse? You may remember, I have a niece in Germany, I travel there all the time. And you know what I think when I'm there, when I see the guys our age? You know what I think when I see them living in their neat little houses, shopping at their supermarkets, driving their nifty BMWs? I think: You bastards, you lost the war, but you actually won—the way you've fared since 1945 . . . you won it . . . or else you won something much better than a war. So . . . stop this blubbering nonsense, take the money, and do something useful with it. You keep talking about your love of travel; here, right here is your chance. We can go traveling—you and I together. I'm friendly with a travel agent in Ashdod, she'll send us on a cruise. How about Scandinavia? The Baltics? Your world. Remember that island? And the lighthouse on the cape? The old sea dog back to his tricks, huh? How does *that* sound?"

David looked at Boris (who was rarely that eloquent) in some confusion. "A cruise?" he mumbled pensively, suddenly drained of his determination to reject the handout. The sun was now descending towards the horizon, growing in size and getting redder as it neared the line where the sky met the sea. It was time for their evening walk. "A cruise on the Baltics?"—"Yes, a cruise—calling into different ports, an Olympic-size swimming pool filled with seawater, all-you-can-eat buffets three times a day. And you know how you are—you'll probably get inspired to write a story about our travels, maybe even a book of stories . . . or poems. You lot need inspiration like we ordinary earthlings need oxygen, and what can be more inspiring than travel?"

David sighed and scratched his recently trimmed beard (Nadia preferred it that way). For a few minutes he stood silently in the center of the room, framed by the balcony door, his silhouette growing more solid and losing its distinctive features against the looming red disc of the sinking sun. "Ok," he sighed again. "You're right. I should take the money, and we'll go on that cruise. But on one condition: I'm going to invite Nadia to join us. She never got a break in her life and I'd like to do this for her. Can you imagine how happy she'll be to learn about the trip? I would gladly spend all this money just to see her smile." Boris should've known better, but there was no point arguing, he would have to accept the inevitable, he would have to adjust. "Of course," he nodded resignedly, "of course, *druzhok*, you can invite Nadia. After all, she is one of us now. She is *our* Nadia."

Nadia's feeble but apparently sincere protestations were overcome in the course of an extended poetry reading that doubled as an impromptu therapy session. David cajoled and cooed. Boris reasoned. Nadia insisted that it would *kill her* (like many Russians of her generation she had a weakness for grand hyperbolic statements) if she was a burden on David; the mere thought that her cruise adventure would be paid for by another person, even by someone she loved dearly, the mere thought of being a liability was *suffocating* to her. David responded with a barrage of quick kisses and fervent assurances of his complete commitment to their relationship; he declared his *horror* (Boris cringed—when it came to hyperbolic statements David was not to be outperformed) at the prospect of spending two weeks at sea deprived of her company. He would not be doing her a favor; it was the other way around. He was pleading with her to let him use money that had just fallen into his lap for the privilege of sharing the joy of travel with her.

But it was Boris's argument that carried the day by outmaneuvering Nadia and leaving her with no other choice but to yield to pressure.

Deep inside, Boris agreed with Nadia's objections to David's offer and almost wished that she had been more forceful in presenting them. Alas, forcefulness was hardly one of Nadia's attributes, while David, when it came to matters of the heart, could be obstinate and unreasonable to the point of self-destruction. Boris broke the impasse by steering the exchange away from the escalating emotional intensity and towards more practical considerations. In all honesty, he argued, the issue had less to do with questions of pride and dignity, even (sorry) love, than with the fact that two age-battered geezers would be taking a major risk embarking on an extended sea voyage without a younger chaperone. David's back has been acting up lately and that seriously worried Boris. David being David refused to make a doctor's appointment and the last thing he, Boris, needed on this trip was to find himself stranded on a cruise ship next to a David immobilized by one of those severe lower-back spasms he'd been suffering lately. So, by coming on the cruise Nadia would be doing both of them a favor. Ok? It's been emotional but enough is enough. So why don't you wipe away your tears . . . and yours, David . . . and let me call Olga-the-travel-agent in Ashdod and start planning for the trip. Ok?

As if hypnotized by this masterful display of practical thinking David and Nadia nodded obediently, looking like too sniffling children—both still tearful after a deep emotional dive but now inexorably coming back to the surface, prepared for that first gulp of air, for the first ray of sun falling on their wet and flustered faces . . .

***

Stockholm was their last port of call and that's where David pulled a David on them—he disappeared . . . The cruise ship turned out to be just as Boris, who read travel brochures for recreation, had imagined it—a fourteen-deck behemoth, with several swimming pools, Jacuzzis, fancy boutiques and gourmet shops, bars, restaurants, and nightclubs. The shameless plenty of the gargantuan all-you-can-eat buffets overwhelmed them and prompted David to reminisce wistfully about his family's wartime depravations and the food rations in postwar Leningrad. David and Nadia shared a cabin, while Boris occupied a single stateroom across the hallway. David spent long hours on the upper deck, holding onto the rails and peering through the Baltic mist. By unspoken agreement, Boris and Nadia mostly left him alone, assuming (correctly) that a maritime reunion with his youth would inspire David to write.

At the very beginning of the journey, soon after they left the harbor in Tallinn, the cruise ship sailed past a massive, irregularly shaped island. In the dusk, Boris could distinguish high cliffs topped by massive pines and a sliver of pebble beach at the bottom of the cliffs. A narrow peninsula reached out into the sea and at its very tip Boris noticed a flashing red dot—a lighthouse. He tapped David on the shoulder: "Do you think it's *that* lighthouse?"—"Who knows . . ." David sounded surprisingly noncommittal. "I'm not even sure it's the right island. Frankly, I'm not even sure if that island ever existed." Boris remembered Marina seated by David's feet on the balcony and gave his friend a puzzled look; a few minutes of perplexed silence ensued, after which Boris opted not to press the question any further—memoirists can be a whimsical lot.

Such interludes of nostalgic introspection on David's part could be occasionally forbidding for the rest of their little group but on the whole did not prevent them from enjoying the cruise. The ship sailed majestically in and out of Baltic harbors, disgorging its passengers for daily excursions, resting comfortably at the wharf while its temporary residents caught fleeting touristic glimpses of other countries: Estonia, Finland, Latvia, Poland, Sweden . . . Stockholm was the last stop of their multistage itinerary. It was the very last port of a long list of ports they had visited and that's where David chose to disappear—as if on cue, immediately after they had completed an exhausting excursion up and down the cobblestone hills of Gamla Stan.

Boris discovered the disappearance as soon as he and Nadia exited the souvenir shop next to the Nobel Museum. Since his early youth, Boris was a lover of pranks and silly jokes. Now he was sporting a plastic, two-horned Viking helmet, while Nadia carried a white carton box that concealed her proud new possession—a glazed coffee mug bearing a print of Stockholm's skyline. They had left David to wait for them by the fountain in the center of the plaza outside. He claimed to have developed an allergy to shopping and begged for a few minutes of peace while Boris and Nadia hunted for souvenirs. Ever since their last call at Gdansk, where he refused to disembark, David had been troubled by nagging back pains and Boris could sense that his friend's enthusiasm for seafaring was beginning to wane. These past few days David remained particularly moody and surprisingly unresponsive to the parade of ports and docks that, Boris assumed, should have evoked in him all sorts of youthful memories and creative urges. He spent most of the time holed up in his and Nadia's cabin and it took them a massive joint effort to cajole him to get off the ship in Stockholm. Boris was growing concerned and deployed an assortment of tricks (hence the purchase of the Viking helmet) to distract David from his brooding introspective state.

They walked around the fountain, but David was nowhere in sight. They circled the plaza which that early in the afternoon was chock-full of tourists and thus presented ample opportunities to conceal the presence of an absent-minded poet. Nadia checked out the lobby of the museum while Boris walked back into the souvenir shop—no trace of David. Boris resolved not to get worried, not yet. But no sooner had he made this decision than he realized that he was worried—seriously worried. They rushed down to the water and walked (ran, really) the length of the harbor-facing side of Gamla Stan. Boris's massive Pentax camera (a recent acquisition and lately the focus of his attention during most of his waking hours) dangled restlessly on a polyester strap, its predicament somewhat softened by intimate proximity to the owner's prominent belly. Boris and Nadia raced up and down the narrow alleys of Gamla Stan and then zigzagged the square in front of the Royal Palace. Nadia tried to reach David on his cell phone, but that would've been a hopeless undertaking even under more routine circumstances—David almost never picked up his phone (also never bothered to learn how to text). More than two hours passed in a desperate search that covered the whole of Gamla Stan and eventually expanded to the park across the bridge. "We need to warn the cruise ship; maybe they can delay departure," sighed Boris panting heavily. He pressed his palm into the left side of his chest, trying to calm his madly racing heart. "Just give me a minute to catch my breath, ok?" he pleaded with Nadia, an unnecessary appeal in view of Nadia's propensity for accommodation.—"Of course, dear, just breathe in, take it easy, *now*—breathe out. Better? One more time: in a-a-a-nd out, in a-a-a-nd out. Feeling better?"

They called their Russian-speaking guide and asked her to contact the ship and notify them about David. Then they debated the worst-case scenario, which envisioned Boris retrieving his valuables from the ship and staying in Stockholm until he could locate the fugitive. Nadia declared that she would never (NEVER!) leave the two of them behind, so Boris had to apply his formidable powers of persuasion to convince her that her presence on the ship could be essential to coordinating the rescue mission. Having secured Nadia's consent to Plan B Boris suggested they focus on Plan A—that is, a last-ditch effort to locate David while they still had some (if barely any) time left. Holding onto each other they marched determinedly through Kungsträdgården, its alleys thronged with tourists, all of them oblivious to the drama unfolding in their midst. The festive atmosphere of the park hardly registered with Boris and Nadia; they remained silent and only exchanged nervous glances each time another departing ship in the harbor blasted her horn.

Nadia was the first to spot David—slouched on a bench by a fountain, a half-obliterated baguette resting on his lap. The bench was surrounded by an impressive posse of pigeons. Deliberately, as if in slow motion, David was tearing off bits of bread and throwing them to the pigeons, who mobbed him unceremoniously and clearly took his generosity for granted. Suddenly Boris felt drained of the energy that had sustained him through the desperate search. His legs grew weak and he only just made it to the bench. He lowered himself heavily next to David. "David . . ." He didn't even whisper, he exhaled. "David, what the hell? What are you doing here?" David raised his eyes and smiled sheepishly: "You told me to meet you by the fountain, didn't you? So here I am . . ." He pointed at the fountain in front of them. David looked serene and it was this serenity that made Boris most uncomfortable. Obviously, it was the wrong fountain.

Boris and Nadia exchanged alarmed looks but by an unspoken agreement decided not to press the issue. "So . . . feeding the pigeons, eh?" David nodded and tapped Boris on the knee: "I have a story for you, Borechka. There was this old Jewish woman living in our courtyard in Leningrad, shortly after the war. She survived the siege and lived alone by herself. I guess the family died in the war, I don't remember . . . But then again, most everyone's family died in the war. She had this thing about pigeons. Every morning she would come out into the courtyard and sit on a bench by an old dilapidated fountain, a remnant of the prerevolutionary halcyon days. For hours on end she would feed pigeons, and I found it puzzling. Bread was rationed, I still remember that hunger—the never-ending, omnipresent, excruciating need. And there she was—this strange creature wasting her ration on the pigeons. I finally asked her about it. And you know what she said?" Boris and Nadia (who had now joined them on the bench) shrugged. "Well, she said she owed them one. During the first winter of the siege they ate all the pigeons in the city, and the cats, and finally the rats. The pigeons were the most nutritious, a true delicacy that sustained her and allowed her to become her family's only survivor (a dubious blessing if you ask me) . . . So she felt this connection to the pigeons, a sense of obligation if you will . . . Later in life I wrote a poem about her but it never got published—the editors thought it too dark, not uplifting enough. You see, nothing uplifting about an old woman, whose whole family perished in the war and who survived on pigeon and rat meat. We were supposed to go through life on a diet of uplifting stories, but that's not the diet that saved my neighbor." Nadia kissed David on the cheek and smoothed the strands of his beard: "What happened to the woman?" David gave her a quizzical look: "What happens to all of us? She died, of course. Maybe she could've lived a bit longer had she not wasted her bread on the pigeons. Maybe the story could've been just a tiny bit more uplifting. But it was what it was . . . Say, it must be time to head back to the ship and, frankly, it's time to head home. You two will have to help me up, I can't get off the damn bench by myself, my back is killing me . . . Hoist me up, but please, please, very gently, it really hurts . . . Yes, yes, like that, and now . . . now lead the way, and while you're at it maybe one of you can explain to me how the hell had I ended up here in this park."

***

"It was a stroke, a minor one but a stroke nevertheless." About a week after their return Boris was sitting in the doctor's office, taking in the news of David's medical condition, and thinking that it could have been worse. The doctor was a friend or rather "sort of a friend." As one of few Russian-speaking doctors practicing in Ashkelon, Victor was in high demand and too many near strangers laid claim on his friendship. Victor appreciated the material benefits that attended to the practice of medicine but otherwise resented his profession, mostly because it exposed him to the excessive demands on his time and privacy. But Victor did respect the imposing Boris and liked David, with whom he shared a connection to the Baltics and passion for Premier League soccer. Usually impervious to the emotional side effects of his vocation he presently felt genuinely uneasy about divulging the results of David's MRI scan to Boris. "Listen, we can deal with the consequences of the stroke; at his age there are no guarantees for a full recovery, but he can do reasonably well. It's this other thing . . ." He trailed off.—"What other thing?"

It was such an unpleasant sensation—as if someone had attached a pump to his stomach and proceeded slowly and methodically to suck the air out of it. Boris sat up. "What other thing? His back?" Victor sighed and reshuffled the papers on his deck. "Well, he feels it in his back but it's not really his back, it's in his lungs . . . Pretty advanced. Stage three, I would say . . ." Breathe in a-a-a-nd breathe out; i-i-i-n a-a-a-nd out. Almost eighty and at this age ("at our age") one should take such sooner-or-later inevitable news in stride. With dignity and without fear . . . Who said that? The words rang in his ears and he knew they didn't belong to him, they came from the outside, not from within. It was different for David—David had his own words, always. *Submit to the inevitable* . . . Boris shifted on the chair uncomfortably, he was annoyed: such an important, such a fateful moment and his brain was being flooded with some secondhand wisdoms. He waved his hand as if chasing off pestering flies. *Submission* . . . it wasn't *his* word, he couldn't remember ever using it, not once. He might not have the right words, but he'd let David search for them, he'd render unto David what was David's. Because *his* was a different mission—he'd focus on deeds. He'd focus on scheduling those chemotherapy sessions and on making sure that David being David didn't miss them. He'd make the doctors' appointments and pick up the pills at the pharmacy and make arrangements with the social services as needed. He'd pick up Nadia in the morning in his regularly serviced and meticulously cleaned Mazda (excellent gas mileage) and bring her to David, and then he'd drive her back home after the Shabbat. He'd do all these necessary things and more, because doing chores made the world go round. And so did love. Words too, of course, but not everyone had words—he, for example, didn't.

Their routine changed gradually, in almost imperceptible increments spread across a twenty-seven-month period—the most meaningful twenty-seven months in Boris's life. Twenty-seven months . . . which turned out to be exactly twenty-four full months longer than initially predicted by Victor. Once they had passed the three-month mark Boris's spirits soared and he developed a peculiar pride in his own omnipotence. Years before, still a young lieutenant in the army, he owned a dynamo torch, a mechanically activated flashlight that worked without batteries. To produce electricity, he had to crank the handle of the dynamo, and as long as he continued to pump the built-in tiny generator (in and out, in and out) the flashlight worked—the harder he squeezed the brighter the light grew. It was sort of like that with David now . . . Late at night new words crowded his wakefulness, Boris didn't quite know where they came from and was content to let them flutter around his head and lull him to sleep: *biopsy, immunotherapy, remission, hope, hope, hope.*

Boris and David made a point of keeping their daily schedule intact—their nightly strolls on the boardwalk, their (increasingly perfunctory) visits to the open-air gym, their early morning and late afternoon swims, their boisterous *boker tovs*. Even the poetry readings on the balcony that continued to attract their fair share of the "fair ladies of Ashkelon," and which now even included the mollified Rosa. Just pump the flashlight, *haver*, just keep pumping that flashlight. Nadia was part of the effort, of course. And David too. He quickly took to referring to his medical needs in first person plural: *We have a chemotherapy session on Tuesday*; *We need to pick up that prescription*; *Did you see the pillbox? Where do we keep it?*; *The first three or four days right after the chemo are tough, but we certainly feel much better afterwards.* Staying afloat was truly a joint undertaking. David wrote a poem about the three of them going through rapids, straining to keep a rickety boat steady amidst the raging whitewater whirlpools. He titled the poem "Our Twilight Adventure" and assured them that he meant it in jest.

David only began to grow visibly frail during the six months preceding the first big stroke. He lost weight and it took Boris considerable effort to drag him out of bed every morning. By midday he would be too exhausted to continue with their regular afternoon swims. They still took their evening walks, but those too were growing shorter by the day. Yet David's obvious deterioration only strengthened Boris's determination to preserve their routine. Nothing is inevitable: you cannot, should not submit to something that doesn't exist—so Boris thought or, rather, intuited.

During those final few weeks of relative normalcy Boris was especially busy. He drove David to his appointments at the clinic, he arranged for a technical inspection of David's gas-guzzling car (ignoring the fact that David had stopped driving it), he even hired a couple of young Arab handymen to repaint the walls in David's apartment. He took a lot of pictures with his camera. Despite his present infirm state David continued to generate an endless stream of problems that needed to be solved or mitigated. "Never a dull moment with you," grumbled Boris after David dropped his partial upper denture into the toilet and then managed to crack the water tank while trying (vainly) to fish it out. "You just never stop, do you?" Boris fumed as he struggled to replace the broken bowl. David smiled meekly: "Don't be cross with me, Borechka. I'll stop soon enough. I promise!" He sounded conciliatory, not accusing—it was one of his "good" days, one of those increasingly rare, post-chemo days without pain. And deep inside Boris hoped that the problems would never cease.

The door was unlocked. Boris habitually shook his head and prepared to deliver his half-sincere daily reprimand to David. But David . . . Boris took in the scene as it presented itself to him and suddenly felt tiny and insignificant, almost nonexistent. "And that's how the world ends . . . ," someone whispered next to him. He spun around but failed to locate the source of the sound. He tried to recall where he picked up this line (he was pretty sure it *was* a line) and . . . couldn't. Maybe at one of their poetry readings? Was it David's? Maybe. It did have a ring of David to it . . . David . . . David was lying on the floor by the sliding balcony door—shirtless, legs splayed, the front of his unzipped jeans visibly wet. He was making faint moaning sounds; his voice was high-pitched and sounded unfamiliar. One eye remained partially open and the eyelid of the other was fluttering tentatively, and it was the sight of that trembling eyelid that Boris found particularly unsettling. Boris was not given to introspection, but he had an out-of-body sensation at the sight of David lying prostrate. He wondered if he could stay in that mode for just a few minutes longer—remaining on the other side of the glass door, looking in from the outside, being separated by an imaginary partition from the immediacy of his grief. Yet he knew that as tempting as it seemed he didn't have the luxury of engaging in such acts of dissociation. He needed to locate David's documents (not an easy task even under ordinary circumstances), especially his *teudat zehut* and medical insurance card. Phone calls were to be made. He needed to call Victor-the-doctor, and Nadia, and the ambulance service—in that order, definitely in that order. And then he would make numerous other phone calls and even now, at this preliminary stage of the coming ordeal, he looked forward to spending time on the phone, knowing from his previous experience with Bella that the phone calls would make things a little bit more bearable, less painfully immediate.

When the ambulance crew had finally succeeded in changing David's underwear and putting on his blue tracksuit (yes, Boris did ask them to do this and the two sullen nurses complied grudgingly) and placed him on the collapsible stretcher, Boris got out his comb and gave David's untrimmed beard a hasty, superficial grooming. He then wetted his handkerchief and tapped David's forehead and neck, carefully brushing off the specks of dust and the minuscule sand particles that collected in the lines and creases of his weathered skin during the long debilitating hours he spent lying on the tiled floor. Boris followed the stretcher as the taciturn nurses wheeled it out of the apartment and towards the elevator—to take David downstairs to the waiting vehicle. He held David's hand in both of his palms, squeezing it lightly but reassuringly. Just before they pushed the stretcher inside the ambulance, David stirred and Boris felt his fingers moving—barely, but moving. Another moaning sound, which at first had no obvious structure to it but then unexpectedly congealed into a nearly inaudible, plaintive sob: "I'm so scared, Borechka, so . . . scared."

The second stroke came a week later and triggered a transfer to Holon and therefore another rearrangement of Boris's daily schedule. David's new doctor—luckily, a Russian-speaker from Ukraine—embraced a professional commitment to unvarnished truths, which a less pragmatic man than Boris would have confused with cruelty. But not Boris—he appreciated the clarity of her pronouncements. "Six weeks," she said, "seven at most."—"I'll be coming every day, even on the Shabbat," Boris said to her, making certain that things stayed clear between them. The doctor looked at him oddly: "I have this weird feeling that we've met before . . . You know what, you remind me of my late grandfather. Yes, that's it—my grandpa." Boris smiled: "Everyone thinks so."—"Only, my grandfather couldn't drive and would've never missed his Shabbat dinner. Otherwise, you look remarkably similar."—"Your grandfather sounds like a charming person," Boris joked and the doctor laughed. An inelegant belly laugh filled the hallway on the sixth floor of the Wolfson Medical Center. "You're funny, you know how to make a tired, overworked woman laugh. My husband should take a couple of lessons from you. Don't worry, we'll take good care of your . . . Is he your relative?"—"My friend, my . . . best friend," said Boris simply and winced at his own words, surprised to realize that this was the first time that he'd been asked to define his connection to David.

He now had his breakfast alone and usually left Ashkelon just after 9:00 a.m., as soon as the rush hour traffic on Route 4 had thinned out. Sometimes (once or twice a week) he picked up Nadia. She waited for him at the curb by a grim block of concrete panel buildings that mostly housed low-income Ethiopian and Russian families and where she shared a rent-stabilized municipal apartment with her ailing son. Boris much preferred driving to Holon alone, Nadia's perpetually alarmed look and the fixed tragic expression on her face made him more uneasy than the sight of David—motionless and hooked up to the vital signs monitor. But she was "our Nadia" and he accepted her presence and never allowed himself to question or regret it.

For those days when he visited David alone (that is, most of the time) he developed a comforting routine, which saw him seated next to David's bed, fumbling with his digital camera or another recently obtained toy—a slick Samsung smartphone. The smartphone in particular offered inexhaustible opportunities to remain preoccupied. Boris spent endless hours downloading apps and absorbing staggering amounts of factoids and sundry news items: the latest exchange rate between the Indian rupee and the Turkish lira, the marital problems of a Ukrainian pop star, the weather in Qingdao, the timetable for an express train connecting Arlanda airport and Stockholm city center . . . He eagerly shared this newly acquired knowledge with the nurses and doctors, as well as with other patients and their visitors, and as a result gained something of a reputation for being an expert on a number of esoteric subjects. After several failed attempts he set up a Facebook profile and used for his avatar a five-year-old photograph showing him and David on the beach, looking surprisingly fit for their ages and humorously posing like playboys. Within a few days he gained twenty-six Facebook friends and was inspired to announce his social network presence with a post: "A cinnamon bun for breakfast." Almost immediately the post got three likes and Boris felt a rush of exhilaration.

After several weeks of daily commuting to Holon, Boris began to view the situation as his new normal. It was not easy to get used to lonely breakfasts and the termination of their nightly walks. Or rather it was an adjustment, and Boris managed it the same way he dealt with other life's changes—with his usual adaptive skill and without much complaining. It was the new normal and he would be content if it continued in perpetuity. He quickly got used to, even enjoyed, his morning, post-traffic drive to Holon; he looked forward to browsing the trinkets at the shopping arcade on the ground floor of the hospital and then spending a few hours fussing with his smartphone and chatting with nurses (many of them were Russian-speakers). He got accustomed to the constant beeping of David's monitor, which initially irritated him but was soon absorbed into the general flow of things, too, became a soundtrack to this new chapter in their story. He found the beeping reassuring, he imagined even that David was communicating with him, constantly alerting him to his heartbeat rate, blood pressure, and oxygen saturation. Boris was thankful to technology for providing them with this reliable channel of communication. Never a Luddite, he now placed his complete trust in the humming and beeping contraption that, from his point of view, served as an anchor preventing David from drifting off into the Baltic fog. It would have never occurred to him to fault technology for failing David. He recognized that even the most advanced machines (even his Samsung smartphone) had their limitations. "They are doing everything humanly possible," he kept telling himself, thinking of the machine that pumped oxygen into David in revealingly anthropomorphic terms.

In his whole life, he never blamed technology, but he was not above blaming people, who, experience had taught him, tended to be less reliable. So when the amplitude of the pulsating charts on the monitor began to diminish (heart rate, oxygen levels, respiration, temperature . . .) he had no quarrel with the machine—the machine was doing "everything humanly possible." He blamed David who so recklessly and selfishly (David being David, of course) was about to upend yet another ritual that had given Boris a reason to get up in the morning. Six weeks . . . almost six weeks . . . just as the doctor predicted. Barely a silhouette under the beige hospital blanket, David didn't really look much like David—with his dentures removed, his sunken cheeks rendered even more hollow by the untended beard (strangely, not all of it grey), he had a severe look about him, which reminded Boris of a painting he saw at the Prado Museum on a trip to Spain he once took with Bella. He forgot the name of the artist but remembered being disturbed by the uncompromising intensity of the work and by the artist's austere vision, delivered in pigments of dark green and vermillion. "Damn, this is the stuff of nightmares," he winked at Bella. Bella chuckled and elbowed him feigning mock embarrassment. Boris knew how to make a woman laugh.

Now he smiled at this memory and instantly recalled that endless October afternoon and how the museum tired them and how they couldn't wait for the excursion (included in the price of their package tour) to be over . . . He checked again the running graph on the monitor—the peaks were growing lower and the valleys in between were gaining in vastness. David was leaving mountain country and entering the flatlands. Suddenly he stirred and took a deep, greedy breath, and it was that gulping sound that forced Boris off his chair and into the hallway. The doctor was already on her way. She touched Boris's listless hand: "I told you—six weeks"—"Yes, you did. Thank you."—"He was comfortable, no physical suffering. And he had you next to him."—"It's true. And I had him next to me. We've had a very good six weeks. Thank you for that."—"You're just like my grandpa, always thanking people," she smiled.—"Your grandpa seems like a very nice person." She smiled again: "He was . . . just like you. Are you OK? How do you feel?"—"How do I feel?" Boris chuckled because he knew exactly how he felt: "I feel like I've been laid off, lost my job . . . again." She sighed sympathetically: "Yes, that's how I felt when I lost my grandpa . . . Oh well, wait for me just outside."—"I'll probably start making phone calls." Boris sounded businesslike, he knew he couldn't just *be* in the hallway.—"You need a phone?"—"Oh, no, thank you—mine is fully charged, I always charge it at least twice a day, just in case. I'll be here in the hallway, making phone calls." The doctor nodded and, before entering the room, gave his shoulder a quick friendly rub. Boris pulled his Samsung out of its belt pouch and called Nadia.

***

The funeral was well attended and Boris even set up something of a reception inside a gazebo that the alternative cemetery allowed to reserve for such occasions. The "fair ladies of Ashkelon" assembled in their full cast of eccentric characters. Nadia and Rosa recited David's poems, drank cognac in dangerous quantities, and eventually fell sobbing into each other's arms. Boris hardly drank and didn't cry—he was too busy overseeing the proceedings and cognizant of his responsibilities as a designated driver. Also, he had a post-funeral, post-David plan that required him to take meticulous care of his health. He had even come up with a name for the plan: "My Last Chapter." David would've cringed at this cliché, but David was busy with his own walkabout down in the flatlands and Boris took his unavailability as a pass to engage in a little literary exercise of his own. Hence "My Last Chapter"—that is, a decision to travel the world and finally put that Pentax to its ultimate good use. Ever since he sold his Moscow apartment and dacha, Boris, the man of means and property par excellence, had come into some serious money—serious enough to sustain at least a few years of his wanderlust. So he resolved to travel.

He flew to Japan with a Russian-speaking group. In Kyoto, he walked through the orange *torii* gates of Fushimi Inari-taisha shrine and took pictures of the hillside sculptures of the mysterious *kitsune* foxes. At a souvenir stall outside the park, he bought a discounted fishnet kimono with a wide, orange-colored belt. Once back in their three-star budget hotel he donned the kimono and asked one of his companions—a vivacious redhead divorcee from Haifa—to take a few pictures on his camera. They pretended it was a real photo shoot and had a lot of fun. The redhead laughed uproariously while Boris struck extravagant poses in the hotel rock garden. "You sweet man, you know how to make a woman laugh," she cooed. For the rest of the trip they would pretend to be a couple—a performance, which, considering their age difference, provoked considerable mirth among other travelers. Later that evening Boris uploaded his kimono pictures on Facebook and waited anxiously for likes. He got four within an hour. A woman, whose name he didn't recognize, left a comment underneath his post: "Looking good! Are you traveling with David?" Boris contemplated the appropriate response and settled on an emoji: a smiley face. The woman immediately liked it. He then posted a sad face and the woman liked it too. He pondered the exchange for a few more minutes and decided that he had failed to adequately respond to her question, so he finally typed "No." Another like. He hesitated and then typed, "Thank you." Who would've thought that this Facebook thing could be so exciting? Certainly not David, who had no understanding of technology. By the next morning the post had garnered eleven likes—a personal record for Boris. "You're becoming a viral sensation," laughed the Haifa divorcee.

They took a cross-country bullet train to Kanazawa where there were more parks to see. Boris and the redhead split from the group and roamed the old geisha district. He took lots of pictures. In one, the redhead pretended to be a geisha; then she took the camera from him and Boris posed as a samurai, leaning against a carved teahouse door. They both laughed themselves to exhaustion. Later that evening their group attended a tea ceremony (included in the package tour) performed in the pavilion outside the Castle Park gates. At the ceremony, Boris found himself seated next to an elderly American couple, approximately his age. Luckily, the tour guide was nearby to translate. The Americans, Patrick and Nancy, hailed from Nevada and were full of excellent cheer. Like most other people, they took to Boris instantly, and they generously shared with him the happy details of their family life: children, grandchildren, and . . . hold your breath, I know you won't believe it because we, ha-ha, look too young for this, but . . . are you ready? . . . two, no wait . . . watch the two fingers . . . TWO great-grandkids! "They are just like the 'fair ladies of Ashkelon,'" Boris noted to himself. Patrick in particular was starving for interaction (or rather the chance for a monologue). There was an urgency to his desire to share: "I've just retired. Can you believe it? My own accounting firm, fifty full years and counting . . . ha-ha, pun intended! And you know what, had it not been for this young missus over here"—a playful nod at Nancy—"I would've kept on working. But what could I do? The girl wanted to travel! Are you retired?" Boris considered the question for a few seconds and nodded: "Yes, recently retired." Patrick sounded almost euphoric: "Just recently?! I knew it! You know what they say, . . . 'birds of a feather,' and so on. I knew you were one of us; the minute I saw you, I told my gal 'This fella, he's just like us—advanced in years but not over the hill.' Recently retired—I love it!" Boris handed his Pentax to the guide and asked her to take their picture—three broad, beautifully dentured smiles, three enthusiastic thumbs up, a young woman in a kimono serving tea in the background. "Are you on Facebook?" roared Patrick "You are?! I knew it!! Birds of a feather! I'll send you a friend request tonight, don't forget to tag me when you post the pic, ok?"

"What a great trip, what a fine idea it was to start writing this last chapter," thought Boris contentedly, lying in his hotel bed (rather too small for his size) and cataloguing in his head the events of the past days, and the laughs with the redhead, also the future Facebook posts and the likes they would yield—the thumbs up, the smiley faces, the wows, the laughing faces, the beating hearts . . . he would surely get his share of those beating hearts. What a fantastic idea it was to buy that Pentax camera.

***

In Vienna, he separated from the group with which he had just toured the castles of Slovakia. This had been his plan all along—to have three days in Vienna to himself. In truth, the idea belonged to his niece who worried that he was spending too much time on tour buses. Boris didn't mind being around other people, but he agreed that a solo stay in Vienna could give him some breathing space. The niece identified an inexpensive hotel with Russian-speaking staff, just a couple of blocks from the Ring, within walking distance of Innere Stadt and the museum quarter. Boris didn't care much for museums, but he would never admit it to his niece (or to any of the "fair ladies of Ashkelon" who would've never taken kindly to such admission). Upon his arrival at the hotel, it turned out that the "Russian-speaking staff" consisted of a middle-aged Serb called Dušan who worked night shifts on the front desk. The room was tiny and not without some visible blemishes: one of the nightstand lamps had a broken switch and an electric socket had detached from the wall and presented an obvious hazard. The bathroom faucet was leaking, while the toilet seat shifted dangerously sideways when Boris tested it with his heft. He considered requesting a room change but quickly decided against it—a broken lamp was not enough of a threat to scare him off.

His niece had recommended the Leopold Museum and Boris decided to give it a try. But it was a disappointment, a real downer. The paintings of broken and distorted male bodies bothered him and some of them, especially on closer examination, were plain "indecent" and made him avert his eyes. He expected art to be visually pleasing and comforting—"something I could put up on my dining room wall," as Bella would say. But most of the paintings on the walls of the Leopold Museum provided no comfort, certainly no more than the night-terror-inducing canvases at the Prado. He left the galleries and found his way to the museum shop where he felt much more in his element and eventually bought a set of colorful refrigerator magnets. "Presents," he explained to the sales clerk who responded with a polite smile.

Boris exited onto the pedestrian square in front of the museum. It had grown dark and the air was crisp and smelled of cinnamon and grilled meat—and something else, something festive and impossible to define. David would've found the words to describe the smells of Vienna in late November. But David couldn't be bothered—being otherwise engaged, strolling across that vast valley to which he descended from his sixth-floor mountaintop in Holon. Boris walked slowly across the square; he noticed that he was limping—his right foot was bothering him again. Victor had diagnosed a heel spur, a trivial but troublesome condition that Boris chose to ignore. But at eighty-three one can hardly afford such carelessness, at least not for too long. He would have to pay Victor a visit on his return.

Christmas markets had already sprung up throughout the city and there was one right across the tram tracks, on the other side of the Ring. The brightly lit trams glided by noiselessly. Back in the Moscow of his youth they thundered and screeched and splashed their head beams on the cracked wet asphalt. In Vienna, even the trams behaved. Boris found the market—its smells and gay holiday lights and Glühwein stalls—more attractive and infinitely more comforting than the morbid art collection he just visited. At a souvenir shack he picked up a nicely framed, postcard-size print of Maria-Theresien-Plaz in winter. "Present," he said to the seller, a ruddy-faced fellow wearing strange leather breeches, which, in Boris's opinion, fitted neither his age nor the weather. At the adjacent stall Boris bought a glass of fragrant hot wine and sipped it with great pleasure, all the while studying the newly purchased print. "This is something I can definitely put up on my dining room wall," he affirmed to himself upon completing the inspection. He was satisfied with the print; at a measly twenty euros it was a bargain.

There was a hole-in-the-wall, all-purpose convenience store next to his hotel, and before turning in for the night Boris paid it a visit. He picked up a pair of pliers and a slotted screwdriver (the one he had in his portable tool kit was too miniature for the task)—he had a job to do and that prospect filled him with a familiar pleasant anticipation. Back in the room, he meticulously prepared a work space and proceeded with a series of repairs: the broken nightstand lamp (fixed), the loose electric socket (reattached to the wall), the leaking faucet (just a matter of tightening a couple of screws), the wayward toilet seat (a slightly more involved task that necessitated another quick trip to the convenience store to buy a mounting kit). Boris then took pictures of all the repaired items and after some internal deliberation posted them on Facebook, accompanied by a satisfied boast: "Done!" Within minutes the post garnered five likes, one of them a beating heart from Patrick. Boris now had fifty-four Facebook friends, and, after months of travel, could claim a truly global reach. In a particularly good mood, he gathered up and put away his tools and took the rickety elevator downstairs. The elevator smelled of boiled cabbage and spilled beer, but Boris didn't mind the odors—on the contrary, they seemed familiar, soothingly domestic, and thus fit in perfectly with his contented mood.

Dušan was already on duty and greeted his fellow Slav with a corny "Privet, *tovarisch*!" But Boris didn't mind corny. In fact, Dušan had unwittingly preempted his own, almost identical attempt at fraternization. "Look." Boris placed his bulky camera on the counter and turned on its LCD screen. He scrolled through the images of the repaired appliances. Dušan acted impressed: "Wow! You fixed these? By yourself?"—"I surely did," nodded Boris. Dušan emitted another emphatic "Wow": "Just wow, *tovarisch*! You remind me of my grandpa in Novi Sad. Ninety-two years old but still going strong! Plants his own vegetables. Always tinkering away in his backyard, always fixing stuff." Boris smiled slyly: "Why is it that everybody always tells me I remind them of their grandfathers?"—"Beats me, *druzhe*, but you certainly remind me of mine." Dušan picked up the phone and briefly spoke to someone in German, then put down the receiver. "Listen, I just talked with the manager; he's agreed to give you one free night at the hotel. He also thanks you for the repairs. You really didn't have to . . ."—"Oh, it's nothing. But hey, much obliged for the free night. A real bargain!" Boris meant it, his delight was genuine—in a lifetime of bargain-hunting he had just chalked up another minor triumph. Later, he would make sure to boast about the freebie on Facebook; he imagined he'd get at least half-a-dozen "wows," especially from some of the "fair ladies of Ashkelon," easily impressed with such displays of business smarts.

Boris smiled at the thought and lifted up his faithful Pentax by the strap. Before taking his leave, he leaned over the receptionist desk to shake Dušan's hand and bid his new friend good night. As he did so he noticed that the counter was wobbly. He stepped back and gave it a tentative shake. Definitely wobbly. Boris lowered himself in front of this substandard piece of furniture to examine it and quickly concluded that it was flimsy, worse than flimsy. It was a shoddily assembled piece of garbage. He shook his head in disbelief and motioned to the Serb, inviting him to appreciate the pitiful state of the workstation: "Don't they have any decent craftsmen in Austria? What kind of sloppiness is this? The boards are all splintering and coming apart . . . two, no . . . three screws and two corner braces are missing. Next thing you know the whole thing will collapse on you." Dušan laughed: "What, now you are going to fix the desk?"—"Why not? I've got my tools upstairs. It'll take but a minute." He was being sincere and he would've done it without receiving another free night in return. "No, please, enough!" Dušan waved his hands. "We want you to be comfortable here. Just relax, Grandpa, no need to rebuild the hotel. Go upstairs, have a drink, go to bed. Man, you're just like our old Luka—always looking for something to do. Don't trouble yourself, go to bed, good night!"

Boris gave him a look of serene bemusement: "Trouble? *Trouble*?! Oh, you don't know what trouble is, young man. You've never met my friend David, have you?" The receptionist shook his head: no, he had never met David. "But of course you've never met him. How could you? And he is not here right now—busy, preoccupied with other matters . . ." Boris trailed off and fell silent for a moment, but then it occurred to him that he had failed to make himself clear to Dušan. "You see, David . . . he is . . ." He continued, haltingly, "He is . . . my best friend, my . . . *very* best friend." The Serb made a sympathetic grimace, but it didn't satisfy Boris's need for clarity. He searched for words that would've made Dušan understand. At first the words eluded him—like mischievous children playing hide-and-seek with hapless adults, they concealed themselves in the nooks and crannies in the lobby of a shabby Viennese hotel and it took him a whole long minute to realize that all this time the naughty, unruly words were hiding in plain sight. And that's when he suddenly felt at ease and smiled with relief because he knew that he had finally found them. "My *only* friend," he explained to Dušan.

Six Trains of No Return

He is probably dead. The way he was drinking, the way he was smoking those unfiltered Bulgarian cigarettes, pack after pack, thirty years on . . . he's got to be dead. I meant to write about him ever since I helped that bleached-haired train conductor, still a young woman but barely, to drag my friend's listless body along the dimly lit, narrow corridor, which smelled pungently of tar or burnt coal or whatever it is you smell at railway stations late in October, just before the early snow. The woman helped me carry him past the endless compartment doors (open, half-ajar, and shut) to be finally deposited on the lower berth of an overnight Leningrad—Moscow train. He and I never got a chance to properly say goodbye—he was *that* drunk and unresponsive—and now when I think about him (which happens once in a while) I think about him as having died long ago. Of course, he may be alive and well, raising (or have raised, really) his kids in a small, God-forsaken, emptied of its population village outside of Vladimir. He may wake up early in the morning, just before dawn, hungover and drained of any will to get up, to keep on going . . . He may light his cigarette and take that first greedy drag and hold the smoke in for a long while like he used to do when we were . . . when we were . . .

A different platform but the viscid smell of overheated bitumen and engine exhaust will linger on for decades, assuming eventually some material form, becoming a linear narrative of a life. His life. In the shapeless mass of subdued new recruits he stood out due to a demonstrative lack of inhibition. There were several such guys among a couple hundred boys, still wearing their civilian clothes, but their heads already shaved and slightly bowed in ready submission. We had just emptied the train after a twenty-four-hour ride from Leningrad. But before the train departed the station of origin from which I had previously traveled so often with my parents or friends, always for pleasure—to see relatives or catch a play in Moscow, to spend the summer in Crimea—they kept us for a night in a holding block adjacent to the depot. It was a Harry Potter sort of experience—the world of the everyday and of the familiar receded into a milky mist and we found ourselves in a parallel space, where mundane sounds and sights lost their immediacy and realness. It was exactly the kind of depersonalized experience that I intuited years earlier when, while walking by the red-brick walls of the city's main penitentiary, I spotted a green prison bus with barred narrow windows idling at the curb. Suddenly the prison gates screeched open and the bus lurched forward towards the slowly widening entrance. I could glimpse the dirty interior of the courtyard and about a dozen men in ill-fitting black uniforms ambling across it, hauling what looked like enormous aluminum canisters and sacks of clothes. For a couple of disturbing minutes, I was treated to a spectacle of alien and forbidding life following its own mysterious course right in the midst of a city that I loved and whose constant presence I felt so intimately—until the day I was drafted.

That airless night in the secret bowels of a railway station would haunt me for years to come; it was a perfect nightmare scenario of forced separation and exclusion: hundreds of strangers suddenly withdrawn from their familiar comforts, not allowed the luxury of knowing their own fate, waiting listlessly for the slaving schooner to enter the harbor, pack them on board, and ship them off to strange lands. The Middle Passage. The metaphor. A stark reminder for those of us (most of us) who cannot preserve our individuality when faced with overwhelming impersonal and dehumanizing forces. And then there are those whose sense of self survives intact inside the hold of a slave ship in the middle of the ocean or in a hospital on the outskirts of town or in a prison camp deep in the freezing provinces or in a swarming-with-multitudes railway station or inside an army barracks.

If anything, he was resilient, his life force warm and contagious, his crooked smirk impish and knowing. He was no stranger to impersonal spaces (hospitals, nightclubs, police precincts, jails) and that experience showed in his masterly performance on the platform, its uneven surface generously covered with spit and cigarette butts and sporting tiny clusters of dusty weeds obstinately sprouting to life through cracks in the asphalt.

I spotted him as soon as we got off the train. In the somber and frightened crowd he exhibited an almost carnivalesque cheerfulness; it did look like he was fully enjoying himself—smoking cigarettes, spitting copiously on the asphalt after every other drag, chatting to his gloomy companions. An officer emerged from the station and approached the uneven file of recruits; he took in the measure of our confusion and sighed with intentional theatricality: "You fucking sacks of shit, just look at you—how are we supposed to shape you up? How do we even begin to make soldiers out of you turds?" It was a performance, of course, but it terrified many of us, nevertheless. Many . . . but not all—certainly not the cheerful one, who apparently found the officer's well-rehearsed outburst quite hilarious and laughed out loud. The officer was not amused: "What's so funny, soldier?"—"Nothing, comrade lieutenant, nothing at all. It's just weird how you called us 'sacks of shit' . . . my parole officer used to call me that. And the shift manager at the garage. And . . ."—"Oh, I see, we've got a talkative one here." There was nothing performative about the officer's speech now, his malice was genuine. "One more word and I'll fuck you up like you've never been fucked up before, by which I mean that I'll let a couple of Tajik shepherds from the Third Battalion play with you tonight. They miss their goats, you know, you'll come in handy. Understood?"—"No sh . . . I mean, yes, sir, comrade lieutenant." The officer let the threat sink in, scanned the silent line, then turned on his heels and slowly walked off to the end of the platform.

I glanced at the offending recruit and was stunned to see that his amusement had not been diminished by the exchange; he looked . . . well . . . entertained, his broad defiant smile (an incisor was missing) betrayed no fear or internal panic. He noticed my stare and winked mischievously in response, then left the file and walked over to take a spot next to me: "No need to shit your pants, my brother, the little jerk wanted to feel important for a minute, that's all. Leo and I . . . I'll tell you about Leo later, Leo is legend . . . we used to mess up these uniformed fuckers at the discotheque in Lenin Park. You ever heard about Lenin Park? In Vladimir? No? Really? What are you—from Mars? It's legend. So Leo and I would beat the shit out of them; then, you know, fuck their girls. Never failed. So much fun! Man, do I have stories to tell you. By the way," he stretched out his bony but muscular hand, a workman's hand, "my name is Yurik. What's yours?"

Yurik and I quickly became inseparable and this unexpected bond came as a blessing during the first six months of service, which were marked by pointless daily humiliations and various absurd and absurdly cruel hazing rituals. Yurik was a few years older and his life experiences differed dramatically from my own, and man oh man did he have "stories to tell"—stories of amorous conquests in shabby dorm rooms, stories of bloody battles royale in Lenin Park, battles involving an assortment of weapons: broken bottles, knives, and homemade brass knuckles. Yurik had a couple of convictions for "hooliganism" under his belt, and his reputation for audacity and reckless behavior followed him into the army—even the sergeants preferred not to provoke him, extending him the same grudging respect that was accorded to a small but tight group of Chechens. There are those who can be broken and cut down to size and there are those who can't—people you would probably have to kill first. Even though Yurik possessed a pair of the kindest, gentlest brown eyes I have seen on any man, it was generally, and with good reason, assumed that he belonged to the latter category. His sinewy body was a canvas displaying abundant evidence of multiple near-death experiences—knife scars mostly, but also several spots of burned tissue, a few awkwardly healed wounds of mysterious origin, some improperly mended broken and fractured bones. In the grimy public bathhouse that our platoon visited once a week he always posed in front of a chipped full-size mirror and examined himself pensively, as if taking in an abstract painting: "Well, the dick is fine, it's a good, solid dick, but the rest of it . . . Man, I can't fucking believe it. How am I even still alive?"

Most likely he was still alive because after his last stint in jail Yurik decided to turn his life around: he obtained a commercial driver's license and landed a job driving long-distance rigs, mostly to Moscow but on occasion as far afield as Kursk and Belgorod. He also married Olga, a comely but stern young woman from his village outside of Vladimir, who took her marital responsibilities very seriously. I always understood that type of seriousness (I sometimes observed it in other Russian women) to reflect the gravity of the task of keeping one's husband alive in a society where men tended to self-destruct. Yurik embraced his wife's determination to keep him in line; there was something almost comical in their shared commitment to the struggle against his worst demons, even though he left most of the fighting to Olga. Not only was he unfaithful to her, but he clearly saw no contradiction between his regular and often ill-considered indiscretions and the strangely old-fashioned view of matrimony that he espoused. It was a self-serving attitude, but there was something genuine in his acceptance of his moral fallibility and his recognition of Olga's right to despise him and punish him for it. They both played their roles well: he, that of a flawed and sinful rake; she, that of his judge and savior. It was a centuries-old arrangement that they had inherited only to claim as their own, and, as it seems to me now, there was something distinctly Christian about it. If he is alive (which obviously I doubt) they are probably still together.

At the end of the fall, we both got promoted to junior sergeants and our little fellowship had expanded to include Sergei, or Serzhik as he preferred to be called. Serzhik hailed from a small provincial town on the Volga. He was tiny in stature but all muscle, his torso covered with poorly executed tattoos that were dizzying in their incongruous assortment of Orthodox crosses, mermaids, and soaring eagles. Just like Yurik he had done time (for knifing a guy who had called him a "shorty") and was now married to a girl determined to keep him off the booze and out of fights (and also away from his beloved Czech motorcycle). Serzhik was a man of few words but huge heart and formidable street smarts. I was mystified by the formality of his epistolary interactions with his wife Natasha. In her weekly letters she addressed him in the second-person plural, using both his first and patronymic names. On major holidays (including ones I would never so much as think of celebrating: Border Guards' Day, Constitution Day, Militia Day, etc.) Natasha sent him cards with more or less the same text, wishing "Sergei Nikolaevich" all the success in his "military and tactical training, good health and"—somewhat puzzlingly since this was coming from a wife holding down the fort five hundred kilometers away—"lots of joy in your personal life."

Our trio functioned as a well-oiled social organism, each member contributing a unique set of skills to its overall coherence. I was the worldly city boy, the "student" who knew how to tell a story or write a touching love letter on behalf of an inarticulate corporal courting a big-bosomed Ukrainian seamstress in town; Yurik was the fixer, someone with a web of useful connections that reached deep into the corners of the military base—the canteen (held by the Uzbeks), the headquarters (held by the Lithuanians), the laundry (held by the Chechens), the garage (held by no one in particular); and Serzhik was . . . Serzhik, the one who was universally liked and respected for his friendly disposition and skilled hands (I also had reasons to believe that he was the smartest of the three of us).

Now, so many years later, I have trouble reconstructing the particulars of our relationship; in fact, I cannot remember what it was about my two friends, with whom I really had almost nothing in common, that made our connection seem so natural and so powerfully meaningful. Did we bond randomly? Did we sense intuitively a potentially perfect or mutually complimentary union? Were we that pragmatic? Hardly. Certainly, Yurik's and Serzhik's pre-army life choices lacked pragmatism. But impersonal settings make people appreciate the value and comfort of personal associations: hospitals, prisons, and army barracks can be fertile grounds for nurturing deep friendships. And the friendship we shared was deep, and rendered even deeper by our vastly different backgrounds and dissimilar life paths that crossed so fatefully in a small provincial town, some one hundred and eighty kilometers west of the Volga.

The newly found closeness and comradeship of our trio faced a test of sorts during a visit to Kovrov by my girlfriend from Leningrad, an event that inspired my two friends to engage the services of a private barber in town and have their belt buckles fashionably bent by a skillful Tajik craftsman, the pride of the Third Battalion. Despite their colorfully varied life experiences neither Yurik nor Serzhik had had much exposure to "city girls" and now both were full of anticipation. Somehow, they had come to see this conjugal visit as a joint venture, to which they contributed a fake pass in my name to help me leave the base for the night undetected, a room in a dilapidated moonshine den that a mean-spirited old witch rented out to soldiers and their consorts by the hour, and tips (unsolicited, unscientific, and potentially hazardous to health) for enhancing sexual endurance. Maya's impending arrival threw a monkey wrench into our routine. I fretted over the maddening unpredictability of the battalion commander: his drinking habits, his occasional meanness, and the bizarre mood swings that could easily derail the planned reunion. Serzhik was primarily concerned not to look or sound "like a dumb fuck" in front of a Leningrad sophisticate, while Yurik worried himself silly with the logistics of my planned two-day absence from the barracks.

On the big day we successfully bribed a young Dagestani guard and left the installation undetected. As the Leningrad train was pulling into the station the three of us observed its slow-motion emergence from an overpass connecting the station square with the repair depot on the other side of the tracks. The overpass was the perfect observation point from which we could watch the approaching train but also scan the square for military patrols—better to be avoided under any circumstances, especially by those with forged leave papers. The train came to a stop, at which point Serzhik bent over the rusty rail and celebrated the termination of its journey by emitting a long and copious spit that traveled gracefully through the crisp autumn air and splattered upon landing on top of the car below. "Alrighty, she has arrived," he declared with a solemn finality. That Serzhik, he had a knack for stating the obvious. Yurik remained silent; he looked nervous but determined.

The strangeness of seeing my girlfriend, someone from a different (normal?) life, completely unconnected to my new reality, making her way down the platform was difficult to shrug off; even more startling was her apparent comfort in these drab surroundings. If she was surprised to see the greeting party, she certainly didn't show it. Her garrulousness and the self-assured way in which she was prepared to communicate with complete strangers seemed to overwhelm my two friends. On a trolley ride to the rented accommodations, they remained quiet, looking almost subdued. Yurik nodded gravely listening to Maya's account of her last few months, which turned out to be eventful in a special Maya way: a study abroad stint in East Germany ("Amazing, amazing, I'm in love with Germany now!"); a difficult conversation with an old boyfriend ("Such a sweet and devoted guy! Breaking up with him was so painful . . .") who needed to be apprised of her new relationship status (Maya and I had started dating just a few weeks before my call-up); another difficult conversation—this time with a Belgian exchange student, who'd developed a mad crush on Maya and thus required to be gently guided away from the unattainable.

Yurik listened to these updates with the look of someone receiving somber medical news. Serzhik was dutifully studying the tips of his meticulously polished military boots, trying to make himself invisible—a task easy enough to accomplish for a diminutive soldier riding a crowded trolley through a provincial Russian town during rush hour. He elbowed me to get my attention, then whispered under his breath: "Hey, do Belgians speak Russian?"—"No, I don't think so."—"So how the fuck did she know that he had a crush on her?"—"They spoke French, I guess; she majors in French"—"She speaks . . . French?!" He rounded his eyes in amazement and issued an almost imperceptibly thin whistle: "F-u-u-ck, f-u-u-ck me." He was genuinely stunned—these Leningrad girls were even weirder than he had thought. "Hey," he drove his elbow again into my side, "I don't get it, she makes it sound like all this business about her breaking up with guys and stuff, you know . . . like it's a big deal. Is it?" He sounded doubtful. —"I guess it is, it is for her. Why don't you ask her?"—"*Ask* her? Are you crazy? I'm not asking *her*!" Serzhik looked at me with exasperation as if even suggesting the possibility of a brief verbal exchange between him and this girl was the height of preposterousness. He sighed warily, shrugged his shoulders to show how hard it was for him to enter the world of a twenty-year-old French-speaking woman from Leningrad, someone who had recently traveled to Germany and broken the heart of a Belgian student: "I dunno, no offense, she is cool and everything, but I kinda wish . . . we could borrow some of her problems."

In the meantime, Yurik had apparently reached the conclusion that it was time for him to show his chops. He cleared his throat, furrowed his brow, and straightened the folds of the standard issue trench coat—a sign that he was about to utter something of critical significance: "Say, I hear you have some excellent museums in Leningrad. I once read a book about the Hermitage Museum and it was exceptionally educational. Also, there is the cruiser *Aurora,* which fired the famous blank shot in October of 1917." I nearly burst out laughing, Yurik certainly didn't sound like his usual self but rather like one of those English-language recordings we were forced to memorize in middle school ("London is a beautiful city. Trafalgar Square is situated in the center of London."). Surprised by this unexpected display of erudition Maya paused, mid-sentence, her elaborate account of cross-border heartache and stared at him incomprehensibly. But Serzhik was more than impressed. Another elbow jab just below my rib cage, then in an excited whisper: "Fu-u-u-ck, did you hear that?! How does he even know this stuff? This fucker is just so *smooth*!"—"But I know all this stuff too and you never called me smooth," I protested feebly, but Serzhik would have none of it.—"Come on, you're different, you don't count." He gaped at his idol adoringly while pulling on my sleeve as if inviting me to share in his admiration: "One smart motherfucker, I had no idea he could talk like that. And about *museums* of all things! F-u-u-u-ck me, damn! The dude can do *anything*." Serzhik's faith in his friend's omnipotence knew no bounds.

The trolley carried us across town: past the low sitting grimy blocks of a heavy-machinery plant that everyone knew manufactured heavy weapons, past a bulky monument to space exploration, and along potholed streets named after dead Jewish revolutionaries (Sverdlov, Abelman, Uritsky)—a peculiar fact of Kovrov's urban geography that immediately caught my attention but was apparently lost on the local population of factory and railroad workers and garrison officers. The city's central part was separated from the outer districts by a shallow river, but the two sides were connected by a disproportionately massive bridge adorned with four oversized statues of grey concrete, each statue presenting an anthropomorphic metaphor of Kovrov's industrial might. Once you've passed the bridge, Kovrov immediately dropped any pretense at being a city and assumed its age-old provincial identity. The outer districts were but a series of overlapping villages, sporting rows of dilapidated one-story houses behind crumbling fences. Packs of apathetic dogs, misshapen mongrels all, lazily sauntered about with no other apparent purpose except to mark the place as their own.

We got off the trolley and Yurik led the way up the narrow unpaved alley to a cluster of weathered cottages that passed on this side of the river for a city block. A couple minutes later we knocked on the door of a shack that looked no different from any of its battered neighbors. This was the infamous moonshine den, the ultimate destination of Maya's fifteen-hour journey from Leningrad. To my surprise, my girlfriend did not seem in the least perturbed by the postapocalyptic appearance of our lodgings; there was something almost otherworldly in her ability to dissociate from her surroundings, an art of distancing from the immediate that I have never been able to perfect.

Yurik knocked energetically on the shaky front door and the neighborhood immediately filled with delighted barking by otherwise bored dogs. Maya laughed at the commotion we had created and pressed herself against my rough trench coat, let me feel her body—a playful reminder of her presence and a promise of joys to come. Serzhik's elbow jabbed me: "Hey, what did she bring?" He was referring to food, of course—soldiers' wives and girlfriends usually arrived at the base laden with foodstuffs and various delicacies that were then shared among friends. We were perpetually famished and the unsatisfying meals at the military canteen only exacerbated our hunger. The rule of thumb was that a conjugal visit should yield a feast for at least three or four people. Maya smiled at me: "What is it? What is he asking?"—"Well, he is asking if by any chance you brought with you any food?"—"Food? All the way from Leningrad?!" Maya sounded genuinely perplexed: "Of course not, why would I haul food halfway across the country?" She dismissed the strange question with a shrug and smiled coyly: "I brought with me something much better than food; I bought some really cute lingerie back in Germany, you'll love it, I promise!" Serzhik couldn't quite hear our exchange and was growing impatient: "Nu, where is the food?"—"Just chill, I don't think she brought any . . ." Serzhik gave me an alarmed look: "Come on, stop bullshitting, no woman would come for a visit without food, it's not like she is visiting you at some fucking Crimean resort. She must've brought something?!"—"She has . . ."—"What exactly?"—"Well, I think it's some fancy underwear . . . from Germany." Serzhik fixed me with a gaze of perplexed hurt, then sighed dejectedly: "Underwear . . . I can't believe this shit . . . She brought her fucking underwear. You know what, I'm done here. If anyone ever asks me 'Would you like a Leningrad girl, sir?' you know what I'm gonna say? I'll say, 'Fuck no, sir, thank you, but most definitely fuck no.'"

Just as Serzhik had given up on Leningrad girls the door cracked open and the proprietress of the clandestine establishment greeted us with a terse "What the fuck?" Yurik gave us a sign to wait and entered into protracted negotiations with the woman, whose bedraggled appearance and obvious state of rather extreme intoxication made me momentarily question the wisdom of Yurik's choice of accommodations. After a few minutes of whispering, which reached us as an unending litany of swear words, Yurik turned around and winked at me victoriously: "It's all good, she wants an extra three rubles; she says, 'They are gonna fuck, it's extra for fucking on the premises.' The sneaky bitch. What else did she think a soldier gonna do when his girl comes for a visit? Watch cartoons?"

I paid the woman, but the transaction failed to lighten her mood. She showed us to our room, which in contrast to the rest of the house turned out to be surprisingly neat if sparsely furnished: a narrow spring bed, a lonely and bare table, a couple of chairs. The walls were pasted with clippings from illustrated magazines, presenting to the viewer a dubious collage of Soviet everyday life as captured by the lens of some ideologically sound photojournalists. The bedside wall was covered by the inevitable tapestry depicting a fairy-tale motif—a young princess of delicate disposition carried on horseback across snowy landscapes by a dorky prince.

Yurik surveyed the room approvingly and voiced his satisfaction with the arrangements, which he promptly conveyed to the landlady who was hovering by the door: "Super. Thank you, Tatiana Petrovna, you're a gem. Now we'll leave our lovebirds to take care of their obvious needs. Be good to them, my dear." The woman waved her hand as if to demonstrate a principled lack of commitment on her part: "What do I care? They paid for two nights, so it's two nights. But I'd better warn them right now: no noise, not a peep. Fuck as much as you want but no noise. Got it?" She peered at Maya—an older woman instructing a younger one: "You scream once and you're out of here. Got it?" Startled, shaken out of her usual unawareness of the immediate by this display of matter-of-fact crassness Maya silently nodded her consent; clearly, she was not in Leningrad anymore. Our lovemaking would have to proceed in silence.

With their task of setting us up in style accomplished my friends prepared to leave. Yurik solemnly shook Maya's hand and fixed her with a stern look: "You treat him right, ok? He is a good soldier, a city boy, that's for sure, but one of the good ones. It's not easy, you know, to be a soldier. Things we have seen . . . you can't even begin to imagine. Treat him good, ok?" Yurik was exaggerating; probably the worst thing I had observed in my seven months of service was when I walked in on our perennially soused corporal Yegorov having clumsy sex with a singularly unfriendly staff typist. It occurred to me at the time that there was something almost otherworldly in witnessing an act of fornication between two individuals who were that disagreeable. But Yurik's attachment to the truth was never more than tentative; facts for him were pieces of a puzzle that never quite fit together but could be rearranged at will, usually to satisfy some overwhelming need of the moment. With him, the need was frequently of an erotic nature.

Yurik asked me to walk him and Serzhik outside, where the two in an almost synchronized move pulled out crumpled Primas stored behind their ears, lit them, and took long needy draws. "I owe you an apology," said Yurik, letting out the cigarette smoke in neat but quickly dissipating circles.—"An apology?"—"Yeah, I'm sorry, brother, but I sort of fucked up . . . I touched her boobs." Serzhik snickered, but Yurik looked decidedly mournful.—"It's ok, it was so crowded on the trolley, some asshole probably pushed you into her." I felt like giving him an easy way out, but Yurik had apparently decided on a full and heartfelt confession.—"Truth is . . . I did it on purpose. She just kept talking, you know. I've never met girls like her, you would never meet a girl like that at the discotheque in Lenin Park. I just kept listening to her and . . . um . . . staring at her boobs and . . . May I say there is quite a bit to stare at there . . . And then . . . and then . . . I just couldn't help it, I sort of brushed against them, sort of like I was fixing my cap and . . ." He showed us exactly how he committed his transgression by slowly moving his hand (the cigarette still squeezed between his fingers) against the front of my trench coat: "Just like that . . . Sorry, you're like a brother to me and it's wrong to touch you brother's girlfriend's boobs." For a second I thought he was joking, but Yurik looked genuinely concerned—his intemperance had crossed some invisible personal red line, some deeply held and unknown to me principle that apparently was important to him. I knew he cared about his friends, but the fact that Yurik possessed a moral code came as a surprise to me. "Will you forgive me?" sighed my distressed looking friend.—"*Of course* I will, there is nothing to forgive really, could happen to anyone." Serzhik made a grimace. He clearly found the exchange hilarious: "Come on . . . *anyone*," he chuckled. "A thing like that could only happen to Yurik."

Having obtained his indulgence Yurik sighed again, but this time visibly relieved. He then tried to give me last-minute instructions on lovemaking, but these quickly became so anatomically explicit that even Serzhik protested their grossness: "Stop it, Yurik, leave him alone, he knows what he is doing, she is his *girlfriend*, he fucked her before and now she is here—all the way from Leningrad, so she probably enjoyed it. No need to worry." Serzhik was a man of very few words, but when he spoke he usually made sense. The pair finally took their leave but not before finishing two more cigarettes while one last time going over our elaborate plan to cover my two-day absence from the barracks. I watched them walking down the alley towards the trolley stop at the corner. I thought how lucky I was to have met these two guys, how their presence in my life made the tediousness of service and the impersonal cruelty that often accompanied it bearable. Yurik turned around and made an obscene gesture, apparently intended as one final encouragement. "Tell

Maya I'll come and visit you guys after our discharge! We'll go to the fucking museums!" he yelled and gave me the thumbs up. He then said something to Serzhik and they both laughed out loud. "Hey," Serzhik waved just before they exited the alley: "I still can't believe she didn't bring you any *food*! And I can't believe she speaks *French*! That's really *fucked up*!" They burst out laughing again and I could hear them still hollering as they turned the corner and disappeared onto the street.

I looked up at the low, overcast sky—trying to find some comfort in its heavy greyness, struggling to compose myself before returning to Maya. Had she noticed how much I'd changed in these past few months? Did she recognize how strange it was for her to be here, to share this dreary garrison town, this squeaky spring-box bed with me? Even if just for a couple of days? We will make love through the night while the idiot prince on the tapestry will keep on carrying his betrothed, galloping across the embroidered valleys and mountains to a nonexistent destination foretold in the tales of yore, while the foul-mouthed moonshine queen keeps brewing her potions, and swearing, and hoarsely yelling at her black-and-white Ladoga television. We will have no choice but make silent love as prescribed to us by the fire-breathing and firewater-brewing landlady. It's a memory that we would keep for years to come after we have long forgotten each other—in a different world, in a different time, remembering in a different language . . . It was time to get back into the house. When I touched the gate handle the first rain drops hit the coarse gabardine sleeve of my trench coat. By the time I reached the porch it had started raining in earnest. Of course, it had.

***

And there he was—Yurik. Just as promised: thin and bony as a rail, grinning broadly (two molars now missing), his thinning hair carefully combed and parted to the right, the neatly creased brown polyester trousers, a crimson-colored polyester shirt—tucked in, buttoned all the way up to his prominent Adam's apple in a style that we Leningrad snobs always viewed as provincial. I had never seen him in civilian clothes, and it took me a few minutes to get used to the spectacle of this new civilian Yurik. He looked festive, expectant but also tense, manifestly out of place in my Leningrad apartment. He greeted Maya by ceremoniously shaking her hand and congratulating her on our marriage and the arrival of our little son, born almost exactly nine months after the army released me. "I knew you guys wouldn't waste any time," he joked. Maya gave him a puzzled look, which was her signature response to most attempts at humor—the joke fell flat and I immediately wished that Serzhik could be there to appreciate his friend's self-confident sophistication in the face of an uppity city girl. But Serzhik was nowhere in sight. In fact, as I quickly learned from Yurik, he was hundreds of kilometers away, back in his hometown—a young father like the rest of us, busy being a family man, staying off the drink and out of trouble, and saving for a new Czech motorcycle. He and Yurik had remained in touch; Yurik was now conveying Serzhik's regards and deepest regrets that he couldn't join our long-awaited reunion.

My youthful mother-in-law served us tea, and Yurik, now seated at the table covered with a white satin tablecloth and nibbling on oatmeal crackers, surveyed the kitchen, which was airy, with potted plants sitting on the window sill and rows of family china and Czech crystal arranged neatly behind the glass doors of kitchen cabinets. He nodded appreciatively: "This reminds me of my late grandmother's apartment." He turned to me quickly and added meaningfully: "The one in Moscow. Remember, I told you about her? *That* one." I did remember. "She was really into music—lots of old records, tons of ancient books gathering dust." He checked himself: "Well, I'm sure they were not just gathering dust, she probably read them all. She always served tea in tiny, flimsy cups, just like . . . this one. Would make funny little sandwiches too. Everything about her was so small, so tiny. One tidy little grandma. Her neighbors always freaked out when I arrived. I would park my rig up front, right down in the courtyard, a real beast of a truck, one of those mean, stinky Kamazes. An exhaust pipe on wheels, we called it. Blare the horn upon arrival, those Kamaz horns are really something. I think they just couldn't figure out how this nice old lady could have a scary truck driver for a grandson. One of the neighbors once complained to her about the truck, so we had a chat—he and I." Yurik sighed melodramatically, took a deliberately slow sip of tea, then winked at us. He was performing now. "Let me put it this way . . . I think he got a new appreciation for the importance of long-haul cargo deliveries. Never complained again, not a peep, not even once."

My mother-in-law was instantly charmed, like many a Leningrad intellectual she liked imagining herself a woman of the people and often bemoaned the dearth of "real men" among her colleagues at the research institute that ungainfully employed her. Having recently observed her falling for a married navy captain, a ruddy-faced fellow blessed with a mouth full of golden teeth and the sunny disposition of someone used to giving random orders to his subordinates, I knew that her class sensibilities were flexible enough (inverted, in fact) to appreciate Yurik's manly elan. And at that moment I could see Yurik through her eyes and also through the eyes of Serzhik, I could see a hard but kindly man, a man of experience, capable of violence and great tenderness, someone refreshingly irresponsible, someone who could be himself without even trying.

Yurik had a return ticket for the midnight Moscow train tucked into the breast pocket of his shirt, right next to a sizeable wad of cash and a passport. I couldn't help but marvel at his daring; it would've never occurred to me to carry my money and documents like that. As so often with him I was immediately reminded of my own aversion to risk, his casual display of unconcern made me slightly envious—I could never learn to embrace his brand of abandon. My mother-in-law was similarly impressed and her instant infatuation with this "real man of the provinces," expressed rather vocally and with her typical lack of inhibition, could not have been lost on Yurik, who knew only too well how to recognize and accommodate female affection. The obvious chemistry between the two was disconcerting to behold and I felt relieved when Yurik and I finally left the apartment on what I expected to be a daylong tour of the city's standard attractions: its museums and palaces and stately cathedrals and granite-clad embankments, all the splendid sites and vistas that I never tired of describing to Yurik and Serzhik in the course of those endless, boredom-laden evenings back in Kovrov.

Yurik seemed at ease, his mood apparently buoyed by his warm reception and the attention lavished on him by my mother-in-law. "Brother," he smiled knowingly, "your mom-in-law is really something, let me tell you. Wow! Not bad, not bad at all!"—"Come on, Yurik, cut it out. She is Maya's mother, have some decency..." I tried and failed to sound cross, it was impossible to be cross with Yurik. Who could possibly be cross with a life force that elemental, that authentic?—"Alright, alright, I take it back, you Leningrad softy. Not a word about your mom-in-law, who by the way is . . . really *hot*!" He laughed subversively, that rogue. It was so good to see him.

We walked to the river and then up the embankment towards the Palace Bridge. I insisted on pointing out all the sites connected to my childhood and adolescence, somehow it seemed important that Yurik knew exactly where I first went to school ("Across the river, you see that tram stop? Right there.") or took long autumnal walks with my dad ("You see the park by the Bronze Horseman?") or lost my virginity ("The grey building by the canal, the third-floor corner apartment... there, there ... I don't know, I don't think you can actually see it from here."). He patiently suffered through my self-referential account of the city's architectural history. We stopped by a newspaper kiosk where he bought two packs of unfiltered Primas—his smoking habit had not changed much and he was visibly irked to learn that I had quit the day I returned home from the service. This was not the only news I had in store for him, though . . .

He stopped in his tracks, swiftly turned around to face me; his look of wide-eyed bewilderment reminded me that of a child suddenly informed by callous parents that Santa Klaus didn't exist. "You're going fucking where?! America?! Like fucking forever?!"—"Yes, we're leaving soon—in a few months . . ."—"But why? Why would you want to leave? You're fine. Sure, the fucking army was a drag, but it's over now. You go to school, Maya is hot (her boobs by the way have gotten even bigger, sorry but I couldn't help but notice, it's because she is nursing), your son is cute and healthy, you even have a sexy mom-in-law! You live in fucking Leningrad, which is like the most beautiful city in the world or the second most beautiful or something like that. Listen, when I told the guys at the garage that I was gonna visit a buddy in Leningrad they were like really *impressed*, they thought it was fucking *amazing*. Why do you need to leave?! Really, why?!"

I didn't know if my arguments would convince him—I replayed them in my head, the good well-rehearsed and thus sufficiently worn-out arguments: freedom . . . freedom to travel, freedom to reinvent myself, freedom to see new places, new faces, speak in a new language, freedom to experience new colors and smells. Colors were important, they would be bright and occasionally fluorescent, the dazzling emerald color of those shoelaces I spotted on a pudgy Swedish tourist the other day. The smells, the scents of the foreign . . . those I couldn't quite fathom, but I did expect them to overwhelm me, to send me into a tailspin of new olfactory sensations. But I was at a loss as to how to explain this to my friend. I thought of saying these words, but frankly, at the moment, they rang hollow in my head, they sounded too feigned. Instead, I opted for a shortcut: "Yurik, the country is changing, people are leaving . . . Jews are leaving . . ."

Yurik let out an exhausted grunt, pensively scratched his chin, lit another cigarette, and took a deliberately long drag, so sustained in fact that it burned in slow motion half of the cig. "Yeah, Jews . . . I see. Too bad, if you ask me, too fucking bad. You know, Serzhik will freak out when I tell him. He already believes Leningrad is sort of like America, so I don't even know what he thinks about the real thing. I'm telling you, he'll go fucking nuts."—"No, he won't,

Yurik; if there is one guy out there who will never go nuts, that's Serzhik." I actually meant it. Yurik used the cigarette stub to light another Prima, then flicked it away.—"I don't know, it's just weird; I mean, remember our fortified district? The bunker? Remember the bunker? The woods? And after all that . . . America! The two girls that we took back to their village? Remember them? And the weirdo on the motorcycle? Remember her?" I did remember, remembering had long become a passion . . .

Yurik's frustration with the news of our leaving surprised me, ordinarily he was not given to displays of sentimentality. He leaned against the embankment parapet; it looked like he was taking in the views of the river: upstream, the dark waters captured the reflection of Peter and Paul's spire in all its gilded glory—the image of the cathedral, remarkably lifelike, trembled, extended across hundreds of meters of the water surface, its tip reaching to the very edge of the granite exterior, where the embankment wall met the water and was caressed by slow, leisurely waves. It was time for a third Prima, the pathos of the occasion could not be easily satisfied with just two cigarettes. "I've been thinking," Yurik slipped the cigarette lighter back into his pocket. "I've been thinking . . . since 'people are leaving,' you know, maybe I'm one of the people. Maybe we should up and go too. Just come to the garage one day and totally freak out the guys: 'Fuck it, dudes, I'm done here, off to America with my army buddy.' If you know what I mean." I tried to visualize the scene of Yurik making a declaration of his imminent departure to a bunch of grizzled but touchingly clueless car mechanics. Clearly Yurik was trying to do the same because promptly he slipped out of his melancholy mood and broke out laughing. "But seriously," he still wanted to finish the thought, "I could be one of the people. What the fuck, I *am* one of the people. Don't forget about my Moscow grandma, the one that always served me tea, *that* one. Never forget about the grandma. You remember her, don't you?" Yes, I did remember.

The Hermitage felt empty. It was free of the usual tourist mobs that besieged it on the weekends. My father often joked that the tradition could be traced back to the fateful storming of the palace in 1917. On a weekday afternoon, save for the occasional school group breezing through, the hallways and the exhibition rooms of the museum were devoid of the droning hum generated by thousands of shuffling feet and low voices of visitors, pierced occasionally by an inspired delivery by one of the museum's notoriously eccentric guides. The reigning quiet was almost absolute—oppressive and intimate at the same time, and it made quite an impact on Yurik, who slipped into whispering the moment we stepped up to the ticket booth.

The marble grandiosity of the interior visibly overwhelmed him. Again, selfishly I wanted to show him my favorite parts of the museum, the nooks and crannies that I had known so well since my early childhood. The usually rambunctious Yurik lost some of his confidence in these stately surroundings; he followed my lead timidly, pausing occasionally at an exhibit that caught his fancy. These were mostly nude Greek and Roman statues, but when it came to their artistic value Yurik appeared to be of two minds. "The dicks are too small," he complained. "Come on, think about it: you make a beautiful statue, tons of marble and stuff, but why can't you make a decent-sized dick? I wonder if it's because of all these school groups . . ." I doubted that first-century Roman sculptors could have possibly been concerned with their work's reception in twentieth-century Leningrad, but the point was a bit too obvious to make. Yurik kept at it, though: "Really, what was that sculpture—the dudes with snakes?"—"*Laocoön*. Father and his sons attacked by giant serpents."—"Yeah, that one. Did you see their dicks? I couldn't see *any*, none whatsoever. No wonder they couldn't handle those snakes. It takes a *real* man, if you know what I mean." I couldn't quite figure out whether he was joking or not; as Serzhik would have said, he was just "being Yurik."

Yurik desired to see a mummy and was excited to find out that the Hermitage housed two. Most visitors rushed straight for the Egyptian one, the desiccated remains of a three-thousand-year-old priest, Petese. But locals in the know harbored a secret: the best preserved of the two mummies was displayed inconspicuously in one of the basement rooms—a remote and often overlooked part of the museum, empty of tourist groups. So empty, in fact, that on a rainy April day in the early 1980s, an Wednesday that felt perfect for skipping the last physics class (my high school was located just a few blocks away from the museum), the niche right behind the enclosure containing the other mummy became the site of my very first "real" kiss . . . For fear of providing an unnecessary distraction from the treasures of the Altai burial mounds I opted not to share that bit of historical trivia with Yurik.

The Altai mummy, resting in dignified repose in its hermetically sealed and climate controlled glass case, made a powerful impression on my friend. "Fu-u-u-ck, it's like being in a church," he muttered.—"I didn't know you went to church . . ." He hesitated for a second, then shrugged: "I don't." He circled the display, bent his neck at an awkward angle, trying to peek under the discreetly placed loincloth: "I can't see anything; wonder if he still got his dick intact. How old is this dude?"—"About two thousand years old, probably older, actually."—"Fuck me, two thousand years . . . there's definitely no dick left there, but man . . . two thousand years . . . You know who he reminds me of?"—"Who?"—"Lenin, of course! In the mausoleum! They once brought our school on an excursion to Moscow, on a bus from Vladimir. I was in the seventh grade . . . eighth maybe. My buddies and I smuggled a few bottles of port onto the bus, so by the time we got to the fucking mausoleum we were pretty sloshed. We walk in, all freaked out and giggly, and the dude is right there in a glass box, only I'm so wasted I see three Lenins instead of one—the fucking Trinity. Three Lenins is three Lenins too many, if you ask me. And in my mind, I go like, 'You fucking Vladimir Ilyich, look what you've done, look at this country where the largest and baddest and most dangerous after dark park in the ancient city of Vladimir is named after you. You turned the country upside down and now you're lying here all peaceful, in a fucking suit . . .'" Yurik touched the glass surface of the sarcophagus, a clear violation of museum rules that elicited an immediate harshly worded warning from a watchful security guard—a bored elderly woman, who had positioned herself unobtrusively but strategically on a chair lodged between the Chinese funerary chariot and a two-thousand-year-old Pazyryk carpet. Yurik raised his hands in the air and, in a conciliatory gesture, presented to the woman his open palms: "Now, now, my dear fellow citizen, don't you see I'm not armed, I mean no harm. My buddy and I are just admiring your little friend right here under the glass. Just before you revealed your presence, I was sayin' he sort of looks like Lenin . . . minus the suit, of course." The woman mumbled something in a tone of habitual annoyance but didn't move from her chair. Yurik gave the mummy one last look over and one last time summarized his impressions of the inspection: "Yeah, definitely like Lenin but no suit. The only difference, really."

In the Rembrandt room, Yurik headed straight for the *Return of the Prodigal Son* and pondered it for a long while. "Reminds me of me and my dad, only . . . in reverse," he remarked somewhat mysteriously. From there he moved on to the *Sacrifice of Isaac.* Upon learning about the subject matter of the painting he immediately claimed that "God or no God" he would never do anything of the sort to his two-year-old. He suddenly grew uncharacteristically serious: "Cutting your own son's throat? That's bullshit, there is no God who would ask you to do this."—"The Bible says he did ask Abraham."—"The Bible got it all wrong. It was not God."—"No? Who was it, then?"—"Come on, think: Who could possibly ask a dude to slice his son's throat?"—"Not God?"—"Certainly not." I was at a loss: "But who?"—"Are you dumb or something? It was the devil, of course!"—"Well, it's not in the Bible . . ."—"Lots of things are not in the Bible. But they are in here." He vigorously tapped his breast pocket, the one bulging with a wad of cash and a passport, to indicate that a virtuous heart was beating underneath. "You see, it's simple. If your god tells you to slaughter your own blood, then this god is not worth shit; you should go out there and find yourself another god, someone who would never place any idiotic demands on you. It's like in the army—there are normal officers and then there are assholes. Remember Colonel Veleiko, that piece of shit? I still daydream about busting his fucking snout in." Yurik punched his open palm with a massive fist, the smacking sound echoed, amplified, throughout the empty hall, bouncing off the walls covered with priceless canvasses and startling a couple of pensioners in front of the painting of Danae welcoming Zeus in her bedchamber. The pensioners hastened to leave the room. Yurik in the meantime remained typically oblivious to his surroundings. "That's it, it's like in the army. Remember how we hated that fucking Veleiko? Remember how we *ignored* him? That's how you do it: you *ignore* the assholes." He pointed at the painting where an insistent angel, a winged tender-faced youth emerging out of a golden glow, had just stayed the hand of the faithful Abraham bent on striking the fatal blow. "The bearded dude, *that* one—he should've just *ignored* the asshole who told him to kill his son. Oh well, I guess then we wouldn't have this picture . . . Listen, are there any paintings of naked ladies?"—"There is one of Danae. She is being penetrated by a Greek god who appears in the form of golden shower."—"What?! Now, that's my kind of god! Wild! Let's go and check it out."

We exited the Hermitage straight into the glorious October afternoon, one of those afternoons that made you doubt if Leningrad's reputation for rain, fog, and gloom was not a myth concocted by some sickly late nineteenth-century poet. It was one of those afternoons when our impending departure for America revealed itself in all its ineluctable monstrosity. It was better not to think about it, pretend for a few hours that there would be many more balmy autumn days just like this one and the city . . . the city is not going anywhere, it will wait patiently for the seduced to come to their senses—it'll still be there for us to walk and breathe when we finally free ourselves from the centrifugal forces of our alienating age and submit freely (and what a freedom in such submission) to our urban fate, to our genius loci.

After several hours in the museum Yurik was starved for a smoke and I had to wait until he finished his second cigarette before we could discuss our plans for the remainder of the day. We left the Hermitage with Yurik in a pensive mood, the moral conundrums of father-and-son relations still on his mind—at least that's how I interpreted his expressed wish to buy a toy for his son. I thought we would have plenty of time to indulge his sense of parental responsibility after we were done with the obligatory sightseeing. We crossed the bridge to Vasilyevsky Island and once on the other side of the river I led Yurik to my favorite spot—the tip of the island, dominated by the two iconic rostral columns where the Neva widened majestically before splitting into a giant snake tongue of two streams that hugged the island and headed out into the gulf. Walking down a cobblestone ramp at the water edge, Yurik balanced precariously on one foot while endeavoring to draw whimsical patterns on the water's surface with the toe of his shoe. In his usual Yurik fashion, he was courting trouble and, as always, his matter-of-fact ignorance of danger reminded me of my own deep-seated inhibitions.

For some time, we contemplated in quiet the vast panorama opening up in front of us. With a smoldering cigarette squeezed between his thumb and index finger like a painter's brush, Yurik-suddenly-turned-artist traced the contours of the rooftops abutting the fortress and raised his hand skyward to draw an invisible outline of Peter and Paul's spire; slowly, he lowered it and sketched another imaginary line along the length of the bridge, moving leisurely down the opposite bank, past the elegant pastel-colored palaces that used to belong to counts with German surnames and dainty ladies-in-waiting—and that now housed regular Soviet citizens and uninspiring Soviet institutions—past the Winter Canal and the recently visited Hermitage, back to the bridge right behind us, to finally complete the airy circle at the very spot of our impromptu observation post. He flicked the burnt-out stub of the cigarette-brush into the water, his pretend outline of the city still hovering over us, gradually dissolving into the real cityscape around. "It *is* really beautiful here," he exhaled, his tone serious, almost grave. "You know, I still can't believe you're leaving. In the army, you kept whining about how much you missed Leningrad. And now I can see why. I can see your point. Look, look at the crazy seagulls, smell the sea . . . You probably don't even notice anymore, but *I* do." He sighed: "It's fucking beautiful. Why leave? Makes no sense to me, no sense at all . . . But . . . whatever . . . Your choice, brother, your choice . . . Anyway, what's next on the menu, boss?"

We certainly had options, the day was relatively young and there was so much of Leningrad to see. We had enough time to take a walk around the fortress, maybe climb the walls built to repulse the rampaging Swedes (the

Swedes never came), check out the cannon that always fired a blank at noon, then cross the bridge and stroll through the Summer Garden—who knows, maybe the Russian Museum would still be open. We could manage another museum, couldn't we? Yurik slowly nodded his tentative consent, but I could sense his hesitation; it was clear to me that he was equivocating, holding something back. "Come on, Yurik, what *is* it? You don't feel like walking? Are you tired?" He instantly looked insulted by my doubting his stamina: "Tired? Are you kidding me? Don't you know me? Of course, I'm not tired! It's just... listen..." He hesitated for a few long seconds. "Listen, don't be offended, ok? I loved the museum and the city is awesome, just like you told me. And I really, really would love to see more of the sites and those marble statues of Greek chicks across the river..." He waved his newly lit cigarette in the direction of the magenta and yellow colored mass of the Summer Garden. "I mean no disrespect to you and your city, and I will definitely come back one day for another walk with . . ."—for a split second he looked genuinely pained—"or . . . *without* you. But right now, right now . . . Oh come on, brother, do I even need to explain this to you? Right now I could *really* use a drink. What do you say? You know a nice place that will welcome two pumped-up-on-culture ex-soldiers? Money," with some pomposity he patted his stuffed breast pocket, "is *not* a problem. It's my treat, don't even think of paying for anything. You move to pay, you die—got it? Do you have a place in mind?"

I should have expected this, but I was being too selfish, too absorbed in my own little farewell project, too keen on stuffing *my* city or, rather, *myself* down my friend's parched throat. I didn't have a place in mind but quickly thought of one, likely the only place in the restaurant-deprived Leningrad we stood a chance of getting in without the benefit of knowing someone (a waiter, a cook, a bouncer) inside. The little Georgian joint was tucked away in a side street in the old residential part of town. Popular with students, local Caucasians, and hard-drinking bohemians it was one of my most cherished secrets—a destination for special occasions. And Yurik's arrival in Leningrad most certainly qualified as a special occasion. We would have to take a tram and endure a fifty-minute rickety ride marked by frequent stops. "A tram?!" Yurik would have none of it. "We ain't taking no fucking tram, we are taking a taxi! From this point on we're doing everything in style. Got it?" Apparently, our Hermitage excursion and the city walk had fallen short of his ideal of a classy day out. With his proposal to cut down on sightseeing and proceed with drinking accepted Yurik came to life. Gone was the languid and melancholy sightseer disoriented by his encounter with two-thousand-year-old mummies and bearded fathers assaulting their sons, and in his stead I recognized the Yurik that I remembered so well—the lithe panther on the prowl, the determined sower of mischief, full of a zest rarely encountered among genteel urbanites. "A tram!" he scoffed again contemptuously and I could see the hunter's glee flickering in his mad brown eyes. We stepped up to the curb and Yurik flagged down a gypsy cab that materialized seemingly out of thin air. The gods of wine and wild frenzy have a way with taxis, I thought.

***

Maya departed in tears. The rain never stopped during the two days of my leave and we spent almost the entire time holed up indoors, in bed—only venturing outside once a day for a quick dash to the railroad canteen secreted behind the tracks in the train depot. The boozy Megaera mostly kept out of our way—mostly but not completely. During the very first night she stormed into the room just before dawn demanding that we pay her extra on account of our "fucking too much." I figured that had been her plan all along and even though we were sound asleep at the time of the storming there was no point arguing with the raging she-devil—we were entirely at her mercy. I coughed up an extra three rubles and she left pacified and then kept to herself for the remainder of our stay. But that was not why Maya was crying as she got on the Leningrad train. She cried, as she confessed to me through sobs, because she was afraid that she would not be able to survive the next eighteen months of our separation. She actually said "survive"—that's how she talked; at that point I still had not gotten used to the emotiveness of her language (that would come later) and felt overwhelmed by the exotically verbose power of her love confessions.

I needed that drug but also harbored a nagging concern, a concern that I dared not share with her for fear of looking weak and vulnerable. It was the time in the service when recent recruits had begun receiving the inevitable notices of romantic termination, dreaded "Dear John" letters. The nights in the barracks were filled with sounds of heartbreak and desperation: some broken souls bawled into their pillows, others lay awake in comatose immobility—both types could be recognized in the morning by the sight of their puffy red eyes. And there were the more assertive characters, those who preferred cursing to crying, the same ones who would startle you by suddenly and violently hitting the cracked, white-tiled wall in the common lavatory, the ones who fiercely masturbated through the night as if trying to beat cruel fate into submission. Yurik, who knew everyone at the base, reported a suicide attempt in the Third Battalion, then another one in the Sixth . . . At nineteen years old, eighteen months seemed like an eternity, and despite Maya's protestations and an impassioned disavowal of the Belgian suitor I remained wary of the future. Her train left the station, but the smell of her perfume lingered, clinging to the lapels of my rain-soaked trench coat, the moist warmth of her kiss still on my lips. The red tail lights of the last car teased me for a while before finally fading into the damp night and it occurred to me then that I would probably never see her again.

A few weeks later, back in the barracks, the memory of the visit had faded to such an extent that once or twice I caught myself doubting its reality. The mind-numbing routine of morning and evening roll calls, of kitchen and bathroom details, and the exhausting, twice-weekly marches to the firing range outside of town had triumphantly reasserted itself. Almost daily I received long letters from Maya; she described in minute psychoanalytical detail her feelings about me but mostly her feelings about her inner self. One letter ran to more than a dozen pages—an epistolary achievement that prompted Serzhik to launch into an unusually lengthy for him deliberation on the fundamental flaws of urban upbringing. Otherwise, the daily grind proceeded apace—at least for a time, until Yurik got news about a death in his family. Uncharacteristically, the vicious Veleiko granted him a few days of family leave—to attend the funeral and help out with other arrangements. Serzhik and I had reason to suspect that Veleiko's magnanimity was of a purely transactional nature. Yurik's departure from the base was shrouded in secrecy and now we anxiously waited for his return—to catch up on news from the outside but also to feast on what surely would be a generous food parcel thoughtfully prepared by his wife, Olga, who, as Serzhik didn't fail to point out, viewed her life obligations very differently from Maya.

Yurik returned from the funeral in a strangely contemplative mood; he was peculiarly absent-minded and preoccupied with something. We spent the day at the firing range and hardly had a free minute to exchange a few words, but he let it be known that we'd have things to discuss after the evening roll call. The hour before bedtime was the most cherished sixty minutes of the day, the only time when the foaming-at-the-mouth officers and sergeants finally left you alone and you could take care of your needs, write or read letters, mend torn fatigues, or simply close your eyes and fantasize about being transported to far more pleasant surroundings.

The three of us huddled in the corner of the sleeping quarters, a few square meters of weathered hardwood floor surface that we had long since claimed for our exclusive possession. Yurik had some news to share, three bits of news, to be precise. "Listen, soldiers, it's like this." He cleared his throat to indicate that what he was about to communicate should not be taken frivolously. "Three pieces of news—one bad, one . . . I don't know . . . kinda weird, the last one actually pretty fucking amazing. So . . . how shall we proceed, comrades?" Serzhik, always the rational thinker among us, smiled knowingly: "Come on, Yurik, stop being so mysterious. You can proceed in this very order: from bad to weird to amazing. Just don't reverse it, ok?"—"Well, here we go, then, first the lousy one: I caught a dose of the clap, a nice little memento from a hot Byelorussian seamstress. Leo and I got smashed after I got back from the funeral and went to the discotheque in Lenin Park . . ." He trailed off as if trusting our imaginations to conjure up the rest of their night. After a short pause he continued: "Did you know that Vladimir has a sister city in Byelorussia? They do these factory personnel exchanges; their girls come here to work at our factory and give the clap to our guys and our girls, I guess, do the same in Byelorussia." Serzhik was rolling around with laughter: "You knucklehead, this nonsense happens to you every other time they let you off the base. I heard the dispensary had a special enamel basin for magnesium baths. Guess how they marked it? No clue? They marked it: 'Yurik's dick.' With a thick black felt pen! You idiot!"

We laughed. Yurik's activities on leave followed a surprisingly predictable pattern and yielded predictably consistent results. "Ok, ok, your dick will be fine. Give us the weird bit of news. Yeah, give us the weird one." At that, Yurik's expressive face underwent a strange contortion, he looked simultaneously bemused and hesitant, bewildered by the outlandishness of what he was about to communicate: "Well, comrades, it looks like . . ." He swallowed nervously. "It looks like I'm . . . Jewish."—"You are *what*?!"—"Well, half-Jewish, to be exact, through my . . . ahem . . . late father." This was obviously too much even for Serzhik who had long since come to expect his best friend to reliably attract absurdity. Serzhik's piercing beady eyes, two black dots of concentrated intensity, fastened on Yurik, weighing his stunning news for accuracy. But truly, how could it be? The port-guzzling and truck-driving brawler, the intrepid provincial Romeo, the battle-hardened habitué of Lenin Park . . . was Jewish? Serzhik let out his signature admiring whistle: "I can't believe it! Yurik, you son-of-a-bitch, there is always something new with you. *Always*! With you, one doesn't have to go to the movies. F-u-u-u-ck! You're incredible!" I immediately felt familiar pangs of jealousy: "Come on, Serzhik, why the fuss? Ok, he is Jewish, so what? I'm Jewish too. Have you forgotten? I've been Jewish from day one, all my fucking life, and you don't seem to be impressed . . ." Serzhik snorted contemptuously, clearly uninterested in my feeble attempt to grab the spotlight: "Don't be ridiculous, you don't count, you're from Leningrad, everyone up there is Jewish. Or almost everyone. But this dude," he grinned lovingly at Yurik, "this dude is different."

Serzhik was right, of course. Yurik's story deserved cinematic treatment and bore little resemblance to the run-of-the-mill urban biographies of college-educated Leningrad Jews. The death in the family that sent Yurik off the base and towards his inevitable mishap in Lenin Park was that of his Moscow grandmother. That he had a grandmother in Moscow came as a surprise to us, a surprise that Yurik apparently shared. It was only at the funeral that he realized that the old lady that he sometimes visited in Moscow—and whose elegantly shabby, full of dusty books and classical records apartment, intimidated him—was his paternal grandmother. "But how is it even possible?!" I wondered aloud. "You never talked with her? You never asked who she actually was?" Yurik appeared genuinely baffled by what in retrospect did look like a spectacular breakdown in communication.—"I know it's pretty weird," he mumbled guiltily. "I would come for a quick visit on a drive through Moscow, park my rig out front. She would always put on some old record—violins and stuff, bring out cups of tea on a tray, no booze, then ask me a few things about my mother, how we were doing, if I enjoyed driving the rig, things like that . . . Come to think of it, it was sort of like in a movie . . . or a dream. She never so much as peeped that she was my grandma. How was I supposed to know? I'm no mind reader."

But there was more to the mystery of his Moscow grandma. While arranging the funeral and going through the old woman's papers Yurik stumbled on a previously unacknowledged family drama that drove him into an emotional whirlpool (and ultimately into the poisonous embrace of the Byelorussian seamstress). His father had been a Moscow-born Jewish painter who early in his career discovered the lucrative vocation of icon forging. The young man traveled around the country copying medieval icons inside dilapidated, boarded-up churches and then selling these remarkably authentic-looking replicas to the gullible or unscrupulous foreigners. To engage in that sort of business venture in the late-1950s Soviet Union was a risky proposition and Yurik's dad's luck soon ran out. The prosecutor asked for the death penalty but, as Yurik noted knowingly, more to show off than actually kill the wayward artist. The man's life was spared, but he got the proverbial "ten" in a camp and after release was banished from Moscow and other major cities. That's how he ended up in a half-ruined village east of Vladimir, a barely existing place, where he worked as a school art teacher, where he met Yurik's mother, where Yurik was born, and where, in keeping with well-established local tradition, he took to the bottle and died of cirrhosis before his son turned seven. Yurik's mother never spoke of the colorful details of his father's biography and for years he simply assumed that the person to whom he owed his patronymic fit perfectly the time-honored life pattern of the village males: he drank and he died . . . young.

For years, Yurik remained untroubled by his father's absence from his life and uncurious about his own family roots. The factory girls, small-time thugs, and other denizens of Lenin Park claimed no family histories and their conspicuous rootlessness never bothered him. He was satisfied to have his mother's last name. By going through the old woman's papers he became aware, for the first time, of the complicated family saga that predated his entrance into a world of reckless living and early departures. "At least you knew her name, right? You couldn't possibly *not* know her name?" I was still trying to come to terms with Yurik's disconnect from his own origin story. "Her name?" He sounded almost indignant now. "What am I, mental? Of course, I knew her name! Here, I want to make sure I pronounce it right . . ." After which he enunciated—slowly, deliberately, with an unmistakable affectation: "Rebecca Isaakovna Mendelsohn."

Serzhik and I exchanged astonished looks. He couldn't be serious, could he? I was struggling to comprehend whether he was mocking us or was truly that innocent of our country's dirty little secrets. "Listen, Yurik." I proceeded slowly, trying to make sure that he was not pulling my leg. "Rebecca Isaakovna Mendelsohn is like the most Jewish-sounding name in the world, it's more Jewish than any other Jewish name I ever heard in my life, and I, as you know," a quick reproachful glance at Serzhik, "grew up in a Jewish family. Are you telling me that for years you visited an old woman bearing this name and had no idea she was Jewish?!"—"I really didn't. Look, it's just a name, people have all sorts of names. Sure, I thought it was . . . unusual, but everything about her was unusual—the books, the tea tray, the old turntable spinning her records . . . She was one strange bird . . . my Jewish grandma. May she rest in peace . . ." He quickly crossed himself. He sounded sincere, he was not joking—my scar-covered, battle-tested friend was an innocent after all.

We fell into a contemplative silence from which Serzhik was the first one to emerge to remind Yurik that he still owed us the last bit of news. And just as promised we were in for a pleasant surprise. Well, more than pleasant. The amazing news exceeded our wildest expectations, for once Yurik didn't exaggerate. The three of us had been assigned to a three-month maintenance detail at the fortified district, deep in the Ivanovo pine woods. Save for final discharge one couldn't hope for more. There was no bigger prize, no more coveted assignment than a stint at the isolated secondary "ghost" base some seventy kilometers north of Kovrov.

Throughout the year the remote area, prepped as a back-up installation in case of a direct (and as we all agreed highly unlikely) NATO hit on the main base, was looked after and guarded by rotating teams of soldiers. A dozen massive log cabins and earth bunkers reinforced with concrete scattered across an area the size of several soccer fields, surrounded by coils of barbed wire and camouflage netting, with a small number of inconspicuous entry points. Reflective of the changing seasons, the camouflage had to be replaced twice a year from a dark-green pattern to snow white. The assignment was labor intensive—the three-person team was responsible for maintaining the integrity of the perimeter, keeping all access roads clear of snow and fallen branches, servicing the back-up generators, and testing twice daily a complex system of pipes that delivered hot air and water to individual structures. But twelve-hour work days and exposure to the elements was a ridiculously small price to pay for three months of freedom: freedom from noxious barrack smells and constantly yelling officers, freedom from regimentation and grueling marches to the firing range, freedom from the grinding need to navigate the minefield of interpersonal and interethnic conundrums—the inevitable byproduct of the forced cohabitation of hundreds of young men who, in most cases, shared little in the way of common culture or even language. Three months of freedom . . . Some desperate souls self-mutilated for the far more modest payoff of two weeks in the dispensary.

Yurik-the-miracle-worker had cast his spell at division headquarters. As befits the true magician who resents revealing trade secrets, when pressed for an explanation he grew serious and vaguely enigmatic. What did we care? Let's say the division commander needed a new timing belt for his jeep. And Yurik, as we may recall, used to work at a garage where they still remembered him fondly and even promised to keep his job for when he was done with his stupid service. So . . . As often was the case with him he urged us to use our imagination. And we did . . . and asked no further questions. Instead, we launched into an inspired planning session—deciding on the needed supplies to request from headquarters, scheduling a clandestine run to the moonshine witch's den, and sketching out a smooth approach to our Lithuanian radioman, the owner of a beat-up and taped-together Vesna cassette player that he was known to loan out for an immodest fee or a favor (and opportunely we had on our side Yurik who was a pro at dishing out and reclaiming favors).

And there was one more . . . thing . . . one additional potential benefit to our upcoming stay in woods. In their infinite wisdom, the Moscow-based cold war strategists had placed the fortified district smack in the middle of the old textile belt, an economically depressed region that Yurik casually referred to as "the women's townships." Local textile factories had fallen into a steep decline since the days of their prerevolutionary economic prominence, but a few of them stayed open and employed an almost entirely female workforce. Men, at least the men in the fifteen to sixty-five age bracket, had no place among this peculiar regional sisterhood. As soon as they graduated middle school, the boys left for vocational training in the city and rarely, if ever, came back. And when, and if, they did return they didn't reappear as men, but rather as prematurely aged human wrecks, as alcohol-drenched apparitions, ground down and worn out by years of hard-scrabble toil and even harder drinking.

The scarcity or unavailability of local men and the permanent presence of the rotating maintenance crew at the secretive military installation in the woods provided exciting opportunities for seasonal romantic adventures, to which most of the townships' residents owed their origin. "You ever fished bream in late May?" Yurik asked slyly. I never fished and, of course, he didn't think I did. "Well, then it's hard to explain, but it's sort of like catching bream in May there. You don't even need bait, no fishing rod. Just wade into the shallows, keep close to the bank, put your hands in the water, don't move too much, wait for a few minutes, sooner or later it'll swim straight into your grasp—that is, if you can stand holding your hands in the frigid Klyazma water for a few minutes. Get it?"

Yes, it was all fairly straightforward. Clearly it was not just snow and pipe cleaning and perimeter maintenance that awaited us in the stately pine forests crowding those slowly dying "women's townships." Yet we hardly needed any extra enticements; no illicit romance in the woods could compare in its attractiveness to three full months of unregimented living, and that's exactly what Serzhik and I claimed to be looking forward to. The rest was noise, the elements of nature, fate, and historical circumstance that we'd accept stoically if the mischievous Ivanovo satyrs resolved to test our virility. The woods were calling, we'd just have to wait for the first snow to powder the dirt Ivanovo track, an old unpaved road winding through the bleak countryside on the way to our temporary autonomy.

The first snow fell just before the November holidays and as soon as the lieutenant in charge of the motor park had emerged out of a seventy-two-hour alcohol-induced celebratory stupor a heavy-set personal carrier transported us, along with a sizeable load of supplies, to the fortified district. The farewell from Veleiko, resentful of the fact that we had been able to secure the assignment behind his back, sounded ominous: "I hope you freeze your asses off, you slimy fuckers. And remember, no food deliveries for you. You run out of supplies, you're on your own—feel free to forage, or beg in the villages, or hunt, or . . ."—he burrowed his fat index finger into Yurik's defiantly puffed-up chest—"just fucking croak, which happens to be my personal preference."

The bastard must've jinxed us because the freeze set in within days after our arrival and we had to adapt to running the secondary military base under extreme wintry conditions—not unlike those that had doomed most of the historically significant invasions of Russia in the past couple of centuries. We incessantly shoveled snow off the access paths, but it accumulated faster than we were able to remove it. Every morning we spent hours shaving off the ice coating that grew mysteriously overnight on the canvas canopy of the perimeter camouflage, but the struggle quickly proved to be futile. "It's pointless, sort of like clipping nails," philosophized Serzhik. We agreed and eventually left the camouflage to its evil fate. We slept in shifts, not out of a guardsmen's sense of responsibility but to avoid carbon monoxide poisoning from the capricious and foul-smelling diesel generator that like a barely tamed mustang recognized only one master—Serzhik. Those were the hardest, coldest days of my life. And possibly the happiest.

The first two weeks were taken up by a frantic struggle against the elements and the faulty equipment and we hardly had time to take in our surroundings, which were snow-covered and spectacular. Endless rows of sky-high pines and graceful spruces encircled the camp; it seemed they had been arranged by some thoughtful giant (Yurik thought it may have been Peter the Great), a meticulous planner and stickler for details. The trees' majestic, centuries-old presence dwarfed our half-hearted efforts at securing this secondary base against NATO, but we had no reason to complain. We were free.

In the evening, we burned wood in a rotund cast-iron stove that generated so much heat so quickly that within half an hour the bunker became barely habitable and we were stripped down to our standard-issue blue underwear and reclining on our bunk beds heaped with malodorous old blankets and discarded padded jackets. The day's fatigue evaporated as we feasted on canned beef and baked potatoes, washed down by strong tea and even stronger moonshine. Those awful Bulgarian cigarettes never tasted better. And in the stuffy greenhouse of the overheated bunker our friendship blossomed, grew even sturdier and more timeless—just like those noble pines outside the camouflaged perimeter.

Conversations were endless, meandering; there was some excitement in identifying common threads in our otherwise dramatically disparate life experiences. We reminisced, we exaggerated our youthful triumphs and downplayed the disappointments, because, you see, everyone needs an exquisitely polished draft of the past—a memory that serves the utilitarian purpose of making you levitate just a few meters above the cozy squalor of the bunker or maybe even above the snow-capped tops of the spruces. We made plans for the future, and those by default included frequent reunions—family barbeques on the banks of the Volga, riotous Crimean vacations, grand tours of Yurik's blood-soaked haunts in Lenin Park or my far safer ones in Leningrad, reunions that we imagined as the centerpieces of our post-military existence, its, as Yurik put it, supporting axel . . . "till death do us part."

Finding a daily rhythm was key to normalizing the Sisyphean toil of snow removal; patterned motions, day in and day out, lightened the burden; they had a way of turning physical tasks into an exercise in applied existentialism. Yurik had told us that once we hit our stride the labor would grow habitual and uneventful, which would allow us to open our eyes and hearts to other pleasures. He meant the women from the textile townships, of course. By now, he figured, the word of our presence in the woods had reached the surrounding villages. He claimed to have spotted the shadows of scouts lurking outside the perimeter late one night. "I'd give it a couple more days," he said. "Remember what I said about fishing? They come to you, you keep still, don't move."

And they did come, unless, of course, one believes that they had always been there—two cone-like figures, bundled up against the gusts of arctic wind that whipped up huge clouds of fine snow. The wind kept the snow suspended and swirling madly for extended minutes before finally relenting and letting it settle slowly and thickly on the spruces. In the icy twilight of the receding day the two girls looked numinous in their immobility. I noticed them as I stepped onto one of the exit paths on my way to mend a tarpaulin recently damaged by the wind. Not a move, not a word from the otherworldly visitors. I greeted them awkwardly, still uncertain of how corporeal they actually were. They didn't respond to my greetings but instead exchanged quick looks and snickered as if entertained by this forest creature's ability to speak. I motioned them to stay put (which was probably unnecessary as they showed absolutely no inclination of moving—they appeared comfortably and naturally stationary) and rushed back to the bunker to announce the arrival of guests.

Serzhik would have none of it. He had far better and more useful things to do—like, for example, fixing a loose valve on the generator and fine-tuning the portable Omega HF receiver that we used for our daily radio contact with headquarters, a brief communication that had no other purpose beyond transmitting a superficial vital sign: all is well, still hanging on out here in the woods, still snowed in. But Yurik, of course, was a different story. He perked up at the news and immediately proceeded with hasty but meticulously thought out and flawlessly executed preparations: a dash of cheap cologne on the neck, a flask of moonshine in the pocket, fresh batteries into the cassette player (check play, check rewind, check fast forward. Perfect—it works!). In less than ten minutes we were outside, introducing ourselves to the girls, with Yurik doing all the talking while they remained singularly unresponsive. "It doesn't look like they are interested in us," I whispered to Yurik. "Not a word, nothing." Yurik dismissed my self-conscious concern with a smug smirk. "Come on, what the fuck are they doing here, then, five kilometers from the nearest village? Remember the fish? The fish don't talk, but they . . ." he winked at me, "but they swim and when well-cooked can be delicious!" He turned towards the girls, whose faces remained largely hidden behind layers of formless woolen scarfs. "Welcome to the base, ladies. You're in good hands now, you're safe with us, just like the rest of the country. No harm will come to anyone, as long as this courageous band of hardened and frost-resistant soldiers is holding down the fort in the woods. Say, will you join us for a walk? We've got booze, we've got music, and our radioman tells me the moon is almost full tonight!" The girls retreated a few steps behind the spruce for a whispered consultation. They reemerged from their hideaway a couple of minutes later giggling and one of them nodded: yes, they would join us for a walk.

The nonexistent radioman hadn't lied, the moon was full or very close to full that night, and by the time we reached the main road it had claimed its prominent spot in the dark skies and loomed large and candescent over the road. The snow reflected its cold light, and the wide white stretch of the road (who in the world had cleared it?) and the snowbanks flanking it on both sides contrasted sharply with the mournful, muted mass of the surrounding forest. In the moonlight, the snow shimmered, giving off a quivering silverish glare as if millions of tiny ice crystals joined to salute the rising moon. Or at the very least to greet the strange little group walking on a path illuminated by the moon, and walking in complete silence, save for the scratchy sounds of music coming from Yurik's battered cassette player. We only had one tape—the new album by a wildly popular boy band that had recently emerged out of some provincial hellhole and quickly captured the imagination of Soviet teenagers who had little choice of musical offerings. The boys' songs were cloyingly sentimental and one could sense that despite their professions of affection for "white roses that I want to cover with kisses and protect against the January cold" the performers' sweet innocence was fake, a saccharine coating for a rough and likely criminal past. But the girls loved it and even began to sing along. All of a sudden, the weird double date in the woods with a couple of Ivanovo girls whose faces we had yet to see started to feel more conventional. A fleeting illusion of normalcy, of course, that didn't wait long to dissipate.

On our approach to a bend in the road the girls stopped abruptly and began to listen intently—not to the music, no, but to some other sound coming from afar. And then I heard it too—a faint, but unmistakably increasing in volume, purr of a motorcycle engine. One of the girls grabbed me by the sleeve and I was surprised by the strength of her grip. "Run!" she gasped and pulled me towards the snowbank. We rolled down the incline into a shallow, snow-filled ravine that separated the woods from the road. The girl continued to hold onto my sleeve as we came to rest in a hollow. "Shhh, be quiet," she hissed. I looked around and saw no trace of Yurik and the other girl; they were probably hiding on the other side of the road. The rumble of the approaching motorcycle grew louder and soon became the only noise. And then there was more—a strange guttural howl that overpowered the crackling of the engine and echoed mightily through the silent forest, sounding at first ominously unintelligible but eventually solidifying into words: "G-a-a-a-li-na! G-a-a-a-li-na! Ga-a-al-ka, you bi-i-i-tch!"

My companion was playing dead, she had burrowed her way deep into the snowdrift, and all I could see now was the pink of her cheek and wide-open eyes with flecks of snow and tiny icicles clinging to her eyelashes. She seemed genuinely panicked, but there was something else, something less definitive, something lighter . . . Hilarity perhaps? "Are you Galina?" I whispered. She nodded bashfully but almost immediately burst out in a silent, barely suppressed laughter. And suddenly I realized that I was looking at a child, the scarfs and layers of clothing concealed a middle schooler. Damn you, Yurik, you and your fishing metaphors! As noiselessly as I could I crawled up the snowbank and peeked just above the iced-over ridge.

About fifty meters ahead of us a motorcycle idled in the middle of the road, one of those heavy old Urals with a sidecar. A bizarre figure straddled the motorcycle, a shapeless form that from a distance and lit by the moon appeared artlessly imposing and godlike. The woods had yielded their deepest secret—a cutout of an enormous equestrian superimposed on the low hanging disc of the full moon. "G-a-a-a-li-na!!" thundered the motorcycle goddess's booming voice, which got louder as it ricocheted among the gargantuan pines, filled the sky, and caused some uncanny tumult deep inside the woods. "G-a-a-a-li-na! Where the fu-u-u-ck a-r-e y-o-o-o-u?!" A heavy spruce branch snapped and crashed into the snow, sinking into its softness. A hefty bird, disturbed by the commotion, alighted from the top of a pine where it had settled for the night and flew off, moving slowly and clumsily and keeping close to the treetops. The giant rider raised herself; keeping her feet firmly planted on the motorcycle footrest, she surveyed the road. She took in the frozen landscape and muttered some words that, I thought, sounded more plaintive than threatening; even from this distance I could see the steam of her breath. I also noted some hesitancy in her posture, which contrasted sharply with the rest of the spectacle and, oddly, made me feel sympathetic to her. Finally, she lowered herself back onto the saddle and gave full throttle to her bulky steed; it veered nervously left and right, trying to find its grip on the icy surface, then jerked powerfully forward and sped off, carrying its oversized jockey towards the enormous moon in futile pursuit of a missing daughter.

The quiet returned but soon enough was violated again—this time by Yurik, who noisily slid down the slope to join us in our hiding place. Yurik looked and sounded annoyed: "That was your mom, right?" The girl nodded. "Ok, kid, time to come clean. How old are you? Fifteen? No?! Fourteen?"—"Fourteen . . ." Her words were barely audible. Not without some theatricality, Yurik shook his head, then sighed and, to my surprise, the sigh sounded genuine: "Fuck . . . You're probably even younger than that . . . Listen, children, we're still going for a walk but not the kind of walk you probably had in mind—we'll see you home, back to the township. And we'll make sure that you're home *before* that crazed biker gets back and whoops your underage asses like, when you think of it, she really should. Understand? Ok, let's go."

On the way back to the bunker Yurik remained uncharacteristically subdued. We staggered down the empty road, passing the moonshine flask back and forth. From time to time, he kicked the snowbank with his kersey boot, provoking a series of short-lived but violent little blizzards. Halfway to the base we dropped into the snow on the road shoulder and stayed there for a good half hour, lying next to each other splayed on our backs like two snow angels. Warmed by our recent adventure and the moonshine we hardly felt the cold. "You know what really sucks?" Yurik sounded melancholy. I waited for him to continue. "What really sucks is that I know exactly what will happen to these girls. I see girls like that in Lenin Park all the time. Sooner or later they're gonna get knocked up by some asshole soldier—right on that bunkbed in the bunker, or under one of these fucking spruces. The crazy mother will watch the kid while her daughter goes off to work at the textile factory. You ever been to a textile factory? Not a fun place, not at all. Within ten years she'll balloon to the size of that motorcycle monster. On the weekends she'll go with her girlfriends to some other Lenin Park—you know, every shithole in this country has a Lenin Park, lots of shitholes, lots of Lenin parks, lots of discotheques, lots of white fucking roses, tons of snow . . ." He grabbed a fistful of snow and rubbed it onto his flushed face, and as he was doing this he kept on whispering: "Tons of snow, tons of snow, tons of fucking snow . . ."

How did we manage to get so drunk on so little booze? The moonshine queen back in Kovrov had certainly perfected her recipe; I dreaded to think of the ingredients that had gone into the concoction that had now drained us of any strength, any fear of falling into a deadly hypothermic slumber. Just don't fall asleep, just don't fall asleep—we're not that far from the sweltering heat of the bunker, not all that far from the dependable Serzhik who has just finished fixing that valve and probably brewed us some tea. He'll be there for us, waiting to hear another ridiculous story of yet another Yurik fuck up, ready to roll on the stained linoleum floor with laughter. So we better get up and get moving before the precious moonshine warmth leaves our skinny bodies and a marauding Snow Queen comes after us to take possession of a couple of hapless soldiers, and certainly, certainly before the fearsome apparition, that lost Horseman of the Apocalypse with a sidecar, that *Flying Dutchman* of a motorcycle reappears from the wintry emptiness and roars down the deserted white highway bringing vengeance on two defenseless snow angels.

***

The entrance to the restaurant was besieged by a small, dispirited mob, whose sight filled me with a familiar sense of futility. The restaurant, like other such establishments in the city, was a fortress, and whatever my other strengths I was not good at storming impregnable citadels. But Yurik was unfazed. Well, more than unfazed—his face glowed with delight and excitement. He scanned the queue with an expert eye and headed confidently for the front door, where his unscheduled appearance evoked immediate protestations and threats of imminent mob justice. A minute later I saw him chatting animatedly with the bouncer guarding the hallowed entrance. The two laughed and embraced, then took a seemingly choreographed step back and high-fived each other, and that's when I noticed the reddish edge of a folded ten-ruble banknote jammed inconspicuously between Yurik's index and middle fingers. Yurik looked around searchingly and quickly spotted me at the end of the queue. He gestured me to join him, his smile warm and self-congratulatory—he was pleased with himself, he wanted me to know that even in forbidding Leningrad, on my own turf, he could be in his element. And he was. Even the indignant crowd had calmed down having accepted the inevitability of his triumph. He was Zeus controlling the thunder, he was Moses parting the waves. He was . . . Yurik.

In less than five minutes we were seated at a corner table in the main dining room, flipping through the soiled pages of the menu and breathing in the kitchen aromas, the pungent scent of fried lamb and Georgian spices. The restaurant was filled to capacity: a group of students from the School of Architecture across the street occupied the largest and rowdiest table, a trio of somber Caucasians huddled over a huge plate of lamb skewers and a battery of empty wine bottles arrayed in a neat geometrical pattern—they acted like they owned the place and I wondered if they actually did . . . There were others: more students, families from the neighborhood, a small group of artillery officers in uniform (Yurik gave them a quick dirty look), and a young couple holding hands across their table and engaged in some sort of staring contest, probably trying to communicate to each other (and by extension, to the rest of the restaurant audience) the intensity of their mutual affection.

At the table nearest to the exit two young women, approximately our age, shared a bottle of Georgian red and a plate of lamb dumplings. They were sitting very straight, hardly exchanging a word, purposely ignoring the half-hearted attempts by the Caucasians to gain their attention. Yurik nodded in their direction and winked at me: "What do you think? Not bad, eh?" I ignored the innuendo and continued to study the menu. He smiled: "Alright, alright, no need to panic, just sayin' there're some good-looking and apparently unclaimed women in this joint is all. So . . . back to the menu . . . Shall we start with red or skip the formalities and move directly to cognac? You know me, I'm open-minded when it comes to liquids." Apprehensive about this emerging trend for the rest of the evening I suggested we go easy on hard liquor and stick to red wine. Yurik shrugged: "You're the boss, all I want is for us to be happy tonight is all."

He turned to the waiter, whose slack posture conveyed a rather extreme lack of enthusiasm for his job: "Ok, friend, for starters, bring us a couple of those Kindzmaraulis and . . ."—he paused for effect—"a bottle of cognac, the Armenian one. And make sure there are five stars on the label; you bring me a three-star bottle, I'll send it right back. Understood?" The morose waiter emitted a snorting noncommittal sound but took down the order. "And while we're at it," continued Yurik, "how about a few lamb skewers, two orders of dumplings, two *kharchos*, a lavash . . . No, make it a couple, and a bunch of veggies—tomatoes, cukes, radishes, scallions . . . the works. Well, you know the drill, right?" The waiter's body language indicated that he indeed knew the drill, even if he didn't care much for it. After he left, Yurik exhaled with obvious relief, as if he had just conquered the last necessary hurdle of this long, full of obstacles day and was now free to relish the well-deserved fruits of his labors. He checked out the hand-holding lovers at the table next to us, rolled his eyes, and winked at me: "Should we hold hands like them? I mean, why not? I haven't seen you in months, you fucker. I missed you, I really did!" I missed him too.

The two bottles of Kindzmarauli didn't last long, and after Yurik ordered two more and the interior of the dingy kebab joint began to feel suspiciously ethereal, it occurred to me that the responsible thing to do would be to call Maya and update her on the current modified state of our city tour. The payphone across the street, by the entrance to the School of Architecture, turned out to be in perfect working order—a little miracle in a city of smashed and disconnected payphones. The fact that, instead of touring Peter and Paul Fortress or kicking up the storm of fallen autumnal leaves in the Summer

Garden, Yurik and I ended up at a crowded Georgian restaurant had no audible effect on Maya; other people's altered trajectories rarely concerned her. Our son was fine, though, enjoying yet another happy day of his nascent life, and upon receiving that bit of day's news from Maya I desperately and futilely searched for a wooden part inside the payphone booth to knock on—a silly superstition to ward off trouble. I launched into a disjointed account of our visit to the Hermitage, and the walk, and the update on Serzhik and his Yava motorcycle, and Yurik's apparent heartbreak upon receiving the news of our imminent emigration, and . . . almost instantly realized that Maya was not listening. I could hear her talking to her mother over the handset—a familiar scene that was all too easy to visualize. Why was she so nonchalant? Didn't she recognize the danger of a night out in Yurik's company? Didn't she care? And here I was, half-drunk in a stinking payphone booth, bothering my rightly self-absorbed wife who had just spent the whole day caring for our son while Yurik and I gawped at ancient mummies and discoursed on biblical filicide. How selfish of me to desire her sympathy. And for what? For being plastered? For being secretly terrified about our looming departure? "Are you still there? It looks like I may be home late, later than I thought. That's ok with you?" Maya didn't quite understand the question: "Ok with me? Why? Sure, you can come home whenever you want. Whatever. Mom wants you to tell Yurik that she found him 'enchanting'—her exact word. You know how my mom is . . ."—"Right, I'll let him know. But what about you . . . and me?"—"What about us?"—"You're not mad at me, are you? Not mad that I'm going to be late? Do you . . . miss me?" I should've known better, subtlety was never Maya's thing. "Miss you? What nonsense, I see you every day. Stop being silly and go back to your friend, make sure he doesn't kill anyone—don't imagine I didn't notice those scars." She hung up, and in the split second before the handset hit the receiver, I could hear Maya resuming her interrupted conversation with her mother. Full of self-pity and weighed down by an oppressive sense of premonition I headed back to the restaurant.

In my absence the seating arrangements in the dining room had undergone a dramatic change. The two stern-looking young women had moved to our table, their relocation, I had no doubt, initiated by Yurik. They seemed to me just as ill at ease, just as taciturn as they did when they were sitting across the room from us. But Yurik was full of smiles and infectious excitement. Red-faced, his thinning black hair plastered in sweaty disarray over his damp forehead, Yurik projected an air of adolescent exuberance. I noticed that his shirt was now unbuttoned down to his solar plexus; a tiny aluminum cross on a crude leather thread rested on his broad but hollow chest. He tilted back on his chair, a glass of cognac in hand, affecting the relaxed posture of an art school model in a state of demonstrative tranquility. Yurik was distinctly and unambiguously in his element. He greeted my return with a sly wink: "Surprise! We have guests. Please, meet and greet the two most beautiful women in Leningrad—Lera and Lisa or, as they are known in their native Belgorod, the L-girls!" Balancing precariously on two chair legs he leaned closer to me and lowered his voice: "Lisa, brother, is all yours."

The women observed my arrival and Yurik's exuberance with a palpable lack of curiosity, like two bored schoolchildren forced to attend a performance that they'd rather skip. I did notice, though, that they were sipping our cognac. Yurik was in his most expansive, unabashedly fabulist mood: "I was just explaining to Lera and Lisa that this here is a really special occasion, a reunion of two warriors, a fraternal meeting of two ex-paratroopers. The shit we've been through, my dears, is simply unimaginable . . ." Now it was my turn to lean close to Yurik: "Stop bullshitting, you know we were never paratroopers, and there is nothing unimaginable in having Veleiko yell at you day and night." Yurik chose to ignore my feeble objections; when epic tales are being woven there is no place for quibbling over minor biographical details. Besides, he had more exciting information to communicate to the Belgorod duo: "But it's a special occasion for yet another reason. My friend here, my recent brother-in-arms, is leaving the country soon. Guess where he is going?" Lera shrugged and sipped her cognac: "I dunno. Bulgaria?"—"Bulgaria?!" Yurik affected an offended look. "Who cares about Bulgaria? I know it sort of sounds like Belgorod, but . . . no, aim higher, my dear, *much* higher." A dramatic pause (Yurik was big on dramatic pauses). "How about *America*?! This decorated vet here is moving to America! How about that?!"

For the first time the girls looked at me with something approximating interest. "Is it true?" Lera asked. "Or just another piece of crap from this bullshit artist?"—"It is true," I admitted with some hesitation. "Well, then," Lera poured me some cognac, making it clear that she was a person of authority. "Let's drink to your safe journey. Remember that Nautilus Pompilius song about America "that I'll never see"? Let's drink to seeing things that we never hoped to see." To my astonishment, she smiled genially, like an old friend returning from oblivion. Yurik gave me a quick celebratory double kick under the table—apparently, he found the toast and Lera's changed demeanor promising. I looked around the restaurant and was surprised to see it bathed in a warm comforting glow; the din was considerably muffled and the diners, even the rowdy students and the unsmiling Caucasians, looked now almost beatific, as if engaged in some delicately choreographed communal ritual of Buddhist introspection. Someone touched my hand—it was Lisa, she wanted us to clink glasses.

We exited the restaurant. At dusk the city was at its most spectral, especially in this old part of town, squeezed between the canals. Trams rumbled down the street towards the distant lights of Nevsky Prospect. An evening breeze carried the usual city smells—the occasionally overpowering stench of exhaust fumes, the fainter whiff of rotting garbage, but also the fresher, gentler, far less offensive scent of the sea. A woman, laden with groceries, hurried home along the canal, the click-clack of her shoes on the granite slabs of the embankment traveling through the neighborhood, amplified tenfold by the echo.

I was prepared to say goodbye to our new friends, but that's not what Yurik had in mind. He pulled me to the curb, out of the girls' earshot, there was something childlike and therefore urgent about his excitement: "Time to party! Where can we take them?" I didn't think we could take them anywhere. It was getting seriously late and back at the restaurant the girls had mentioned the curfew at their friend's dorm where they were staying. To me, that was a clear enough indication that the night's pleasures would be limited to lamb skewers and five-star Armenian cognac. And the furtive touch by Lisa's hand, just before we clinked our glasses—that touch was enough.

Lera and Lisa smoked cigarettes a few meters away, waiting with apparent indifference for our little summit to be over. I thought Yurik was beginning to look and sound positively demonic: "Do you guys have a Lenin Park around here? You know like a place where you can take girls after hours? Come on, there got to be a Lenin Park in this city, it's named after the dude!"

I couldn't think of such a place. There was, of course, a huge park on the outskirts—the popular Victory Park by the Gulf that my dad and I used to frequent on the weekends. For hours on end, he played speed chess with disheveled, eccentric-looking men at the specially designated pavilion while I roamed the alleys of the park or rode my bicycle to the stadium that looked like a gigantic fort guarding the entrance to the Gulf. So yes, there was a park that I knew fairly well, but it was a good hour-long tram ride away and . . . Yurik interrupted me with visible frustration: "What, a tram?! Are you nuts?! We'll go in a taxi! Remember, no trams today. Everything is on me. Only the best, only the very best, my brother!" He rushed back to the girls and launched into an animated oration. I couldn't quite catch the words, but I saw Lera and Lisa exchanging puzzled looks and shrugging their shoulders. To my great surprise, Yurik returned from the exchange in even higher spirits: "Ok, it's a go. Stay here, entertain the girls. There is a liquor store by the tram stop. I'll be in and out." And he took off like a madman. How did he know there was a liquor store around here?! Some of life's mysteries are destined to remain unsolved.

In no time Yurik was back from his liquor run, jubilantly waving two liter bottles of Armenian port. A few minutes later we were in a gypsy cab, expertly commandeered by my increasingly delirious friend, speeding off towards Victory Park. Yurik nestled one of the port bottles between his bony knees and dexterously tore off the plastic cap. "Here," he offered the bottle to the driver, "you go first, boss." The driver, one hand resting on the wheel, took a long swig straight out of the bottle and grunted approvingly. Yurik had just made a new friend for life. The girls and I were squeezed tightly in the back seat of the tiny Lada, and . . . I couldn't lie to myself anymore, their proximity was thrilling. As the car crossed the bridge and passed by the now lit up fortress that we had failed to visit earlier in the day, I felt Lisa's hand on my knee. I turned to her, but she seemed oblivious, completely captivated by the illuminated cityscape gliding by outside the car's window; her hand, I began to suspect, had its own mind.

I had never been in Victory Park after dark and was immediately struck by its nocturnal emptiness. In contrast with the city center, the air here was fresh and fragrant, full of yearning-inducing sea smells and the comforting tang of autumnal decay. Yurik, who had an intimate familiarity with nighttime parks, was impressed, even humbled, and immediately announced that this was far, far superior to Lenin Park in Vladimir. We walked to the water's edge on the tiny municipal beach. The sliver of dirty, wet sand was littered with debris, dog poop, and sundry traces of recent human visitations. We loitered there for some time, sipping port and taking in the night views of the Baltic, made visible by scattered boat lights, the insistent searchlight mounted atop the stadium across the tributary, the lighthouse in the distance, and the reflected glow from the island fortress, some twenty kilometers away out in the Gulf... The girls voiced their appreciation of the view, but Yurik showed little enthusiasm for sightseeing and insisted that we needed to find a perfect spot to finish off the remaining port in style.

He raced through the park like an experienced greyhound in search of a duck downed by a hunter. Trusting his instincts, we followed him closely and soon found ourselves in the middle of an abandoned playground, which Yurik quickly determined to be the "perfect spot" he'd been looking for. Lera looked around doubtfully; she probed the splintered outer rim of a dilapidated sandbox with the toe of her shoe and the pressure proved to be too much for the sandbox walls, which collapsed as if they were made of the very sand they were guarding. "*This* is perfect?" Her sarcasm was of a habitual kind, not vicious. Yurik grinned like a maniac: "Of course it's perfect! It's amazing! Look!" He dashed across the playground towards a massive piece of equipment, whose exact purpose was not easy to ascertain in the dark. I stepped closer and realized that it was a rusty merry-go-round, its colors long faded, its paint peeling off the rounded rails like fine aspen bark. Yurik roared with delight and jumped onto the wobbly platform. He then turned to me: "Hey, push me, brother, push me real hard, make me spin, make me go crazy!"—"You're already crazy!" I laughed . . . but pushed. The mechanism squealed, complaining bitterly about this latest after-dark indecency, about being forced out of retirement to entertain a group of drunk park invaders led by a frenzied joyrider. "Push me harder!" Yurik screamed again. And I pushed and pushed, and the merry-go-round started moving—at first with screeching hesitancy, but then, awakened to its true calling, faster and faster, hitting its stride, spinning confidently around its axel. "Enough already!" I yelled at Yurik. "You'll get nauseous!" Yurik grabbed the rail and, keeping his feet firmly planted on the platform, bent backwards, as if trusting himself to some unseen dancing partner, his face turned up towards the dim stars. "I never get nauseous," he laughed. "Never! Push harder, harder!" And I pushed—because when Yurik got like that, who in the world could possibly say no to him? Even Lera and Lisa seemed to be entranced by this spectacle of abandon; they stared at the spinning merry-go-round in amused disbelief. "What a clown, what an idiot clown . . . in a red shirt," Lera laughed, but I heard unmistakable notes of tenderness in her voice.

Finally, I stopped pushing and the wheel immediately began to slow down and eventually ceased spinning altogether. Yurik crawled off the platform and, breathing heavily, dropped on the grassy patch next to it. The beam from the stadium searchlight swept across the playground and I could see the huge dark semicircles of sweat spreading from his armpits down the sides of the shirt. He motioned me to come closer: "Remember, remember, how in the army we always talked about happiness? Remember how we were gonna be happy after the service? Like no one would ever stop us from being happy? No fucking Veleiko, no fucking artillery patrol! Remember?"—"Yes, of course, of course I remember . . . So?"—"*So*? *So*? Don't you get it? *This* is happiness. Right here, right now! It doesn't get better than that. *That's* what we were talking about. Our happiness . . . it is here, I see it, I smell it, I *feel* it! Oh, come on, you see it too!"

He closed his eyes and for a second I thought he was fading, but no, he wasn't, not yet. He indicated that he wanted to get up and needed some help: "Give me a hand." I helped him get off the ground and in doing so noticed how drunk he really was. But not so drunk as to forgo the concluding part of the night's program, not so drunk as to skip the coda to the day's symphony. "Lera and I are going for a walk," he announced solemnly while trying to regain his balance. "I'd like to take her on a little excursion around the park. Lera, my dear, may I?" He extended his hand, inviting her to join him. I fully expected Lera to brush him off while doling out a weighty dose of her signature scorn. Strangely, she didn't. She put out her cigarette and got off the rickety park bench that she and Lisa had mounted to better observe Yurik's wild ride. She sighed for dramatic effect, but when she spoke she sounded almost business-like: "Alright, you little fool, let's go for a walk. Just make it quick, we need to be back at the dorms . . . Wait, can you even walk, Charlie Chaplin?" Yurik smiled condescendingly: "Of course, I can walk, come here, I'll show you how to be happy in a park, not everyone knows how . . . just me and that other Vladimir delinquent, Leo. Ever heard about Leo? No? Didn't think so. No worries, I'll tell you all about him. He's a legend." He turned to me and Lisa, who had not moved from her perch on the bench: "You two lovebirds, behave, don't do anything we wouldn't do." They both laughed, suddenly and unequivocally a couple. I watched them stroll down the poorly lit alley, hand in hand, towards the darkening mass of lilac bushes. When they entered the cone of light thrown by a lonely park lamp, their shadows grew enormous and I caught myself admiring the smooth cohesion of their step—they could have been married.

Lisa shivered visibly, she looked nervous. "It's getting cold," she complained. "Come over here." I took off my jacket and helped her wrap it around her shoulders—an ancient ritual of caring that all the Russian men I knew performed with great seriousness. I sat down next to her on the bench and she immediately scooted closer, leaning against me, still shivering. "I'm cold, soldier, I'm really cold," she breathed warmly into my ear. She touched my neck with the back of her hand: "You see how cold I am? What are you gonna do about it, soldier?" Was this the happiness Yurik raved about just a few minutes ago? Was this the happiness we imagined during those frozen nights in the overheated bunker? She slipped her hand underneath my t-shirt and I felt it crawling slowly up my spine all the way to my nape, then reversing its movement and tracing it back down, each vertebra counted on descent with a light tap: one, two, three . . . "I'm marking you," she said. "That's what all witches do—we mark our prey." And sure enough, I felt bewitched and longed to kiss her but also tell her about those nights in the woods and the dreams of happiness and freedom the three of us swapped casually while resting on a pile of decommissioned blankets. I wanted to explain to her why sitting next to her on a shaky park bench, getting goosebumps from the night breeze coming from the Gulf, or, more likely, because of the ice-cold touch of her fingers burning my skin under the t-shirt, why all the disparate elements of this endless day would inevitably come together and congeal into an artifact of memory to be cherished. That's not what I said, though, not at all. "I'm married. I'm sorry, I should've mentioned this earlier. But . . . I'm married." Lisa sighed overdramatically and threw up her hands in mock disbelief: "Oh, no, not *you*, not *married*! Woe is me!" She laughed. She didn't appear to be upset, but her merriment also seemed slightly forced. "Listen, I'm a big girl and not really an idiot. Do you think I'm blind? You never even bothered to remove your wedding ring, not like that Rambo out in the bushes, who took his off (I noticed!) just before he came up to our table at the restaurant."—"I'm sorry . . ."—"Oh, come on, what's there to be sorry about?"

Lisa pulled away from me, got out a cigarette, and, squinting against the flickering light burning down the match, lit it. She readjusted my jacket on her shoulders, indicating that she was not ready yet to part with it. The night chill was now becoming difficult to ignore. She finished the cigarette and glanced at her watch. "Damn, it's getting really late; we should be getting back to the dorms soon. I didn't come on this trip to spend the night on the streets or sleep in a park." She laughed again, but this time the laughter sounded genuine. "Stop looking so serious, lighten up a little, no one has died. You're married, that's wonderful. 'Good on you,' as they say in the movies."

She moved closer to me again and curled both of her hands over my arm: "Don't get any ideas, I'm just cold, that's all. Friends should help each other out and I'm freezing right now—so, here, be a friend, give me a hug." I freed my arm and put it around her, letting her adjust to the shape of my body. "Thank you, that's much better," she whispered. "I feel like falling asleep, right here next to you. Did you know that that's how people die of hypothermia? They fall asleep in the cold and never wake up. Don't let me fall asleep, ok?"—"Ok," I agreed. "I won't." I suddenly remembered the frozen immediacy of that snow-covered road under the moonlight and the approaching rumble of the ghostly motorcycle. I saw two tiny figures in the snow, prostrated on their backs with their faces turned up towards the gigantic, looming moon. "No," I repeated, "I won't let you fall asleep."

Lisa remained quiet for a few minutes; just as I was beginning to think that she has indeed fallen asleep, she stirred: "Is it true what that clown said? That you're moving to America soon?" I nodded gravely.—"Yes, I am moving to America," I sighed in a manner far more tragic than had been intended.—"Oh, come on. What's with all this drama? It's like everything about you is so damn serious—your marriage, your America. Look at me. I've never been anywhere; this is the first time in my life that I have left Belgorod, in fact. You know what, I'm jealous that you'll travel and see all these new places. No need to mope. You'll meet new people. You know, people live everywhere, and everywhere they're human—in Leningrad, in Belgorod, in your crazy America . . . Just people."

Could she be that wise? That perceptive? Or did people just say such soothing things out of habit or because they heard them said in the films? Where does one get the right words? She shuddered ("Cold! Cold! Cold!") and cuddled up to me, making herself even more comfortable; my arm was going numb because I dared not move it for fear of ruining our instant companionship. I felt her lips brush against my neck, just above the collarbone. "It's nothing, don't get too excited," she smiled, "it's just a little thank you for keeping me warm. Your marriage is safe, no worries . . . By the way, do you know that I used to be married too?"—"*Used to*? What happened?"—"What happened? What usually happens? He drowned . . . Moron left me a widow at twenty-two."—"I'm sorry . . ."—"Yeah, well, I don't even know if I'm sorry. I guess I'm sorry, but mostly I'm mad at him. I told the idiot a thousand times not to go near the Donets when drunk. The river is tricky, especially by the railroad bridge—it's like a whirlpool down there. But he and his buddies . . . Sort of like your joker friend . . ." She motioned with her chin towards the lilac bushes. "I know the type . . . So the three of them wade into the water, only two come out. They were so wasted, they didn't even realize that one was missing."—"I'm sorry."—"Thanks, life goes on, as they say. But I have something to live for. Look—here . . ." She rummaged in her purse and fished out a small picture of a blond, unsmiling toddler. "Here, see . . . my son, my little boy, my everything."—"He is very . . . handsome," I lied.—"I know." Her smile was warm and earnest. "He is the best thing in the world, my mother is watching after him, but he knows I'll be back soon. I promised to bring him a toy from Leningrad. He must be already asleep by now, probably dreaming about his new toy. What should I get him? What do you think?" Oh, a pang of conscience—we had forgotten to buy a present for Yurik's boy, who was about the same age as Lisa's. She didn't wait for my response, she had moved on to a new subject: "Do you believe in God?"—"In God?!"—"Yes, in God. Do you believe in God?"—"I don't really think I do. Never really thought about it much . . ."—"Well, I do, always have."—"But you said you were a witch . . ."—"So what? Witches can believe in God too. He's always been good to me, he listens to my prayers." I thought that a strange confession from someone who had recently lost her husband to drowning. "So you're in luck, because I will pray for you too now," Lisa continued. "I won't pray every day or even every week, but once in a while I will and you'll feel it. You probably won't even know what it is because you will have forgotten me by then, but you'll feel this, you know, warmth, and when you feel it you'll know that someone is praying for you."

A lonely figure appeared in the alley and moved towards us. As if on cue, the searchlight illuminated the playground and the alley and we saw that it was Lera—walking briskly, alone. She looked . . . it was hard to tell what she looked like. Annoyed? Amused? She waved at us: "The rocket launch has been scrapped, the cosmonaut is unconscious. Hope you guys had better luck." She brushed tufts of grass and tiny twisted twigs from the front of her skirt. She didn't appear particularly upset. "You'll find your buddy out there in the bushes, passed out. You'd better fetch him and make sure he makes that Moscow night train." She turned to her girlfriend: "Lizok, I hate ruining your bliss, but we really have to run, they are locking up the dorm in forty-five minutes." Lisa wiggled herself free of my jacket (and my arm) and got up. Lera shook my hand ceremoniously: "It was nice meeting you. Tell your friend he was fun until he . . . wasn't. One more thing: I had to borrow a fiver from him for the cab fare. I never take other people's money, especially the money from passed out people, but we don't really have a choice here, we need to get back to the dorm before they lock us out. Tell him I'll pay him back if our paths ever cross again."

Momentarily, I felt the piercing pain of separation and it took me a few seconds to compose myself, to think calmly that yes, of course, they have to run, they have to get back to the dorm, and eventually back to Belgorod, where a little boy is fast asleep in his bed in one of those faceless, soulless block apartments, not far from the fast-flowing river that had recently claimed his father, watched over by a weary middle-aged woman. Of course, they had to run. And they did. And that was that. Well . . . almost. Because about fifty meters away Lisa stopped in her tracks, turned around, and started walking hurriedly back towards me. "Come here," she motioned impatiently. We met at the very edge of the cone of light cast by the lamp. She was shivering again and slightly out of breath. "I couldn't leave like that without saying goodbye," she sighed. "I'd like to give you something to remember me by, something small, you know." She brought her face very close to mine and for the first time I realized how pretty she was. "We're friends, right? So I'll give you a kiss, not a girlfriend kiss but a friendly kiss, you know, like I'm your sister. Do you understand?" I nodded, but I didn't. "Come here, closer, closer, here . . ." she whispered. That kiss . . . there was nothing friendly about it. She pulled away from me. "You see, it could've been nice, it could've been *very* nice," she smiled. "Now you'll remember me, I've branded you for life. That's what we witches do." She turned around and ran down the alley to catch up with her friend. And *that* was that . . . I looked at my watch. We would still be able to make the Moscow train, provided I could locate the comatose Yurik, lying somewhere in the lilac bushes, and transport him to the station.

***

And that's how I got to say goodbye to my friend—in a coach compartment on the midnight Leningrad-Moscow express, late in October. I gave the irritable bleached-haired conductor my last three rubles, in return extracting from her a promise to make sure Yurik got off the train in Moscow. "Ok, but only if he doesn't throw up," she warned me grimly. "If he pukes, I'm not cleaning up after him, I'll kick his ass off the train in Bologoye."—"He never does," I assured her. It was true, he never did. With fumbling care, I adjusted his pillow and covered him with a blue woolen blanket. I was about to leave the compartment when he opened his eyes and his lips formed a familiar crooked smile. He whispered something inaudible; I couldn't quite hear him and moved closer, placing my ear right next to his lips. And then I heard it: "Don't fuck it up . . . my brother . . . I love you . . ." The conductor tapped me impatiently on the shoulder and motioned for me to get off the train.

The metro was already closed and I had no money left for a cab, so I walked. I walked down Nevsky, past the buildings that I knew so well, so intimately. They were destined to become memories too. I crossed the bridge back to the island, retracing our steps earlier in the day, and paused on the other side to take in the night view of the city, trying to make that memory permanent. The rituals of departure are like copper etchings, I thought. Later that night, I lay in bed next to Maya, her breathing calm and even. Our boy's breathing was heavier than hers. From time to time he stirred in his crib and whimpered quietly, almost imperceptibly. I listened to him, filled with tenderness and pity—as always. And then I tried to think of Yurik—passed out on that bunk bed, under a filthy blue blanket, carried by the night train towards Moscow. I tried to think of his next day as a story of his return journey, which with time would gain a life of its own and morph into a tiny and insignificant artefact of history.

In that story, I see him woken early in the morning by the rude train conductor. The train has arrived in Moscow and he is the last one to disembark and walk down the platform towards the arrivals hall. His hangover is wicked, and his head is throbbing, and he needs a smoke to better compose himself before venturing to make the transfer to another train station. He also needs a drink, desperately. The line at the beer kiosk is your typical morning affair: the down-and-outs in search of relief, the train station transient types, but also the more conventional lot—those who drink beer instead of coffee on their way to work.

He smokes greedily; one of the local clochards bums a cigarette off him. He doesn't mind, he is generous, booze and cigarettes are to be shared—a glue holding humanity together. He finally gets his beer and blows the foam off the top. It's warm and watered down, but it's, you know, beer and it revives him. He is now strong enough to get on the metro and endure the thirty-minute ride to Kursk railway station to catch the commuter to Vladimir. The four hours on the train he mostly sleeps, pressing his burning forehead to the cool window glass. The window is streaked with dirt and grime, but he remains oblivious. He frequently wakes up and steps into the gangway for a smoke. There are gaps between the metal plates of the gangway floor and while smoking he observes the endless, thunderous parade of sleepers racing down below.

In Vladimir, he has a few hours to kill before the scheduled afternoon bus back to his village. Thankfully, the station kiosk still has some beer on tap—that late in the day it's mostly water, but it doesn't really matter, not that much anyway. He walks slowly up the hill to the cathedral and lowers himself onto a grassy slope—hands first, then the rest of his aching body. He still has time for a nap; and if he oversleeps, so what, there'll be another bus later in the evening. He lies on the faded grass in his favorite snow angel position and drifts off almost immediately. The tired late October sun beats down on his stubbly chin and sore eyelids and makes him smile—the sun is his friend, it'll wake him up in time for the bus.

It's one of those beetle-like Lviv buses that connect Vladimir with the bleak expanse outside the city. If he is lucky he'll find a seat by the window, but it's unlikely. Most of the passengers are older women on their way back to their villages from exhausting grocery trips to Moscow—and he always gives his seat up for a woman. Or for anyone who is older. That's one of the few moral principles that he holds dear. The bus will leave the terminal after a delay (it always does) and rumble through the city on the way out into the countryside. As soon as the bus reaches the outskirts it picks up speed considerably, it needs to go fast to gather enough torque to climb the hills on the other side of the Klyazma. The road is full of potholes and the ride is bumpy; the bus has been in service since 1971 and the suspension is shot to pieces—too bad for the riders but, truth be told, many of them experienced worse. The bus rolls by the textile factory and the ball-bearing plant, and soon after it crosses a weather-bleached city limits sign it is finally free of Vladimir's industrial drabness. The bus races up the provincial highway and each time it gets to the crest of another hill it grows smaller in size, slowly melting into the landscape—until it is only a tiny, rounded dot, like the chaffer beetle on which it was apparently modeled. And then, in an instant, even the dot has gone, vanished, swallowed up by the vast and indifferent country.

Red Dress*

In Prague. He arrived from Amsterdam by bus—his first such trip, and for a few hours, he thought of himself as one of those carefree hitchhikers whose oversized backpacks accentuated their worldly elan, their gravitas. He was not free of worries. Quite to the contrary: he was full of them. But as long as he stayed on that bus, he could feign nonchalance. A free spirit is easy enough to fake.

And he had some experience. It used to be his habit to plop down on the steps of the metro escalator during rush hour. Sitting on that escalator seemed like the most iconoclastic act in the world. And it probably was. The other riders disapproved and either demonstratively ignored his performance or scolded him for it. The nastiest of them, the grim Soviet urbanites, mocked him. The less imaginative ones called the police, the *militsiya*. No, he didn't really feel free, not at all. He felt the humiliation deeply.

But in Prague... It was easy to find a cheap short-term rental. A worn-out young woman approached him at the station as he exited the bus. She spoke some Russian and a smattering of English—enough to explain what she had to offer: a top-floor one-bedroom in the old district, a few tram stops from the railway station, no elevator. That was fine, better than fine. Remarkably cheap. And he didn't need the elevator. *Would he be staying alone?* "No, a friend will arrive this afternoon." *A woman?* "Yes." *That's fine. Just don't throw any parties. Some Russians like throwing parties.* "No, of course not, no parties, it's just going to be the two of us. And, frankly, I'm not really a party type."

After this exchange, they didn't have much to discuss. They took a tram together and got off after a short ride. She led the way up a steep street to an old residential building that looked remarkably similar to the one in which he grew up. The pavement was cracked, and he caught glimpses of the old cobblestones underneath the veneer of dirty asphalt. The chipped marble staircase—a wide, late nineteenth-century affair, its surface polished to perfection by generations of shuffling feet—again reminded him of childhood.

---

* First published as "Red Dress," *Fatal Flaw Literary Magazine* 6 (April 2022).

They climbed the stairs to the fifth floor, their steps echoed in the stairwell and bounced off the graffiti-covered walls. He exchanged the money for a key. The landlady left her phone number in case of emergency. There was no phone line in the apartment, but he could always find a payphone.

"I couldn't find a babysitter for more than two days," she announced to him at the airport, dodging his welcoming kiss. He immediately felt tense—a familiar, unpleasant feeling. She had always set the parameters for their time together—ever since, some two years earlier, she took him by the hand at that party in Mark's art studio. She led him to the bathroom. "Wait," she said then, the first thing she had said to him since Mark introduced them hours earlier. She left and soon returned with a pile of towels, which she spread on the floor to cover the tiles. "Here." She pointed at the towels. He was taken aback by this display of unsentimental practicality. They made love in almost complete silence. She moaned a little, a self-directed sort of sound, as if she was having a quiet conversation with herself. Even inside of her, he felt superfluous, absent from the scene. He didn't know then that the sensation was not fleeting. Afterward, he attempted pillow talk, but she shrugged at the foolishness of holding such conversations beside a leaking faucet. He volunteered to walk her home. She said, "Sure, why not?"

They walked through falling snow. He racked his brain to find words that wouldn't make him sound dull. But every single word that came to his mind sounded like a disastrous cliché that he dreaded to utter. She didn't seem like someone who would forgive a cliché. Finally, she relented. "Do you keep track of the number of your lovers?" she asked. He did. Of course, he did. She spread out her gloved hands as a peace offering. "You're my number ten if you care to know," she said.—"It's a nice, round number," he joked.

It was easy to absorb such revelations at the beginning of a fling. Flings allowed for banter. Flings were like easy friendships until they withered away or else turned into something one couldn't control. Later, her confessionary tales would haunt him. Tossing and turning on a mattress in his East Village sublet, he couldn't stop thinking about those other nine. From thousands of miles away, he tried to invent ways to emasculate them, to reduce them to insignificance, to dust. But for that, he needed to know more about them, about each one of them—and that's where he set up a trip wire for his own inflamed imagination. He would roll off his mattress, pick up the phone, and make another forty-dollar phone call—just to hear her tired voice, attuned to its modalities, trying to get the full measure of her mood, searching for scraps of tenderness.

In Prague, on the bus from the airport, she fell asleep on his shoulder, which grew numb because he was afraid to wake her. She always complained about lack of sleep. He fretted that she wouldn't like the apartment and wished he had the money for nicer accommodation. But he didn't really have any money. At the final stop, he gently roused her.

"What? Already?" She sounded annoyed, and he felt like apologizing for everything that provoked her: for the bumpy flight from Moscow, for the bus that didn't take long enough to get to the city center, for the necessity (once again) of finding a babysitter, for the shabby apartment that awaited them, for his own anxiousness, for Prague—in all its drab, post-socialist glory.—"We're almost there. Just ten more minutes and we'll be home."

How strange that he already thought of a newly rented fifth-floor apartment as *home.* In the apartment, she undressed and went straight into the shower. He waited nervously for her to return. He tried to read but couldn't focus; he couldn't even pretend to read. He paced the living room until she finally opened the bathroom door, wrapped in a towel, and let him embrace her. "I missed you so much, so much," he whispered pitifully. She smiled—a condescending smile, a smile that gave him some hope—untucked the towel and let it drop on the floor.—"You're such a fool," she said with a sigh. "You act as if I were unavailable. But here I am, right here with you in Prague. Ok? Now come here." She took his hand and nodded at the massive, unsteady-looking futon in the corner.

Later that evening, they walked around Prague and it almost felt like a regular sightseeing trip. Before they left the apartment, she unpacked her bag and put on a snug-fitting red dress that he had never seen before. "I bought it for the trip," she explained. "Mother thought it was way too tight on me, so I thought, 'Perfect—I should go ahead and buy it.' Don't get too excited, I didn't buy it because of you."

They approached the clock tower in the Old Town Square just in time for the hourly show. The four figures framing the clock came alive, turning the arrival of the top of the hour into an animated performance. "Look," he said. Eager to show off, he pointed out the figure of a skeleton. "Death marks the passage of time. But the sinners—the other three figures—refuse to accept it. See how they shake their heads?" She shrugged.—"That's understandable," she said. "No one wants to grow old. But you can't argue with Death; it's silly. They can shake their heads all they want, but the skeleton will still strike on the hour. It's fate. How old is the clock?"—"I don't know. Sixteenth century or something?"—"Well, you see," she said. "It's what . . .

five hundred years' worth of dead people? Proves my point." It probably did. He was not sure.

They crossed the Vltava via Charles Bridge, whose length was occupied by a parade of souvenir stands and roaming hawkers. They bought a bottle of red wine, which he was prepared to drink straight out of the bottle, but she insisted that they buy plastic cups. They drank the wine on a park bench on the slope overlooking the river. Sightseeing boats dotted the water. The illuminated Old Town shimmered on the opposite bank. Prague Castle loomed grandiose behind them. "What an unbelievable view," he said. He meant it.—"It's alright," she said. "I've seen worse." Her smile was vacant, vaguely standoffish. She had a way of smiling like that, as if establishing a defensive perimeter. "I'm exhausted. Let's head back. We can grab something to eat on the way back to the apartment. Did you notice that weird café near the Jewish cemetery? Did you see its name? Pushkin! Can you believe it? Why would they name a café after a poet? But, whatever—we can still buy something there and pretend the name means nothing to us."

Back in the apartment, they made love again. And then again. The second time, she grumbled, "You're wearing me out. I'm not used to these acrobatics. I'm an overworked single mother, remember? Enough, let me sleep, ok?" She kissed his neck, and at that very second he thought that he could not be without her—not even for a day. He would not be able to go back to his studio in Alphabet City. He could not spend another lonely night on that mattress, her voice ringing in his ears, obsessing about those nine who had known her body. The tension, the angst, the exhausting, unending lust would never go away. He was still hard. That inability to relax, let the tension out of his body, created panic in him. She felt his erection and slowly ran her fingertips along the rigid shaft, all the way up to the smooth and vulnerable tip, which she flicked lightly—a casual dismissal, not a promise of relief. "Oh, no, not again," she said. "What is it, a circus performance? You need to let me sleep, dear. Get some rest. You're being too dramatic." She pulled away and rolled over to the other side of the futon, next to the wall, where she buried her head under the pillow and said goodnight.

There was no release. And he took no pride in his stubborn erection. It scared him, made him worry about tomorrow and the day after tomorrow when she would be back in Moscow and he . . . What would he do then? After she had left again? He eventually dozed off, but real sleep evaded him. *These days I sleep fitfully. Not so much sleep as a strange state of semi-wakefulness. I see images floating just above my eyelashes; sometimes, it's the faces of my late parents, but it's often just landscapes, riverbanks, gorges. Things like that—sort of like an Andersen fairy tale.* His gravely ill father confided this to him a few years later, three days before he died. It would be their last phone conversation. "Dad, I know exactly what you're talking about," he told him—a response that puzzled his father, who was too weak to demand a full explanation.

He woke up in the middle of the night to the steady sound of rain beating on the rusty cornice outside the window. He crawled out of bed and tiptoed across the room. The street below showed almost no signs of life. It was possessed by the rain, by the streams of water that flowed down the incline towards the poorly lit tram stop at the corner. The water collected in vast puddles before the dark mouths of the courtyards opening onto the street. He spotted a lonely drunk splashing through the puddles, moving slowly uphill on a precarious but determined mission to reach the peak.

She stirred in bed. He tensed up, fearful he had interrupted her sleep. Suddenly he heard a muffled sound. She was not asleep. She was crying, her face pressed into the pillow. He leaned over and touched her shoulder, but she waved him off with a vehement shrug.

"What's wrong? What can I do?" he pleaded with her, understanding full well what was coming.—"Fuck you," she sniveled. "There is nothing, nothing that you can do. You're weak, indecisive. You're a disappointment."

He stared at the wallpaper. Its flowery pattern reminded him of his childhood room that he shared with his parents. Once, when he was seven or eight, he was awakened at night by his mother's sobs. And there was another sound: the drone of his father's whisper, cajoling her, talking her out of her tears. He had pressed his tiny palms against his ears and entered a realm of silence, where he remained for what seemed like hours. When he finally allowed himself to hear again, all was quiet in the room; his parents appeared to be asleep. The next morning, they looked their normal selves and he promised himself to forget the bad dream. Only, one rarely forgets such dreams.

Facing him on the bed, she continued. "I thought I wanted to be with you. I thought you were different. But you're fucking weak. I was so happy, so happy . . . last year. Last year? It feels like last century." She recoiled as he reached to comfort her. "Don't touch me. And I don't even like Prague, and I don't care about the clock and the old square, and what's his name? Kafka? I don't care about him, either. And Pushkin . . . Why did they name a beer hall after him? I'm so tired of this. I want to be home with my daughter. There is no future. None." She turned her tear-smeared face to the wall and refused to talk to him again.

They didn't speak on the bus to the airport. She knew how to remain silent and her silence drained him of any will to live. There was no joy. He thought of a possible dramatic resolution to this crisis, of some bold move that could make her looming departure less final. But the closer they got to the airport, the less likely such an intervention seemed. He was losing her. She was right, he thought. He was weak.

At the terminal, without so much as looking at him, she headed straight for passport control. He lingered by the barrier. In films, he had seen miraculous happy endings at airports. Last-minute changes of fortunes. He watched her present her ticket and passport to the border guard, who examined them briefly and stamped both. She crossed the border and stopped. His heart jumped. *Will she run to him? Will she offer him one last chance?* She motioned for him to come closer. He obeyed instantly. "Shit," she said. "I left my red dress in the apartment. Just the perfect ending to this nightmare." He saw a ray of light. Here was some hope, at least.—"I'll get it for you," he gushed. "I'll go back right away and get it for you."—"Don't bother, the flight is in an hour. It's just shitty all around, that's all."—"I'll get it for you." He pleaded with her. "I'll get it and mail it to you. I promise." She looked at him doubtfully, then waved her hand dismissively.—"Ah, you promise. You and your promises. I don't believe you." She shook her head and turned on her heels. A minute later, she disappeared into the terminal.

Some years later, he would reread Stefan Zweig's *Amok* to better understand the state he was in during those last two days in Prague, the feverish days after her departure. He rushed back to the apartment, but the landlady had already cleaned it and left. He roamed the neighborhood looking for a working payphone and finally located one across the street from the tram stop. He called the landlady's number that he had kept in his pocket. A child answered the phone, but they couldn't understand each other. He stayed close to the payphone and continued to call every half hour. Each time, the same child answered. "Krasnoye platye!" he yelled into the receiver. The child responded in Czech. "Tvoje matka tam?" he yelled. The child hung up and stopped answering the phone.

Exhausted, he looked up at the sky. It was dark. Night had descended on Prague. She must have landed in Moscow already. She was probably back with her daughter. The thought of her being, this very moment, two thousand kilometers away seared him with pain. He couldn't go on like this.

He found a cheap hostel hidden from view in a small alley by the river. The room sported a dozen beds, half of which were occupied. He didn't really care. He asked a woman at the front desk to wake him at six. That turned out to be unnecessary; he couldn't fall asleep. At five, he quietly got up, picked up his bag, and left the hostel.

It was still semi-dark outside; he walked through the empty city to the railway station and deposited his bag in one of the lockers. Half the night he had agonized over the appropriate time to call the landlady and, without much reasoning, resolved that seven o'clock would be just right. To his delight, she picked up the phone. *Oh yes, it's ok, not too early, she was about to leave for work. And yes, she got the dress, she wanted to return it but had no idea how to find him. And no, unfortunately, they cannot meet right now—a company bus is picking her up in ten minutes to take her to her forty-eight-hour shift at a steel factory in Kladno. And if he wanted to get the dress that day, he would have to come to Kladno—an hour's journey from Prague by bus or commuter train.*

They agreed to meet by the factory gate during her afternoon break. It was still early, and he could have spent a few hours strolling about Prague, but he was too anxious, too depleted by insomnia to indulge in sightseeing. He took the earliest commuter to Kladno. Once there, he found an empty bench in a small park by the station.

It was a workday morning with few people strolling through the park. An old woman, in a blue polyester windbreaker, occupied an adjacent bench. A paper bag filled with breadcrumbs rested on her lap. Now and then, she fished out a handful of crumbs and spread them generously on the ground in front of her, much to the delight of the fluttering pigeons. Such scenes were all too familiar. They belonged to his own past, his Leningrad childhood. The pigeons looked exactly the same: greedy street urchins whose brutishness he disdained. But he felt, in his heart, for the old woman feeding them. She belonged to a timeless breed of caretakers—survivors of wars, famines, foreign occupations, and endless personal tragedies. The compulsive pigeon feeders of his childhood were like this woman. Only, they did not wear polyester windbreakers.

He met the landlady by the factory gate. She looked even more tired than she did when she approached him at the bus station two days ago. She handed him the dress in a plastic bag and hurried back to her workroom. There was a rundown post office around the corner from the station. He made it there forty minutes before closing time to mail the package to Moscow. The clerk, a friendly middle-aged woman, spoke basic Russian. He tried to extract from her some assurances that the package would reach the addressee. She couldn't give him any guarantees. "Russia, you know . . ." She made a noncommittal gesture with her hand, conjuring up the unpredictable fate of postal packages crossing the Russian border. "Hopefully, it will arrive . . . at some point." He had hoped for more, for something more definitive, for at least a semblance of certainty to relieve his anguish. But certainty remained unattainable. There was no release.

Back in Prague, he managed to place a phone call to Moscow. She picked up. The connection was poor, but he was glad of it. At least he could pretend that the hostility he discerned in her voice was the function of faulty, dated equipment. He told her he had tracked down the dress and mailed it to her. "Whatever," she said. He told her that hearing her voice always made him nervous. She said nothing. He told her how much he missed her, how desperate he was for her. This desperation caused him to lose sleep and focus. She cut him off mid-sentence: "All you ever talk about is yourself. Always." There was a long, static-filled silence. And then she told him it was over. No more extensions, no third chances.

Over. Over. Over.

***

"I only have an hour," she announced briskly. Instantly he experienced a long-dormant sensation—a tiny knot tightening in his stomach, a fleeting sense of déjà vu that dissipated as quickly as it arrived. "It's been a *craaazy* day," she continued, almost without a pause. "A partners' meeting at the office, then a parent-teacher conference at Adam's school, then I had to take him to his swimming lesson, dash back to work, back to the pool to pick up Adam and deliver him into the arms of his piano teacher. Damn! At least the other kid is all grown up. Who wants to be a modern woman?"

The rooftop bar of the posh hotel in Chelsea was too swanky for his taste. She had texted him the address last night, soon after he checked into his Airbnb off Russell Square. He was not surprised by this expensive choice; he had come to expect no less from the moneyed Russian cohort in London. She exhibited the telltale signs of wealth, which were clear even to him: a Patek Philippe watch, an inconspicuous ring of white gold encrusted with tiny stones (diamonds, he assumed), a white leather Gucci bag. He ordered a martini; she asked for a glass of red wine. The martini was excellent: well balanced, not too dirty, terribly expensive.

She had pecked him on the cheek when she first walked in. Now, she critically examined his face and produced a handkerchief to wipe off the smudge of lipstick. "One would think I'm marking you. That's what they call a kiss of death, right?" she said, laughing. He smiled back. "You look great, terrific." She shook her head.—"Bullshit, I'm old. No one is getting younger, my friend, *no one*. Each year it takes more effort to remain presentable. Effort and money." She looked at him. "It's so much easier for you men. So totally unfair, but that's how it is. How long has it been? Twenty years?"—"Twenty-one."—"Whatever, just proves my point."—"The passage of time . . ." She shrugged.—"It's a cliché, but sure."

She received a text and appeared momentarily distracted by it. "Sorry, work stuff. So, where were we?"—"The passage of time."—"Right, yes. Anything to slow it down. I work out like a maniac. I mean, whenever I get a breather. 'A gym rat with a yoga mat.' That's what my housekeeper calls me. Did I tell you? We just bought a new place in Notting Hill. So now our whole life revolves around the house. Well, and Adam, of course." He didn't remember her being that chatty and so eager to share the details of her life. She took another sip of her wine. "And my housekeeper. She's Ghanaian, and really something. I absolutely adore her. She tells me white women are terrified of their bodies. Can you believe it? I think she's right. It's so strange, I never thought of myself as a white woman. Not until we moved to London."

He found it very easy to talk to her. There was a warmth and genuine friendliness about her that he didn't recognize. It seemed as if he had just met a pleasant, if slightly too talkative, stranger. And then he remembered. "Oh, I almost forgot. Did you ever get that package I sent? The red dress?" She looked at him uncomprehendingly.—"What red dress?"—"The red dress I sent you from Prague. Or, rather, from that other town—its name escapes me now." She struggled to remember but finally gave up.—"Nope. Sorry, I don't remember anything about that dress. A red dress, you say?"—"Yes," he said, rummaging inside his computer bag. "The one you wore in Prague." He pulled out a photograph. In it, she stood leaning on the balustrade of Charles Bridge in a red dress, looking past the camera. She took the photograph from his hands and studied it.—"Shit. I used to be so thin. Why did you have to show it to me? No one is getting younger and especially not thinner."—"What about the dress? Do you remember it?"—"I don't. Sorry. You have a better memory than I do. It's unfair, so unfair."

Another text message interrupted them. Again, she apologized for getting distracted. "I would've turned it off, but I can't. My business partner is a major pain. Well, since we're sharing photos, let me show you my fam, the two handsome boys—the hubby and Adam." She showed him photos on her iPhone. The kid looked about twelve, sporting an Arsenal jersey, blond with dark-brown eyes and dimpled cheeks. A cute boy next to his good-looking father.

She ordered another glass of red, asking the server to make it quick, she would be leaving soon. When the glass arrived, she lifted it against the sunlight. The wine absorbed the light and filled with cloudy crimson. "You know," she said, slowly, "sometimes I wonder. Especially after a couple of these." She set the glass down on the table. "I wonder . . . that's the wrong word. I need to be careful here. I am curious . . . yes, curious what it would've been like if . . ." She smiled innocently, apparently unsure about her inebriated flight of fancy. They fell silent, but the brief pause was not too awkward. She shuffled in her seat. "Well, curiosity killed the cat. That's what the English say, and let me tell you, these chaps have a way with words."

She asked for the check. When it arrived, she cupped her hands over it, refusing to let him pay. "My treat, my pleasure." After paying, she picked up her phone and ordered an Uber. "Well, I have to run now," she said. "But listen, you should stay here a bit longer, order their carpaccio. It's the best in London, at least that's what the website says." She smiled again, an open, friendly smile. "And the museums are all within walking distance. The British Museum and the Victoria and Albert are open late on Fridays. I think the V&A has a special exhibit on vintage dresses or something. Jesus, I sound like a tour guide. But you'll enjoy it. Shake hands?"

They shook hands across the table. She picked up her bag and was about to leave, then paused, furrowing her brow: "Wait a minute," she said. "Would you believe it? I do remember that dress. Yes, of course I remember it. It did arrive . . . a few months later, I think. You know, the Russian post . . ." She made a waving gesture with her wrist that brought him back to that agonizing afternoon in Kladno—the Czech postal clerk unable to assure him of timely delivery. The memory flickered for a second, too brief to knock the wind out of him. "I can't believe I forgot about it," she continued, sounding bemused by her own forgetfulness. "I never wore it again. Well, let me qualify. I tried to wear it once, on a date. Even put the dress on but decided it would be too . . . I don't know. Weird? Too dramatic? So, no, I took it right off. And you know what, you shouldn't have shown me that photograph—I look so thin, so very young in it." She sighed. "Alright then, now I really must run. The Uber driver is texting me. Don't be a stranger, ok? Next time you're in London we'll have you over for dinner. You should meet my adorable boys."

And she was gone. He stayed for another half hour as she suggested, sipping his second martini and answering work emails on his phone. A late afternoon visit to the British Museum sounded like an excellent idea, and he would enjoy the walk through the park. Ever since his elementary school days he'd had a sentimental attachment to London's landmarks, whose names were hammered into his head in tedious English lessons: the Tower of London, Nelson's Column, Piccadilly Circus, Hyde Park and Speakers' Corner, the British Museum. And he grew up addicted to long-winded British novels—Dickens, Galsworthy, Maugham—that, in his imagination, forged an intimate connection to the distant city. If only someone had told him back then that, one day, he would walk the same streets and visit the museums and swap memories with an old friend while sipping a martini in a rooftop bar.

He left the bar in a good mood. He chose not to think this through, not to search for the origins of the joy that now overwhelmed him. His flight was not until the next evening. There was plenty of time for museums, for sightseeing. He might even return to this stylish hotel. Why not? Sure, the place was expensive, but the martinis were wonderful. He felt so free, so relieved in a way not experienced since childhood when sudden bursts of happiness sometimes lit up his days. But that was long ago. And even then he understood that joy could not be preserved, that it lacked permanence, that sooner or later life interferes and drains it of its essence.

A Phone Call*

—Hello?

—You have exactly twenty seconds to guess who's calling you!

—I really . . .

—Come on! *Guess*!

—I can't . . . but you sound . . . familiar?

—Well, thank you, that's at least something . . . *Familiar* . . . And you sound so *formal*. Is it because I'm calling you at work?

—No, it's because I'm still trying to figure out who you are . . .

—Ok, fine, let me help you, let's see if your brain cells are still intact. Close your eyes, meditate for a second—imagine that you're back in Leningrad, late 1980s, it's May or June, the white nights, the bridges are up (aren't they always up during the white nights?). You and I, the two of us, are stuck across the river. I'm wearing a light muslin dress with draw strings up front. Off-white color with floral pattern. You tell me I look like a Latvian peasant and that no one in Leningrad would wear a dress like that. Then you kiss me . . .

—Jesus . . .

—Well, you do. You did. Don't you remember?

—Vaguely, it's all a bit generic. But I can't help thinking that I recognize your voice.

—Of course, you do. How could you not? You poor fellow, your poor, poor brain cells. I am . . . are you ready? Gulp for air, my friend, take a deep breath, then hold it in for a few seconds. Now . . . exhale . . . I am . . . N.

—?

—You remember me now, don't you? If not then I'm hanging up and . . . I dunno . . . swallowing my favorite poison? I know it's been a while but we're not *that* old. At least that's how I prefer to think about it: not *that* old. I even wrote you a few letters when you were in the service. Not often, but I certainly did. For my twentieth I had a nice picture taken—wearing that

---

* First published as "A Phone Call," *BigCityLit* (Winter 2021).

floral dress. I looked *radiant* in it. Not my word, by the way—yours. I mailed you the picture and that's what you said in your thank you letter. Your words, not mine. *Radiant.* Like a radiant Latvian peasant, right?

—Oh god, yes, of course! N.! That picture, I still have it somewhere in my army archive. Actually, just last summer I was going through the folder and found the photo. You did look radiant in it! Glowing!

—Finally! Dude, time has not been kind to you. A bit slow, aren't you? Ha! How did you manage to make it in America? My sister-in-law lives in Baltimore. She says, in the States, you slow down, you die. Just kidding. Actually, not kidding—I'm pretty sure she meant it. Whatever . . . Yes, glowing . . . That photo—I had just found out that I was pregnant. Literally a couple of hours before the picture was taken. My first husband, you see, not a happy story.

—So you must have a grown-up child . . .

—No and yes. That one didn't grow up, was not even born—a miscarriage, and a bad one too. Probably for the best; the father was really fucked up in his head. He came back from Afghanistan, all messed up. I felt sorry for him, mostly sorry, I think, but also all these other feelings . . . Wonder what they were, actually . . . My mom took one look at him and said: "Run, you fool, run!" My mom is a wise woman, I should have listened to her more often. But who listens to their mothers when you are twenty? I did run eventually, of course.

—So what about the yes part of your answer?

—Oh! Two kids: a boy and a girl, both students now, fantastic children, just fantastic. She's studying to be a hairdresser, he is going to be a programmer, like his dad. His dad, of course, is Robert—my number two. Can I tell you something important about Robert?

—Yes, please tell me.

—Robert is . . . I don't know how to put it . . . He is part of me, we're *so* together, I don't know if it's even possible to be as close as we are. Maybe I'm revealing too much . . . I've had a drink, so never mind me . . . Never mind if I blabber too much. But I know you care about me, so you don't mind if I make a fool of myself, do you?

—No, of course not, and you're not making a fool of yourself. I'd love to learn more about your life.

—You're really nice—that's exactly how I remember you: my polite and *intelligentnyj* Leningrad boy. So sweet. But back to Robert . . . yes, we've been together for so long that I can't even imagine his absence (God forbid, knock on wood, I'm fucking superstitious). You know, I hope you don't mind my saying this, because exes can be weird, you know . . . but Robert and I have not slept in separate beds in twenty years. Not once. My girlfriends don't believe me, they all have separate bedrooms. But I can't even imagine spending a night without Robert next to me. It's like leaving a limb outside before you walk in the door.

—I'm really happy to hear this. So few happy couples out there and every unhappy couple . . .

—I know, I know, you don't have to quote Tolstoy at me, I am not one of your students. Say, they probably all have crushes on you, no?

—No, not in the States. Here, students don't have crushes on their professors and, frankly, it's hard for me to see them that way. They are just . . . I dunno . . . kids.

—Kids?! You're not teaching elementary school, are you? How old were we when we . . . well, when we first met?

—Eighteen? Nineteen?

—Right, and we were young, to be sure, but hardly kids. I was planning to marry you, for God's sake. And then your army, and my marriages, and your leaving for America and getting married (or was it the other way around?) and never writing me one fucking letter. In twenty years! That's not kids' stuff. That's fucking adult stuff.

—You . . . were planning to marry me? I had no idea! Did we . . .?

—Yes, *yes*! Those brain cells, those poor brain cells—you don't remember anything, my poor dear. Ok, let me pour myself another drink, I need it right now. Here, wait . . . I'll explain it to you. In case you haven't noticed yet (being so slow and everything), I'm really good at explaining things. Do you know that I googled you?

—No, but now that you mention it, I did wonder how you'd tracked me down. And I'm happy you did. Just curious . . .

—Drink and google, buddy. It used to be drink and dial, now it's . . . google. I heard you on the radio. Don't ask how and why, just heard you on the radio, and then . . . well, googled. You're like the easiest guy in the universe to find—your life's like an open book. I even found a website where your students complain that your classes are boring. Bastards! And you, you probably never even googled me. Don't you drink anymore?

—I do—of course. I mean, I do drink, but . . .

—It's ok, no worries, I'll let you off the hook. For now. And you wouldn't be able to find me by my maiden last name anyway. So I choose to think that you did google me but nothing came up, right? Don't say a word! Let's pretend that's exactly what happened. And I'll take this silence for a yes. Yes? Thank you, dear.

—. . .

—Are you still there? Listen, I'm calling you for a reason. The weather has been just awful around here. We now live close to the sea, in Robert's family home; it's a large Finnish A-frame, 1929 construction, which is just wonderful when the sun is shining . . . But you know, the Baltics is not the Mediterranean, it's capricious like . . . like I used to be at eighteen. When the fog rolls in it gets dark and damp and soggy. The wind howls, it comes from all the different directions at once and chills your bones and pierces your soul. I hope I'm not sounding too poetic to your taste. Hope not, I'm always suspicious of poetry. What I'm trying to say is this: it's fucking cold here half of the year. But not just that, that's not the only thing (*obviously*) I'm trying to tell you. Damn, I'm being too chatty . . . Look, I did call you for a reason. Can I confess? Are you ready? You'd better sit down . . . Oh, hell, what am I saying . . . Ha-ha . . . You're *already* seated, you're in your *office*. I'm calling you at your American office to tell you something that I have never shared with any living soul. Except for Robert, of course, because Robert and I—we share everything, we keep no secrets from each other. It's a simple thing, a fact of life, of *my* life, that I believe you should know: I have never gotten over you.

—What? I mean, that can't be true. Twenty years? You disappeared so long ago. You lived your life . . .

—Sheesh! Please, don't say a word. You really don't have anything to say, because it's not your story, it's mine. I never stopped loving you. As simple and as complicated as that. Robert knows. I told him when he and I started dating that there was someone in my past that I just couldn't forget. I asked him if he could live with it. He said yes, absolutely. And he has lived with it all these years. He is the best thing that ever happened to me, I would never live with anyone but him. And he knows it—in his strong and calm and confident Robert way. Falling asleep next to him makes a day worth living. Our bed is up in the loft, the window opens onto the dunes—you can hear the waves from where we sleep. And the mattress is super comfortable, with memory foam, it's IKEA.

—Sounds cozy—a sea view, an A-frame loft . . . You know how many people would like to have this life?

—I know, I am not ungrateful. Ungratefulness is one of those deadly sins, right next to lust . . . or sloth . . . one of those. I am not like that. In a way, that's why I've loved you all these years—out of gratitude for that week we spent together in your apartment on Petrogradskaya. It was a high point, but also a vanishing point. You were about to be drafted, and I knew that we wouldn't be able to continue forever. We didn't make any plans, but you couldn't get enough of me. I felt so . . . wanted. There was a moment when I thought that maybe we could get married, you know—to make the moment last a bit longer . . . Am I making you uncomfortable?

—Well, it's not that . . . It's just . . . Did you say Petrogradskaya . . . ?

—Yes, your apartment, steeped in silence, just the sound of our lovemaking, and the old clock ticking. What's that line? "The apartment is quiet as paper . . ." It's not like me to recite poetry. Blame it on the wine, I guess. Sorry, I don't want to make you uncomfortable, and God knows I don't want your students to see you blushing later—they might write some nasty stuff about you on that weird site. Why do they even let them write such things about their teachers? And your mother, of course. *She* was unhappy! What, some crazy Polish *shiksa* ensnaring her precious Jewish son? She would've never accepted me! I knew that the moment she snubbed me when you brought me over.

—That certainly doesn't sound like my mom. Or my dad, for that matter. They never encouraged me to date Jewish girls. In a way, it was sort of the other way around . . . Also, that thing about Petrogradskaya . . .

—Don't interrupt me, please. You keep interrupting . . . I know professors are used to hearing the sound of their voices, but just give me a few minutes, bear with me . . . Remember that old Soviet film *I Ask to Accuse Klava K. of My Death*? The Soviet Union was a dump, but they did make some amazing films. Remember the final scene from that movie?

—No, I don't really . . . Sorry.

—Why "sorry"? Stop apologizing. You keep apologizing—like befits a good Jewish boy, a good Jewish son. No need. So, the film . . . The guy in the film can't get over a snooty brunette who has tormented him since kindergarten. There's another girl, who is in love with him—your typical love triangle—and the main character is trying desperately to fall in love with the good one. And he just can't . . . But the other girl is wise (sort of like my mother) and she knows that no matter how hard he tries he'll never love her, because you never really get over love. You never do. They showed that film last year on the Russian channel and that final scene just floored me, I couldn't stop bawling. Robert knew instantly why I was crying. My Robert . . .

—I think I remember the film now. Some provincial town, where everyone is smartly and fashionably dressed, they all seem to be chess players, sculptors, and math wizards. The teenagers dance freely in a brightly lit city park to Afrique Simon's "Hafanana." All lies, of course. But a lie, when properly remembered, can become the truth . . . Just before, you mentioned Petrogradskaya . . . Why? I never lived on Petrogradskaya. I'm from the other side of the river. And my mother . . . what you've described doesn't sound like her. Not at all. She would've never called you a shiksa; I don't believe she knew a single Yiddish word. Just not that kind of family. And I don't recall her being all that possessive. And my father . . . he had something of a blond Slavic fetish. Never practiced what he preached, but preached it he did, nevertheless . . .

—A father? I don't remember him. It was just you and your mom . . .

—*And* my father, *and* my grandma—we all lived together *on the other side of the river.*

— . . . Now you're confusing me, and you should never do that to a woman who has just had a couple of glasses of Malbec. And not just any woman—one who has spent more than twenty years preparing to make this phone call. I'm not twenty like I used to be but far from senile, and you should know, men still check me out. I get catcalls all the time. My sister-in-law tells me in America guys get sent to jail for catcalling. Not in our little progressive republic by the sea. Thank God. Why are you confusing me so?

—I am sorry . . .

—You are sorry again. You should be. You do remember the bridge though, don't you? The raised bridge? I can hear you nodding. You remember the kiss, right? Ah, another nod—I hear it. We cross the bridge by the fortress and walk past the mosque. It's chilly so early in the morning and you're holding me tightly, and I think that all I want is to feel your presence. You're so skinny, a waifish Leningrad boy. Back then I had a weakness for the type, there were so many of you: all polite, shy but hungry—hungry for me. Your mother sensed danger right away—a C-cup-sized Polish shiksa equals *danger*. That whole week we hardly left the room, we avoided her. She made terrible racket in the kitchen and dropped pots and cutlery on the floor every ten minutes—just to make her displeasure known. Duly noted, madame, duly noted. All this nonsense was like an aphrodisiac to me . . . Then, later, after they had drafted you, I kept having weird sex dreams. About us. That's why I hardly ever wrote to you, I just didn't know how to put all those feelings on paper . . . "The apartment is quiet as paper" . . . All those yearnings . . . so exhausting. I slept around a lot after they had taken you away from me, lots of bed-hopping. Each new guy had your eyes, I chose them that way—your chestnut-brown eyes stayed with me even after you left . . . What did you say?

—The eyes . . . My eyes are not brown, they've never been brown. What color? Hard to tell . . . I think they are sort of green or light grey. Definitely not brown . . . And my mom . . . And the bridge . . . The other side of the river . . . N., I'm pretty sure it was not me.

—Not you? And you said it so easily: "Not me" . . . Like a little kid, like you've been waiting for it all along. My little stonewaller . . . "Not me, I didn't do it." Ha-ha. You're funny. But I still love your voice. It's ok, don't bother to apologize. God, you're really into apologies. But that's so you and I love you for that. Robert—he never apologizes. You know why? No? Because he has absolutely nothing to apologize for. His eyes are not brown, by the way, they are . . . well, not brown.

—Listen, I do remember you. Of course, I do. And I am really sorry that it was not me. And I am not apologizing for saying "I'm sorry" . . . Old friendships—they are important to me too. Memories are important, we learn from them . . .

—And that's something you would say. Shit, I'm almost out of wine and the wind is picking up again. What is it exactly that you've learned from this memory?

—My insignificance, I guess?

—Ha! That's a good one. You're my history professor and your eyes are definitely brown, chestnut brown. Do I care what you have to say now? No, not really. Class dismissed, as they say in the movies, especially in that one about Klava K. Poor Klava, it's all her fault. The wind is blowing like *crazy* . . . squalls . . . can you hear it? Wait a sec, I'll put the phone on speaker, I want you to hear the gusts. It's high tide too. Can you hear it? The wind is playing catch-up with the sea. The sea is winning. Robert will be back home soon. I hate it when he drives in this weather. He and I will sleep together tonight on our memory foam. We always do. In more than twenty years, not one night apart. Not once . . . A day worth living . . . I may call you again . . . Don't worry, on *this* number—at your office, not at home. And if there is anything you have to say to me, you can say it now . . .

—Thank you.

—"Thank you" . . . "Thank you" is good. Sufficient. Sort of perfect for the occasion. You are gifted with words, my brown-eyed Leningrad boy. I know you think it's not you. Such delusions . . . And *now* I'm officially out of wine. Too late to drive to the store, too late. And the wind . . . howling . . . The chill. Let's do it again soon, ok? Let's do it again. Good night, my love.

Forgetting Mariam*

"Did it hurt?" He made an effort to sound tender. They were spooning after sex and she took his question for pillow talk. "Hurt? You silly. I'm just noisy. It didn't hurt at all. It was nice." Playfully, she pressed her buttocks into his groin—a lighthearted sign of no regrets harbored. "It was *really* nice. Did you know that by touching a man with her bare butt a woman signals trust?" She was full of such little wisdoms. He couldn't see her face but knew that she was smiling, the sly and contented smile of a woman flattered by her lover's concern. Her lover, her man . . . well, that was an overstatement. To say the least. But at that moment, at that early morning moment, it did feel like they belonged to each other. One-night stands can be like that—deceptively intimate, out-of-thin-air immediate. "Instant coffee, one-day mayflies, or, if you prefer a cliché (which I know you always do), a flash in a pan," that's how his ex, Lisa, talked about her own past casual hookups.

Lisa's sarcasm drove him mad and eventually drove him away. At least, that was the convenient explanation he came up with and then perfected in the course of numerous faux-therapy, post-breakup sessions with his friends and occasional lovers. She drove him away, which really meant that he was a coward and a weakling—an unpleasant but easily provable fact that Lisa never failed to bring up in their increasingly rare phone conversations. It was an amicable divorce and, as such, a source of some pride for both of them. What could be more civilized, Lisa quipped, than parting ways like true adults? He agreed, but a divorce is still a divorce and occasionally a thought of Lisa made him wince—as if someone had pricked at a tender spot with a tiny safety pin. And presently he promptly felt that quick pinprick, but it only lasted for a second, half a second to be exact, and the discomfort was gone before he'd been able to process it. Not now—now was different, now he was lying in bed next to Mariam, her trusting butt pushed up against his wooly lower stomach, his right arm over her side, under her warm armpit (Lisa's voice again: "Remember how back in childhood they would stick a

* First published as "Forgetting Mariam," *San Antonio Review*, no. 5 (Summer 2021), 79–99.

thermometer under your arm? Remember how desperate you were for the mercury to hit the magic thirty-seven degrees and then move just above the fateful red dot? You got a fever, sweetie, no school tomorrow. Oh, the joy, the happiness of having a fever!"), his hand cupping the fullness of her breast, its nipple flattened innocently against his palm. He was hugging her so closely that his lips touched the small of her neck, he felt his nose tickled by a coarse wayward curl that had broken out of her black frizz, also tickled by the barely perceptible and still unfamiliar odor of her post-love sweat.

Mariam laughed: "Hurt?! Oh my, it's like you're not Russian anymore. They must've added something to the water in America. Or what is it you drink over there? Coke? Budweiser? Whatever it is—you have stopped being a Russian man. You even made love like a polite foreigner. You'll start speaking Italian with me next. I once had a fling with an Italian guy. On Cyprus. Just as sweet before sex as after. Not Russians though, oh no, siree, not Russians. Our guys, they just come and go . . . if you know what I mean."—"What about Armenians?"—"How would I know? I never slept with an Armenian. My daughter's father, by the way, was Jewish—just like you. You know what my grandma used to say about Jews and Armenians? No? Get this: 'We Armenians should always take care of the Jews. You know why? No? Because if there are no Jews left, the world will notice that we're next on the list.' Funny, don't you think? My grandma was a riot!" Tenderness—effortless now. But how real? He was old enough to know that about himself—that instant attachment to the immediate, the fleeting intimacy with a stranger, a "perfect stranger," as they say. Only in this case the cliché didn't work. Mariam laid no claim to perfection and she was hardly a stranger. Not *exactly* a stranger—they probably said that too. Mariam shifted, adjusting more snugly to the shape of his body, and once again he sensed her smile: "Look at you. Getting hard again, my little childhood friend?"

No, not a friend, not really. Neither a stranger nor a friend. Their shared childhood was a myth—to a point, of course, as there is a kernel of truth to any myth. That obsessive German, Heinrich Schliemann, found his Troy precisely because he trusted a myth, was guided by it, in fact. Schliemann quite literally unearthed Homer's Troy (or what he took for Homer's Troy, anyway), but *he,* he had not been looking for Mariam, having little interest in relics of the past. He had managed to lead a life free of such pursuits, and fairly successfully . . . to a point. Lisa used to fault him for this lack of curiosity. "Painfully unimaginative," he overheard her once describe him over the phone to a girlfriend in Belgium. At least he *assumed* she was describing him.

At the time he thought she was being unfair, but, grudgingly, he had to admit to himself that Lisa's disdain for him was not entirely baseless. Unforgiving and cruel—yes, but hardly baseless. And now, again, with his lips touching Mariam's round shoulder, his hands cradling her breasts, he felt far removed from the original myth of their relationship—he cared about it as little as he did about the hulk of that lost ark resting forlornly on the side of an Armenian mountain. He was no Heinrich Schliemann, and he didn't discover her on a mountain slope—the day before, he ran into her on Nevsky Prospect. You always run into someone on Nevsky—it's one of its well-publicized and much written about oddities.

She recognized him first and having assessed quickly his state of incomprehension proceeded to tease him affably: "No, I'm not your college girlfriend. Actually, not an ex at all, so you can relax. Breathe evenly. Think harder. I can't believe you don't recognize me! This chance encounter will live in infamy." She laughed and he instantly liked the sound of her voice, even though he still had no idea who this cheerful woman was. He liked her cheerfulness too—it communicated good humor and friendly intentions but somehow managed not to slip into something grotesque. He couldn't help but appreciate the masterful balancing act (eccentricity, so common and even cultivated among his old St. Petersburg acquaintances, was not his thing). But still, he couldn't remember her.

"Alright, alright," she patted him on the shoulder in a mockingly condescending gesture. "I'll help you out. Look, here," she tapped the bridge of her nose with an immaculately manicured index finger. "I used to have a unibrow—right here. You see? Like that Mexican painter, Frida Kahlo. Did you see the movie? No? You should, it's quite good!" It was time for him to fake recognition, but he couldn't; somehow, he knew that this handsome, dark-haired woman (two perfectly trimmed black eyebrows belied the unibrow reference) would immediately call his bluff. She studied his face for a few seconds and sighed, now slightly annoyed: "Come on, how many lives have you lived? Think: junior high class, a new girl, transferred from Baku . . ." And suddenly he remembered, more than remembered—he felt transported by some gentle but powerful force into that classroom with its view of the canal. The classroom walls were painted an indistinct beige and displayed half a dozen portraits of bearded classic writers. A Mayakovsky quote was featured on a poster above the blackboard: "I would learn Russian simply because it was Lenin's language." It all came back to him now—the wet granite embankment outside the classroom window, the endless rainy afternoons, the rush of exhilaration, the sense of common purpose, the excitement, the feeling of disgust. Yes, he remembered now: "Wait a minute . . . Are you . . . are you . . . Mariam?" She made a quick show of demonstrating her relief: "Phew, finally! *Of course,* I am Mariam. The last name has changed—I lost it to my first husband, along with my virginity . . . the usual. But the first name has sort of stuck with me." She smiled at him warmly; apparently, they had moved past the teasing stage and towards a genuine reunion.

To his surprise, Mariam was aware of the general outlines of his post-high school life trajectory: the army, his first marriage, emigration to Israel, then another move—to New York. She even knew that he had kept his apartment in the city and visited regularly from the States. How in the world did she know all of this? "Ah," she shrugged, "St. Petersburg pretends to be a major metropolis, but we all know that it's really just a small provincial town where every piece of news travels fast and rumors even faster." No wonder he had some difficulty recognizing her. Somewhere along a twenty-year stretch of the road she had shed more than the Kahlo-like unibrow and her Armenian last name. There was no trace of that cornered little ferret scowling at her relentless pursuers. Her joviality seemed natural, he saw no signs of playacting: she appeared to be genuinely pleased—with the balmy June morning, their chance encounter right outside the metro station, with her own ability to attract and command attention. At once, he shook off the interfering vision of a stuffy classroom in mid-afternoon and saw her as she was—an attractive brunette, assured of her powers. And she could read his thoughts too. "An ugly duckling, my late grandma used to call me."—"Well, not anymore," he smiled.—"Nope." She shook her head: "Not anymore—the ugly duckling has grown up and matured into an ok duck."

She was a doctor, a pediatrician, with her own practice. In a city where, after the Soviet collapse, rank and status had come to define (and often ruin) personal relationships, she clearly passed the success test. Her daughter was . . . she was the same age as Mariam when they first met. Even more strangely, the daughter attended the same high school, which, as Mariam quickly explained to him, was now considered among the most prestigious in the city and catered mostly to the elite: "The place is corrupt to the core. You wouldn't believe the bribes I had to dish out to get my daughter in. But the teachers are excellent. There are even a couple of holdovers from *our* time." To him, that "our time" struck a discordant note: she claimed a shared history that, in fact, covered less than a year. Did she forget? Her harried mother withdrew her after that spring quarter. Did she forget? He couldn't tell. But he could tell that Mariam had a gift, and he wondered if it was related to her professional occupation. The gift was a skill—a particular knack for initiating the stranger (*sort of* a stranger, in this case) into her world. Within a few minutes of the conversation, he had developed a strange sense of familiarity that he experienced almost as a sense of déjà vu: their common past didn't have to be a fiction, their fluke late morning encounter on Nevsky didn't have to be accidental.

That evening he was throwing a going away party that was intended to double as a real farewell—it was time to sell the apartment and finally put some distance between the corporeality of New York and his exhausted St. Petersburg fantasy. Would she care to stop by? She sounded delighted with the invitation, but she probably often sounded like that. Yes, she would, absolutely. How nice and spontaneous of him. Would it be appropriate to bring along her "guy"? But of course, the more the merrier. He gave her the address—just a few blocks away, around the corner from the Catholic cathedral. The invitation made it easy to say goodbyes—as usual, he had intuited a way to evade permanence. Indecisiveness—that's how Lisa identified this feature of his. Lisa was a definitions expert. Lisa was decisive. Lisa was many things . . . A quick pinprick, an instant dimming of the morning light—just for a second, a split second, to be precise. He looked up: the tiniest of cumulus clouds had brushed by the edge of the sun but, as if burned by this proximity, instantly separated themselves from the brightness and floated on—towards the gulf.

On his walk back to the apartment, he compiled a mental list of items to buy for the party. He also thought of Mariam and how, for a few minutes, he experienced her life as his own. Those thoughts, though, didn't stay with him; the lazy morning was about to become much busier and he had other things to worry about—a shopping list, packing, and a phone call to the realtor. But Mariam . . . One runs into people on Nevsky—the prospect, he read somewhere, was likely designed specifically for such happenstance. It was not running into her that was surprising. The surprising part was Mariam herself. She'd fared well, and that simple thought filled him with relief. She has fared really well. Who would've thought? . . . That ugly duckling, that cornered hissing ferret . . . Will she come to the party? He considered the odds, weighed them carefully, and decided that she probably wouldn't.

But she did. She came late and alone. Of course, at the peak of the white nights the notion of "late" was relative to one's personal conception of time, and his tended to follow the never-setting Northern sun. In Mariam's case, the notion of "alone" similarly assumed a certain relative quality. He was mixing drinks in the kitchen and didn't hear her ring, and by the time he spotted her in the living room, Mariam had already established herself as the heart and soul of the party. Being the center of attention came naturally to her. Someone had placed a drink in her hand and now she was perched on the edge of a coffee table, gyrating slowly to the music, laughing at something one of his guests, the fashionable conceptual poet Yegor, was eagerly whispering in her ear. Yegor was on his highest conquest alert, and he was also the most alpha of the several other men who circled the coffee table like purposeful sharks. She waved, indicating the hilariousness of this almost comical encirclement and mouthing a mock appeal for help: "SOS, I am completely surrounded!" He could see that she was in her element, though. She didn't need his help.

* * *

He remembered his very first impression of her, mainly because it had been at odds with his upbringing and previous life experiences. Their elderly physical education teacher, a wounded World War II vet, often referred to him (and others) as "sheltered." The teacher, a true man of the soil, resented his young urban charges, who'd had the audacity to grow up in peacetime. "You don't know shit, you don't even know how to hate," he sometimes castigated them. For the veteran, life was a field of battle, and all those devoid of martial instincts elicited his contempt. He enthusiastically cheered the invasion of Afghanistan but not for any patriotic or geopolitical reasons. After the Soviet tanks rolled into Kabul, he (correctly) concluded that the "soft asses" would finally learn what "killing and getting killed" was like—somehow, he believed that to be an essential educational experience. Sadly, his prediction would prove to be only too true for several of his students . . . But before Afghanistan had a chance to test some of them, most of them would be tested by Mariam, who was transferred to their high school at the beginning of their freshman year.

Years later, on those rare occasions when alcohol or a particularly poignant literary association prompted him to travel down memory lane, he wondered about the source of that all-encompassing and eviscerating hatred that he felt towards the disheveled, black-haired girl with a unibrow. Her manner was both obsequious and unfriendly, servile and hostile at the same time. She transferred from a school in Azerbaijan and rumor had it that her transfer was the result of a near-death experience in her Baku school yard, where Mariam, one of very few Armenians, was set upon by a bunch of local boys. Hearing that was hardly a surprise—being Jewish, even at this early age, he well understood the limitations of the vaunted "friendship of peoples." Yet the harrowing story of Mariam's Baku ordeal somehow failed to make her a sympathetic character—to the contrary, it simply served to confirm her instant pariah status.

His best friend, Dimka, thought she looked feral: "What a savage creature she is, just look at her—hideous, vicious, s-o-o-o ugly!" And indeed, he couldn't stop looking at her: her beat-up woolen slippers, her brown stockings of rough cotton—full of unpatched holes and perpetually loose at the knees; her stained uniform blouse with a pinafore strip slipped down to the elbow, revealing the contour of an overdeveloped breast. The sight of that breast, unusual on a girl her age, made him anxious and fueled a desire to . . . to do what exactly? He was not quite sure but eventually came to believe that it was a desire to hurt, to inflict pain, to see this wild-eyed girl, her mouth distorted in a mad grin (a scream?), writhe in agony. The novelty, the intensity of these emotions overwhelmed him but also made school infinitely more exciting. And he couldn't fail to notice that most of his friends, boys and girls, had a very similar response to Mariam. Suddenly, the cliques, the insignificant rivalries and minor snubs, were all but forgotten. Their shared hatred of the new Armenian girl unified them and there was sweetness in that unity. The war-loving phys ed teacher had nothing to worry about after all.

The taunting ensued within days, if not hours, of Mariam's appearance in their classroom. They mocked her "Southern" accent and made fun of her awkward gait. One day, most of the girls in class came to school sporting massive penciled in black unibrows. On their daily walks home from school, strolling up and down the tree-lined boulevard, Dimka and he concocted elaborate plans to better humiliate Mariam. All their creativity and the pulsating teenage energy went into this scheming. During that school year, they lived the most fulfilling, the most horrifyingly exciting months of their youth. Through trial and error, they learned to pace their attacks. They learned how to escalate, how to withdraw quickly only to return when they were least expected, how to besiege and wear out the besieged. Both of them hailed from bookish Jewish families and their familiarity with literature and artistic precedent came in especially handy. As the ringleaders of the ongoing assault they gained in popularity, a reversal of fortunes for which they were thankful.

Never before had he felt so close to his peers, and he cherished the joy of being accepted on his own terms. Or so he thought.

Their harassment of Mariam grew progressively more physical in nature. This progression had an inevitable logic to it, and he recognized it as necessary, akin to the laws of physics they were learning during that fall quarter. The first tentative kick in the hallway during recess proved to be tremendously satisfying. After school they paced the length of the boulevard discussing the experience and analyzing its most minute details. Mariam's response to mistreatment was puzzling, but its very strangeness inspired them to further mischief. She defied expectations and, by acting unpredictably, greatly enhanced the entertainment value of the torment to which they subjected her daily.

It was a truly incredible show, marked by surprising plot twists, punctuated by seemingly spontaneous flare-ups and dramatic lulls in action. Mariam vacillated between displays of extreme distress and over-the-top merriment. One moment she would be wailing hysterically—her face all red, covered with tears, and with beads of sweat clinging to her unkempt unibrow. But within minutes a bizarre transformation somewhere deep inside her would generate a bout of laughter. She would lash out against her tormentors, trying to kick them in the groin, scratch them, gouge out their eyes with her dirty, gnawed nails. Just as they grew seriously worried (but there was some sweetness in that fear too) about the ferocity of her response she would retreat into a hallway corner, covering her face with her unwashed hands, whimpering pitifully, pleading for mercy. All of this was disorienting and . . . extraordinarily exciting: the unpredictability, the depth of her humiliation, the exquisite cruelty of their assault, the implicit danger of going too far. Mariam's flair for the dramatic added to the intensity of those several months. On one particular occasion, Dimka, relentless in his ingenuity, dropped a plate of meatloaf and mashed potatoes (their standard school cafeteria fare) into Mariam's lap. The whole cafeteria went silent, students flocked around expecting a scene. And Mariam didn't disappoint. Scowling at the nervously expecting mob she scooped up a handful of the steaming mess from her lap and proceeded to methodically smear it all over her uniform, especially over the bulging breasts, and then all over her red and sweaty face. She sneered, seemingly uncontrollably. The mob was stunned, taking in this act of extreme self-abasement in disbelief. How do you truly torment someone who is willing to drink the chalice of humiliation to the dregs? His hatred of this strange, large-breasted

Armenian girl couldn't be any more visceral, and at that moment he knew they would have to up their ante.

***

As so often happens at such parties the host had far less fun than the guests. He didn't mind, not really, but at some point it did register with him that he had barely left the kitchen. He walked down the corridor—most of the remaining guests (the crowd had thinned out considerably) were hanging out in the living room. He passed around drinks and headed back into the kitchen. The guests protested and he promised to be back shortly. The door to the study was slightly ajar; he peeked in and saw Mariam and the conceptual poet next to each other on the daybed—they were energetically making out. Pale midnight light filtered through the muslin curtains and gave the scene an artificial and even borderline comical quality; he smiled to himself and quietly closed the door. Over the years he had observed or participated in quite a few such scenes; for him, they were part of the White Nights canon, along with the echo-filled courtyard and the pallid sunlight penetrating through the parted drapes at midnight, along with boozy companions, conceptual poets all, even those who were not. It was time to close that chapter and to make a decisive break (don't say a word, Lisa) with this chimera, which really was nothing but his past masquerading as an elusive and uncertain present. But first, he would have to wrap up the party and embrace his friends one last time before locking up behind them and heading back to the kitchen to do the dishes. Before . . . heading back to New York.

Mariam leaned against the door frame, eyeing him with apparent amusement. He wondered how long she had been standing there. Doing dishes could be therapeutic for him—a perfect time to be lost in thought, or whatever passed for a thought at 2:00 a.m. in late June, just before the restless sun began its morning ascent. She found the sight of him entertaining: "How cute—doing dishes all alone. I can't tell you how touching this is to observe." He gave her a wan smile: "Where is the poet? I thought you were into him?" She touched the glass kitchen door with her forehead: "Oh, nice, feels so cool . . . The poet, you say? Yeah, I was . . . for a minute, but then he recited a couple of his poems and the spell was broken. It's a common St. Petersburg misconception that reciting poetry leads to a fuck. I mean, it may . . . occasionally, but he should've done better." She stepped inside the kitchen and picked up a dish towel: "Here, let me help you, I'll dry."

For a few minutes they remained silent, working in tandem. Her motions were quick and expert. Then she paused: "Do you think I'm promiscuous? You can be honest." He looked at her, confused: "Promiscuous? Why, of course not. You're a grown-up and can do whatever you want. Who is to judge you?" She considered his response briefly and shrugged her shoulders—his open-mindedness failed to satisfy her: "It's a nice thing to say but quite meaningless. It's an American thing to say too." He objected: "Now you're sounding accusatory. And I'm not really an American, not exactly."—"True, not exactly, but close enough . . . You know, I had this teenage fantasy of sleeping with an American guy. I guess many of us did at the time. But it never happened. A German happened, a couple of Italians, even one Swede (which was a mistake), but not an American."

He tried to understand her, to follow her train of thought, but decided that he could do no better than reiterate his original response: "No, seriously, I don't find you promiscuous. Not at all. You're vivacious. My ex would accuse me of using a cliché, but . . . you know . . . your presence lights up the room. Zest for life, as they say. Don't laugh, I mean it." But she did laugh: "You're funny and . . . sweet. My grandma always said that I had a magnetic personality. 'Be careful,' she would say, 'with that personal magnetism of yours.'" She made her eyes rounder and changed her voice to an affected croak that brought to mind a *Lord of the Rings* movie: "I'm dangerous, young man, *very* dangerous." Who *was* she? This being St. Petersburg she was likely a literary character or else pretending to be one. He rummaged through his memory of their high school curriculum for an appropriate reference. One of those phantasmagorical tales by Gogol (they had run into each other on Nevsky Prospect, hadn't they?)? A Dostoyevskian feverish dream (the White Nights reigned indisputably just outside the kitchen window, did they not?)? But none of the references fit—Mariam's Southern vitality, her "zest for life" defied the rain-soaked St. Petersburg literary standard. She was in a league of her own—a woman apart.

Together, they finished up drying the dishes. She placed the wet towel on the checkered oilcloth covering the kitchen table and looked at him expectantly: "So what's next, my childhood friend?" Was she teasing him again? Challenging to come back with a joke? He glanced at the wall clock—it was almost three in the morning and the short-lived night outside had already receded into memory. "I can call in a cab," he suggested cautiously, not quite knowing what was expected from him. "You could," she agreed . . . most unhelpfully. With her manicured finger (the same one with which she had pointed out her absent unibrow) she drew an invisible whimsical pattern on the oilcloth. "Would it freak you out if I told you that I like you?"—"I like you too . . ." His good manners seemed to annoy her and she dismissed them with a casual flip of hand: "Listen, you don't have to be so polite—I'm not used to it and, frankly, it gets old quick." But almost immediately she relented: "Ok, sorry, I didn't mean to be brusque. It just sounded so . . . I don't know . . . so fake, I guess . . . *I love you, honey—I love you too.*" She uttered the last phrase in heavily accented English, lampooning an imaginary American couple. And yet she came across serious enough but also somehow bewildered—as if caught off guard by her own frankness.

"I hate these nights without darkness," she continued after a short pause that he failed to fill. "I've lived in this city for most of my life now. You may not remember, but my Russian used to be accented; I dropped that stupid accent, those soft fucking consonants—the curse of the Caucuses—decades ago. I've never been back to Baku, certainly not back *there*—what sane Armenian would ever go back to that bloody oil rig? I'm not suicidal, you know . . . So, that's it—a Southern beauty coming into bloom under the gray skies of your precious Northern Venice. And, would you believe it, I still don't feel at home here, especially during this time of year, when the cursed city denies me even the most natural and easily obtainable thing in the world—a few hours of solid darkness. Just give me eight pitch-dark hours—to rest, to make love with a stranger and afterwards pretend that nothing happened. It's easier to pretend in the dark, it's more expedient for forgetting . . ." He thought that it was exactly the opposite for him and then wondered if Mariam had not inadvertently stumbled onto a new fault line between the North and the South. For a second, it felt like a momentous insight on his part—a flash of new understanding. But to keep up with Mariam one had to forgo the luxury of such theoretical detours. "It'll probably feel incestuous," she said.—"What do you mean?" He pretended not to understand. She let out a tired sigh: "Oh, stop it. Let's not play games? You understood me perfectly well." He fidgeted and busied himself with the folded kitchen towel. Why in the world did he fold it? It was still wet, and he must've spent a full minute looking for a perfect drying spot in an almost empty kitchen before finally deciding to spread it across the radiator.

All along, he felt Mariam's presence and knew that as soon as the towel conundrum had been solved he'd have an even more complicated one on his hands. "I'll call you a cab," he offered again, trying to sound as matter-of-fact as possible. She smiled condescendingly and he immediately became embarrassed by his own insincerity; he wished for an easy way out. You run into all sorts of people on Nevsky, and some of them, the dark-haired Caspian beauties, for example—the fully grown ducks of transplanted pedigree—are liable to offset your recently (and barely) restored life balance.—"Don't be so tense." Mariam was standing right behind him now. Quietly she leaned into him, letting him appreciate the generosity of her body, its willingness to be available to him. On her own terms, she was giving him a way out. "You don't really have to call a cab," she whispered into his shoulder.

***

After the outrage in the cafeteria, the school was buzzing for weeks. Conflicting and often ridiculously exaggerated accounts of Mariam's awesome and horrifying performance spread throughout the grades. After classes, he and Dimka spent hours on the boulevard, strategizing for an appropriate and appropriately fearsome response. Raising the ante indeed: the months of hounding of Mariam were set to culminate in a stunning grand finale—a meticulously choreographed coup de grâce, staged with a nod to their cinematic and literary influences. The school was gripped by anticipation and again he found himself at the center of attention—by general consent it would fall to him to administer the final judgment. *Vox populi, vox Dei*—the people have spoken and, by popular acclamation, appointed two thirteen-year-old Jewish boys their honorary ambassadors and . . . executioners. They were humbled and overwhelmed by the honor, but as befitted true Stoics they embraced the challenge. Mariam's pain and symbolic destruction would be the price of their popularity.

Spring stirred late that year, but once it did the telltale signs were everywhere. That spring had come out of the pages of the Russian literature textbook they were reading in class: blackened patches of muddy snow, crusted into permanence around the rusted pole of the bus stop sign; innocent rivulets, streaming down the boulevard, carrying with them the pathetic remnants of winter that had survived until April buried inside snowbanks—sundry branches and twigs, cigarette butts, black and soggy leaves. Renewal was in the air, but first the city had to purge itself of its dead and dirty wintry secrets. Hence the rivulets of melting snow transporting their ragged debris to the sewers that were hidden under heavy manhole covers or down the slope towards the canal. One evening his mother came back home from work in a particularly light-hearted mood. She was carrying a tiny bouquet of yellow mimosas and humming a lovely tune—spring, she declared with her usual flourish, had finally arrived.

Fridays were bookended by chemistry classes—stale affairs, taught by a perpetually bored young woman, whose lack of enthusiasm for her subject rivaled that exhibited by her pupils. Under ordinary circumstances, the end-of-class bell occasioned a virtual stampede of students desperate to put some distance between themselves and the glossy periodic table on the classroom wall. But that Friday proved to be different—there was no crush for the exit. The students left the classroom in an orderly fashion and once outside almost immediately reassembled in a neat formation. A casual observer would've been puzzled by this seemingly spontaneous expression of social cohesion. But the mob, as mobs sometimes do, had a purpose, it adhered to a script, which was intuited, not rehearsed. Many years later he could still remember the excitement of that assembly; he could see his friends' faces—open, eager, and glowing with anticipation. What could be friendlier than a jubilant crowd at a public execution? The condemned is lavished with warmth and appreciation, her body in its impending agony will provide unprecedented entertainment to the masses, who will draw on the pending spectacle to affirm their own claim on life. They fully embrace this connection between another person's destruction and their own survival. They acknowledge and celebrate it.

It was clear to him that Mariam knew what was coming. Trapped inside the formation she acted with uncharacteristic restraint. Some of his favorite books contained famous execution scenes and, strangely, they often described the doomed as serene or resigned to their fate. When finally facing the executioner's axe, the nefarious and irresistible Milady de Winter in *The Three Musketeers* accepted the inevitable and bent a proud head to her pursuers' will. In *Darkness at Noon,* Arthur Koestler's Rubashov saw his own execution as historically necessary—a feat of dialectical reasoning worthy of an old Bolshevik. Mariam was hardly familiar with these literary precedents, but she fell right into this well-worn pattern. She walked silently (a dead woman walking), her feet in her oversized and crumpled slippers shuffling on the hardwood floor of the main hallway. She walked (was led) past the stinking gym, past the foul-smelling cafeteria, past the indifferent-looking Lenin statue—a tribute to another great dialectician, someone who had no trouble recognizing historical necessity.

The procession left the school building and continued on towards the soccer field in the back. And that's where Mariam's demeanor suddenly changed, or rather reverted to its usual ferocity. She was hissing, and spitting, and swearing at the spectators. With piercing howls she threw herself at her tormentors—again and again. But the phalanx didn't budge; he had never observed such determination in the ordinarily immature faces of his school friends, those "soft asses" par excellence. Like silent Spartan warriors, like wordless Zulu fighters, step by slow step they reached the middle of the field, and only then their ranks broke, allowing them to retreat to the field's fenced edge. Mariam was left behind—spinning, and pacing, and hissing, and glowering, and cursing them in the foulest language. But he contemplated her without his usual disgust. He didn't hate her anymore. A strange calm descended upon him—a calm that came, he realized, with a great sense of responsibility. Just the two of them remained in the middle of the field, united by a script that, they both knew, could not be altered. Mariam's behavior underwent yet another change—her frenzy subsided and what was left of it transformed into heavy panting. She looked disoriented, as if she were an actor who'd suddenly forgotten her lines. "What now?" she asked him, annoyed, her voice rasping. She was asking for guidance . . . *What a strange girl,* he thought. *What a weird girl . . .* He explained to her what needed to be done ("Get down on your knees, lower your head, don't move.") and to his surprise she complied. He didn't feel entirely present at the scene but, rather, floating above it, overhearing someone who looked and sounded like him issuing orders to a red-faced, dark-haired girl with a unibrow.

That scene would come back to haunt him. Not because it became a defining memory, but simply because he once saw it re-enacted on television. He was holed up at a conference hotel in Toronto, flipping through channels, and generally feeling depressed about the predictability of his life and career choices. CNN was running a special about the horrors of Taliban rule in Afghanistan: the bearded morality police riding armored-plated "tacticals" with mounted machine guns—check; the destruction of the Buddahs of Bamiyan—check; the enthusiastic crowds in a soccer stadium . . . He sat up in bed, fearing what was coming next. But it was all too obvious: a tactical drove onto the soccer field and two bearded guards helped a third figure—a woman in a blue burka—climb down from the truck bed. The camera swept across the crowd, capturing the joyous and expectant faces of the men there—young and old—and the children of both genders. The woman's pain would be their joy, her impending destruction would give them reason to live, her spilled blood would course through their veins and animate their bodies. The guards led the woman to the penalty kick spot and said something to her. She lowered herself on the ground—so compliant, so dutiful, so willing to oblige. Who was she? Someone that submissive . . . what had she done to deserve this? This penalty kick with a piece of lead? This rapt attention of a captive audience? The guards took a few steps back and cocked their AK-47s . . . And that's when he heard himself scream. Desperately, he fumbled for the remote, dropped it, picked it up again, and finally managed to turn off the fucking television just as the guards pulled the trigger.

Respectful of the script, Mariam did as she was told. One couldn't wish for a better acting partner. Without so much as trying she exhibited a keen and natural talent for the stage. Her wild fluctuations—from timid acceptance to rage to bashful supplication—served to entertain. Even facing certain harm, she continued to work for the audience; she insisted on working *with* it. Now safely stationary, folded in a prayer pose, Mariam kept herself close to the ground. He couldn't see her face but imagined it distorted by a frantic grin. Such a grin would've been appropriate for the occasion. Or so he thought as he embarked on a ceremonial jog along the field's perimeter. He held his fists high up in the air—like Mohammad Ali, who was so popular with them at the time. The crowd chanted its support. He felt the warmth of the April sun on his cheeks; he took in the sight of the fluttering sparrows hovering over the canal, celebrating the arrival of spring. The crowd chanted its love—for him, for the late and much-anticipated spring, even for Mariam, who remained motionless at the penalty spot. He completed his lap of honor and positioned himself at a distance of some twenty meters from the folded heap that was his classmate. The time for action had arrived; it arrived along with the seasonal warmth and the happy sparrows ducking in and out of the lilac bushes along the canal. He would administer justice; he would administer a penalty kick for the ages. He was rumbling in the jungle, he was Mohammad Ali dispatching George Foreman, he was the mysterious and honor-bound Count de la Fère in *The Three Musketeers,* condemning his beloved to death.

Time stood still as he sprinted across the dusty ground towards Mariam. Never a great athlete, he had not run before as fast or (Dimka would assure him afterwards) as gracefully. It was important not to slow down, not to ruin the carefully choreographed ritual slipping or stumbling at the last minute. He kicked. The exact moment of impact didn't register with him, but, in slow motion, he observed Mariam jerk forward, her arms and legs flailing. The consummate performer to the very end, she kept rolling, and rolling, and rolling, until she came to an abrupt stop against the rusty goal post. He finally saw her face again—flushed and sweaty as always, its features distorted by a primordial scream. What a triumph! He had done it for his friends, for their love and acceptance on this radiant April afternoon. He had done it for their sense of togetherness and purpose. Mariam may have failed to appreciate it, and understandably so. Writhing in pain and humiliation, wiping away her tears, inspecting the torn sleeve of her tattered school uniform, tapping tentatively at the raw gash on her elbow, she was in no position to recognize the value of his sacrifice. He'd done it for her too. He thought that maybe in a week or two, in a month, he would be able to explain to her the full and complex meaning of what'd just happened. He would have to make sure that she remained calm and didn't succumb to one of her frightful fits of fury. He'd explain to her the historical necessity of his act, its ultimate logic. The law of physics. She would understand. She would be able to understand . . .

Only, they didn't have another chance to talk. A few days after the historic "penalty kick" Mariam's mother withdrew her from school. The head teacher explained that Mariam was never a "good fit." The students agreed.

***

She kicked the crumpled sheet off the bed and, having thus liberated her body, stretched with obvious pleasure. "Oh, Mariam," she yawned. "Oh, Mariam, you slut. You did it again. And with a childhood friend no less. What would your grandma say? Your black kerchief-wearing, the Catholicos-worshipping grandma? *Shameless, so utterly shameless,*" she said, parodying her grandma's raspy accent.

Mariam got out of bed and walked over to the window, only to pause briefly in front of the windowsill. Then, with a yank, she opened the curtains. He couldn't help but notice how comfortable she was with her own nakedness. For a couple of minutes she studied the courtyard down below, then made a diagnosis: "Your typical St. Petersburg courtyard—pretty dreary-looking, if you ask me, even for this time of year." She turned around and eyed him quizzically: "I just had this weird vision. I saw you crossing the courtyard. A sickly Leningrad boy . . . You know, you all looked like goldfish to me, very vulnerable, worthy of my pity. In your silly blue uniform, your stupid school attaché case in hand. Remember, those used to be all the rage back then. They looked like bricks bound in leather. Probably just as heavy.

What did you call them? *Diplomats*! That's it—*diplomats*! And you certainly looked like one carrying it. An important diplomat on his way to school. The number six bus, right?" He nodded, mesmerized by her performance, but also by her silhouette against the light that had flooded through the parted curtains.—"You are shameless," he said quietly. It was a compliment, and she received it as such.

It was almost eleven. Mariam came out of the shower and dressed quickly. She asked him to walk her to the metro station. No, forget about a cab. Apparently, you've never heard about the latest natural phenomenon at this degree of Northern latitude—it's called *St. Petersburg traffic*. She had to be in the office by noon; no cab would be able to cross town in under an hour. "Let's walk . . ." And they did. They crossed the courtyard and he put up a little show for her benefit—swinging in front of her an imaginary diplomat, adjusting an invisible school uniform. They walked out onto the street, which was choked with traffic but somehow still felt desolate. They passed the old bus stop—the number six had stopped running years ago, but the authorities never bothered to remove the dilapidated yellow sign. They pretended they were waiting for the bus to carry them to school. "What a pity it's not coming," she smiled.—"It must've broken down, never left the depot," he joked. She shrugged. She smiled. She took his hand when they were crossing the street but once on the other side forgot to let it go. They kept on walking, holding hands, and that added intimacy felt appropriate to the occasion. "Your hand is soft," she informed him. For a second he was taken aback and protested: "Soft? It shouldn't be soft. How can it be soft? After all the hours in the gym?" She pecked him on the cheek: "No need to get all worked up about it. It's just a comment. And don't you worry—I noticed your body, actually gave you a quick professional examination while you were asleep. I am a doctor, after all. It's pretty hot. *All* of it. You have nothing to worry about. And your hands . . . They aren't rough, aren't calloused. They are like a reflection of your inner self—*gentle* is the word. You're a *gentle* man, my childhood friend—a little goldfish that jumped out of the fish tank."

He noticed that they had reached the very place where she first approached him the previous day. Mariam laughed: "My, my, my . . . how symbolic indeed. It's like we've gone full circle in"—she checked her watch—"almost exactly twenty-four hours. Do you believe in numerology? I don't." Yes, just twenty-four hours. Or twenty years. Or choose your own number and imbue it with meaning—turn it into a memory heirloom. "Will you write to me?" She sounded casual, not anxious at all. Nothing heavy about her touch—it was a light touch indeed. "But of course!" He came across too eager to please and she instantly caught on to it.—"Oh, come on . . . Just say yes—like in 'yes, I will write to you.' Drop the 'of course'—no one was asking for it."—"Yes, I will write to you . . ."—"You see, that's much better, more natural, no peer pressure as they say."

By the station entrance, she spent some time kissing his face, avoiding his lips but compensating for this oversight by planting numerous quick kisses on his cheeks, forehead, neck, his eyes, even his smooth earlobe. "I'm kissing you into oblivion," she explained enigmatically. Not much of an explanation, really, he would have to consider it later. But not now. Now they needed to say goodbyes. He detested the ritual. Another late start to another day, one of his last in an exhausting city that refused to let him go, that kept him tethered to his own shadow.

Goodbye, Mariam. I can't tell you how lucky I am to have run into you. You made my day and you most certainly made my night. I just hope it was good for you, I hope it was worth it . . . I hope . . . As if reading his thoughts she looked at him with hesitant curiosity; she brought his hand up to her face and pressed it against his palm, she kissed it tenderly. "It was worth it," she said. "It was wonderful. And you know what the best part was?" She was being playful again—she had to be before separating herself from him for good. One has to cut earthly connections before descending deep into the metro. And that's what she did—with a wink, with a laugh, with an impish response to her own unvoiced question: "It didn't hurt, my darling, not at all."

Nora's Caravan*

Perched against a fluffy pile of IKEA pillows Nora watched the camels cross into her field of vision, framed by the glass panel of the balcony door. An early evening quiet filled the room, the pale rays of the setting sun reflected off the ceramic floor tiles and played havoc with the otherwise stately outlines of her beloved possession—a bulky mahogany armoire. It was acquired at the Elite Wholesales Furniture Emporium in Newton, Mass.—an acquisition intended as a testimony to her exquisite Leningrad taste and American success—and it loomed large in Nora's life story. Although it was a story of great suffering and resilience, Nora wouldn't have it any other way. In Boston, her American coworker, Amy, once told her, "Nora, your life reminds me of a Hollywood movie—so many struggles, so many missed chances, but you always triumph." She meant well, but Nora was not pleased, she bristled at the very idea of a happy ending. "Hollywood? In your Hollywood, they make you believe that everything will eventually work out, but it never does. Life is a war that cannot be won." She liked making such pronouncements—for the theatricality, to be sure, but also because they made her American interlocutors uncomfortable.

Americans have had it too easy, she thought. Their infantile optimism shielded them from the stark realities of the wildness and savagery of the "real world." *She* knew because she had come from that world—from the wild—and she could still sense the heat of the scorching fires licking at her feet, the stench of burning flesh still filled her nostrils. She couldn't abide not being dramatic—*that* would've been a betrayal of her "life story," as the well-intentioned but hopelessly naïve Amy would put it. Amy had no clue, none of them did. No wonder most of her Boston coworkers voted Democrat—all desirous of happy endings, all believers in hope and change and other feel-good nonsense that only existed in their popcorn-fueled imaginations. It pained her that Alex had bought into these rosy visions. Of course, he had—

---

* First published as "Nora's Caravan," *BigCityLit* (Winter 2024).

he was weak and malleable, which sort of worked . . . so long as she was the one bending his will.

The armoire was a statement of faith and an award for her daring flight from the netherworld. Its hulking and unequivocal presence served as a constant reminder of her successful escape. In the meantime, the first of the camels had reached the outer edges of the frame and the animals now formed an unsteady procession that from her perch reminded Nora of a clothesline stretched out between the two panels of the balcony door. How far away are they? Half a kilometer, at least . . . She could see that far after her cataract surgery in Ashdod. The measly five hundred meters was nothing, she could see further—thousands of kilometers into the distance. She could see Alex. She could see *right through* him . . . She caught herself humming a long-forgotten tune of her youth: a song by a bandana-sporting bard, Novella Matveeva, who crooned about heartache reimagined, old raincoats left hanging on rusty nails as souvenirs of loves that never were. Matveeva was as anti-Hollywood as one could be, as one should be. And, surprisingly, one of her songs was about a camel caravan crossing the desert. Nothing in the desert, half-whispered Matveeva to the strumming of her guitar, is what it seems. The desert comes alive with colorful fantastical visions of fata morgana, dreamy images that promise and distort, that beckon only to disappoint. But camels . . . they remain indifferent and tread their set path, harboring no regrets, uttering no complaints:

My caravan was traversing the desert
My caravan was traversing the desert
The leading camel deep in melancholy thought
And the rest of them following him
And their heads were moving slowly
As if they knew something but kept silent
As if they knew something but didn't know
How to share what they knew: with whom, when, for what purpose.

Lines so simple and lulling; the words of one who prefers not to explain. Such words are impossible to translate into English.

A Bedouin boy on a battered motorcycle accompanied the camels: at first, he idled at the edges of the frame, then revved the engine and sped the length of the caravan—a quick flash across the screen. The camels kept on moving—graceful, stately, and completely uninterested in the motorcycle. Like in a movie theater, Nora thought. Lately, she had developed a habit of comparing her lived moments to movie scenes. Both the star and the director of the film, she recognized the thrilling but also, importantly, the therapeutic potential of this innovation. Her approach to live filmmaking differed radically from the Hollywood concoctions she despised. *Her* movie would seethe with passion and tension, but there would be no resolution, no ridiculous happy endings. Alex wouldn't be able to exhale a sigh of relief. Her friends back in Boston, and especially Gala, would not have the satisfaction of picking her up at Logan and hosting a welcome back party with stupid balloons and Gala's ever gallant hubby, Misha, flipping hamburgers in the backyard.

Gala, despite their shared Soviet past, always struck her as a well-meaning fool, who would like nothing better than a tear-stained reunion. In their last Skype conversation Gala pleaded with her to reconcile with Alex and "respect his life choices." She begged her to return to Boston. What an idiot! What a blithering, blabbering, kind-hearted dupe! Probably voted for Obama too. And to think that she had known them for close to half a century. Wasn't Gala paying attention? Didn't she realize that Nora never, *never* betrayed her principles. "It's a slippery slope," she'd barked at Gala. "Gala, you are always ready to slide down the slippery slope and you want to drag me along? To squeeze in next to you on the sled and hurtle merrily downhill, leaving everything that's sacred and right behind? Leaving Alex behind? In the clutches of that horrid, twice-divorced Moldovan whore? No, Gala, you definitely have not been paying attention, and if you so much as breathe another word there will be no more Skype calls. I can do wonderfully without the Skype calls, thank you very much. My friendship (and you should know this) is not unconditional—loyalty is the condition. And I have everything that I need right here—my little country that fills my heart with pride and sweet tenderness, a view of the Judean desert in bloom through my bedroom window, a bottle of Armenian cognac (the select five-star brand), a pack of Davidoff Golds, a brightly colored pill case: Monday, Tuesday, Wednesday . . . all the days of the week through Yom Rishon. And most importantly, I have my honor intact, my principles uncompromised."

Nora was done explaining herself to her Boston friends. What was that saying she liked quoting so much? *If there is a need to explain, then it's futile to explain.* Something like that—as always it sounded perfect in its original Russian. And there was another one that she never tired of hurling at her adversaries, even before her relocation to a real, bona fide desert: *I'm not gonna bother proving to you that I am not a camel.* She'd spent enough time in the States to know that the phrase sounded borderline insane in English, but that knowledge never stopped her from deploying it in both languages. You think we owe each other an explanation? Forget about it, don't waste my time. And really, how could you explain betrayal? How could you make the kindly and unprincipled Gala recoil in horror at the idea of Alex betraying his mother? How could you make Alex, her sweet little Alex (not so little anymore at forty-five, what with all that weight he had put on now that the Moldovan bitch was busy plying him with *mamaliga* and that revolting stuffed cabbage dish) . . . yes, her *formerly* sweet little Alex or better yet her "sweet little Alex" in quotation marks . . . *that* Alex, her faithless and weak son Alex—how could you make *him* shudder at his own disloyalty? "Respect his life choices" . . . Well, here she was—on the edge of the desert, breathing in the arid medicinal air of Arad, smoking her Davidoffs, sipping her cognac, respecting his fucking life choices. And it's not that she didn't warn him, she did—more than once, more than a hundred times; she warned him about those provincial sluts, brazen and irrepressible like weeds: you kick them out of the door and they'll climb right back in through the window. It's impossible to get rid of them . . . short of radical measures. Moving to Israel was a radical measure—an act of inspired nationalism that doubled as a devastating rebuke to her son. It felt so right and appropriate, having been let down by the most important, the only important human in her life, to seek solace in the bosom of *her* people.

Those people, though . . . they defied her idea of them and tested the limits of her tribalism. The Bukhara Jews, the Moroccans, the Ethiopians, the Black Hebrews, the *shtreimel*-wearing Haredim . . . And those ramshackle Bedouin encampments on the edges of the city . . . the proverbial big tent, the Jewish family that she had yearned for, seeking protection against the indignities inflicted on her by the only person who really mattered. She desperately wanted to become one with this place. Back in Boston, when haranguing her baffled friends, she tapped into the deepest well of emotional theatricality to declare her attachment to the land of Israel. The pushback from shell-shocked friends was feeble, they knew better than place themselves in the way of Nora's passions. Like most of her other life decisions, this one was articulated in such extreme and intemperate terms that the doubters didn't dare to protest.

***

Extravagant articulations of emotion came naturally to Nora, who'd had close to eight decades to hone the skill. She learned early on in life that very few were capable to withstand a torrent of over-the-top superlatives without giving ground. She first discovered the potency of the trick at that horrid deathtrap of a boarding school in Western Siberia, where she was moved from besieged Leningrad in the autumn of 1941. Her father stayed behind to defend the city and, as she would find out after the war, lasted until December. Her mother . . . the Germans began strafing the train as soon as they reached Luga. The attacks seemed like an afterthought, the Luftwaffe had more important targets to play with—weapons depots, grain elevators, military barracks. The bombers were sweeping in at a frighteningly low altitude, breezing leisurely over the train—a cooldown after the main mission. Sometimes they didn't even shoot, their ammunition spent elsewhere. When they did strafe the train, they tended to target it without precision. Mother should've not poked her head outside, she should've known that even satiated predators can be deadly. So . . . an orphan.

The Siberian school contained multitudes, which is to say, dozens of children from Leningrad and smaller cities overrun by the Germans, most of them now parentless. At the time she couldn't understand why some of them blamed kids "like her" for the loss of their parents. Seventy-five years later, Nora remembered a few of the children, mainly those who attempted to bully her but were eventually tamed by her primal scream, by the power of her emotions. She remembered Pavlik, a boy her age evacuated from Pskov. "Comrade Stalin is defending the Jews," he explained to Nora during recess. "He is very kind, but because of his kindness the Germans shot my parents."—"But the Germans shot my mother too," objected Nora. Pavlik would have none of it.—"It's a lie," he smirked. "Jews are never harmed; others die for them." And that's when Nora discovered the power of her scream. Poor Pavlik would never know that he served as a test subject for a weapon that Nora would wield with such deadly efficiency for the rest of her life.

She swapped Boston for Arad in the same dramatic fashion that some thirty years earlier she had exchanged Leningrad for Boston. But in some ways, this latest passage proved to be infinitely more performative. Her Soviet exodus followed a well-trodden path that bore the footprints of almost a million of her fellow Soviet emigres, including a number of close Leningrad friends (Gala and Misha, for example). "I feel like a guppy fished out of the aquarium," she shared with Gala soon after they had reunited in Brookline, Mass. "You see, it's like being stretched out in someone's palm, all rainbow colored and tremulous, exposed and therefore unique." She took a sip of her favorite cognac; Gala nodded obligingly as she often did when forced to endure one of Nora's soliloquies. "It's all an illusion, of course. For them," her index finger stabbed the air in the direction of the bay window—the vastness of America unfolded outside of it, "for them, we're indistinguishable from one another—just a school of fish, an enormous school of fish crossing the Atlantic."—"And whose palm is it?" asked Gala—haltingly as Nora rarely responded well to interruptions. "How the fuck do I know? God? Uncle Sam? Senator Kennedy of Massachusetts?" Gala winced—she was squeamish when it came to cursing. And so, generally, was Nora—squeamish, yes, but not above transgressing, especially to impress her audience, or just to make Gala squirm.

From Leningrad to Boston she had traveled in a metaphorical herd, holding Alex's hand, figuratively and literally not letting it go; one with her son, but the two of them also forming a constituent part of the great migration. Crossing the Atlantic with a flock of migrating birds, many thousands of them, all ferrying suitcases and shipping containers full of Czech crystal and hard covers of Russian classics. No husband, though. Nora could live perfectly well without a husband, especially without the one who had gifted her with Alex. Job well done, now get lost. That was the official version of her separation from the man who at their alimony hearing, conducted in a featureless, malodorous courtroom, called her an "evil gargoyle" and boasted of his many infidelities—ill-advised behavior at a divorce trial, but something that clearly gave him enormous satisfaction. She couldn't care less; the loser was a certified nobody, not deserving of their company—hers and Alex's. Getting rid of the cheating bastard was "the best thing that ever happened to me"... Again, the official version of events that would be presented to the world having passed her personal censorship.

Her escape to the Judean desert thirty years later—"My Exodus," as she predictably referred to it—would proceed in accordance with a different script, one that didn't exist. Misha, aghast at her decision, said as much: "No sane person, no one in her right mind, and no one, forgive me my bluntness, at your age has ever done this!" Yet Misha's opinion didn't matter to her. She would travel alone, disconnected from any larger historical patterns, at least from the most obvious ones, not holding anyone's hand, certainly not the hand of Alex. Alex's hand, just like all the other parts of his body (which she had never learned to see as separate from her own), was now occupied otherwise.

What did she expect? Did she have a plan beyond the practical steps required for relocating? Where did she see herself in five years? What a stupefyingly idiotic question to ask someone like Nora. Funnily enough, she was asked precisely that when interviewing for her first job in the States. A stout, kindly HR person, his pinkish bald spot glistening with sweat, prodded her ever so lightly towards the correct response: "Do you see yourself succeeding at our company? In five years?" In five years?! What hubris! Americans, even the mild-mannered bureaucrats, believe they can control their destiny. They plan their weddings several years out, make hotel reservations months in advance. Ridiculous. Life is not a river to be dammed, its course adjusted or reversed to your specifications. The Soviets tried that trick in Central Asia and look what happened: Remember the Aral Sea? Exactly. No, you don't make plans, you make moves—sensational ones, fueled by extreme emotions. Nora had no idea whether she would succeed at her new place of employment. Five years?! "I cannot promise you that," she hissed. "Five years is a long period of time. For all I know, I may be dead in five years." Then she fixed the visibly uncomfortable interviewer with an intense stare: "You could die too. It's quite possible that five years from now both of us will be dead." Somehow, she still got the job, and drew all the wrong conclusions from that one-off accident.

She didn't expect Alex to drop his pathetic Boston life—six-figure salary, four-bedroom house in Newton, shiksa whore in the kitchen—and follow her, Nora, to *Eretz*. A vision of the last scene. The two of them lighting Shabbat candles by the balcony window, the camel train in the distance gradually dissolving into the quickly thickening Levantine darkness. She pours out two tumblers of cognac for them to share; her recently purchased Hyundai Elantra is parked outside the building in the designated parking spot that came with the apartment; the day after tomorrow, after Shabbat, Alex will drive her to a doctor's appointment in Ashdod; he'll sit still in the waiting room of the doctor's office, while she is undergoing all the necessary exams and renews her prescriptions. Her pill box is never empty, not these days, not at her age. Afterwards they'll have a lunch of *khachapuri* and *khinkali* at that friendly Georgian beachside café. What a lovely last scene, with the camera panning across the breadth of the Mediterranean horizon, then zooming out . . . Will never happen, of course. Her life is a movie, no doubt, but it's a different sort of film. No happy ending, remember?

***

Farida will take care of things. What do they call her? Another strange Hebrew word—a *metapelet,* Nora's caretaker. "Oh, you now have a nurse?" the feeble-minded Gala innocently blurted out during a Skype call. Nora bristled indignantly: "I don't need a nurse! I'm not one of those Brookline old hags! I still drive, which by the way *you* never learned to do. No, she is my *assistant,* helping me out with the chores and such." But Gala, whose many virtues did not include circumspection, pressed on: "Farida . . . She is Muslim, isn't she? It's a Muslim name. Isn't it funny that now that you have moved to Israel you have a Muslim . . . *assistant*?" Momentarily, Nora was taken aback: such ignorance. Muslim! What does she know?! Listen, you fool, you hardly know what you're blabbering about, you'd better keep quiet about serious matters that you're too limited to understand. She doesn't say it exactly like that, despite her perennial disdain for Gala she is eager to preserve the connection, these Skype chats sustain her in her profound loneliness. Instead, she snorts contemptuously at the screen: "No, she is my *metapelet,* a beautiful Hebrew word." Nora claims to "absolutely love" her "native" language, which she neither speaks nor understands. But she derives such pleasure from knowing that it's all around her, its guttural sounds, those throaty "khs" filling her with delight and a sense of belonging. Farida speaks it fluently, even though she is not Jewish. An Uzbek? A Tatar? Nora always forgets to ask, too busy oversharing with Farida the minute details of her own odyssey.

In her sorrow over the loss of Alex to a Moldovan carpetbagger, in her fierce commitment to an illusion of independence, in her stubborn refusal to accept reality as it presents itself to her, stripped of fiction and allegory, Nora is not about to admit to her growing affection for Farida. She is contemptuous of sentimental human attachments, especially to strangers, to those who cannot possibly share your values or your grief. Only the tribe can do this for you, the tribe will protect you from the species of the wind-swept outside that are keen, hell-bent in fact, on tunneling their way inside your warmly lit world. The multitudes of hate-filled and antisemitic lie-spouting Pavliks, and the cheating, good-for-nothing husbands, and the dour Soviet apparatchiks, and all the grasping provincial tarts, whose whole purpose in life is to ensnare, and to disrupt, and to claim your own flesh and blood as their own—the strangers, the trespassers, the meddlers, the appropriators. But the tribe . . . where *is* it? In search of its protective shield, its metaphorical Iron Dome designed for her own needs, she had secured a refuge in this God-forsaken, yet God-blessed, desert.

The town is drab and feels alien, she rarely leaves her apartment. The irony of it, the irony of her tribe appearing like a still from a *National Geographic* documentary about a remote community of exotically attired locals, whose ways she cannot begin to comprehend. She never cared much for documentaries. "It's like a miracle, I instantly felt at home here!" she announced to Gala and Misha within days of her arrival in Arad. "It's like returning home after decades of wondering in the desert." Gala thought the analogy strange and topsy-turvy: "What are you talking about? You're in the desert *now*; you have literally *moved* to the desert . . . from Boston." That idiot, what does she know? What does she understand? Hidden from the elements behind Misha's broad frame: fifty years of no problems, fifty years of being led by her hand, fifty years and counting. She understands *nothing*! Those free of hurt are incapable of understanding.

But Farida understands. Farida, a stocky, fast-moving, and fast-talking woman, shows her kindness. More importantly, she shows respect for Nora's misfortunes and doesn't dismiss Nora's grievances glibly, absorbing the torrent of lamentations with unaffected ease. Grateful, Nora is willing to forgive even Farida's lulling, singsong accented Russian. So what if she *is* a Muslim? After all, the two of them hail from the same one-sixth of the earth's landmass, now rearranged in a new geopolitical constellation, where such distinctions didn't matter. Only they *do* matter, just ask any Pavlik. And yet, and yet . . . Farida is hardly a stranger, even though her claim on this patch of the Judean desert is rooted not in a three-thousand-year-old prophesy, but in the vagaries of post-Soviet disintegration.

Muslim or not, Farida isn't above sharing a snifter of cognac when they assemble in front of Nora's flat-screen Samsung TV to watch the evening news on a Russian-language Israeli channel. A breakdown of the day's events is delivered in urgent Russian by a gaggle of boisterous presenters. The rightwing and unapologetically nationalist tone of the news analysis satisfies Nora's deeper political cravings, while having no visible effect on Farida. "Damn right!" reacts Nora to another swipe by a paunchy talking head against the evil machinations of the appeasers. Farida glances briefly at the screen and takes the measure of the expert. "God, isn't he fat?" she pronounces to Nora's great indignation.—"Fat?! What do you mean 'fat'? He is smart, he sees right through these leftist hoodlums. If we had more like him back in the States maybe the country wouldn't be going down the drain right now!" Farida, ever nonchalant, waves her freshly refilled tumbler: "Ah, politics, just politics, all the same everywhere: people barking at each other like dogs. Woof! Woof!" She imitates the barking sounds, then laughs, and the sound of her laughter envelopes Nora and drains the pent-up tension out of her tired body. "Norochka, my lovely, don't you sweat over such silly things. Here, let me top off your glass. Here! *L'chaim,* my dearest!"

Such are their rituals of sisterly bonding, set against the backdrop of Nora's two-bedroom apartment, with its whitewashed walls and ceramic flooring, purchased for cash with the proceeds from the sale of her Brookline condo. Predictably, Alex denounced the transaction as fiscally irresponsible madness, failing to realize that he had forfeited his right to express an opinion about her affairs. No person, living or dead, could pass judgment on her "last chapter." For that's how Nora, with her penchant for grandiose formulations, saw her present state—her last chapter or maybe even, she thought to herself slyly, the epilogue. Or . . . an afterword to summarize the progression of humiliations, insults, and unearned misfortunes that have landed her—wronged, exhausted, but unbent and unbroken—in Arad. Goodbye, Alex, my dear chubby boy, sail on or, rather, spin your wheels in that mamaliga-reeking kitchen. Free at last, free of your mama's concerns and fears (all justified, of course), free to choose as you please, even if what pleases you makes your poor mama shudder, her lonely misery the price of your liberation. But at least one of us knows (feels it in her gut) that the promise of freedom is but an illusion, just another pipe dream, pushed by the loveless ones. The land of the free is the land of the unloved, the land of the damned, the land of exile.

Baruch atah Adonai Eloheinu, thank you for Farida, thank you for a stranger, who knows how to love and be loyal. Farida will take care of things, nothing fazes her. Gala and Misha—immersed in their comforts, shielded from the angry winds by their self-serving naivete and lack of imagination—have no appreciation for the bonds of unlikely friendships. When everything else fails, as they say. And everything else has failed—everything! Which, of course, is what has brought her to this comfy setup inside the movie theater of her life. With little effort she had secured the best seats in town—propped up on the cushions, tucked in neatly by the thoughtful Farida. Farida will be back in the morning; she'll take care of things. In the meantime, Nora can sit back and enjoy the view of that moving caravan. She can sip her cognac and maybe, ah, what the hell, one last Davidoff before bedtime (Bedtime? She is already in bed.), one for the road, one for the flinty caravan trail.

"Don't forget the pills, sweetie," Farida reminded her before leaving the apartment. And she promised not to. And as everyone who has ever crossed Nora's path knows only too well, she's good at keeping promises. Alex knows. And Misha knows. And the dim-witted Gala would've known had she ever paused to think. The pills are right here, on the nightstand, next to the cognac, next to a half-empty pack of Davidoffs: a merrily colored plastic box, whose seven square compartments represent the days of the week and are loaded up with every conceivable pharmaceutical wonder. Today is . . . what? Monday? Yes, *Yom Sheni.* One of the very first things they teach you at the ulpan are the days of the week. And that's about the only thing she has retained from the two-week language course for new arrivals. She quit, the class gave her headaches, and the very thought of having to turn in home assignments was both demeaning and inducive of hypertension. But not before she had learned the days of the week. *Yom Sheni* is followed by *Yom Shlishi,* which is still a long way from *Shabbat.* One can cover the distance by living it out or else by cheating: by jumping the hurdle of the plastic partitions separating the tiny squares. There was a book . . . There is always a book . . . A strange fantastical tale by two science-fiction author-brothers, wildly popular among her Leningrad friends. And what a peculiar title too—*Monday Begins on Saturday.* She was never big on anything outlandish and didn't care much for the book. But its title, so openly disdainful of the linear conception of time . . . that title intrigued her, largely because it appealed to her rebellious spirit. Rebels know how to cheat time and bend it to their will. If only she could focus well enough and stop worrying about tomorrow or the day after tomorrow; if she cleared her vision of the haunting images of that man-child Alex, she would skip a week, and another one, and yet another one . . . Her *Yom Shlishi* would arrive on *Shabbat.* And how liberating would *that* be? She would soar high above the roofs of Arad and swish through the night air—down to the Dead Sea, up to the domes of Jerusalem, onwards to the glistening spires of her forgotten Leningrad. She would take in the earth below, *breathe* it in, become one with it, because it'd be a movie, *her* movie, its very last scene. The camel caravan out in the distance, now a slender, barely visible thread of tiny dots, weaving its way through the desert. It's getting darker, but she can still see them: a bird's-eye view of the last speck of an animal crossing the balcony window frame, lingering for a brief second, and then . . . gone.

Bar Beach Police Station*

In the last year of the twentieth century, I flew to Nigeria from Chicago via St. Petersburg, Helsinki, and Amsterdam. If you get a kick out of experiencing intense and disorienting contrasts, try that route. My childhood friend Alex drove me to Helsinki from St. Pete. Alex was driving like a madman—honking incessantly, tailgating, yelling at slower traffic. Just past Vyborg a traffic policeman signaled us to stop. Alex slowed the car to a crawl but didn't come to a halt. We continued to roll along the curb, with the police officer trotting next to the driver's side window and Alex feeding him hundred-ruble notes: one, two, three . . . Enough? No? Ok . . . four, five . . . Eventually the cop (who never stopped jogging next to the moving vehicle) gave a sign that he'd received enough and wished us a happy onward journey. "Those greedy assholes," grumbled Alex and floored the gas pedal.

Soon after, we crossed the Finnish border; and the minute we did, Alex miraculously turned into a sensible just-under-the-speed-limit driver. I looked at him, surprised.

"You see, it's a civilized country, they got laws, and you can't really bribe anyone," explained my friend.

We both sighed. Him, with visible regret; me, with some relief. My flight was early in the morning, and we slept in Alex's Audi hatchback parked in some field, not far from the airport. Ah, childhood friendships . . . so special . . .

I had a long layover in Amsterdam, which was great, because I was able to drop by another childhood friend's place on Keerkstraat and take a shower. After a day of travel Dina's and her husband Florian's flat felt like a safe and welcoming harbor. Florian was watching the news, which happened to be from Nigeria. Nigeria was very much in the news at the time due to the recent suspicious death of the country's dictator, General Sani Abacha. Florian looked worried and suggested that, instead of flying off to Lagos, I stay with them in Amsterdam. Florian and Dina are among the most hospitable people I know; they are always hosting someone, sometimes for months on end. It's

---

* First published as "Bar Beach Police Station," *New England Review* 43, no. 3 (Fall 2022), 169–79.

been more than twenty years, but they are still at it. It would've been nice to stay with them, but I really couldn't. We hugged and I left for the airport to board my flight to Lagos.

The first few weeks in Nigeria were surreal, exhausting, maddening, exciting. The place was outrageously corrupt, palpably dangerous, and, in the aftermath of Abacha's demise, overflowing with wild political rumors. But I also kept meeting the most wonderful and warm people, who were eager to take me under their wing and help me out in any way they could. The mixture of dysfunction, brutality, and generosity would've been disorienting had it not been so familiar. In many ways, it felt like my native Russia. Strangely, Nigeria proved to be easier for me to figure out than the US (still a work in progress).

That year Lagos was simmering with anticipation. My colleagues at the Nigerian Institute of International Affairs (NIIA) on Victoria Island warned me that another coup was inevitable. They hinted darkly that Abacha had not died a natural death. Frankly, I would've been surprised had it been otherwise. And then there was this whole business of "armed robbers." Every few weeks the army and the black-uniformed police fought pitched battles against gangs of marauding vigilantes ("area boys") on the outskirts of the city. By December, the unrest would reach a boiling point and erupt into open warfare on the mainland. The posher neighborhoods of Victoria Island and Ikoyi remained relatively safe, but I was advised to drop my habit of hitching *okada* rides to the University of Lagos campus. Instead, I now spent most of my time working at the institute library.

On the weekends, my friend Isaac and I would go to one of the city beaches—Bar Beach or Lekki Beach—to hang out under a rented canopy of palm leaves, which gave a lot of shade. We bought weed from the Hausa beach traders, who, once you've made your first purchase, would never leave you alone. Isaac and I swapped life stories. His were infinitely more colorful—stories of stowaway migrations, trans-Saharan crossings, and extreme violence. Often he spoke of the deep, redeeming faith that he had never abandoned. Isaac was one of the most fearless, tough, irrepressible but also gentle people I've ever met. The world goes around because of people like him. He now lives in New York and works as a nurse; once every few months he texts me his blessing and a reminder that he owes me a trip to visit his home in Ghana.

When things turned particularly crazy on the other end of the pothole-riddled but majestically zigzagging Carter Bridge that separated us from the mainland, the institute's security personnel grew increasingly worried about my presence on the premises. As the only white person in the immediate neighborhood, I stood out and, they feared, could attract some unwelcome attention. They also informed me that they had spotted a silver Peugeot with diplomatic plates idling outside the gate. They were concerned about this car, but I suspected its appearance had nothing to do with the ongoing unrest; it was likely connected to a couple of weird encounters I recently had with the staff of the Russian embassy, located a few blocks away.

The embassy building loomed like an impregnable fortress, and the security guards stationed by the fence acted as if it were one. On a few occasions I tried to gain access to the embassy library, which I thought might contain primary sources relevant to my research. My attempts at making an approach invariably turned into awkward affairs. The staff became immediately suspicious of my intentions, and once they found out that I wanted to work in their library while not possessing a valid Russian passport they were not pleased. Not pleased, but curious.

"Who the fuck are you and what the fuck are you doing in fucking Nigeria?"— that's how the consular official, a skinny but menacing guy in his twenties, tried to clarify the situation.

We were speaking in Russian by the guard house, across the street from a fast-food joint that pretended to be a McDonalds. I could see that my explanation (a graduate student on a research fellowship at the NIIA) failed to satisfy him. "What is it you want here?" he asked, lighting a cigarette. I didn't want to smoke but figured that under the circumstances it was the wise thing to do. And for a few minutes we smoked in silence. "It's hot as fuck here, like . . . all the time," he finally opined. I nodded an affirmation; it was easy to agree since the guy was stating the obvious. "So what is it you want from us?" he continued, after taking another drag on his cigarette.

"I'd like to be allowed to work with the press releases and other documents at the embassy library . . ."

He looked at me pensively, then let out a delicately trimmed stream of smoke: "Are you fucked in your head? What moron would ever let you do it?" It sounded better in Russian: "Ты что, совсем охуел? Какой же мудак тебя туда пустит?"

We shook hands over nothing and I headed back to the institute. But from that point on I would keep running into this foul-mouthed consular official whenever I went to the store to get some bottled water, or to the counterfeit McDonalds to grab a meat pie, or to the internet cafe by the beach (an unpleasant forty-minute walk), or with Isaac on the weekends to "Why Not?," a Lebanese bar whose name accurately captured its prevailing ethos.

So that particular library collection turned out to be off-limits. Thankfully, the NIIA library proved to be a treasure trove, and I soon settled into a routine of spending most of my days there, with occasional trips to the archive in Ibadan, a hundred-mile drive north of Lagos. As I said, the Nigerian colleagues were very supportive and generally laid-back. On one occasion I tried to pay for my lodgings at the hostel, but the administrator refused to accept my money.

"It's quite all right, no need to pay," he said, waving away a stack of soiled naira. "You're welcome, we're happy to have you with us. One day I'll come and visit you in America and you'll be good to me." I promised to be a good host to him. Throughout my stay in Nigeria, I would end up making a lot of such promises. Every single one of them, except for the one I made to Isaac, has remained unfulfilled.

I stepped outside the library to stretch my legs when a shabby guy approached me. His dirty shorts were fraying at the edges, his beat-up flip-flops seemed to exist separately from his feet, and sort of followed him around. After a few months in Nigeria I knew what to expect—he would ask for money. And he did. His wife was in the hospital, the surgery was scheduled for tomorrow, if he didn't raise some funds the doctors wouldn't operate. I knew the drill and gave him whatever I had in my pocket, probably a couple hundred naira (about two dollars). He seemed pleased with the haul but still asked for more, as there was a script that had to be followed. We both understood it. I wished him and his nonexistent wife well and headed back to the research room.

A few minutes later, the institute's security chief, a mild-mannered man in his sixties, came up to my desk in a state of unusual agitation. He wanted to know the details of my brief chat with the man in shorts. I couldn't understand why he sounded so concerned and assured him that whatever worry he might have on my account was most certainly misplaced. He didn't look reassured and suggested that we should take a quick ride together to the Bar Beach police station to "sign an affidavit." At that point I had been in Nigeria long enough to know that it was advisable to steer clear of the police, unless one had an unlimited supply of cash and an irresistible urge to part with it. In other words, it was a bit like Russia—the similarities between the two places never failed to impress me. No, I really had no desire to visit the compound by Bar Beach. I had passed by it on my walks to the internet cafe, and its heavy gates of weather-ravaged corrugated metal sheets looked anything but inviting.

The security chief sighed with sad resignation: "Are you sure you don't want to go?" Yes, I was sure, but I also felt sorry for him, mostly because I couldn't fathom the reason for his alarm. As far as I was concerned, there was absolutely nothing to fret about: Ok, I exchanged a few words with a beggar outside, I gave him some money—just one of many such transactions happening every minute in this overwhelming and mad city of broken traffic lights and unfinished skyscrapers. The pungent smells from the lagoon a couple of kilometers away reached the courtyard of the institute. With no evidence at all I connected these acrid-smelling whiffs to the rainbow film of oil that covered much of the water of the lagoon and stretched out into the ocean as far as the eye could see, and I couldn't separate the omnipresent toxic odor from the spectacle of black police uniforms. I once shared this association between the smell of petroleum and the sight of the police with Isaac and asked him if it made any sense to him (things he and I discussed . . .). Isaac shrugged: "It depend," he said. That's how he often responded to my questions—a shrug, a quick laugh, "it depend."

The security chief and I reached an agreement. It was still Tuesday and he'd let me work in peace until Thursday. We'd go to the police station on Thursday after lunch. "Can the signing of the affidavit wait until Thursday?" I asked him. He assured me that it most certainly could. I still thought that this whole affidavit business was absolutely unnecessary, a total waste of time, but I also sensed that the security chief was following some unknown to me protocol.

During those first few months in Nigeria, I made a conscious and often exhausting effort to understand and respect the local customs (including the bureaucratic ones). It seemed an enlightened graduate student thing to do. Also, a reasonable safety precaution in a country seemingly poised on the verge of another military coup. Isaac thought I was trying too hard, but of course he would think that. Isaac once bribed the Ukrainian captain of a Panamanian-flagged reefer ship with a hundred-gram gold bar to deliver him to Cadiz. After a week of hiding under a bunk in the engine room, half-deaf from noise and half-conscious from fumes, Isaac arrived in Cadiz, where he was instantly apprehended by the immigration police and placed in detention. His deportation proceedings would take months, and in the meantime he picked up some conversational Spanish and learned how to play backgammon from an Egyptian asylum seeker with whom he shared his cell.

Strangely, Isaac had very fond memories of his year-long stay in the Spanish prison; among his numerous life experiences, the Cadiz fiasco qualified as one of the milder ones. So he believed I was overthinking the whole affidavit situation. I asked him why the security chief acted so anxiously. Isaac thought for a second. "He thinks the beggar was a spotter," he said.

"What does it mean?"

"It means the area boys sent him in to find out where you're staying at the hostel."

"Should I be worried?"

"It depend." He then laughed. "No worries, I'll stay with you in your room for a few days."

On Thursday, we didn't go to the police station. My colleague Adisa volunteered to drive me to Ibadan for a day and I couldn't pass up on the opportunity to spend a few hours at the national archives. On the way back, the car broke down and we were picked up by a yellow minibus headed to Surulere. Then the minibus broke down just before the Ketu junction, and Adisa and I hailed down an *okada* that delivered us to Victoria Island after sunset. The nights were pitch-dark, even on the island, and full of the sounds of streaking *okada* engines and occasional laughter erupting in the courtyard of the Cuban embassy next door. I asked Adisa about the car. He looked concerned, as if I'd asked him something he really didn't want to think about until the next morning.

Isaac was waiting for me in my room, all good cheer and smiles. I noticed a sawed-off broomstick placed inconspicuously by the closet door. I picked it up, only to discover that it was unexpectedly heavy. "Lead," explained Isaac.

"Do we really need it?"

"It depend," he said.

I really had no desire to visit the Bar Beach police station on a Friday afternoon.

The security chief was seated at his usual spot by the front door of the library. He listened to me with a set solemn expression on his gentle face. "It's ok," he said. "It's ok, I can see you're busy, we don't have to go there today, the affidavit can wait until Monday. Especially because they are not releasing the inmates on Fridays, the offender will have to stay in jail until Monday anyway . . ."

I thought I'd misheard him. "What offender?"

"The beggar, the one who begged you for money."

"He is in jail?!"

"Of course! Where else would he be? We caught him soon after he talked to you on Monday, no, wait . . . on Tuesday."

Too many days in the week and one guy, one guy in jail, for . . . talking to me. Awful. Worse than awful.

"Why didn't you tell me?! I thought it was just a formality. I didn't realize someone actually got locked up for talking to me!"

The security chief nodded agreeably. "I told you we should go to the police station, but you were busy. And yesterday you traveled to Ibadan. I heard Adisa's car suffered a malfunction on your way back. What happened? Did he succeed repairing it?"

He sounded so formal: "succeed repairing it." This placid guy and his old-fashioned English, and that other skinny one, wearing tattered shorts and flip-flops like flattened pancakes—in jail. I had spent the previous few weeks feeling elevated by my ability to adapt. I got an instant high out of my self-conscious efforts to identify common threads that connected me to Isaac, and Adisa, some of the "Why Not?" regulars, and the Liberian *okada* driver, who used to take me to campus before the latest violence had made such trips unsafe. Apparently just another self-serving illusion on my part, one of many . . . And I couldn't stomach the thought of someone stuck in a dirty, overcrowded cell inside the Bar Beach police station's jail on account of chatting with me . . . Ok, on account of "spotting" me. What did *I* care? He can spot me all he wants—my presence here is hardly a state secret, even the lamplighters from the Russian embassy seem to be aware of it.

Maybe they'd let him out on Friday afternoon? As a nice, goodwill gesture to this visiting foreigner, who is more than willing to sign any fucking affidavit they desire? We were deep into the Christmas season, after all. I wondered if it meant anything to the black-uniformed cohort at the Bar Beach police station. I had an eerie sensation that this had all happened before, in some other life. Then I remembered: Leningrad. I must've been six or seven when my mom spent a few weeks in the hospital, recovering from a spine injury. I missed her terribly and kept nagging my dad to get her to come home. The agony of waiting reached its crescendo on one Friday afternoon when Dad headed to the hospital to pick up Mom after the discharge. To my horror, that evening he returned home alone—no Mom in tow. The hospital bureaucracy had taken too long to process the discharge papers and by the time it was my mother's turn their workday had come to an end. "You will have to return on Monday, we don't discharge patients on the weekends," some pale-eyed and thin-lipped nurse explained to my father. My mom too must've been a spotter. The time warp of that weekend was still with me. I could certainly do without another one. "We need to go to the station right now," I entreated the security chief.

He considered my plea for a few seconds, checked his watch, then nodded: "Alright, then. Please, allow me to finish up my duties here and then I'll accompany you."

We walked the familiar route: by the noisy Cuban embassy, over a bridge of uneven cinder blocks linking the two sandy banks of a ditch that crossed the island (its purpose remained unclear to me), past an old rosewood tree with, bafflingly, a "Passport Photos Here" sign nailed to it. It took us less than twenty minutes to reach the gates of the police station and another thirty to explain to a bored constable the purpose of our visit. "Give him a little something, give him twenty naira," said the security chief.

I did as told, and the policeman, having pocketed the money, finally detached his bulk from the gate that he'd been propping up and walked towards a low building that I assumed to be the station. He returned a few minutes later and unhurriedly unlocked the gate.

The stench inside the station was overpowering. I looked at the security chief, wondering if he smelled what I smelled. By all outward signs he didn't, appearing just as calm and proper as he did every morning when I greeted him at the institute's entrance. It was difficult to reconcile his Victorian formality with the spatial and aesthetic confusion of our surroundings, with those offensive smells. But he remained calm, as Isaac remained calm in the Spanish jail, as Alex remained calm at the wheel of his Audi, while conveying a stack of banknotes into the waiting palms of a traffic police officer. How does one preserve this sort of serenity in the face of a world that offends and disappoints and makes mockery of morality? Just last week Isaac and I were spending a lazy afternoon on Bar Beach, sharing a joint, watching the gray, oil-filmed waves licking the pebbles. "You see that corner of the beach?" Isaac pointed out a narrow strip by the cabanas, where the local traders roasted meat.

"Yes. So?"

"They used to shoot people there."

"You're kidding, right?" I didn't think the joke was funny.

"No, I'm serious. Those rusty petrol barrels, right there, stacked up. You see? That's where they executed the robbers. I'm telling you, Nigerians are rough."

Now, inside the Bar Beach police station I remembered that conversation and thought that signing the damn affidavit (why do they call it an "affidavit"?) was the least I could do. The sergeant on duty led us into his office, which was sparse, its walls painted a disturbing green. A portrait of the new president hung slightly askew on the wall above the desk. The president in the portrait wore a traditional Yoruba dress and a pair of sunglasses, exuding self-confidence and haughty benevolence. And so did the sergeant while inquiring about the purpose of our visit. The sergeant, hefty and in crisp, freshly pressed uniform, also had sunglasses on and sported a cool black beret that bore a strange silver insignia—an eagle perched atop an elephant. I really didn't know what to make of any of it. "It's a two-stage process," explained the sergeant. "First you are asked to formally identify the prisoner in question. Then you have to sign the affidavit. Understand?"

I nodded, still struggling to reconcile all this primness in manners and neatness in dress with the shabbiness of the interior of the station. And with the fetid smell that induced in me a peculiar sensation of levitating, much like the effect of those joints expertly rolled by Isaac. The smell grew in intensity as we exited the office and walked down a feebly lit corridor (the sergeant still wouldn't take off his shades) towards a partition of thick vertical bars. We got closer and I could now see a mass of people behind the bars and hear the droning of voices, interrupted by occasional yelps and bursts of laughter. Oh, that's how they did it: they had divided up the corridor by an iron curtain and turned the remaining half of the hallway into a cell. They didn't even bother to build a proper jail. On our approach the prisoners rushed the bars, yelling requests, demanding attention.

And then I heard: "*Oyibu, oyibu,* I'm here, my friend, I'm here!" It was the guy, the beggar. Somewhere along the way he had lost his flip-flops and t-shirt, but it was him. He had forced his way to the bars and was now crying out to me, smiling deliriously: "*Oyibu, oyibu*! How are you, *oyibu*? Tell them we're friends." I had never seen anyone so seemingly delighted to see me.

The sergeant observed our reunion through the shades, then pointed a massive finger at the inmate: "Do you know him?"

I nodded eagerly: "Yes, that's the guy. He did nothing wrong, he is a good and friendly person. I gave him some money because I wanted to help; it was *my* idea. I can vouch for him. You really must let him go. Please. I will sign the affidavit."

The sergeant's face remained expressionless, separated from the immediacy of the scene by the black ovals of the sunglasses. We were standing in semi-darkness, in front of the steel bars, amidst the terrifyingly foul smell of the dozens of neglected bodies . . . and I still had not seen his eyes. He appeared slightly contemptuous (of me? of the guy in the tattered shorts?), but he probably always looked like that—the learned demeanor of someone bestowed with the power to lock and unlock prison cells. I wondered if he would relent. He did—ultimately—and motioned me to follow him back to the office.

In the office, I took the seat across the enormous desk from him. The sergeant pulled a blank piece of paper out of one of the drawers and pushed it towards me. "Here, sign the affidavit," he said. I signed the blank sheet. He studied my signature pensively, then sighed: "It's expensive."

"What is expensive?"

"The upkeep of the prisoner is expensive. He's been here since Monday . . ."

"Tuesday," I corrected him.

He froze and immediately I knew that I should not argue with someone who never takes off his sunglasses.

"You're right, sir, since Monday. My mistake."

"All right, then: Monday, Tuesday, Wednesday, Thursday, Friday . . . We don't release prisoners on the weekends so . . . Saturday, Sunday. Seven days. Meals, sanitation procedures, guard duty, cleaning . . . All very expensive."

"How much?" I asked.

The sergeant didn't bother to respond. I took out a wad of cash and started counting out hundred naira notes:

"One hundred, two hundred, three hundred, four hundred . . . Enough? No? Five hundred, six hundred, seven hundred . . ."

Through the dust-coated glass of the office window filtered in an unsteady orange glow—the sun was setting across the lagoon. Thousands of kilometers away Alex was driving his Audi on a snowy highway by the frozen Gulf of Finland, the wipers going steady, pushing the fast-falling snow off the windshield. As always, he was speeding, indifferent to the dangers of slippery winter roads, oblivious to the presence of a ghostly traffic policeman jogging effortlessly through the icy air alongside the car, his felt-booted feet not touching the ground, his waiting palm outstretched, like in a Chagall painting.

Later that night (much later) Isaac and I were seated at our usual corner table at Why Not? Michel, the Lebanese proprietor, had brought out a battery of stouts and local Star lagers. I had spent the previous hour unburdening myself to Isaac, trying to assuage my guilty conscience. He listened to me politely, but my angst didn't resonate with him. I described to him the interior of the jail and mentioned the sour stench permeating every nook and cranny of the Bar Beach police station. I talked at length about the poor wretch in his threadbare shorts, whose toothless smile still haunted me. Isaac set pace to my lament by tapping his fingers on a cool bottle glass, against the soundtrack of the humming of the generators outside. "Nigerians," he said. "Nigerians are rough. I told you, remember? Nigerians are rough."

I noticed the skinny Russian diplomat at a table by the stairs. He was drinking beer in the company of a morose heavy, whose nationality was betrayed by an incongruent ensemble of dark-blue socks, sandals, and a knockoff Armani t-shirt tucked into cargo shorts. The skinny meanie waved at me with a half-empty bottle of stout, then got up and stumbled over to our table. "Want to come over and join us?" he said to me, ignoring Isaac.

"Would love to, but I can't, I'm here with a friend."

"Your friend . . ." He finally looked at Isaac. "The manager at the hostel. I know. We know."

I pretended to be surprised. "How do you know?"

The Russian appeared pleased with himself. He finished off the stout and placed the empty bottle on the table in front of me, just a notch too aggressively. But whatever.

"Enjoyed your trip to the police station?" he said.

"You know that too?"

He winked at me and pointed his index finger towards the ceiling fan: "*We* know."

"It was a misunderstanding . . ." I tried to explain, but he waved off the explanation.

"Who fucking cares? Do you think I care? I don't. Want to come over for a drink? Your last chance."

I shook my head. "I can't. Sorry."

"Oh, well, have it your way. We'll see you around."

"We?"

He chuckled, then pointed his finger again at the fan: "Up there. You understand, right?" He lowered his finger until it was level with Isaac's face. But he was not looking at Isaac, he was looking at me: "You really should hang out with your own kind. Safer that way."

Another chuckle. The diplomat turned around and walked unsteadily back to his watching post by the stairs, where his comatose friend waited patiently for his return. No, I definitely didn't want to hang out with "my own kind."

"Did you speak Chinese with him?" Isaac asked me unexpectedly.

"Chinese? Why would I speak Chinese? I don't speak Chinese . . ."

"Well, I told you about Gloria, right?"

Yes, numerous times. Gloria was one of Isaac's several girlfriends, and she worked the reception desk at the Chinese embassy on the island. Judging by what Isaac had communicated to me about her, Gloria was high-maintenance and status-oriented. The job at the embassy placed her at the higher end of some Lagos table of ranks and she rarely failed to remind Isaac of this fact. Even though he was far from being faithful to her, Isaac was perpetually preoccupied with mollifying Gloria. I couldn't quite figure out their relationship, but, frankly, I could never understand other people's relationships. It was on his regular visits to the embassy that Isaac was introduced to the Mandarin of Gloria's Chinese coworkers and bosses and apparently concluded the language to be the lingua franca in use by other foreigners on Victoria Island. But maybe he was just making fun of me and the narrow-framed drunk Russian who'd rudely pointed a finger at him.

"Are you joking? We spoke Russian."

Isaac seemed neither impressed nor convinced: "It sounded like Chinese. The guy was rough. Russians are rough."

"That's how you describe everyone: Nigerians are rough, Russians are rough . . ."

"No, not everyone," disagreed Isaac. "Ghanaians are not rough, Spanish are not rough, Cubans are not rough . . ."

And that's how we talked deep into the night—our Friday ritual of effortless bonding. The generators hummed ceaselessly outside, where the damp air hung heavily and the nocturnal insects made a terrible racket, too boisterous even for Lagos. A few kilometers away a haggard middle-aged man slept on the dirty floor of his cell inside the Bar Beach station. He didn't need to be there; he was not a robber and I was not his prey. I had conveniently convinced myself that the sergeant would release him on Monday because I signed the affidavit, my signature instantly recognizable on a blank sheet of paper. The sergeant would perform that quick bureaucratic act, an easy act of mercy—release a prisoner. He'd unlock the metal barred door without removing his sunglasses. The grateful detainee would step out of the cell and shuffle down the airless hallway towards the exit. Free at last, he would touch the street dust with his naked feet and pause to savor the moment, absorbing the noise of the traffic, inhaling the fumes emitted by the *okadas*, greeting the young sun with a relieved smile.

A Walmart Love Story*

Petite filet mignons at the Walmart Supercenter in Honesdale, Pennsylvania, sell at eleven dollars and eighty-two cents a pound. I pick up four wrapped in plastic film and place them in the cart next to the romaine lettuce and two organic English cucumbers. There are nonorganic cucumbers in the adjacent section, and they are a dollar eighty-five each, as opposed to two dollars and ninety-six cents for the organic ones. Eleven eighty-two, one eighty-five, two ninety-six. How do they ever come up with these figures? I overpay for organic produce because overpaying at Walmart Supercenter is really a sign of class. Or hubris. Or aspiration. Or my recently acquired class-consciousness.

The woman in the cereal aisle draws up her cart next to mine, then overtakes me—I'm moving too slowly, and violating the six-feet rule is her way of alerting me to this fact. She probably drives the same way—one of those perpetually honking tailgaters, always in a rush, forever annoyed with us, the five-miles-above-the-speed-limit drivers. The woman sports snugly fitting camo pants covering the tops of her grey Caterpillar work boots. She is so unapologetically busty that I immediately suspect outside intervention. The prominence of her breasts is accentuated by a tight, pink "Women for Trump" t-shirt. I try to avert my eyes, but there is a magnetic quality to the woman's proximity, and I can't avoid the sight of the outsized white capital letters, pushed forth by the assertive power of her flesh. Her hair is bleached and ponytailed, her skin deeply tanned, and a sorrowful Jesus on the cross is inked on her forearm. She wears a mask the color of the American flag. Actually, she doesn't, it's some other mask, but I can't help seeing stars and stripes—the stripes are faded, the stars emit an unsteady whitish glow, traveling at a speed of light from some distant galaxy. Everything about her is just so tight, so seamlessly assembled. I'm certain she hunts, and I can easily visualize the truck she drives. Her in-your-face sexuality strikes me as determined but self-conscious; she looks so tough but at the same time strangely vulnerable. The mixture of girlishness (pink), militarism (camo pants), voluptuousness

---

* First published as "A Walmart Love Story," *Anti-Heroin Chic* (November 25, 2020).

(her boobs), right-wing politics (the white lettering), religion (Jesus on the cross), counterculture (Jesus on the cross). I wonder if she prepped for this Walmart stop, conceived it as a statement of purpose. How carefully did she choose her outfit? *Did* she choose it? I wonder what she made of me. Did she even notice? Or was I just a slowly moving obstacle to be honked at and pushed aside, out of the fast lane?

We might fall in love, and fall hard. We're so different but are drawn together by the power of opposite attraction. I can see myself hunched over on a plastic chair inside that rundown laundromat on the corner of High and Church, waiting patiently for the droning dryer to stop. I'll carefully fold her undies, her tube socks, and, extra carefully, the pink t-shirt with the white capital letters: the "T," the "W." These laundry rituals are the most boyfriend thing in the world. A dollar seventy-five per load, plus another dollar twenty-five for the dryer. (Again, how do they ever come up with these figures?) I think of an old Soviet film that I always loved—*The Forty-First*. A story of doomed love between a Bolshevik sniper and the wounded White Army officer whom she captures. A devastatingly romantic film. She loses her head over him and even tosses aside her weapon, which had previously claimed the lives of forty other White officers. But this one is different—he's the enemy but also the love of her life. You watch the film and desperately wish for the merciless dialectical wheel to come to a halt. And for a while it appears that the two may just escape the bear hug of history, if only it left them alone—to heal their wounds, to make love on the sandy Aral shore. But they can't help themselves, they can't stop choosing sides. Eventually he tries to escape, and the woman retrieves her discarded rifle and once again lives up to her reputation as one of the best shots on the Caspian front.

At the cash register she is right in front of me—six feet away—unloading boxes of frozen pizza and Frosted Flakes onto the conveyor belt. The cashier's name tag says "Maryanne"; she must be in her eighties and moves very slowly, slower than I moved in the cereal aisle. Every single cashier at this Walmart seems to be way past retirement age, all fully masked—this country is seriously messed up. I fear that my huntress will get annoyed, start honking. But she now exhibits a new, endearing side of her personality—she is being patient while Maryanne struggles with the price scanner. There is something wrong with the credit card and she ends up writing a check. It's been a while since I've seen someone write a check in a supermarket—the act seems as foreign now as it did the first time I observed it back in 1991, also at a Walmart store, my very first Walmart.

"You have a blessed day, honey," she says to Maryanne, who nods in response and also utters a few parting words, the sound muffled by her mask. There is a small bottleneck at the exit, occasioned by an elderly gentleman whose job apparently is to monitor retail traffic. He has a small device in his hand, which he clicks each time a customer exits the store. The woman is once again right in front of me, leaning on her cart, her fingers performing an impatient drumroll on the handlebar. Her butt is tautly camouflaged, and relative to her prominent bosom it appears quite small. Once again, I avert my eyes, but not before I take note of a dark brassiere clasp clearly visible through her t-shirt. The brassiere will require a gentle washing cycle and I'm definitely not putting it in the dryer—it'll ruin it. As soon as we exit into the parking lot she pulls down her mask and inhales with relish. She turns around, not because she noticed me (I don't think she did), but out of necessity to share this moment of relief with another living soul. I am that soul and she smiles at me and, unexpectedly, the smile is radiant and innocent. "Jesus, fresh air, at last!" she says. I too remove my mask and smile back at her, my kindest, most gentle, most sincere smile. But I don't say a word, I don't want to confuse her with my accent.

The Jaws of Victory*

That spring of 1988 was a spring like no other. At the end of March, the elderly minister of defense issued his biannual decommissioning order. It was published in all the major newspapers—a small and inconspicuous-looking item at the bottom of the back page of the *Izvestia* or *Pravda,* or that idiotic army paper that we loved to mock (the *Red Star*?). However, for those of us who had been drafted in the spring of 1986, it wasn't so "small." My best friend and fellow infantry sergeant, Yurik, used his connections outside the base to procure multiple copies of the papers carrying the order that heralded our freedom. We then carved out the tiny squares—to be ironed into plastic sheaths and carried around in the breast pockets of our fatigues, a symbol of our enhanced social standing, and a memento to be preserved for future generations.

Yes, technically we were still soldiers but only barely; we were more like civilians in waiting. Even the officers, especially the young lieutenants, began to treat us with a certain respect and consideration. We were *dembelya*—soldiers on the brink of discharge, inhabiting a liminal space between serfdom and emancipation. The ambiguity of this status was a source of both excitement and anxiety. The days dragged on. We smoked a great deal in silence. We tried to read but couldn't. We hung around with the Uzbek kitchen cohort at the canteen. After hours, the Uzbeks grilled pork. Makhsudbek, the head chef, assured us that it was lamb. Not pork, no. Pork was not halal and he would never touch it. Only he did, of course. Yurik delighted in observing Makhsudbek's contortions and played along, praising his magic culinary touch and the delicious "lamb." I remember thinking how easy it was to manufacture one's own truth, to turn fiction into reality by giving it a name.

Those final weeks—they crawled. Some of us were counting the days; the more anxious souls were counting hours. In the meantime, in those rare moments when we could find it in ourselves to pause our dreams of freedom—home-cooked meals, sex, family reunions—certain thoughts and

* First published as "The 'Jaws' of Victory," *WordCity Literary Journal,* no. 14 (March 2022).

questions crept in. Something strange was afoot beyond the fenced-off perimeter of our sleepy military town. In early March, a huge fight broke out between the Azeri and Armenian privates of the Third Mechanized Infantry Battalion. Apparently, the brawl's origins could be traced to an interethnic conflict unfolding in a mountainous region some 2500 kilometers away from our base. Afterwards, our company commander, a wounded Afghan vet, looked worried: "Not a good sign; when this sort of hatred bubbles up to the surface, countries fall apart. Trust me, I've seen this shit happen in real time." Captain Oganesian was a kindly psychopath, damaged by the horrors he witnessed during the battle of Zhawar. An ethnic Armenian, he was a pleasant enough guy when sober.

There were some other indirect signs of a seismic shift occurring in the enormous country beyond our garrison town. In his regular letters to me, my father started making constant opaque references to "something new that I've read, something that could have never been published before." In one of his last letters he had mentioned a vacation he was planning for my post-discharge weeks. We would go to a Lithuanian resort, famous for its sandy dunes, but more importantly, for its public library, which was well stocked with subscriptions to Moscow's literary magazines. "We'll read," my dad promised. "We'll read and read and read. There's so much to read now." All this sounded disorienting. After two years of isolation from the outside world, I harbored less ambitious expectations.

And then there were the letters from my girlfriend, a prolific and emotive writer. During her previous semester she had gone on a study abroad trip to East Germany and returned overwhelmed by the experience. In her letters, she kept referencing locations with strange-sounding names: Leipzig, Halle, Jena, among others. Apart from some of my commanding officers, who had fought in Afghanistan, Angola, and Central America, she was the only person I knew who had been abroad. "It's almost as if you are dating a foreigner," opined the all-knowing Yurik, who in his twenty-two years on earth had never crossed the borders of the Vladimir region. Before serving in the army, he had done eighteen months for aggravated battery in a penal colony for delinquents. The charges resulted from an epic fistfight between Yurik's "crew" of local thugs and a group of artillery cadets. The two factions clashed on the hardwood dance floor of Vladimir's most dangerous spot—the Park of Culture and Rest of the Toilers, named after the city's namesake, Vladimir Lenin.

The park, and especially its famed dance floor, were key to Yurik's personal story and identity. It was on this sacred turf that Yurik's homeboys and the cadets vied for the affections of a trio of Ukrainian yarn spinners, who happened to be on a summer training assignment at a local textile factory. It was certainly not his first fight at Lenin Park, but it was one that went particularly badly for Yurik: blood was spilled and the militia caught Yurik literally red-handed—in possession of a well-sharpened metal object of some unknown industrial origin. Predictably, the cadets were let off the hook, while Yurik, who was not a future Soviet army officer like them but rather a disposable local hoodlum, was turned into a handy scapegoat. The battered artillerists moved on with their army careers. Meanwhile, Yurik was sent to a juvenile detention center, conveniently situated just outside Vladimir's city limits. So no, there wasn't much globe-trotting on his resume. Besides, Yurik's geographic ambitions were modest, and he most certainly never expected to set foot, for example, inside the German State Library of the University of Jena (Thüringer Universitäts- und Landesbibliothek Jena), first founded in 1558; or even anywhere near this famed library—on the cobblestones of Jena's old town, where, in 1806, Emperor Napoleon triumphantly rode his grey Arabian past the philosopher Hegel.

Besides her serialized travelogue, my girlfriend's letters contained other intriguing cues, pointing to a world apparently changed beyond my immediate recognition. Take the Belgian exchange student, for example, and his mad crush on her. In several of my girlfriend's letters, she went to great lengths to describe the ups and downs of their relationship. "Ups" for her due to the excitement of being pursued by a bespectacled native French-speaker; "downs" for him, I assumed (naively, Yurik thought), because of my continuing albeit long-distance presence in her life. The Belgian's heartache was of little interest to me—far less interesting than the mere fact of his corporeal existence: a flesh-and-blood Belgian was walking the streets of my city, wooing my girlfriend. I had never met a Belgian before, but I did have a one-franc Belgian coin in my collection, which bore the image of a young woman, depicted in profile, wearing a headdress. The coin was minted in 1976, the year I started elementary school. Before the army, I considered it one of my cherished possessions. The Belgian student probably had a pocketful of such coins—loose change for him, no doubt.

It occurred to me that it would've been nice to meet him in person, to become his friend. It was a strange aspiration on my part, but the perceived end of history can be a time of moral confusion. "I told you," Yurik said, "dating your girl is totally like dating a foreigner. It's almost like being a foreigner. Remember those Cuban lieutenants, who were assigned to the

Second Battalion for training last year? It's probably sort of like that, like being around them. Fun!" Yurik's associative thinking often left me scratching my head.

It was Yurik, of course, who first got wind of the opening of the first ever "commercial" video salon in town, on the premises of the workers' canteen at the railroad depot. The canteen was one of our favorite spots in a drab garrison town that had few gastronomical options. Once a week we would sneak off the base for a couple of hours and head down to the depot, where Galina the cook, whose long-suffering and callused heart always softened at the sight of Yurik, treated us to a generous meal of meatloaf and mashed potatoes, accompanied by a glass of sour cream.

We usually showed up at the depot soon after the lunch hour rush to avoid unfriendly witnesses (some of our officers' wives worked at the railroad yards), and the even less friendly black-striped patrols from the tank division, who had it in for us red-striped infantrymen. Galina watched us eat with motherly tenderness, giving most of her attention to Yurik and making sure that his glass of sour cream remained at least half-full. "You little soldiers," she would sigh, "you silly little soldiers. Don't they feed you at that base of yours?" An invisible but powerful bond connected her to Yurik, or rather, as she herself put it, to "his kind." The two of them understood each other without exchanging too many words. They came from similar places and shared the same lane on life's journey. She was not unkind to me, but I was clearly a stranger (and strange) to her. Not Yurik, though. She'd sigh (she sighed a lot) and point at Yurik with a wet kitchen towel: "Your buddy here will be alright. He's a city boy, a student. But you, sweetie . . . ah, you're trouble. I just know, know your type, seen too many of you." Sadly, she was right.

Our meal was usually bookended by the passage of the Gorky—Leningrad express, which sped by without slowing down because the station was too insignificant even for a five-minute whistle-stop. I'd look on longingly at the tail end of the quickly disappearing train. In fifteen hours it would pull into Moscow Railway Station in Leningrad, just a ten-minute walk from my apartment. In fifteen hours the train would arrive in a city that I missed so much, a city where my girlfriend was busy with her classes, while also tending to the broken heart of an exchange student from Belgium.

The canteen didn't entirely abandon its primary purpose, but its backspace was suddenly taken over by a couple of heavy-set individuals clad in black leather jackets. The two were men of few words and direct action. Within days they'd erected a partition, cordoning off the back portion of the dining hall by means of thick black drapes. Behind the drapes they lined up a few chairs in front of a plastic café table, flimsy and unstable on its rickety aluminum legs. A TV was placed atop the table, elevated on a pile of plywood offcuts for a better viewing experience. The TV was connected to a device that Yurik told me was called a *vidak*. I had never seen a video player. The contraption, when described by Yurik, sounded futuristic. The men in black, as I now think of them, were the harbingers of a brave new world awaiting us in the months and years ahead; they were "guests from the future," who alighted on the dirty linoleum floor of this decrepit canteen to show us the way and guide us towards the flickering lights of the end of history.

We planned our first visit to the video salon meticulously. Yurik engaged one of his numerous contacts to secure a copy of the hourly schedule of the patrolling units, especially the notorious ones from the tank and artillery regiments (both black-striped and therefore potentially hostile). The staff officer on duty that day was an amicable drunk, temperamental but otherwise not a threat. Yurik sweet-talked him into a minor dereliction of his duty to immediately report any discovered absentees from the base. The kindly major agreed to look the other way for a couple of hours, and a pack of Bulgarian TU-134 cigarettes sealed the deal. Most of the officers were conveniently absent from the barracks, practicing their BMP-driving skills on the slopes of the tank range by the river. The roar of the engines echoed from afar, the distant sound mixing soothingly with the chirruping of spring birds fluttering above the deserted marching grounds. That springtime of 1988 felt like peacetime, a time of renewal.

Around midday Yurik and I scaled the fence and sprinted as quickly as we could towards the muddy alleys of the civilian district. We aimed to put some distance between our uniformed bodies and the heavily patrolled perimeter of the base. We reached Abelman Street in record time. For some unknown to me reason, half the streets of this sad garrison town bore the names of martyred Jewish revolutionaries; perhaps not surprisingly, ideological zeal and provincial naivete were twin features of the local municipal government.

Abelman Street was no Nevsky Prospect, but it did offer a few reminders of civilian life: there was a trolley route, a fire station, a movie theatre called Little Star, and a café with the same name. The street dropped down to the main square by the train station, bypassing a brutalist administrative building that also housed a one-room post office.

For me, that building held a special significance; every couple of weeks, I would leave the base and head down Abelman Street to the post office, where

I would try to call my girlfriend in Leningrad from one of the two wood-paneled phone booths that occupied half of the waiting area. Sometimes the telephone gods smiled and the calls got through. Yurik would stand outside on the lookout for military patrols. He was preternaturally good at spotting them, and every so often his shrill warning whistle pierced the grey concrete and forced an unceremonious end to my static-ridden attempts at romance.

But this time around we didn't stop at the post office. We didn't even slow down. Instead, we marched past the station and onto the depot.

"It's an American film," Yurik had explained before we left the base.

"What kind of an American film?"

"Who knows. It's American, alright. Galina told me it was about a dinosaur, a kids' movie, but funny. She'll reserve two chairs for us, at a ruble a head."

"Do you remember the name of the movie?"

"Who cares? What's with all these questions? But actually—wait. I do remember. I think that it sounds like something dental . . ."

"Dental?!"

"Yes, something like 'fang.'"

"Oh, like Jack London's *White Fang*?"

"Jack who? Never heard of him, but yeah, something like that. Wait a minute, no, not *White Fang*. It's a different word. It's . . ." Yurik creased his brow and looked into the distance. Then he fished an unfiltered Prima out of his inside pocket and lit it expertly with a match. He took a long careful drag on the cigarette and slowly let out the smoke as a series of tiny shapely rings. Apparently, the exercise cleared his head, because suddenly he remembered: "It's called *Jaws*! Yes, *Jaws*. I told you it had something dental about it. I have an exceptional memory for such things. It's an American movie about a dinosaur."

About ten minutes into the film I began to suspect that we were not dealing with a kid-friendly dinosaur. It had to be a different, far deadlier beast. There were eight of us, seated on plastic canteen chairs arranged in two rows in front of the TV. I did some quick math in my head: eight rubles per screening, probably five screenings per day, would yield forty rubles. This was a princely sum—about half the monthly salary my mom earned as a kindergarten teacher.

The owners of the *vidak* knew what they were doing; they were part of a strange new species that had captured the spirit of the time. They came from the future and that future smelled like money. It also smelled a little bit like Galina's signature meatloaf and almost imperceptibly like the sea breeze caressing the sandy beaches on Amity Island, off the coast of New England. The moviegoers watched the horror unfolding onscreen in total silence—so serious and set in their determination to persevere that one would think we were attending an organ recital at the Philharmonic. Everyone was smoking, Yurik excessively. Now and then he shifted uneasily in his chair and swore under his breath. It was strange to see him so tense and uncomfortable in these surroundings. In the course of the two years of our friendship, I had come to believe that nothing, nothing at all, could throw Yurik off balance. He was a fearless thug, a seasoned dance floor brawler, a battle-scarred risk-taker, who knew how to hold the world in his cold stare. Nothing could faze my friend. He had never sidestepped a fight. At the age of seventeen he went to prison and emerged from it unreformed in terms of his addiction to danger. Who would've known that in this late Soviet dusk, perched on a shaky plastic chair, enveloped by cigarette fumes and the stale aromas of a railroad canteen, he'd finally meet his match.

We lasted until the moment when oceanographer Hooper discovers the half-devoured body of Gardner, the fisherman. Suddenly, Yurik leaned into me, breathing hard, his heavy-lidded brown eyes full of angst and terror: "Fuck it, just fuck it. Let's go!"

I was only too happy to follow suit. On the other side of the partition we bumped into Galina, who was peeling potatoes, dropping the skins into a misshaped aluminum basin. She examined us with vague curiosity. "How is the film?"

Yurik waved his hand, "What film? These Americans are a bunch of sickos. And that's their idea of a kids' movie? Fuck that. We're out of here!" Galina gave him a look of tender concern, sighed, and continued peeling potatoes. I figured she had never stepped behind the black curtain. Just like us, she was not of that particular future.

Outside, we smoked silently for a while until Yurik asked, "Do you think they are doing this on purpose?"

"Who is doing what on purpose?"

"What do you mean 'Who'? Who! The Americans, of course! Setting up these fucking video salons, destroying our morale, bringing the country to the brink, one fucked-up movie at a time."

Frankly, I didn't believe we needed any outside intervention to extinguish our morale. A few years later, Yurik would come to Leningrad on the eve of my impending departure for the United States to say goodbye. He didn't look all that great and showed signs of wear. His drinking habit was all too obvious. It was a sad and memorable day. By the time I was able to load him up onto the Leningrad—Gorky express he was too weak with booze to talk. I hugged him for the last time, since I knew I'd never see my friend again. As Galina had said: "Trouble, trouble." She knew his kind only too well.

But that would happen later. For now, we were still smoking outside the canteen, exhaling our fear in tiny, perfectly round white rings. The light wind, coming from the river, carried off the smoke towards the slopes of the driving range, where the tanks moved across the familiar obstacle course. At this distance, the tanks looked like toys—as if some invisible toddlers were playing war.

"Look at them," Yurik said, pointing at the range. "What a fucking waste of time and diesel. Moving around like some stupid chafers, and it's not even May." May held a special meaning for us. It was the month of our promised discharge.

At the corner of Abelman and Sverdlov we were sighted by an artillery patrol. The officer hung back, but the two soldiers gave lazy chase. When they got closer, I could tell by the look of their ill-fitting uniforms that they were young recruits, "spirits" as we called them. We had nothing to fear, as they clearly had no desire to catch us. We trotted unhurriedly along the perimeter fence until we reached a convenient spot to climb over it. Our two pursuers, now out of their officer's field of vision, paused and motioned to us, indicating their preference to see us escape.

Yurik's mood had apparently brightened. "Poor fuckers," he said, nodding in the direction of the stationary patrol. "Black-striped but still good guys, despite this obvious handicap. And the saddest thing is that we're almost free and they've got another two years of bullshit ahead of them." We smiled knowingly at each other, gave appreciative thumbs-ups to the recruits, and approached the fence. It was a spring like no other, the last spring of service. The snow had almost entirely melted and only remained in darkened dirty patches along the banks of the river and by the tank tracks of the driving range. The Cold War was drawing to an end and history's last chapter was upon us. Only, we didn't know it. Not yet. Not ever.

Acknowledgements

I owe a debt of gratitude to the exceptional editorial team at the Academic Studies Press. Working with such a dedicated and responsive group of literary and publishing professionals was a pleasure.

I am fortunate to be employed by an institution that values creativity and recognizes the connections between scholarly and artistic pursuits. My colleagues at Seton Hall University—and especially my colleagues in the Department of History—encouraged me to see this project through with their open-mindedness, collegiality, and genuine commitment to intellectual versatility. For their support and friendship, I am sincerely thankful.

Professor Maxim Shrayer, editor of the series, embodies the ideal of a "writer's writer." His own scholarly and literary achievements are matched by a rare generosity of spirit toward fellow authors. This book would not exist without his thoughtful guidance and his gentle, insistent encouragement, for which I remain indebted.

Writing is often a solitary endeavor, but it flourishes in a community of fellow creatives who understand both its obsessions and its demands. I have been fortunate to receive encouragement and insightful feedback from many colleagues—writers, editors, historians, artists, fellow globetrotters—whose own work I greatly admire and whose opinions are important to me: Carolyn Kuebler, Pavel Lembersky, Nina Kossman, Olga Stein, Howard Fishman, Angela Ajayi, David Galef, José Manuel Prieto, Christopher Cappelluti, Marek Kulig, Michael Goro, Alla Borisova-Linetskaya, Victoria Goro-Rapoport, Leonid and Lena Zeiger, Alexander Slobodkin, the late Vadim Genin, Anatoly Molotkov, Harvey Asher, David Kennedy, Kristina Gorcheva-Newberry, Olga Zilberbourg, Elena Gorokhova, Sasha Vasilyuk, Patryk Babiracki, Mikhail Iossel, Mark Molesky, Nathaniel Knight, Dermot Quinn, Nila Friedberg, Dina Fainberg, Vera Kaplan, among many others. They truly care and that is something I deeply cherish.

My luck is to have in my life a very special and talented person – my wife Alina. A tough but fair critic, someone who is naturally allergic to even a hint of insincerity and hypocrisy, she helped me tame some of my less restrained tendencies towards hyperbole and exaggeration. She has reminded me, time and again, of the truth every writer must hold onto: less is almost always more.

Since he was little my son Yan has been one of my closest friends. His opinion of me and his perspective on the world have always mattered profoundly. We like and take each other seriously, which is a wonderful thing for a father-son relationship. When I write I often think of him.

And of course, my deepest gratitude belongs to my remarkable parents, Lena and Grisha. Their love, sacrifice, and unwavering support made everything possible. This book is dedicated to them.

www.ingramcontent.com/pod-product-compliance
Lightning Source LLC
Chambersburg PA
CBHW060625310726
48982CB00003B/674

* 9 7 9 8 8 9 7 8 3 0 7 8 7 *